Alex Bell was born in 1986 in Hampshire. She studied Law on and off for six long years before the boredom became so overwhelming that she had to throw down the textbooks and run madly from the building. Since then she has never looked back. She has travelled widely, is a ferociously strict vegetarian and generally prefers cats to people.

By Alex Bell

LEX TRENT
FIGHTING WITH FIRE

ALEX BELL

headline

First published in Great Britain in 2011 by
HEADLINE PUBLISHING GROUP

1

Cataloguing in Publication Data is available from the British Library

ISBN 978 0 7553 5519 8

Typeset in Aldine401 by Ellipsis Books Limited, Glasgow

Printed and bound in the UK by
CPI Mackays, Chatham ME5 8TD

HEADLINE PUBLISHING GROUP
An Hachette UK Company
338 Euston Road
London NW1 3BH

www.headline.co.uk
www.hachette.co.uk

For Trevor Bell – father, friend and Sam-I-Am.

'There are two routes to happiness . . .'
Thanks for always helping me get more!

ACKNOWLEDGEMENTS

Many thanks to my agent, Carolyn Whitaker, and my editor, Hannah Sheppard, for all their hard work, comments and feedback on this book. Thanks also to Sam Eades, Celine Kelly, and, indeed, everyone at Headline for making the second Lex Trent book a reality rather than just a fantasy in my head.

My family, as ever, have supported me throughout the writing process, and been appropriately enthusiastic about the end result.

And, as always, I duly acknowledge my pets – my three cats, Cindy, Chloe and Suki, and new addition to the menagerie, my Great Dane, Moose – who all keep me company whilst I write. And I would also like to acknowledge my skeleton, Erin, invaluable writing aide, friend and confidant.

CHAPTER ONE

THE PENALTY TASK

Lex Trent dangled from the tree branch hundreds of feet above the ravine, his tenuous grip the only thing between him and instant death . . . Well, perhaps not *instant* death, as such. It would probably take a good thirty seconds to fall all the way to the jagged rocks below. He risked a glance down.

'Thirty seconds at least,' he muttered. 'Probably more like forty.'

Not that he had any intention of falling. He couldn't use his left hand because that would mean dropping the golden egg his arm was clamped around. He was, therefore, dangling from the tree branch one-handed, which explained why he was having some difficulty pulling himself to safety. It was quite a conundrum. If he dropped the egg he'd have his left arm free and then he'd be able to get himself back on to the branch. But the fact was that Lex would sooner cut off his own foot than willingly drop a solid-gold egg. It was not in his nature to voluntarily relinquish treasure – especially treasure he'd had to work so hard to get. There had to be another way . . .

He risked another look down. Then he looked at the egg. Then he looked at the branch he was clinging to, noting the fact that it was creaking in rather an ominous way. His hand was getting very tired and his arm felt as if it was about to pop right out of its socket or, quite possibly, had already done so. He didn't want to let go of the egg, but he didn't want to fall to a messy, untimely death either. He could feel the weight of the silver whistle tucked beneath his shirt against his chest and a spectacular, horrifying, genius thought occurred to him. But how long would he need for it to work? Twenty seconds? Thirty? Would there be enough time? The smallest miscalculation and he would end up painted on to the rocks below. He ought to think about it very, very carefully before he—

And then the branch snapped and he was free-falling.

For such a young person, Lex had done a fair amount of free-falling in his time. But this was the first occasion he'd ever fallen from such a significant height. He may have been the luckiest guy in the world but he would have to be made out of sponge to survive that fall. So as he fell through the air, the wind whipping his hair, struggling to maintain a grip on the egg with one hand, he fumbled desperately for the whistle around his neck. He got it between his lips in a record-breaking five seconds and blew for all he was worth.

No sound came out, but that was normal. It was such

a high frequency that it was undetectable to human ears. A precious ten seconds passed and Lex continued to fall with no sign of rescue. He carried on blowing the whistle – even more desperately now. Surely *one* of them would hear and come to his aid?

Ten more seconds slipped past and by that time the jagged rocks were looking uncomfortably close and pointy. Lex didn't have time to waste on swearing out loud but he swore in his head as he frantically blew on the whistle.

Fifteen seconds, max. That was all he had left before he was just a smear on a rock. What an undignified end that would be ... But then a great monstrous thing wheeled overhead, there was a raucous cry, a flurry of feathers and, just before Lex was impaled on one of the rocks below, two clawed feet wrapped themselves around him, sticking into his ribs rather painfully, and then he was moving away from the ground rather than towards it as the griffin took off with Lex firmly gripped in its talons. He really must teach the griffins to swoop *under* him so that he'd land on their backs rather than being carried off in such an undignified manner, like a mouse being taken away by an owl. Still, he had the egg and he was still alive, and that was all that really mattered.

Lex's great silver ship soon came into view, nestled grandly amongst the clouds. The griffin soared over it and then dropped Lex – slightly prematurely – when they were still about ten feet above the deck.

He had time for a brief shriek before hitting the wooden boards hard with a loud thumping sound. The egg flew out of his grip, bounced and rolled a little way across the deck. The griffin landed beside it lightly and gracefully a moment later. Lex would have lifted his head to glare at it but he was too preoccupied with the searing pain in his wrists, his arms, his legs . . . Lex had never broken a bone before but there was a first time for everything and it certainly felt like every bone in his body was now broken.

'You bloody great stupid, blundering, brainless bird!' he gasped. 'You've practically killed me!'

'Killed you? Lex, really, what a melodramatic exaggeration,' a familiar voice remarked. 'There's hardly a mark on you. Do get up and stop making such an exhibition of yourself.'

A hand gripped his collar and dragged him to his feet. It was with genuine surprise that Lex found he was able to stand. Lady Luck was quite right: he did not appear to have any broken bones or any bones sticking through his skin or any other ghoulish injury whatsoever. He did, in fact, appear to be fine apart from a few light grazes and one bruise on his right knee.

'And don't take your bad mood out on the griffins,' Lady Luck said, running her fingers down the feathers of Monty's neck.

'I'll take it out on whoever I like!' Lex snapped.

He stomped across the deck to retrieve the golden egg.

'Oh my Gods!' he exclaimed, horrified. 'It's dented! The egg is dented! Just look at it! It's practically worthless now! All that work for nothing!'

'That is utter nonsense, Lex,' Lady Luck said calmly.

Lex glared at her ferociously. There is nothing more irritating to someone who is already in a bad mood than being told that they are talking utter nonsense.

'The dent won't make a scrap of difference to the value of that egg, as you well know,' Lady Luck went on, brushing an imaginary fleck of dust off her white toga. 'And it's not like you're going to be allowed to keep it, anyway. How much longer are you going to sulk like this? I have to say it's getting rather tedious.'

'I'm not sulking!' Lex said sulkily, dropping the egg carelessly on to the deck. 'I'm justifiably furious! I'm understandably livid! I'm rightly vexed! I'm validly seething! I'm—'

'Save your silver tongue for someone who cares, my sweet.'

'I *hate* him!' Lex spat viciously. 'I hate that stuck up git!'

'Then beat him,' Lady Luck replied. 'Give him a good thrashing in the Game and make sure you win.'

'I *will* win!' Lex replied. 'I've never been so determined to win in my life!'

'I'm very glad to hear it,' the Goddess said sharply. 'The Game starts in twenty-four hours and you must be ready. I don't want any more of this nonsense, Lex, I mean it. Hate Jeremiah all you like if it's going to help you win the Game but don't let him get the better of you again. You're lucky you didn't get disqualified this time.'

'*Lucky*?' Lex spluttered indignantly. He pointed at the golden egg on the deck and said, 'There was nothing lucky about retrieving that thing; there was just an awful lot of pluck, courage, wit and—'

'Yes, dear, you did very well,' the Goddess said soothingly. 'And now that you've successfully completed the penalty task, they'll have to let you back into the Game. Now, give me that egg and I'll go make sure it's all smoothed out.'

Lex picked up the egg and moodily handed it over.

'Thank you. Now you'd better set sail for the Sea Volcanoes straight away. You're behind the others already and you don't want to be late for the start of the Game.'

And with that she disappeared, taking the egg with her.

CHAPTER TWO

THE OUTLAW, JESSE LAYTON

Four Days Earlier

When Lex walked into the Guild of Chroniclers in the heart of the Wither City, he fully intended to do things right this time. He'd just had a little smirk over the Royal Monument and left his old companion, Mr Montgomery Schmidt, standing there. His suggestion that the lawyer tag along on the upcoming Game had been turned down, as Lex had known it would be. He would certainly never have made the offer in a million years if he thought there was even the remotest possibility that the lawyer might accept. He may have come to feel a tiny inkling of liking, and even respect, for Mr Schmidt, but the man was still a doddering old fool and Lex was not going to allow himself to be hampered by him a second time. The first occasion had not been his fault. He hadn't been aware then that the Binding Bracelets would tie him to someone for the entire course of the Game. Now that he did know, he was going to make his choice very carefully indeed.

Schmidt had told him that, in light of his previous adventures, Chroniclers were practically clamouring to go on a Game with him. And that was true, so far as it went. The problem was that, once Lex had managed to convince the clerk behind the desk that he really *was* Lex Trent, the man had showed him the books and Lex had been . . . well. . . not much impressed, to put it frankly.

Each Chronicler had a photo and a profile and whilst most of them had quite impressive résumés so far as writing was concerned, it was a totally different story where *adventuring* was concerned. They all had that pale, weedy look of those who never venture outside unless they have to. And over half of them were wearing tweed jackets. Plus, almost all of them seemed to suffer from an interesting variety of allergies. Allergies, tweed, rather anxious-looking expressions on their round, pale faces . . .

'I might as well take another lawyer and have done with it!' Lex exclaimed. 'At least they have quick minds, if nothing else! Is this the best you've got?'

'What exactly were you expecting, Mr Trent?' the clerk asked politely.

'Well . . . I don't know . . . Someone who doesn't look quite so wet behind the ears! Someone who can have my back and hold their own in a fight and be good under pressure and think on their feet and be cool in a crisis. You know, that sort of thing.'

The clerk looked quite alarmed. 'I don't think we have anyone like that on our list, sir,' he said. 'These are *writers*.

But you can look through them all if you like. We have hundreds of names. I'll go and fetch the other books for you, shall I?'

Lex sighed. 'I think you'd better.'

After a disgruntled few hours spent turning mildewy pages, Lex had a list of five names, but he was scraping the bottom of the barrel even with them. The clerk said they could set up face-to-face meetings with the five he'd picked out and if one of them was suitable then they could take things from there.

Lex was not at all happy. In his head he had thought that he would stroll into the Chroniclers' Guild and find a perfect abundance of suitable writers. He had not expected this delay in finding someone and it was making him anxious. The Binding Bracelet on his wrist was a time bomb just waiting to go off. He had put on as much clothing as possible, to the extent that he looked rather like a prophet, but if someone were to have direct skin-to-skin contact with him, even accidentally, then the Binding Bracelets would separate, one would fasten about that person's wrist and they would be the one Lex was stuck with for the rest of the Game. It had happened once and he did not intend to let it happen again. His companion this time would be *his* choice, and his choice alone. But he didn't want to rush it either. He wanted someone who was going to be perfect. You could never have too many advantages when it came to Gaming with the Gods, after all . . .

So he left the Chroniclers' Guild with plans to come

back the next day and meet the five he had picked out. All of them were fairly young men, in good health and most definitely *not* wearing tweed. Nor would they die if they accidentally smelled a peanut from across the room. There had been nothing in their profiles that had ruled them out but then there had been nothing that had particularly recommended them either. Lex was disappointed for he had been hoping one of them would jump out at him. After all, his own grandfather had been a Chronicler and yet he hadn't been a total weed . . .

But it turned out to be quite irrelevant in the end anyway because, that night on the ship, Lex managed to wheedle a little clue out of Lady Luck as to where her round of the Game was going to take place. And as soon as he heard the words *Dry Gulch*, his eyes lit up and a spectacular, stupendous, stunning plan began to form in his mind.

'Why are you grinning like that, Lex?' Lady Luck said sharply.

'Oh, I'm just excited about seeing the Wild West, my Lady, that's all,' Lex said reassuringly. 'I've never been. And I love seeing new places.'

It was quite true that he had never been there before, but he most certainly knew about it. He'd read books and heard stories and seen pictures. And he knew all about the legend of Dry Gulch House and would have done even if it hadn't involved Carey East's family, for Lex made it his business to know about any legend involving treasure . . .

Carey East's uncle – Nathaniel East – had been the loony of the family. Cracked in the head, so they said. But the Easts had always had money and influence so, rather than sending him to an asylum, they packed him off to conquer the Wild West. One might argue that that was something of a cruel thing to do considering the fact that Nathaniel was, after all, a complete nutter. But it was better than an asylum. And Nathaniel did have moments of lucidity. Which was why the East family were – just about – able to get away with referring to Nathaniel as an eccentric. So he had gone out to the West and, as the East family had no doubt secretly hoped, he eventually came to something of a sticky end there. But not before he built a house in Dry Gulch. It had been constructed to Nathaniel's own special, secret specifications and was therefore . . . something of an oddity, to put it mildly.

Lex had seen drawings of it. He had also, during one of his many visits to the Wither City library, looked at a grand total of five sets of building plans for it. They were all different. Try as they might, no architect seemed able to pin the building down on paper. It was full of secret passages, and it was generally agreed that they probably hadn't all been discovered yet. There were staircases that led nowhere, and doors on the top floor that opened right out on to nothing. There were windows set into the floor, and corridors that started out a normal size but gradually narrowed to the extent that the only way a grown man could get to the end of them was to crawl on his hands and knees. The furniture was nailed down in practically every room. Even the individual billiard balls were nailed to the snooker table. This may have been an interim measure before Nathaniel found a witch to cast a sticking spell over the contents of the house. After that, almost nothing could be removed from the walls or the floor. The house looked just as it had done for over a hundred years.

Nathaniel lived alone in the house for five years before, one fateful day, he was ambushed by a savage gang of outlaws. The group killed Nathaniel and took over his house, but not before Nathaniel had time to hide his most precious possession – a magical double-bladed sword known as the Sword of Life that he had supposedly been given as a reward for some service he had done a witch. The sword was said to be capable of cutting any material and killing any creature. It was a hero's sword, made for noble quests and daring adventures. And – most importantly of all – it could *give* life, as well as take it away. All the years of life that the sword took from the men it killed were stored within the blade itself – until the day when someone took them out. The sword could not bring people back from the dead. Nor could it heal grievous wounds. But if a person was already alive and healthy then it would extend the natural period of their life. They would still die if they, for example, walked off the edge of a cliff, or had their head chopped off, but the *natural* period of their life would be extended and some of their youth would be restored.

Lex wanted that sword. He'd wanted it ever since he

first heard of it. It was rumoured to have a hundred years of life stored within the blade. Just think how *invaluable* such a thing would be! For the Games and for his thieving and scams. He could extend his own life by a century or more, and carry on adventuring well past the age he would otherwise be able to.

The problem, however, was that the sword was hidden somewhere inside Dry Gulch House and had not been found in over one hundred years of searching, despite the fact that the house had been combed through from top to bottom. Many people said the sword wasn't there at all and possibly never had been. They said it was a myth. Lex didn't believe it. He thought the sword was there and he'd always intended to go and look for it one day. Now that the Game was to take them directly to Dry Gulch, the opportunity was just too good to miss.

But the problem was that only cowboys and outlaws were allowed inside the house now. After Nathaniel East had been killed, the leader of the gang who'd attacked him – one Elijah Deadwood – had claimed ownership of the house and since then it had been passed down through the Deadwood family to this day. It was a rough, tough sort of place. Not at all the kind where Lex could just stroll in as himself if he didn't want to get his teeth knocked out. So, if he was going to make it past the front doors, he would have to learn how to be a cowboy – or at least pass himself off as once convincingly – and he had a sneaky feeling that that was probably going to be easier said than done. Some things you can teach yourself, but others you need help for, and Lex was certainly astute enough to know the difference.

'I suppose I absolutely have to have a companion by the time the Game starts, do I?' he said, without much hope.

'Oh, yes,' the Goddess said at once. 'You won't be allowed to start otherwise.'

'That's what I thought.'

The question, therefore, was how on earth was Lex going to find an outlaw from the Wild West in the Wither City within the next few days? Although the odd cowboy passed through from time to time, they were certainly not common for the simple reason that cowboys did not tend to have much money and so could not travel across seas very easily unless they went as stowaways.

The next morning, however, Lex was aware of a flurry of activity as soon as he stepped out on to the harbour. Something was obviously going on, but then something usually was so he didn't pay it much heed as he pushed his way past the closed-up stalls, being careful to keep his arms tucked in and not touch anybody.

He was in a little winding street about five minutes away from the Chroniclers' Guild when there was a shriek and someone yelled, 'It's him! It's the outlaw, Jesse Layton! He's getting away!'

Lex's ears pricked up and his head snapped round just in time to see a palomino horse come galloping around the corner, hooves skidding on the cobbles, nostrils flaring, eyes rolling. It was a magnificent creature quite unlike the workhorses Lex was used to with their dull eyes and lowered heads.

And the man on its back was just as conspicuous for, in his flared trousers, checked shirt and wide-brimmed hat, he was a cowboy straight out of the pages of a Wild West novel.

Lex only had time for a brief look before he had to jump back against a shop, flattening his back against the wall to avoid being trampled by the huge horse. They fled past and, without a second's thought, Lex raced after them. When he reached the square with the Chroniclers' Guild and the Royal Monument he saw a whole lot of policemen rushing off in the direction of the city gates. He was about to follow but he stopped. It was too obvious. To escape the police, you had to do what they weren't expecting you to do, and, if this cowboy had ever been chased before, he would know that. Lex looked around the square. What would *he* have done? Sent the horse off in the direction of the road leading out of the city, that much was obvious. And then . . . His eyes swept the square until he found what he was looking for: The Old Bear pub wedged in beside the Monument Restaurant in the far right hand corner.

Lex headed straight for it, went inside and – because he knew what he was looking for – found him at once. Right at the back, at a table all to himself, sat the cowboy, his hat pulled down low over his face and a pint of ale in his hand already. Lex walked over, pulled up a chair and sat down opposite him.

'Are you really an outlaw from the Wild West?' he said.

The cowboy looked up slowly, tipping his hat back with his thumb. Now that Lex could see him properly, he judged him to be about forty years old, with an unshaven face, a nose that had clearly been broken at some point in the past, crow's feet at the corners of his blue eyes and a long pale scar that stretched from just below his right eye all the way down to his square jaw.

'Is it that obvious?' he asked. He spoke with a drawling accent Lex had never heard before.

'Take your hat off!' Lex said urgently.

The cowboy stared at him. 'Now why ever would I do that? This here is my lucky hat.'

'It's going to get you caught!' Lex replied, forcing himself not to glance nervously around the bar. 'They probably won't recognise your face but they'll be looking for your hat. Your best bet would be to give it to someone else. Preferably someone who's of a similar height and build to you.'

A gleam appeared in the cowboy's eyes. 'The old decoy gag, eh?' He whipped off the hat to reveal untidy, longish brown hair. 'You're not as honest as you look, are you, friend?' he said. 'I take it you're not thinking of trying to turn old Jesse Layton in to collect the reward money?'

'I think you can help me,' Lex said.

'Probably, but I don't help anyone but myself for free.'

'Perhaps we can help each other.'

'Can you make the sheriff and his men disappear into thin air?' Jesse asked, staring out of the nearby window.

'No, but I can—'

'Then I don't think you can help me much, kid,' the cowboy said. 'Just keep your mouth shut, eh?'

And with that he grabbed his hat and ducked under the table. A moment later the door opened and five police officers walked in, staring suspiciously around the room. Everyone fell silent at the realisation that there was about to be trouble.

'Listen up,' one of the officers said. 'We're looking for a dangerous outlaw by the name of Jesse Layton. Someone said he came in here. Any of you lot seen 'im? He's a big fella with one of them cowboy hats, spurs on his boots and the like.'

'He was here,' Lex said before anyone else could speak. 'But then he left. Went out the back door not five minutes ago. If you hurry, you can catch him.'

The police were halfway to the door when a nearby woman pointed and shrieked, 'There's a man under the table!'

'Oh, don't worry about him. He just can't hold his drink—' Lex began, but it was no good. The police were doggedly coming over to check it out.

Sensing what was about to happen, Lex jumped up from his seat and hurled himself to one side, thereby narrowly missing getting hit in the face with the table as Jesse burst out from under it, knocking two policemen down before they even knew what had happened.

And then there was a bar-room brawl.

Lex had seen fights break out like this before but he

had never seen anyone as quick on their feet as Jesse Layton. Despite the fact that there were five policemen there, he very nearly got away. Lex ducked behind the bar as soon as the fighting started, whilst all the other customers headed straight for the doors. Lex was rather disappointed that no one got thrown along the bar, knocking all the glasses off to smash on the floor, for it was the kind of thing you expected in a brawl. Jesse got cornered against it at one point, though, whereupon Lex promptly handed him a glass bottle.

'Thanks, kid,' the cowboy said. He actually took a swig from it before smashing it down on the counter and then wielding it in such a threatening manner that the advancing policemen took a few nervous steps back.

'I ain't going back to Cactus Valley! You hear me? Not now, not ever! I'm dangerous and I'm desperate and the first guy who tries to arrest me is going to be eating broken bottle for dinner!'

Oh yes, Lex thought, *this is the man I need, no doubt about it*. He was perfect! What luck that he should have come to the Wither City right at this particular time! Lex even wondered whether Lady Luck herself may have given a helping hand in bringing the two of them together. The cowboy certainly looked like the sort of person she would choose.

'I'm going to back out of here nice and slow,' Jesse said. 'You goons stay there and we won't have any upsets.'

He made it right to the doorway when a sixth policeman appeared behind him and whacked the cowboy so hard round the head with his truncheon that Lex wouldn't have been surprised if it had actually come off his shoulders. He couldn't help but wince as the bottle fell from Jesse's hand to smash at his feet and, still looking faintly surprised, the cowboy thumped down on to his knees to crumple, face down, on the floor.

The policemen all started cheering and congratulating themselves but Lex was livid with anger. 'You better not have done him any serious injury!' he fumed at the officer with the truncheon.

But the policeman just shrugged and said with a grin, 'The reward poster says, "dead or alive".'

'Clearly you don't know who you're dealing with,' Lex said coldly. He pointed at the prone cowboy. 'This man is a companion to one of the players in the upcoming Game.'

'Huh. What would you know about it, boy?' the officer sneered.

Lex drew himself up to his full height – which still wasn't really all that impressive – and said, 'I am Lex Trent, sir, and as you no doubt know, Lady Luck is my patron. This man was supposed to be my companion and your idiot henchman has fair near bashed his head in! If he's not fit to play I will be very unhappy indeed and, what's more, Her Ladyship will be extremely upset with all of you! And you'd be simply amazed at just how unpleasant your life can become when Lady Luck is upset with you! I hope the reward money turns out to be worth it!' And then, because these *were* policeman who couldn't be counted upon to understand sarcasm, he added bitingly, 'But I doubt it very much!'

Lex was pleased to see that they were now all looking rather worried.

'I had no idea,' the officer with the truncheon said, dropping the thing as if it had suddenly burnt him. 'None at all. I'm ever so sorry, Mr Trent, truly I am. Please give my apologies to Her Ladyship, too. We'll take your friend to the hospital straight away—'

'Hospital?' Lex interrupted. 'Don't be silly. It was only a little knock on the head; I'm sure he'll be fine. Take him to a prison cell.'

The policemen exchanged uncertain looks.

'But . . . sir . . . you said—'

'Look, I'm not going to ask you again. Put him in a cell and send for me as soon as he wakes up. And don't say anything to him in the meantime.'

The officers still looked rather confused but they readily agreed to what Lex had said. No one wants to be plagued with bad fortune for the rest of their days and everyone knew that Lady Luck was one to hold a grudge.

Lex wanted Jesse Layton as his companion for the Game and he was certainly not averse to forcing him into it using the Binding Bracelets, but he would much rather that the cowboy came willingly. He knew from experience that unwilling companions tended to complain an awful lot, and if there was any complaining to be done then Lex liked to be the one to do it. Besides which, Jesse teaching Lex how to be an outlaw was probably going to work much better if the cowboy didn't hate his guts for dragging him along on the Game against his will. So the trick was to make Jesse believe that going with Lex was a *good* thing – something that was most definitely in his own interests. And that was likely to work better if he believed the alternative was getting shipped back to Cactus Valley in handcuffs, ready to face the noose. So Lex had him packed off to the police station and didn't even feel the tiniest bit guilty about doing so.

When word was sent to his ship about an hour later that Jesse Layton had woken up, Lex did not rush down there straightaway but left it several hours until the evening. Better to let the cowboy stew a while, thinking about the fact that he'd been caught and was going to be sent back home for the reward money and then hanged by his neck until he was dead. A few hours spent dwelling on that was bound to make any alternative that didn't involve getting strung up seem extremely attractive.

When Lex turned up at the police station at about six o'clock that evening he was slightly disappointed to find that Jesse Layton did not appear to be as distraught as he'd hoped. Lying on his narrow bed in the cell, his hands were clasped behind his head, his hat was pulled down over his eyes, his long legs were stretched out with his ankles crossed and he was singing a rather cheerful little song about a bandit who killed an awful lot of people before setting fire to a village and riding off into the sunset.

'He's been singing like that for the last hour,' the policeman whispered.

Lex gave him a cold look. 'Perhaps that whack on the head from earlier has left him brain damaged. Go away. I want to talk to him in private.'

The policeman hurried off and Lex stopped outside the cell. 'Hey,' he said, looking through the bars. 'You in there. Remember me?'

Jesse stopped singing and tipped back his hat. ' Why, if it isn't the kid from the bar come to visit me.'

'I'm not a kid. I'm seventeen. My name's Lex Trent.'

'Jesse Layton,' the outlaw replied pleasantly.

'Haven't you heard of me?' Lex demanded.

'Should I have?'

'You do follow the Games in the Wild West, don't you?'

'Oh, sure. If it's anything to do with gambling, we've got it.'

'Well, I played in the last Game and won it.'

Jesse raised his eyebrows. 'And you still have both arms and legs. Good for you.'

'I'm about to play in another one. I'd like you to be my companion.'

That got the outlaw's attention. He sat up, swung his legs on to the floor, leaned forwards with his elbows on his knees and said, 'And why's that, friend?'

'Well, it's a Game. Obviously I need someone who can take care of themselves. But, more importantly, I need to learn how to pass myself off as a cowboy within the next few weeks.'

'You?' Jesse said, looking Lex's skinny frame up and down. 'That won't be easy.'

'I'm a good mimic,' Lex said. 'And a quick learner.'

'Why do you want to learn, anyway?'

'I have it on good authority that the final lap of this Game will take us to Dry Gulch. I want to get into the house.'

'Oh, you're a treasure hunter,' Jesse replied with a grin. 'I have to say you don't look like one. Take it from me, kid – Dry Gulch House ain't your kind of place.'

'Have you ever been there?' Lex asked, hopefully, for it was always better to have a guide with first-hand experience.

'Sure,' Jesse replied. 'Once or twice. But you heard what I said to the police back there. I ain't never going back to Cactus Valley.'

'I don't want you to go back to Cactus Valley, you simpleton. I want you to come to Dry Gulch. Besides, I hate to break it to you, but you *are* going back. You're sitting here in a prison cell! So either you return to Cactus Valley in handcuffs with the authorities or you go back to Dry Gulch a free man with me. You'll have to play the Game and teach me everything you know whenever we get a spare minute. If you don't think you're up to it, say so now and I'll find someone else.'

'Hey, I never said I wasn't up to it,' Jesse said. 'And I guess Dry Gulch is a fair few miles away from Cactus Valley.'

'You understand that once you start the Game you're in it for good? These bracelets will keep us tied to each other.' Lex held up his wrist to emphasise the point. 'So don't think about trying to run away because it won't work. And *I'll* be in charge, understand? You'll have to do as I say, not just because I'm saving your neck by getting you out of prison here today, but because I'm the player and you're the companion, and companions must always do as they're told.'

'You've got an awful lot of arrogance and self-confidence for such a youngster, don't you?' Jesse said mildly. 'Still, anything's better than getting sent back to hang.' He folded his arms and looked at Lex through the bars. 'Well? Aren't you going to ask me what I did to make 'em send out those reward posters?'

'I don't care about what you've done,' Lex replied. 'All I care about is how you're going to help me.'

Jesse grinned and then shrugged. 'Well, all right then. I can tell already that you and I are going to get along just fine.'

Lex had to agree. He may not have trusted Jesse – for he could recognise another scoundrel when he saw one – but he did like him.

'I do have one condition though,' Jesse said.

Lex stared at him. 'You're hardly in a position to be making conditions.'

'I dare say not, but I'm making one just the same. My horse, Rusty: he'll have to come with us.'

'I'm not sure that's a terribly good idea,' Lex replied. 'You see, I have three griffins and they try to eat just about anything that moves.'

'I don't go anywhere without him,' Jesse replied firmly.

'I even brought him with me when I fled from the West. I sure as hell ain't leaving him behind now.'

Lex sighed. 'All right; I suppose we can keep him separate from the griffins. He was picked up on the road and taken to the city stables earlier today. I'll pay the release fee to get him out.' He pulled off his glove, extended his hand through the bars and said, 'Now, if that's all, I'd like to make this official. This is your last chance to back out.'

But Jesse looked at his hand for only a moment before clasping it firmly with his own. Instantly, the Binding Bracelets split in half. The black one remained firmly fastened around Lex's wrist whilst the white one shot off on to Jesse's. Lex felt a profound sense of smug satisfaction for he was sure he had chosen the perfect companion. Jesse was tough and big and seemed relatively smart for someone with such a lot of scars and stubble. And to think that he had almost chosen one of those wimpy, peanut-fearing writers. He shuddered at the thought of it . . .

Jesse smiled and said, 'So are you going to get me out of here or what?'

Lex explained very carefully to Jesse how the Binding Bracelets worked – if they didn't eat every meal together they would switch bodies and they would *stay* in each other's bodies until they managed to find their way back to each other and eat together again.

'You don't say?' Jesse said, examining the white bracelet fastened to his wrist. 'But I can still drink, right?'

'Yes. You just can't eat on your own.'

'What about chewing tobacco? Will that make us switch?'

'I don't think so,' Lex said, frowning. 'You don't swallow it, do you?'

'Jeepers, kid, 'course I don't swallow it!' Jesse said, grimacing at the suggestion. 'You gotta spit it out.'

'A disgusting habit,' Lex replied scathingly. 'But not one that should make us switch. Chew and spit all you like.'

After collecting Rusty from the stables, Lex and Jesse made their way back to the harbour. Several people shot the cowboy sharp looks, for many had seen him galloping through the town just that morning with the police giving chase behind him. A couple of particularly slow-on-the-uptake people even felt the need to shriek, 'It's him! It's the outlaw, Jesse Layton! He's getting away!'

'Oh, give it a rest,' Lex replied. 'He's not getting away, he's playing in a Game. Look.' And he grabbed Jesse's wrist to hold it up and display the bracelet. That promptly made people back off and leave them alone. No one tangles with the Gods on purpose, after all.

'This is my ship,' Lex said with a flourish once they'd reached the harbour.

The gigantic, gleaming silver thing was tied up like the rest of the boats but, unlike the ships belonging to the gypsies, traders and tourists, Lex's ship didn't bob on the water but floated in the air instead. For it was, of course, a magic ship that Lex had stolen from an enchanter during the course of the last Game. The enchanters were powerful, magical men and so stealing from one of them was extremely dangerous and practically unheard of. Most people were therefore terribly impressed and even a little in awe of Lex when he showed them his ship.

He was therefore less then happy when, after regarding it for a moment, Jesse said, 'Ugly-looking thing, ain't it?'

'*Ugly?*' Lex spluttered indignantly. '*Ugly?* You've got to be kidding! Can't you see how large and powerful and silver she is?'

Jesse shrugged. 'Prefer the gypsy boats myself.'

Truth be told, Lex had preferred the gypsy boats too at one time, for they were decorated in many fluttering flags and painted with colourful sea monsters. But whilst they may have *looked* pretty, they couldn't fly over land or travel across a frozen sea or soar up into the sky or survive being attacked by sharks or water witches. Plus, anything Lex owned instantly looked all the more beautiful to him for the simple fact that he owned it.

'I stole it from an enchanter,' Lex said, just in case Jesse had somehow missed that point.

But the cowboy just nodded. 'Yep. That's what I figured.'

It seemed he really was determined to be distinctly unimpressed. It occurred to Lex that a writer would probably have been falling over themselves to congratulate him and tell him how wonderful he was and how heroic and daring and brave and the like. In reality Lex would have been thoroughly sick of this within about five minutes but still he couldn't help wishing that Jesse would be just a little bit impressed with the ship. He sighed and said, 'Well, come on then.'

The ship's gangplank had been destroyed during the course of the last Game so, for much of it, the ship had only had a ladder running up its side. This did not make for happy disembarking, especially when it was raining and slippery. So Lex had had a new gangplank put in. It was only one of many improvements he had made to the ship once he'd known for sure that the enchanter wasn't coming back for it (on account of being turned into a little doll and imprisoned in a glass bottle).

He had spent some very happy days during his three months back at the family farm working on and improving the ship. There were still a lot of rooms inside it that he'd never been into and these were all marked with a giant X. He'd originally intended to go through them all but, after one slightly unfortunate incident when he tried to remove the rabid, fire-breathing rabbit that had attacked him once before, and the thing got out and . . . well . . . set fire to the barn, Lex's brother, Lucius, had forbidden him from going into any of the other unsafe rooms. Of course, Lex didn't usually listen to a word Lucius said but, on this occasion, he had to agree. An extremely flammable farm really wasn't the place to have fire-breathing things running amok in a livid rage. So he had left the doors with strange noises behind them well enough alone. For all he knew, this might mean that he'd have a ship full of dead monsters at some point for, if they were sealed into little rooms with nothing to eat, they would surely starve. But the fire-breathing rabbit had been sealed in the room for at least four months without food and, nevertheless, seemed to be extremely active when it finally did get out.

'Some parts of the ship are off limits,' Lex said as he, Jesse and Rusty walked across the gangplank. 'You can't go into any room with an X on the door.'

'Why not?'

'Because I haven't had the chance to check what's in there and it's usually something dangerous that wants to eat you. But the corridors are safe and any room that doesn't have an X on the door is fine.'

Lex opened the door, they stepped into one of the ship's corridors and were immediately enveloped in the scent of carpets. When he'd first got the ship it had been covered in mirrors and marble – even the floors – which hadn't made for a very cosy feel. So Lex had had carpets put into all the rooms he was able to use. It had cost him a pretty penny, of course, for the corridors alone required several huge rolls of carpet. But Lex had sold some of the treasures he'd found on the ship to raise the money. Lucius pointed out that Lex could have spent the money on improving and modernising the farm, not to mention replacing the barn that had been burnt down. Lex resisted this particular line of thought most strenuously at first for the very idea of spending his ill-gotten gains on a *barn* of all things was quite sickening. And it was hardly *his* fault that the rabbit had headed straight for it, damn the thing . . . But, in the end, he gave Lucius some money for a new barn just to stop him from going on and on and *on* about it. You let one fire-breathing bunny loose and no one ever lets you forget it . . .

But the corridors, kitchen and bridge were now all carpeted. And Lex was very pleased with the result. He had even rolled around on the new carpets a bit when they'd first been put in – after vacuuming them first, obviously, so that he wouldn't get all those little bits of fluff sticking to his clothes and hair.

They found a room down below to put Rusty in. Then Lex gave Jesse the tour – showing him the kitchen and the bridge and the room where he would sleep. Lex was planning on sleeping on the bridge as he'd done in the last Game. It was the only room in the ship that had windows, the other rooms all being rather dark, claustrophobic little boxes. As one of the biggest rooms, not to mention the fact that it was the highest, Lex felt the observation deck had rather a nice status-symbol feel to it and saw it as his due to sleep there. It, too, was now carpeted, with a grand four-poster bed and a wardrobe and a little coolbox with some food in it in case he fancied a midnight snack, and a couple of big, squishy armchairs. It was the perfect set-up.

Jesse's room, on the other hand, was a small, sparse place with white marble walls and just a mattress and a blanket on the floor.

'They're new,' Lex said, a little defensively. 'The room isn't big enough for a proper bed. And at least it has a carpet.'

'Don't matter anyhow,' Jesse said. 'I'll sleep down below with Rusty.'

Lex shrugged. 'Suit yourself.'

When they went up to the bridge there was a white griffin the size of a small horse lying on Lex's four-poster bed. Half eagle, half lion, it was sprawled there looking rather pleased with itself.

'That's Silvi. One of the griffins I told you about. She's the friendliest. You can probably stroke her without her taking your hand off. But be careful around the other two.'

'She's not as big as I would've thought,' Jesse said, nevertheless looking impressed for the first time since boarding the ship. 'Baby, is she?'

'Three months,' Lex replied. 'Her brothers are much bigger – they're almost full grown already. They're probably out on deck. Come on, Silvi.'

The griffin jumped off the bed, loped over to Lex and stayed by his side as they went out to the open deck. The other two griffins were indeed there and were much larger than their sister, coming up to Lex's shoulder. They were both lounging contentedly in the sun, although they lifted their heads when Lex and Jesse came on to the deck.

'The grey one is Lukah,' Lex said, pointing. 'And the black one is Monty. Watch out for him; he's really bad tempered and he doesn't much like anyone but me. They'll probably get used to you in the end but for now don't touch any of them except Silvi.'

The only other people who had met the griffins were

Lucius – who'd practically cringed in terror whenever one of them came near him – and Zachary, whom the griffins had all taken an instant dislike to, quite possibly because Lex had turned the man into a ferret during the course of the last Game. The griffins seemed to be able to smell it on him still, even now. It made a pleasant change to show them to Jesse when the cowboy was quite obviously as impressed by them as he should be.

They had been up on deck for only a few minutes when Lady Luck appeared beside them.

'This is—' Lex began, intending to introduce Jesse.

But the cowboy, it seemed, needed no one to do the introductions.

'The Goddess of Good Fortune, of course,' he said, sweeping off his hat with a flourish and giving a gallant bow. 'My Lady, I would recognise your beauty anywhere.'

'Dear me, how sweet you are,' Lady Luck fluttered girlishly. 'Lex, who is this charming—'

'Jesse Layton, ma'am. At your service,' the cowboy said, straightening up and actually taking one of the Goddess's gloved hands to press a kiss to the back of it.

Lex was quite, quite horrified. How had he not foreseen this? Lady Luck *loved* scoundrels and rogues and rotters and rascals. Lex himself was, of course, all of those things but so, clearly, was Jesse. And whilst Lex was usually glad of his honest face – for it made scams *so* much easier when you looked like a gutless twerp – he had to admit that, on occasion, the scarred, stubbled, rugged look would come in handy, too.

'Oh, good choice, Lex,' Lady Luck gushed. 'I like this one much better than that lawyer.'

'Yes, I'm sure he'll do just fine,' Lex said, practically slapping Jesse's hand out of the Goddess's and giving him rather an evil look as he did it.

He did not mind double-crossing Lady Luck and, indeed, he had done it before, but he was not favourably inclined towards being double-crossed himself and a God could only have one player. Lex didn't like the way the Goddess was looking at Jesse – not one bit.

'Is there something you want particularly or have you just dropped by to get in the way?' Lex snapped.

'Someone got out of the wrong side of bed this morning,' the Goddess huffed and Lex cursed himself for being bad tempered when Jesse, drat him, was being so pleasant.

'I just thought you'd like to know,' Lady Luck said coolly, 'that I have it on good authority that Kala is planning to use Jeremiah East as her player.'

'Jeremiah . . . East?'

'That's right,' the Goddess said with a smile. 'The grandson of the famous Carey East himself.'

CHAPTER THREE

JEREMIAH EAST

This was the first occasion in a long while that the Game had been announced ahead of time. Since the last Game, and Lex's spectacular victory, interest seemed to have increased in the players themselves and it was now a little bit about hero-worshipping as well as about the gambling. There was even to be a feast, two nights before the Game was due to start, when the Gods would officially name their players.

Lex was quite beside himself with excitement to hear that Kala, Goddess of the Stars, was going to be using Jeremiah East, the grandson of the great adventurer about whom he – and, indeed, the rest of the world – had heard so many stories, most of which had been written by Lex's own grandfather, Alistair Trent, as Carey East's Chronicler.

Lex was not the only one who had found out about Jeremiah ahead of time. Word had got around that the young nobleman was coming to the Wither City and it was not all that hard to put two and two together. Carey East and Alistair Trent had been a famous pair in their time and already the newspapers were making a big to-do about the possibility of their grandsons being pitched together in a thrilling Game of wits and derring-do.

Jeremiah's ship arrived in the Wither City the next day. Quite a little crowd had turned out to welcome him and people lined the harbour, stuffed in like sardines around the closed-up stalls of the midnight markets. Lex had considered watching the proceedings from the deck of his own ship so as not to get jostled and shoved by the masses but decided against it for the simple reason that he just couldn't wait to meet Jeremiah. So he went down to the docks and Jesse went with him to see what all the fuss was about.

Lex had met Carey East just once, almost eleven years ago, when he and Lucius had been six years old. Their parents had been killed about a year previously when a water witch sank their boat, and Alistair Trent had retired from adventuring to look after them. When Carey East came by for a surprise visit one day, he brought presents for both Lex and Lucius and stayed with them until the next morning. Lex had never seen his grandfather so happy and he remembered Carey East being a large, loud, bluff, yet refined man. Of course, Carey East died two years later whilst battling with a sea serpent. But he had been the most famous, the most noble adventurer the world had ever seen and Lex was extremely proud of the association the Trents had with the Easts – a strong, unbreakable tie between two fine families stretching back across three generations . . .

So, when the gangplank was lowered over the side of the grand ship, Lex was right there beside the red carpet, next to the mayor himself. When Jeremiah appeared at the top of the gangplank there could be no doubt whatsoever that it was him. He was, to put it frankly, the most handsome person Lex had ever seen in his life. People started to cheer and wave flags. It didn't matter that the only noteworthy thing Jeremiah East had done so far was to *appear* in view; he simply looked like the sort of person people cheered and waved flags at. The people who didn't have flags waved their hats. Lex had neither a flag nor a hat so he merely contented himself with grinning stupidly. Usually he would have been a little bit jealous – all right, *extremely* jealous and irate and resentful – that someone other than himself was basking in the limelight. But when people cheered for Jeremiah and his family, Lex couldn't help feeling that they were cheering for *his* family, too. For weren't the Trents, after all, indistinguishably bound up with the Easts?

Jeremiah momentarily looked taken aback by the crowd's reaction but then raised his hand to gracefully acknowledge the applause before walking down the gangplank. He wore a royal-blue coat with shiny golden buttons that was probably worth more than all the items of clothing Lex owned put together. He must have been at least six foot, with black hair swept boyishly back from his forehead, blue eyes, white, even teeth and the fine-boned features of a true aristocrat. You could even see it in the way he held himself – with his shoulders back and his head high so that he sort of looked down his nose at everybody. He looked much older, somehow, than his twenty-one years.

'He fancies himself something rotten, doesn't he?' Jesse remarked. He stood on Lex's left hand side, lounging with his hands in his pockets. 'Snot-nosed kid, if ever I saw one.'

Lex gaped at him. 'Snot-nosed— That's Jeremiah *East*! He's refined, that's all! He's from one of the most noble families in the world!'

Jesse shrugged placidly and said nothing. Lex turned back in time to see Jeremiah step on to the harbour and shake hands with the mayor.

'Welcome to the Wither City, Mr East.'

'I'm very happy to be here,' Jeremiah replied graciously.

'This is Lex Trent,' the mayor said, indicating Lex at his side. 'He, of course, is—'

'Oh, a pageboy. How considerate,' Jeremiah said. 'My servants have my luggage in hand but you can take my sword if you think you can manage not to drop it. It's very heavy.' And with that he unbuckled his sword belt and thrust it into Lex's arms.

For perhaps the first time in his life, Lex was momentarily speechless and could only gape at Jeremiah in stunned silence, horribly aware of Jesse sniggering beside him.

'Oh dear,' the mayor said, flapping his hands in an embarrassed fashion. 'This isn't the pageboy, Mr East. This is Lex *Trent*.'

'Trent?' Jeremiah repeated with a slight frown. 'Can't say I recall any Trents. You're not at the Academy, are you?'

Finding his tongue at last, Lex said, 'My grandfather was Alistair Trent.'

Now, at last, recognition seemed to finally dawn in Jeremiah's eyes and he said, 'Oh, the Chronicler's grandson. I suppose you want my autograph. I'm afraid I don't have a pen on me right now but catch me later and we'll see what we can do. I assume we're to be put up in a tavern whilst we're here?' Jeremiah said, turning back to the mayor. 'We've had a very long journey and are anxious to settle in. Can you have someone show us the way?'

And before Lex knew what was happening, Jeremiah had grabbed back his sword and they were all walking away, leaving him standing with Jesse in the crowd.

'Don't see what all the fuss is about, myself,' the cowboy said, before wandering off, no doubt in search of the nearest tavern.

Inwardly, Lex cursed himself. He didn't know what had come over him. Under normal circumstances he would have said, '*I*? *I* want *your* autograph? Oh, come now!' in the most obnoxious tone he could muster. But he had been utterly unprepared for Jeremiah's manner. He had had a nice little image in his head of the two of them embracing like brothers, the crowd going nuts, photographers flashing their cameras, maybe even a bit of confetti thrown their way . . .

'Good heavens, it sounds like you were expecting to

marry Jeremiah, not merely meet him for the first time!'
Lady Luck said when he expressed his disappointment to
her, later.

'Our grandfathers were best friends,' Lex protested,
turning pink. 'That should mean something.'

'Well, perhaps he was just tired from his long journey,'
the Goddess replied airily. 'I'm sure the two of you will
get on like a house on fire at the feast this evening.'

Lex just grunted at this. Jeremiah had not seemed at
all tired to him. He had just seemed like rather a jerk, in
spite of the shiny gold buttons and the tall, dark, handsome thing he had going on. Lex found it difficult to
believe that Jeremiah's attitude towards him would be in
any way changed that evening. He was therefore surprised
when Jeremiah caught him as he was passing the Town
Hall later that evening and said, 'Look, Trent, I'm sorry
if I seemed a bit abrupt with you earlier. Long journey
and all that. And I didn't realise you were going to be,'
he lowered his voice a little, 'a fellow player.'

No excuse, Lex thought silently. Everyone knew his name
by now because of what he had achieved in the last Game:
all the records he had broken, all the things he'd done
that had never been done before – like being crowned in
the Golden Valley and going down to the Lands Beneath.
Those things hadn't been *easy*. They had been tremen-
dously difficult and yet Lex had pulled them off spectacularly well. He deserved a bit of respect for that, surely?
Even from someone as high born as Jeremiah East. Lex
had to resist the urge to say fiercely, 'I *was* a king for five

seconds, you know!' just in case Jeremiah *didn't* know, which really didn't seem at all likely.

'Come on,' the nobleman said, 'let me buy you a drink.'

'I don't drink,' Lex replied, still rather suspicious of this sudden change of heart.

'Oh, that's right, you're not eighteen yet, are you?' Jeremiah said. 'Well, don't worry, I expect we can sneak one through.'

'No, it's nothing to do with my age,' Lex replied. 'I just don't drink.'

For someone who put such a high premium on having a sharp mind, a quick tongue and always being one step ahead of everyone else, Lex stayed well away from drink and drugs of any kind. But Jeremiah once again seemed to misunderstand him, for he said, 'Dear me, you are a stickler for the rules, aren't you? I used to be like that – terrified of breaking a rule and getting into trouble. Don't worry. You'll grow out of it in time.'

'I'm *not* scared of breaking the rules—' Lex began at once, rather heatedly for the very suggestion couldn't have been any further from the truth. If he wanted to drink alcohol then he most certainly would – rules be damned. It was mere coincidence that his own preference happened to coincide with the rules just this once.

'Well, a pint of Grandy then,' Jeremiah interrupted, in such a jovial voice that Lex had to refrain from his protests because to continue them would appear churlish. 'You can still drink with me and the lads if you just stick to the soft stuff.'

And Lex found himself being manoeuvred into the tavern that was attached to the Town Hall. Well, what could it hurt? The feast wasn't due to start for another hour. He had told Jesse where and when he had to be there and he was sure the cowboy would turn up because there *was* going to be food and he knew that Lex could force them to switch if he wanted to, just by biting into the nearest pork pie. Besides which, a cowboy never passes up the chance of free food. When they went into the building, the hall was on their right and the tavern on their left. As they walked past the doorway Lex noticed that the hall was already set up for the feast – with rows of long tables lining the huge room and colourful bunting hanging from the walls and the ceiling.

'My friends were going to meet me here,' Jeremiah said as they walked into the tavern. 'Oh, yes, there they are at the back.'

The feast was invitation only – so that just the important people would be there and not any plebs gobbling up the free food and drink. It seemed that quite a lot of people had had the same idea as Jeremiah and his friends, to come to the tavern for a couple of drinks first, for the place seemed to be stuffed with city officials and lawyers and important men who were no doubt all on the guest list. Jeremiah bought a round at the bar and then they went to the table at the back where he introduced Lex to his five friends. Lex could hardly tell them apart for they were all tall, dark and handsome with names like Jones and Smith, and they all persisted in calling each other things like Jonesy and Smithy and Williamsy and Easty. It was quite baffling to Lex who, of course, had not been privately and expensively educated at the prestigious Academy.

'What are you drinking, Trenty?' one of the friends asked, peering at the pint of Grandy with a puzzled expression.

'Don't call me Trenty,' Lex said.

'He's having a pint of Grandy, poor boy,' Jeremiah said, thumping Lex on the back so hard that his face almost ended up in his drink. 'He's not eighteen yet.'

'You don't say?' One of the friends – Lex thought it was Jonesy – practically goggled at him in astonishment. 'I didn't realise they let children play in the Games!'

Lex stared at him. With a tremendous effort of will he just about managed not to hurl his Grandy in the twit's face. 'I am seventeen years old,' he said coldly. 'In the last Game I defeated a minotaur and a medusa simultaneously; I became a king – my name is on the Royal Monument in the square out there; I went on to the Space Ladders; I saw an underworld pass by with my own eyes; I went down to the Lands Beneath and – at the end of it all – I won the bloody thing!'

Lex felt extremely vexed. There was something most undignified about having to tout his own victories in such a way. Usually, whenever anyone said anything to him about the previous Game, Lex made a great show of being modest about it. 'It was nothing,' was his usual response. But he was only going to say that if the person he was speaking to knew full well that it was quite far from nothing. Modesty only worked when people knew just how splendid he really was. And these nobles didn't seem to have the faintest clue.

'You did *follow* the last Game, didn't you?' he said.

'On and off,' Jeremiah said. 'But we had studying to do, too, you know. After all, we *are* Academy educated.'

'Well, some people have to bother about things like that I suppose,' Lex said.

The root of the problem was that Jeremiah and his friends seemed like stuck-up snobs to Lex, and Lex seemed like an irritable little upstart to them.

It was Jeremiah who came up with the brainwave of spiking Lex's drink.

'Take him down a peg or two, eh?' he said to Jonesy when they were getting another round at the bar. 'Do him the world of good.'

Perhaps it was because Lex had never drunk before, perhaps it was because he hadn't eaten much that day or perhaps it was simply because he was so skinny . . . whatever the reason, it turned out to be an unfortunate fact that Lex could not hold his drink. It went straight to his head. One minute he was sitting there feeling quite normal, the next he was slurring his words and talking in a much louder voice that he would normally. He was hardly aware of this himself, although he did notice that the others seemed to have distinctly warmed to him and they were now all having rather a good time when they hadn't been getting on at all well before.

The really unfortunate thing about it, though, was that, when each of Jeremiah's friends went up to buy their rounds, they too thought it would be a splendid idea to add a little something to Lex's drink. By the time an hour was up, he was thoroughly drunk and just trying to get his muddled head around why he wasn't feeling normal when someone tapped him on the shoulder and he looked round into a familiar face.

Mr Montgomery Schmidt, through a series of unfortunate mishaps, had been Lex's companion in the last Game. He was a tall, thin old lawyer with the sense of humour of a dead mollusc. He certainly did not look at all amused right now as he addressed the table with his sternest expression.

'You reprobates! You ought to be thoroughly ashamed of yourselves!' He pointed at Smithy and said, 'I saw you, young man, not a moment ago spiking that drink at the bar. Don't drink it, Lex.'

'*You* spiked his drink?' the others all said at the same time, then they grinned foolishly at each other as they realised what must have happened.

'You mean to say that you have *all* . . .' Schmidt trailed off, horrified. 'Good heavens, the feast is due to start any minute! Come along, Lex, you'd better get some fresh air—'

'I don't need your help,' Lex said, waving the lawyer's hand away. 'And I'm not drunk.'

He stood up to prove his point but that instantly made him feel ten times worse. His head spun, the room tilted, he lost his balance and staggered. Instinctively, he reached out to stop himself from falling but only succeeded in dragging a whole table down with him in a spectacular crashing and rolling of tankards.

Oh my Gods, he thought, face down in spilt beer. *I really am drunk!*

It was even worse than he had imagined it would be. No quick thoughts were coming into his head; no snappy comebacks were presenting themselves in his mind; no brilliant, genius plans were clamouring for his attention. This must be what normal people felt like *all the time*! He was dimly aware of Jeremiah and his friends cheering and clapping behind him like this was all some huge joke. Schmidt grasped Lex's collar and dragged him upright as Jeremiah and the others got up and made their way to the hall, still laughing heartily.

'You've got to go in, Lex,' Schmidt was saying urgently. 'The feast is about to begin. Where's your companion?'

'Well now, what's going on here?' asked a drawling voice.

Lex looked round to see Jesse strolling through the now-almost-empty tavern towards them.

'He spiked my drink!' Lex croaked.

'Who? Him?' Jesse said, squinting at Schmidt doubtfully.

'Not me, you fool! Jeremiah East!' Schmidt snapped. His eyes went to the Binding Bracelet on Jesse's wrist. 'Oh, good, you're him. Look, you've got to get in there. Get him . . . Get him some coffee or something. Try to sober him up enough so that he can disguise it. He'll be in terrible trouble if they realise he's drunk; he's underage.'

'Not a problem,' Jesse said. 'I know just the thing. Come on, kid, we'll have you dried out in no time.'

The cowboy had to hold on to Lex's arm quite tightly to make sure he didn't fall down again as he practically dragged him through the hall, which was now bustling with people who were all talking and laughing noisily as they waited for the fun to begin. The grand table on the raised stage at the end of the room was for the three Gods – Lady Luck, Kala and Thaddeus. Filling up the rest of the stage was a huge crystal ball of the type you got in stadiums. When the Gods announced their players, the whole thing would be broadcast to other crystal balls around the world so that everyone might know who was playing in the Game. Then the food and drink would be brought out and the feast would start.

Luckily, the Gods had obviously decided to be fashionably late and had not arrived yet. Jesse dumped Lex down in a chair at the end of one of the three long tables set up in the room and then disappeared, saying something about going to get him some coffee.

The situation was an absolute nightmare. People had noticed him come in and Lex was aware of people pointing at him, for no doubt they recognised him from the previous Game and his presence there at the feast confirmed what the newspapers had been suggesting – that Lex Trent really was going to go up against Jeremiah East in the next Game. The people seated near him at the table wished him good evening and Lex shouted something back. Thankfully, the fact that it was so noisy in the room meant that no one noticed he was speaking louder than usual or that his words were on the slurred side.

Jesse came back just at the moment that the Gods materialised on the stage beside their table. Their image appeared inside the crystal ball, too, as it began broadcasting and, instantly, everyone was on their feet and applauding. Jesse dragged Lex upright and, with a great effort of will, he managed not to sway where he stood.

Lady Luck was dressed in her usual white toga, her blond hair piled up on her head and threaded with pearls. Kala was much smaller than the Goddess of Luck, with very tiny hands and feet and a small, perfect face that made her look rather like a china doll. Her dark brown hair fell about her face in tightly coiled ringlets and she wore a long blue dress with tapered sleeves. Thaddeus, on the other hand, looked more like a demon than a God, with his pointed ears and pointed chin, goatee beard and slicked-back black hair. He wore a dark cloak that fell all the way down to his ankles and had a high collar that came up around his ears.

Lady Luck raised her hand for quiet and, once the applause had finally died down, she stepped forwards and said, 'Thank you, my friends. Please, be seated.'

Everyone sat down. Jesse quietly pushed a steaming mug of what appeared to be strong black coffee towards Lex, who started trying to sip it surreptitiously. But the truth was that he was suddenly beginning to feel rather sick. And there was a ringing in his ears that meant he could hardly focus on what her Ladyship was saying. He tried to tell himself that it would be all right. The Goddess would give her little speech, the players would be introduced, Lex would stand up and bow graciously and try to look daring and heroic for ten seconds and then the feast would begin and he could quietly slip away to be sick somewhere.

Lex realised the first player was about to be introduced when Lady Luck stopped talking and Thaddeus stepped forwards.

'I, Thaddeus, God of Illusion, will be using as my playing piece, the enchantress known as Lorella.'

Lex looked over to the far end of the room where a young woman stood up. An enchantress? Now that was a surprise, for Lex had been expecting an enchanter. She looked young, too – surely not that much older than Jeremiah. But then, Lex knew that looks could be deceiving where enchanters were concerned. The female variety were much rarer and their magic much weaker – parlour tricks in comparison with the male enchanters. Pretty magics and the occasional love spell were about the limit of what they could achieve. Lex had seen several enchanters before, but he had never yet seen an enchantress.

The first thing he noticed about Lorella, even through his drunken haze, was her exceptional beauty. The entire hall seemed to still at the mere sight of her. Her hair was a royal, vibrant blue and fell long and loose down past her elbows. Her eyes were the exact same shade – like two sapphires set in her fine-boned face. She wore a grey dress that clung about her lithe form, leaving only the white skin at her throat on display. Everyone broke into rapturous applause and Lorella inclined her head gracefully before resuming her seat.

Kala then stepped forwards on the stage and said, 'For my player, I shall be using the nobleman, Jeremiah East.'

On the middle table, Jeremiah stood up and there was, if possible, even more thunderous applause for him than there had been for Lorella. It was just that he looked so dashing and noble with his dark blue coat and golden buttons and clean-cut good looks. The crystal ball loved him. If anything, he looked even more handsome in there than he did in real life. He and Lorella both looked so *smart*. It made Lex horribly aware that he was, at this moment, wearing a shirt that was covered in beer stains. This was all horribly wrong. Lex was supposed to be the *best*! The smartest, the handsomest, the daringest . . .

Jeremiah gave the crowd a dazzling smile and a graceful bow before resuming his seat.

Lady Luck then stepped forwards and a great sense of panic swept over Lex. He was concentrating on sitting very, very still because he was sure if he moved so much as a muscle he would be sick and yet, any second now, he was going to have to stand up and try to look impressive and wave and bow without giving away the fact that anything was amiss. He could see Jeremiah and his friends looking his way and sniggering already.

'I, the Goddess of Fortune and current Gaming champion, shall be using as my player the thief, Lex Trent.'

The applause for Lorella and Jeremiah had been enthusiastic but the audience practically wet themselves when Lex's name was mentioned. No one had forgotten what he'd done in the last Game – how exciting and thrilling and entertaining the rounds had all been because of him. Through the haze of his intoxication, Lex felt a glow of smug pride. Jeremiah certainly wasn't looking so pleased with himself now, he noticed. Lex was the favourite, Lex was the champion, Lex was the one who everyone loved . . .

He got up from his seat and bowed so low that his nose practically touched the floor. Then he straightened up – his head protested at the sudden shift, nausea rose up viciously in his throat and there was an abrupt tapering off of applause as everyone watched, shocked and dumbstruck, as Lex Trent threw up where he stood, before crumpling up to pass out underneath the table.

CHAPTER FOUR

THE MORNING AFTER

Lex woke up the next morning with a dry mouth, a sore head and sensitive eyes. And, to top it all off, he was in a cell.

'Howdy,' said Jesse, who was also in the cell with him.

'Urghh blurghh,' Lex replied, unsticking his tongue. 'Gods, my head!'

The questions *what's going on?* and *where am I?* rose in his throat but Lex refused to ask them because they were . . . silly. The sort of silly thing silly people said in silly situations. Lex prided himself on always knowing exactly what was going on and exactly where he was. And exactly how he was going to get out of it, too, come to that.

The 'where' part was obvious, anyway. Lex recognised a cell when he saw one; after all, he'd been in them before. It was the 'why' that took him a moment. He'd been at the feast . . . with the Gods . . . and he'd been unwell, suddenly – wasn't that it? But it hardly seemed fair to lock someone up just because they'd been ill. Lex was just considering the horrible possibility that he had some sort of dire, incurable, highly contagious disease when it all came flooding back to him in rather a sickening way.

'Jeremiah East spiked my drink!'

'Yep,' Jesse replied.

'I was drunk!'

'Yep.'

'I was sick and then . . .' The fact that Lex couldn't remember what had happened after that seemed to be a pretty clear indication of what had taken place.

'Yep.'

'Is that all you can say? *Yep*?' Lex raged, rounding on him viciously. 'It's not even a proper word! That's the best you can do? Why are you even here?'

The cowboy was sprawled on his bed, leaning back against the wall with his arms behind his head and his ankles crossed, hat tipped back, watching Lex lazily. He shrugged slowly in response to the onslaught of questions and said, 'Beats me, partner. First time I ever got locked up for someone *else* getting drunk. Maybe it's because they don't want us switching bodies. Or could be because of all this talk of us being disqualified, I guess.'

'Well, I think it's an absolute disgrace!' Lex seethed, imagining the awful scene of his being carried away to prison last night whilst everyone no doubt roared their stupid heads off with laughter. '*I'm* the victim here! That good-for-nothing, arrogant, snot-nosed brat, Jeremiah East, is the one who ought to be—' He broke off suddenly to stare at Jesse. 'What did you just say?'

Jesse shrugged. 'When?'

'Just now. You said . . . You said something about us being . . .' Lex could hardly bring himself to say the word, '*disqualified*! Surely you don't mean . . . from the *Game*?'

Jesse sat up on the bed. 'Their high-and-mightyships, Kala and Thaddeus,' he said gravely, 'are demanding it.'

Lex gaped at him like a landed fish for a moment before managing to croak, '*Why*?'

'Underage drinking at an official feast is disrespectful to the Gods, they say.'

'Since when has any player been disqualified for being *disrespectful*? Besides, *it wasn't my fault!*'

Jesse shrugged. 'Don't matter so far as they're concerned.'

Lex stared at him for a moment longer, trying to get a grip on the awful mixture of panic and rage rising up inside. Then he crossed the cell to grip the bars and shouted as loudly as he could, 'I demand to speak to someone in authority *right now*! Hey! *Hey! CAN ANYBODY HEAR ME*?'

'Shut up, kid,' came the muffled response from behind the closed door that led out to the office.

Lex scowled blackly. How old did he have to be and how many extraordinary things did he have to do before people stopped referring to him as *kid*?

'Where the hell is Lady Luck?' Lex fumed, rounding on Jesse again. 'Have you seen her?'

The cowboy gave a lazy shrug. 'Last time I saw her was at the feast.'

'You mean she hasn't been here to see me? Not once?

Surely she doesn't think I got drunk on purpose, does she?'

Before Jesse could answer, the office door opened and Lex whirled around expecting and hoping to see his patron Goddess, but seeing Mr Schmidt, dressed in a suit and carrying a briefcase, instead.

Lex stared at him, experiencing an uncomfortable moment of *déjà vu*, for he had been locked up in this very prison right before the last Game and Schmidt had appeared on the scene unexpectedly then as well.

'You're not here to testify against me, are you?' Lex demanded, looking at the lawyer through the bars.

'The thought had crossed my mind, but no, I'm not. I'm here to help you.'

'You mean you can get me out of prison and back into the Game?' Lex asked excitedly, gripping the bars tightly.

'I can get you out of prison,' Schmidt replied, 'but you're going to have to get yourself back into the Game, I'm afraid.'

'What does that mean?'

'There was a special hearing in court today to decide what's to become of you. Thaddeus and Kala were all for disqualifying you straight out but Lady Luck insisted on there being a hearing.'

'Why in the name of the Gods wasn't I there?' Lex demanded. 'Surely I deserve a say in the matter, don't I? I mean, it was *my* hearing! What about due process? What about *habeas corpus*? What about the prosecution's burden of proof? I should have had the chance to tell my side of the story!'

'The hearing was set early – deliberately early, I should imagine. You weren't in a – ah – fit state to attend. I volunteered to attend on your behalf.'

Lex pinched the bridge of his nose. He had a thumping headache and all this was not making him feel any better. 'Did they come to a decision?'

'The Gods are imposing a penalty round on you. Only if you complete it successfully will you be able to rejoin the Game.'

'What about Jeremiah? Doesn't he have to play a penalty round, too?'

'There's no proof that he spiked your drink.'

'But he *did* spike my drink. He and his friends *all* did! You saw them!'

'I saw one young man doing it; I never saw Jeremiah East himself in the act. However, I informed the court that it was my belief Mr East had shared some of the responsibility.'

'And?'

'He's denying it and so the Gods are not prepared to do anything. Lady Luck wanted him disqualified but Thaddeus and Kala refused because there was no eye witness.'

Lex groaned and resisted the urge to shoot his arms through the bars in an attempt to grab the old lawyer by the throat. 'For once in your life,' he said between gritted teeth, 'why couldn't you just have *lied*?'

Schmidt gave him a disapproving look. 'I'm not like you,' he said coldly.

'A fact for which I am eternally grateful!' Lex snapped. 'Fat lot of good you are! Why did you even go to the hearing at all if you weren't going to bother to help me?'

Schmidt regarded him in silence for a moment before saying in that same frosty tone, 'Seems to me that you've always managed perfectly well at helping yourself, Lex. So I don't think I'll give you this key the warden gave me a moment ago.' He drew the cell key out of his pocket and held it up to the light. 'I think I'll just leave it here and you can get it yourself, and good luck to you.'

Instantly, Lex changed his tone to sound beseeching and repentant but Schmidt had never been taken in by these acts, and he wasn't taken in now. Calmly ignoring Lex, he dropped the key on the floor outside the cell, just out of arm's reach, and then turned away towards the exit.

'You ungrateful wretch!' Lex shouted after him. 'How many times did I save your neck during the last Game?'

Schmidt glanced back over his shoulder, pointed at the key on the floor and said, 'Now we're quits.' Then he disappeared through the door and was gone.

'Of all the contemptible, lowlife, despicable things to do!' Lex fumed. 'I'll get him for this!'

He got down on to his hands and knees and reached one arm through the bars but the key was out of his reach. 'The way my luck's going at the moment I might as well shoot myself and have done with it!'

'Ah well, another couple of hours hanging out here won't kill us,' Jesse said calmly. 'Try and relax.'

'What's the matter with you?' Lex retracted his arm

and then turned to glare at the cowboy. 'Do you *want* to stay here in this vile cesspit?'

Jesse gazed about as if half expecting to find himself in different surroundings from the last time he looked. 'Vile cesspit?' he said. 'This? Kid, you should see the prisons they got back west. And even then, prison life ain't so bad. You're warm and you got a roof over your head. Besides, there's good eatin' in prisons.'

'There's "good eatin'" on my ship, too! So come over here and give me a hand, you dolt! Your arms are longer than mine; you might be able to reach the key.'

But, although Jesse tried, the key was out of his reach, too, and, although Lex yelled for the guards until he was hoarse, it seemed that they were not in an accommo- dating mood – after all, they didn't want to upset Lady Luck, but nor did they want to enrage Thaddeus and Kala. When Gods start squabbling, it is usually best for humans to stay well out of it.

When Lady Luck finally appeared, over an hour later, the first words out of her mouth were, 'Oh, that dear man! Lex, however are we going to repay him?'

'Eh? Who? What the heck are you talking about?'

'Mr Schmidt, of course! We agreed to defer to an anony- mous panel of human judges, you see, to make it fair, but I'm afraid I wasn't doing a very good job of presenting our case and we were on the verge of losing them when the lawyer swept in and asked to be heard and he spoke so convincingly that the judges decided to give you another chance, Lex! Isn't it wonderful? I shall certainly be sure to send that dear man a bit of extra good luck. We're greatly indebted to him.'

This little speech only had the effect of annoying Lex even further, especially since Lady Luck had never had a good word to say about Schmidt when he and Lex had been playing in the Game together. It reminded him just how fickle her Ladyship really was and, considering the look she'd given Jesse when she met him, it made Lex nervous.

'Brilliant! I'll send him some roses or something once the Game is over!' Lex said moodily. 'Perhaps even a fruit basket, too! Now, if it's not too much trouble, do you think you could see your way clear to passing me that key so that we can get out of here?'

The Goddess picked up the key and unlocked the door to let them out of the cell.

Lex stalked through the open door first, followed by Jesse.

'Much obliged, ma'am,' the cowboy said, tipping his hat to her, causing her to flutter girlishly in a way Lex found extremely irritating.

'Don't call her "ma'am"!' he snapped. 'She's a Goddess, not some flouncing, gartered, powdered cancan strumpet in one of your cowboy saloons!'

'Really, Lex,' Lady Luck said peevishly, 'you're the most miserable company when you're sulking like this.'

Lex scowled but bit his tongue. The truth was that he felt very much like hitting something. The Goddess of Luck left in a huff, saying that she would meet Lex back on the ship later on, when he was in a better mood, to discuss the penalty round.

'Just get on the ship and start heading for the Jespa Mountains,' she ordered before disappearing.

So Lex and Jesse made their way back to the ship in silence. Lex regretted being rude to her Ladyship at once, for it meant he had to walk back through the town himself rather than being magically put back straight on to the ship and he was utterly horrified to realise that people they passed in the streets were actually *sniggering* at him! *Him*! Like he was some sort of loser! Some no-hoper who was bound to die some horrible death or at the very least suffer some disfiguring accident in the very first round! All because he had let his guard down just long enough for Jeremiah East to spike his drink! It was almost more than Lex could bear and he had never been more utterly determined to beat someone in his life than he was to absolutely *thrash* Jeremiah in the upcoming Game.

He did his best to ignore the sniggering and pointing, and walked through the town with his head held high. Soon they were back on the ship preparing to depart for the Jespa Mountains. There were no cheering crowds, no screaming fans to see him off at the start of the Game – just a few dockhands dawdling about on the pier, eating their pies and smoking their cigarettes.

Lex threw the ivory Swann of Desareth into the basin on the bridge. With the ship then able to read his thoughts and respond to them, he went up on deck to check that all the griffins were on board before taking off. Unfortunately, Jeremiah was also on the deck of his own ship at that moment and, as the two ships were moored side by side, he was close enough to see Lex appear. The nobleman gave him a wave and called across a cheerful greeting. 'Hello there, Trenty! Awfully sorry about last night, old chap. Bit of a misunderstanding! But don't worry – if you faint again, I'll catch you and earn myself some extra hero points!'

'I can tell you're a newbie,' Lex called back in a voice of ice. 'There's no such thing as hero points, you idiot! There are just winner's points. I'll get you back for last night, though. Have no fears about that. You've no idea what you've started.'

Jeremiah just laughed and looked supremely unconcerned. Lex couldn't stand talking to him a moment longer so he threw out his arms in a dramatic gesture and commanded the ship to rise. It shot up into the sky so fast that Lex's hair was whipped back from his head. It occurred to him belatedly that he should probably have given Jesse some warning, but it had been worth it to cut Jeremiah's laughter short and get a glimpse of the startled look that came over his face.

Lex knew – as a cheat and a fraud – that it was always a good thing to be underestimated by people. It was definitely a good thing to be underestimated by a fellow competitor. But for some reason having Jeremiah East look down at him like that hurt his pride. As the enchanted ship sailed up into the clouds, Lex sternly told himself that, not only must he accept Jeremiah's low opinion of him, but that he must *cultivate* it and, at all costs, resist the temptation to show off like that again.

CHAPTER FIVE

THE SEA VOLCANOES

Lady Luck caught up with them on the ship later that evening and told Lex the penalty round was that he must retrieve one of the giant mountain eagle's golden eggs from one of their mountain nests: difficult and dangerous for most normal people, but not too much of a problem for Lex because the fact that he had a magic flying ship meant that he could start right at the top of the mountain rather than climbing up it by foot. Clearly Thaddeus and Kala either didn't know about his ship or they'd forgotten it. Without it, it would have taken Lex days – possibly weeks – to get to the top, and by that time he would have missed the start of the Game. No doubt, that was what they'd intended.

But, as it was, he was not overly worried about the penalty round. After all, it wasn't even a race between him and the other competitors this time, it was just a question of completing the task, and Lex had complete confidence in his own capabilities. He'd get that blasted egg, he'd jump through hoops if they wanted him to, and it would only make his eventual glory and triumph all the sweeter . . .

Lex and Lady Luck were sitting in the squishy armchairs on the bridge. Jesse was there, too, sprawled on the floor with his back against the wall because he said he found it more comfortable than sitting in the chairs or perching on the window seat. To Lex's irritation, Silvi – the female griffin – had settled herself down next to Jesse and was currently sleeping with her head on his lap.

'You do realise she's dribbling on you, right?' Lex said, hoping that the cowboy would push Silvi away and that she'd then go over to him instead.

But Jesse just gave a lazy shrug. Lex hated it when Silvi dribbled on him but that was because he was an absolute stickler for cleanliness whereas Jesse did not seem at all bothered. After all, he was a rough-and-ready cowboy, sorely in need of a shave and a haircut, so what was a bit of griffin drool to a person like that?

When he first sat down, Jesse had lit up a thin, vile-smelling cigarette but Lex ordered him to put it out, on principle. If Lex was going to learn how to be a cowboy then he was going to have to get used to the disgusting scent and taste of tobacco but he was damned if he was going to allow his bridge to smell like an ashtray.

'You smoke outside or not at all,' he told Jesse sternly, whereupon Lady Luck had simpered that she'd always liked a man with a cigar.

'It's not a cigar! It's a weedy cigarette; a disgusting habit

62

and a mark of gross stupidity! Don't you know those things kill you?' Lex demanded.

But Jesse just said, 'We all gotta go sometime, partner.'

Lex felt his lip curl in derision at the obtuseness of that statement. It was a sign of an amateur not to think things through and Jesse's remark clearly showed that he didn't know what the heck he was talking about. Lex knew everyone had to die sometime, but he did not particularly fancy dying slowly from some Gods-awful disease of the lungs, coughing and spluttering in agony all day and night, wishing to the Gods that he'd smoked a few less cigarettes and done a bit more exercise. Lex loved reckless adventuring so much that he was absolutely determined to continue it for as many years as possible. There was therefore no way on earth that he was smoking so much as one single cigarette, not even to achieve the scam of convincing other cowboys that he was one of them. He would find some way around it. He would find some way to cheat. He wasn't going to poison his own lungs for anyone or anything.

'Well, I'd better be off,' Lady Luck said once the penalty round had been explained. 'I'll see you tomorrow, Lex.'

She stood up but, before she could leave, Lex said, 'Is there anything else I need to know? About the Game, I mean? Seeing as I missed most of the feast.'

'Oh, no, dear. You've done it all before; you know what to do.'

Jesse looked up. 'Er . . . *some* things are gonna be different this time round though, ain't they?'

'What do you mean?' Lex asked sharply.

'There were some new rules announced at the feast.'

'Oh, yes,' Lady Luck said. 'So there were. Dear me, how silly to forget that.'

She sat back down in the armchair and started fussing, rearranging her long white skirts whilst Lex resisted the urge to throttle her. New rules! *New rules* and they'd only thought to mention them to him *now*! If it hadn't been for the cowboy he wouldn't have found out at all!

'Tell me everything,' he said. 'That's if you think you can remember it all correctly.'

The Goddess pouted and said, 'Don't be churlish, Lex. I must say I'm starting to tire a bit of all this sulking. You were so excited and delighted when I told you there was going to be another Game and I thought we were going to have such fun together, just like we did last time.' She almost looked tearful for a moment and Lex was just experiencing a faint flicker of guilt when she suddenly turned cold and said in rather a vicious voice, 'I most certainly can remember the new rules if you think you can sit still and listen to them without interrupting me!'

Lex nodded, accepting the dressing-down meekly because it didn't do to upset any of the Gods too much, even his own.

'Right then,' Lady Luck said – the angry look instantly gone from her face and replaced with a pleasant smile. She plucked at her skirts and patted her mass of blond hair, checking that the strings of pearls threaded through it were all in place. Then she lifted her head and said,

'After the last Game and your spectacular victory there was a lot of renewed interest in the Games not just for gambling purposes but for the sake of pure entertainment. You simply wowed everyone with what you achieved last time, my dear.'

Lex usually lapped up praise but even this didn't make him feel much better as he recalled how people had been pointing and sniggering at him back in the Wither City. They may have loved him for a while but fame was a fickle thing and it seemed quite clear that everyone was absolutely determined to transfer the adoration they'd once had for Lex on to Jeremiah East for no other reason than that he looked the part and had a famous grandfather. Sometimes it just seemed like there was no justice in the world at all.

'So this time,' Lady Luck went on, 'we have changed things a little and added a few extra rules, just to spice it up and make things more interesting.'

Lex thought it had already been pretty interesting, what with the constant mortal peril and threat of a sticky, messy death, but he listened intently to what her Ladyship was saying, anyway. Change was always a good thing for Lex because it gave him an advantage in that he adapted very quickly to it – much quicker than most people did, in fact. So the more different it was, the better, because Lex could embrace change whilst everyone else got thrown by it. It was just like when he'd been at school and always preferred unscheduled closed-book exams because, whilst his classmates had been twiddling with their pens, desperately trying to remember a few pertinent facts, Lex had been scribbling away, reading from the library in his head, for he could remember practically every word he'd read.

'The basic structure will be the same,' Lady Luck said. 'There will still be three rounds, each one chosen by a different participating God. But this time the dates and locations of the rounds were announced in advance at the feast. This was so that people could start getting excited about it but also so that they're better able to book time off work. We want as many spectators as possible, after all—'

'Hang on,' Lex interrupted. 'Are you saying that everyone already knows where the rounds of this Game are going to be?' He bit his tongue to keep from adding – 'Everyone but *me*?'

'Yes, dear. They don't know exactly, of course, that would ruin the fun. But they know the rough area. Kala is up first. Her round is to be at the Sea Volcanoes. Thaddeus's round will be on one of the Lost Islands. And mine will be at Dry Gulch.' The Lady patted down her dress absent-mindedly and said, 'I think I have a spare copy of the itinerary in here somewhere . . . Yes; here it is.'

She pulled a crumpled piece of paper out from the front of her dress and handed it to Lex, who just about managed not to grimace. 'What else do you keep down there?' he asked.

The Goddess rolled her eyes and said, 'You'll find the

dates written down on that. The rounds are each a week apart – we thought it would be easier for the spectators to get days off from work that way – so you'll have a bit of time in between and there are inn rooms booked for each of you at every location to make use of or not as you like, but I thought you'd probably just choose to stay on the boat.'

'I will,' Lex replied. 'Everywhere but Dry Gulch. I want to stay in Dry Gulch House the week before the third round.'

'Don't be silly, dear,' Lady Luck laughed. 'Only cowboys are allowed to stay there. Surely you know that? There are enough stories told about the place, after all.'

'Exactly. Jesse's going to teach me how to pass myself off as a cowboy so that I can look for the Sword of Life.'

'Oh, I see,' the Goddess replied, sounding unsurprised. 'Well, if anyone can find it, dear, it's you.'

'Right.' Lex pocketed the itinerary, intending to examine it more closely later, and said, 'Well, what other new rules are there?'

'We've altered the way the points' system works slightly,' Lady Luck replied. 'Now you don't just get points for winning the round – you can also get hero points, too.'

'What are they?' Lex asked suspiciously, remembering how Jeremiah had mentioned hero points to him back at the Wither City.

'We're trying to decrease the death rate a little, you see,' Lady Luck replied. 'It ruins the Game a bit if too many people perish in the first or second round. It doesn't make the last round so exciting if the players aren't all there. So, starting from this Game, if you see another player in mortal peril during the course of a round and you save their lives rather than leaving them to die, you'll be awarded hero points, which will contribute to your overall score. Ditto if you perform some particularly noble or self-sacrificing or just generally heroic act during the round.'

Lex pulled a face. He didn't like the sound of that one bit. 'But wouldn't that mean that someone – say me – could win the round but end up with the same number of points as someone who didn't win, just because they happened to perform a few so-called heroic deeds?'

'Well, theoretically, I suppose,' Lady Luck replied. 'The hero points don't apply to your companions though. Otherwise we could be in a situation where the player was constantly saving their own companion in a contrived manner and being awarded points for it. So the hero points only apply between players.'

'Are there any other new rules?' Lex asked, hoping that there weren't, for he didn't much care for the ones he'd learned about so far.

'I don't think so, dear. Do you remember any other new rules, Jesse?' she asked the cowboy.

Jesse shook his head. 'Can't say that I do, ma'am.'

'No, I think we've covered everything, Lex. Now I really must go. You need to get a good night's sleep before the penalty round tomorrow.'

So the Goddess took her leave and Jesse went down

to the hold below to sleep with Rusty. Silvi looked like she was thinking of following him but Lex called her back. She was *his* griffin after all and he was used to her sleeping on his bed. During the course of the last Game he had shared this room with Lucius and Mr Schmidt and it would have seemed quite lonely there all by himself without the griffin.

Lex got into bed and Silvi curled up next to him. Lex lay awake for a while, stroking her feathers and thinking about the upcoming Game. He'd had rather an undignified start, it was true, but the Game itself would be glorious. He was quite sure in his mind about that . . .

The next day, Lex completed the penalty task fairly easily with only the minor hiccup of almost falling to his death. Fortunately, the black griffin, Monty, saved him just in time and Lex completed the task all in one piece and with the golden egg that was his ticket back into the Game. The ship then set sail for the Sea Volcanoes where the first round was to take place – right at the very edge of the world.

When the first Adventurers started exploring a hundred years or so ago with their Chroniclers, many did not come back. There were countless theories as to why this was the case. Some believed that they got lost; others thought the Adventurers settled in new, tropical lands full of lush greenery and beautiful, half-naked women serving them coconut milk all day long; and some believed that they simply got eaten by sea monsters.

It was only later they suspected that most of the missing Adventurers had inadvertently sailed right over the edge of the world. The evidence for this was the sudden appearance of the Sea Volcanoes. They towered up out of the ocean and, like icebergs, there was even more of them beneath the surface. They were situated right at the very edge of the world, keeping the water in. And all along their base, down on the seabed, were the wrecks of thirty or forty sunken ships.

But the strange thing was that the ancient maps had no record of the Sea Volcanoes, and some Adventurers swore that they'd been in that area before – almost close enough to see the Edge itself – but that the volcanoes hadn't been there then. There was no official explanation but it was widely believed that the Gods had put the volcanoes there later because of the fact that the location and the currents in this particular area meant ships were susceptible to sailing right over the Edge and the Gods wanted to put a stop to it. It wasn't difficult to believe. After all, the Gods did live in the Lands Beneath and anyone would start getting a bit fed up after the twentieth ship came crashing down from the Lands Above, breaking things and cluttering up the landscape. If any ship were to get near to the Edge now, it would just be smashed against the volcanoes and sink to the seabed.

The Sea Volcanoes were a striking, majestic sight, rising up out of the water like noble guardians of the ocean and the men who sailed it. What made the sight particularly rewarding as Lex's enchanted ship approached it was that

Saydi's sun was in the sky that day. As the Goddess of Beauty, Saydi's sun made the air sweet and fresh, and brought loveliness to the landscape whether it was sunny or rainy.

Today, Saydi had cooled the rays of her sun enough that star-sleet fell softly from the sky. This was a special kind of sleet that only Saydi could produce. It sparkled silver like the stars, twinkling and shimmering as it fell, until finally it faded away like a dying glow-worm. It did not leave the skin wet, for it would not do for people to be uncomfortable and thus less able to appreciate Saydi's beautiful handiwork. So, although Lex stood at the prow of his ship surrounded by falling star-sleet, he was not wet. The sleet broke apart when it touched his skin, fading away and leaving behind nothing more than a faint tingling. But the sleet did not disappear when it touched the cold volcanoes and they currently looked like they were covered in a silver, sparkling coat of star-frost.

It was breathtakingly lovely, complemented by the calm dolphin-grey sea and the two-tone sky. It was bright blue where Lex had come from but, as they got nearer to the Edge, it became darker until it was a sort of velvet navy colour on this side of the Sea Volcanoes, melting into star-spangled black beyond them where the sky gave way to space.

There was even a café built on stilts at the base of the volcanoes. After all, when a mysterious volcano range suddenly appears on the landscape and may erupt at any moment, what could be more natural than to build a café right there beside it? Actually, it only served tea and scones, so it was more of a teashop, really, than a café. And a ridiculously overpriced teashop at that. But why not? The Sea Volcanoes were, quite literally, at the edge of the world, which meant that only the very rich could come here. Lex knew the type: men with monocles and women who thought nothing said sophistication quite like a hat piled high with fruit.

There was a little pier at the café only big enough for about four or five boats. One large tourist boat was moored there already but Lex could see no sign of Jeremiah's boat, or Lorella's – assuming that she was even coming by boat.

Ha, he thought smugly to himself, *even with the penalty round slowing him down he was still the first one here!*

He was early, in fact. The round wasn't due to start until twelve noon and it was only just gone eleven o'clock. But it never hurt to scope out the surrounding area a bit first. Lady Luck had told him that the Sea Volcano teashop would be charging more than double what it usually charged because, today, its patrons would be having the honour of witnessing part of the Game *first hand*, and that was quite something even if it didn't extend past seeing the players turn up.

There were a lot of posh-looking people currently on the teashop's veranda, sitting at the tables with their scones and tea, or else standing at the railings, gawking at Lex's beautiful enchanted ship as it approached. Lex manoeuvred it into the pier and was gratified to see that all the toffs were on their feet by then, applauding him from the veranda. At least they were clapping this time rather than laughing. It boosted Lex's confidence a little and almost made him think better of what he was about to do. Almost. When the ship came to a halt he gave them a sweeping bow and a wave before disappearing back inside. The ship was huge and he was confident that no one down on the pier would have seen his face too clearly from that distance, which was good because he wanted to have a little wander about down there without people being all over him.

He went down to the enchanter's wardrobe. When he'd first acquired the ship, the wardrobe had mostly been full of the tall, pointed hats the enchanters favoured, which had been very useful to Lex because it transpired that enchanters kept some of their magic in their hats, which meant that, when Lex put one on, he could perform a bit of magic, too. Of course, human minds weren't built for magic and Lex put himself in terrible danger each time he used it. There had been a couple of rather horrible side effects and talk of brain haemorrhages and unpleasant things like that.

Lex had therefore faithfully promised his brother, Lucius, that, no matter what happened during the course of this new Game, he would never put an enchanter's hat on again. Lex hadn't exactly been lying when he'd said that . . . but he'd only half meant it. He certainly meant to avoid the hats if he could help it but . . . if the situation was *really* desperate, to the point that he didn't have anything to lose by trying, well, he certainly wasn't going to rule the possibility out completely.

Unfortunately, it seemed that Lucius had somehow sensed this proviso in his brother's promise and, one night shortly before he left, Lex had woken up at about three o'clock in the morning to the sight of a huge fire flickering through his bedroom window. His first thought was that the fire-breathing rabbit he'd inadvertently let off the enchanter's ship was now back. He leapt out of bed, dragged on some trousers and was still doing them up as he ran out into the house, screaming for Lucius and Zachary.

'Wake up! Wake up! It's back! The fire-breathing rabbit is back; the barn's on fire!'

He ran out of the house with Zachary moments behind him only to find that Lucius was already there. And it was not the barn that was on fire. It was a big bonfire of twenty or thirty enchanter's hats, now blackened, shrivelled and ruined.

Lex stared at the bonfire in silent, speechless horror for a long moment, vaguely aware of Zachary stomping into the house, back to his bed. Then he turned to stare at his twin who stood there with his arms folded and a grimly determined expression on his face.

'What have you done?' Lex croaked. 'What have you *done*, you *idiot*?'

'I knew it!' Lucius replied, actually having the *audacity* to look *hurt*. 'I knew you hadn't meant what you said when you made that promise! That's why I knew I had to get rid of the hats.'

'You . . . you . . .' For once in his life, Lex could hardly find the words to express himself. It wasn't just that one of the most rare and powerful magical advantages he had was now lost, it was the fact that Lucius had taken it upon himself to go into *Lex's* ship and destroy *Lex's* things.

'Those hats saved your life!' he fumed, pointing at the smoking, blazing bonfire. 'When you were sent down to the Lands Beneath, do you think in a million years that I would ever have been able to get you out if I hadn't had one of those to get me there in the first place?'

'You got yourself there but Lady Luck got us out,' Lucius said, raising his chin stubbornly. 'If you'd used that hat a second time you'd have killed yourself. I know you, Lex. Your definition of an emergency would have been losing a round. You wouldn't have kept the hats just for matters of life or death. You're more likely to kill yourself with those hats than you are to save yourself. That's why I'm getting rid of them. Hate me if you like; I don't care. You're the only family I've got left and it's bad enough that you're playing in another one of those awful Games at all. I'm helping you.'

Lex looked at his brother, firelight flickering over a face that was identical to his own despite the fact that the person behind it was so different. How could Lucius not *understand*? How could he not appreciate how important it was to *win*? How could the thought of losing to someone else not make him feel positively *panic-stricken*?

Lex was strongly tempted, in that moment, to hit his brother for the first time in his life. But he clenched his fists and resisted the urge, contenting himself instead with snarling in a vicious tone, 'Next time you "help me" I promise you'll regret it! I won't forget this, Lucius! Never!'

And, exercising an impressive amount of self-control, Lex turned on his heel and stalked back into the house without slapping Lucius, or shoving him, or scratching his eyes out, or anything.

So there were no longer any enchanted hats in the wardrobe on the ship. Lex nurtured some faint hope that one might turn up elsewhere at some point, for there were plenty of rooms he had not gone into yet and you never knew what might suddenly appear on this ship. But for now at least, he had a total lack of magic hats. He did, however, have a lot of different disguises in the wardrobe. He'd purchased them before he left because, as any thief or con man knows, disguises are very important. Not to mention ridiculously fun.

Lex picked out the Trent Lexington costume – a character first created when he'd been a relative newbie at robbing and scamming, and was practising pickpocketing in the Gaming stadiums. He'd realised that people were much less likely to suspect you were a petty thief if you looked like a posh twit. The costume therefore consisted of a daft-looking frock coat (with tails and everything), fine black trousers, a white shirt and cravat, a top hat, a pair of gloves and – most importantly of all – a stick with a shiny gold knob at the end. Oh, and a monocle. Lex had added the monocle only recently because he thought it might help with disguising his face if anyone were to think that he looked familiar. For starters, it magnified his right eye in rather a startling way whilst at the same time forcing him to squint with his left. Lex was extremely pleased with the effect because, as well as disguising his face, it also helped give him the sort of pained, constipated expression that one rather expected to see on a spoilt young nobleman.

Lex was just admiring his reflection in the mirror when Jesse wandered into the room and visibly jumped at the sight of him. Then he realised it was only Lex and a smile crept over the cowboy's face as he crossed his arms in front of his chest and leaned against the doorframe. 'And just where are you going in that get-up?' he asked, eyebrow raised.

'Just to have a little mingle in the teashop,' Lex replied with a shrug. 'You can stay here on the boat.' Jesse looked like showing signs of protest but Lex cut him off before he could do so: 'I'll bring you back a scone. There's no need for you to come; you'd stick out like a sore thumb and I want to blend in.'

Jesse shrugged. 'All righty. Guess I'll just hang out here with the griffins then.'

'Yes.' Lex nodded. 'I'll see you later.'

He walked out of the room and downstairs. He'd been a little worried that getting off the ship without being seen might pose a problem but it seemed it would not be too difficult because the toffs had all gone back to their tea after the ship had docked and they'd realised that it wasn't going to be doing anything exciting for the time being. If there's one thing you can absolutely rely upon remaining the same, it's the love rich people have for their crumpets and scones.

Just to be on the safe side, anyway, Lex opened the door on the side of the ship that faced away from the teashop. From there he was able to jump on to the tourist boat docked alongside and walk off its gangplank on to the harbour. If anyone saw him alighting from the boat they would merely think he was a young lord who had been taking a nap and no one had bothered to wake him up when they arrived. He plastered a miffed expression onto his face and then stalked on to the veranda, immediately adapting his Trent Lexington walk and mannerisms, head held so loftily high that he was practically viewing the scene through his nostrils. It had taken him a fair amount of practice to walk like that without losing his hat, for it had a tendency to topple off his head when he stuck his nose in the air, but he had mastered the knack eventually.

'Ai simply can't *believe* that you didn't wake me up, Mama!' Lex exclaimed in a loud, snotty voice to no one in particular as he walked through the veranda, thus creating the distinct impression that he was part of some unfortunate family there. Then he opened the door into the tearoom, walked in and said loudly to the room in general, 'Ai say! Are you still serving elevenses or aren't you?'

'We are, sir—' the server began but Lex cut him off.

'Well, what does a fellow have to do to get some crumpets around heyah? Do *you* think this is acceptable?'

'If you'd just place your order with me, sir, I will gladly—'

'Oh, very well, very well,' Lex said irritably, as if placing his order was a great inconvenience to him. 'Ai want a pot of tea. And ai want crumpets.'

'Butter or jam with the crumpets, sir?'

Lex turned his head, looked directly at the server – who was not much older than he was – and affected an expression of utter horror. 'Do people really eat *jam* with crumpets nowadays?' he asked as if it was the most disgusting thing he'd ever heard of. 'My heavens, you'll be asking me if I want *ham* with crumpets next, I shouldn't wonder. Butter, boy! I want butter, naturally.'

'I'm very sorry, sir,' the server replied, completely unaffected by Lex's tantrum, thus proving that he must have worked at the Sea Volcanoes teashop a while now and so was accustomed to rudeness. 'Would you like milk with your tea, sir?'

'Yaas, naturally.'

'I'll bring it right out to you as soon as it's ready.'

'Very well.'

Lex turned and walked back to the door, managing to collide with someone who was coming through it from the other side. It was a woman with a silly hat and an expression that indicated she'd just been drinking cups of vinegar outside rather than tea. She also looked rather like she might have been crying in the not-too-distant past.

'Watch where you're going, young man, really!' she said huffily.

'Ai'm very sorry, madam,' Lex apologised in his best sulky voice. As he walked out to the veranda he could hear the woman berating the server for the fact that there hadn't been enough butter on her crumpets. He grinned inwardly at the heavy weight of her purse, now stowed away inside his pocket.

He'd wanted to come to the teashop partly because it seemed rather a shame to come all the way to the Sea Volcanoes and not sample crumpets at its famous teashop (even if he did have to wait until he was back on the ship with Jesse before he could enjoy them), but mostly he'd wanted to come for a little sport. Lex had moved on from petty pickpocketing. His crimes were more sophisticated than that now. But he still liked to keep his hand in every once in a while, just to reassure himself that he hadn't forgotten how. Of course, this was hardly a sensible time for thieving right when the Game was about to begin and he'd been in prison and threatened with disqualification once already. But a teashop just stuffed *full* of toffs like this . . . Well, expecting Lex not to try to rob them would be like expecting a wolf not to go after a paddock full of fat, stupid sheep who were all bleating at it in a distinctly taunting sort of way.

The veranda commanded a spectacular view of the Sea Volcanoes rising up out of the water and there were twisting black rails all the way around the perimeter to stop rich fools from walking straight into the sea. The tables were placed at a spacious distance from one another and covered in crisp, spotless white tablecloths on which stood silver teapots and plates of scones and crumpets.

Lex surreptitiously eyed the tables, chose a likely looking one with only two men already seated, walked up to it and sat down before saying, 'Do you mind if ai sit here? Ai'm waiting for my elevenses but ai'm afraid ai've just had the most devilishly trying time of it with that fool server in there.'

'It's like I was just saying, isn't it, Forsythe?' boomed the man to Lex's right. 'You can't get the staff these days.'

'You're quite right, Easty, quite right.'

'Easty?' Lex blurted, looking up sharply. 'Are you, by any chance—?'

'That's right. Humphrey East. My boy, Jeremiah is playing in the Game,' the man said, practically swelling with pride where he sat.

Lex had to force himself not to goggle at him in sheer disbelief. Now that he looked at him more closely, he could see that there *was* a slight resemblance. They both had the same dark hair and haughty look, although Jeremiah's father was getting on for being a bit on the rotund side – too many hours spent lounging in fine armchairs, enjoying expensive brandy, had ruined what had probably once been an impressive figure. Lex supposed it made sense that Jeremiah's father would be here at the commencement of the first round. After all, the Easts obviously had more money than sense and so could easily afford to shell out for this little tea party in order to gloat over the first-born son. And if Lex couldn't find some way to turn this to his advantage, then he wasn't half the talented cheat he thought he was.

'Mey name is Trent Lexington III – of the Galswick Lexingtons, you know – ai was at the Academy with your son.'

'Really?' Humphrey East said, grasping Lex's hand and shaking it emphatically. 'Glad to know you, my boy. Glad to know you. Although I can't say I remember Jeremiah writing home about you.'

'Ah . . . well,' Lex looked uncomfortable as he drew back his hand. 'I don't expect he used mey real name. They used to call me Old Squiffy.'

It had been an educated guess on Lex's part but, from what little he understood of private schools, it seemed that there was always one unfortunate boy who got landed with the nickname 'Old Squiffy'. Whether or not Jeremiah had ever had such a friend, Lex couldn't tell, but it seemed to go down well enough with his father, who threw back his head and laughed. 'I say, Forsythe, do you remember the Old Squiffy from our school days?'

The two men had a good chuckle and Lex let them have it. He'd experienced a momentary flicker of concern that they might work out the Trent Lexington thing. After all, they must have known that one of the other players in this Game was called Lex Trent. But that was toffs for you. Money had made them stupid. Lex could have announced himself as Tex Lent and they still wouldn't have put the pieces together. In fact, that wasn't a bad idea, Lex thought. He rather fancied calling himself Tex. He would have to think up an alter ego for Tex Lent at some point when the circumstances were right . . . But not now, when Trent Lexington suited the situation so perfectly.

A waiter appeared at that moment with Lex's tea and crumpets, closely followed by the woman in the daft hat that Lex had knocked into on the way out in order to pick her pocket. He almost choked on his first mouthful of tea when, instead of walking past their table as he'd expected, she pulled up a chair and sat down instead.

'Wilhelmina, my dear, this is Trent Lexington. One of Jeremiah's school friends, come to watch him play. Isn't that nice?'

'Pleased to meet you, ma'am,' Lex managed. So this silly old bat was Jeremiah's mother. And Lex had her purse in his pocket! It was only with a great deal of self-control that he managed not to smirk where he sat.

'Likewise, I'm sure,' the woman said, still looking rather tearful. Perhaps she was fretting about the possibility of poor dear Jeremiah getting killed in the Game. Lex was glad in that moment that he had no such fussing relatives – except for Lucius – inconveniencing him and cramping his style. Who needed parents, anyway?

Lex took another gulp of tea and thought hard. Time to get to work. But how to go about it? He could hardly come straight out and ask Jeremiah's parents if their son had any useful little weaknesses or character flaws that a scoundrel might try to exploit. They may not be the brightest pair he'd ever met but even *they* were surely likely to get suspicious about those sorts of questions.

'Ai can't tell you how much ai'm rooting for Jeremiah!' he gushed. 'I do so hope that he wins!'

'Of course he'll win!' Mr East boomed, as if the very suggestion that he might not was absurd. 'The boy was born and bred to win!'

'Yaas, of course he was!' Lex agreed before making a show of looking around for non-existent eavesdroppers, lowering his voice and saying, 'And ai'm quaite sure that that phobia of his won't interfere with his ability to play the Game one jot. Not one single jot.'

Mr and Mrs East instantly both looked rather annoyed and Mrs East said huffily, 'It's perfectly natural for a young man his age to be afraid of rattlesnakes.'

Lex wasn't sure what the *young man his age* bit had to do with it but he just nodded along, anyway.

'Absolutely!' Mr East agreed. 'Mark of intelligence, if you ask me! Besides, there's hardly going to be any rattlesnakes in *there*, are there?' He pointed at the silver surface of the sea.

'No, sir,' Lex replied. *But we'll see what we can do about that* . . . 'But what about that other thing?'

Guesswork, once again. There was no guaranteeing there *was* another thing, after all. And, indeed, for a moment both of Jeremiah's parents looked blank.

'Oh, perhaps he didn't tell you,' Lex said, looking embarrassed. 'Perhaps ai shouldn't have said anything.'

'Don't be absurd!' Mrs East snapped. 'Do you really

think our son would have told *you* things that he didn't tell *us*? I expect you're referring to that upset with the brandy at the Academy. But Jeremiah doesn't drink anymore,' she said, fixing Lex with a frosty look.

'Doesn't drink, you say?'

'Not one drop. He knows his own limitations. We brought him up in such a way as to make sure of that.'

'I say, perhaps we oughtn't to be talking about such things out in the open like this,' Mr East said, suddenly catching on to the impropriety.

Lex nodded his agreement. It was almost time for him to go, anyway, but there was just time to do one last bit of damage first. He leaned forwards across the table a little and said, 'Ai daresay ai shouldn't tell you this, but ai have it on good authority that this Lex Trent fellow Jeremiah's up against is absolutely *petrified* of bats.'

'Bats?' Mrs East said sharply. 'Bats, you say?'

'Yaas, bats. Little winged rats, you know.'

In fact, Lex had no phobias. None whatsoever. He wasn't scared of heights or spiders or rats or bats or snakes or anything. These were irrational fears and simply baffled him. There'd have been about as much truth in the statement, *Lex Trent is scared of the colour blue*, as there was in the statement that he was afraid of bats. In fact, he rather liked bats. They were sweet little things when they didn't have their fangs out. But he may as well toss a bone Jeremiah's way and see if anything happened, although he suspected the nobleman wouldn't have the wit to make good use of the information. It would take a special kind of cunning to produce a bat in the middle of the Game, after all. Lex would have managed it somehow, but he doubted Jeremiah would. Still, hopefully he might waste a bit of time and energy in the attempt.

'Ai have a friend who knew Trent when they were law students back in the Wither City,' Lex said. 'And apparently, one night, a swarm of bats descended on them and this fellow Trent went absolutely nuts. Freaked out altogether, so old Jonesy said. Practically wet himself.'

'You don't say?' Mr East said, stroking his chin thoughtfully. The man was so transparent he might just as well have been made of glass.

'Best not tell Easty though, eh? Ai mean, it wouldn't be sporting, would it? And ai'm sure Jeremiah doesn't need tips like that to win. He can win without them.'

'Of course he can!' his parents said in perfect unison.

'Of course he can,' Lex echoed.

CHAPTER SIX

THE DEAD SHIPS

Lex left soon after that, stuffing a couple of crumpets into his pocket to enjoy with Jesse later and then going back to the ship the way he had come, through one of the tourist boats, taking the opportunity to pinch a few more wallets along the way. He was pleased to find that he hadn't lost his touch. He barely had to brush past someone and their wallet would be in his pocket. It was ridiculously easy and the reason, as he remembered now, that it had ceased being fun. There was no exciting challenge in it.

That was why he had moved on to daring cat-burglar exploits as the Shadowman, pinching spectacularly valuable things from museums, until he'd got caught up in the last Game and someone had shamelessly stolen his alter ego. He'd therefore been forced to re-invent himself as the Wizard. The tiny enchanter's hats he now left as his calling card were magical. A little bit magical, anyway. If you said *Abracadabra* then a small flame shot from the tip. Lex had found a magically refilling cupboard of them on board the enchanted ship and had no idea what they had originally been for, but they worked very well as his calling card now because the fact that they were magical meant that they could not easily be reproduced by copy-cats. Which meant that Lex got to keep all the glory and notoriety for himself.

He slipped back on to the boat, quickly got changed and then went up to the top deck where Jesse was watching the other ship come in. Lex had noticed its approach from the teashop and had realised then that it was most definitely time to go. It was Jeremiah's ship. He recognised it by the mermaid rising up along the prow and the painted blue and gold exterior. It was a grand ship in a boring sort of way, he supposed, but it couldn't possibly compare with the gleaming, silver enchanter's ship, where even the sails were made out of metal, and ancient, magical black runes were painted all along its sides.

It was fast approaching midday – the allotted time for the start of the round – and even the toffs were no longer showing much interest in their crumpets. They were all lined up eagerly, waiting for the other players to arrive and for things to get interesting.

Finally Jeremiah's ship pulled in next to Lex's. Lex couldn't prevent his lip curling as he saw that it clearly ran on wind and oar power – not on magic. It was really quite pathetic and he felt a glow of smug satisfaction at the fact that Jeremiah had been forced to dock his ship right next to Lex's and thereby emphasise the fact that the two really were in completely different classes. There was much cheering from the toffs below, though, and Jeremiah appeared up on deck to give them a bow, whereupon the crowd went crazy in quite an over-the-top way, in Lex's opinion. After all, Jeremiah was only *bowing*, not throwing fistfuls of money down at them. But he was wearing fancy clothes with shiny buttons again, and had that handsome, noble look, and that sort of thing mattered to some people. Or, at least, it mattered to the stupid people, concerned only with appearances rather than actual talent. Lex wasn't overly bothered by it, for he had no time for stupid people and never had. And never would, either.

He hadn't seen Lorella – the enchantress – arrive in the Wither City and so did not know what sort of transportation she was using. He sort of expected it to be another enchanted ship, similar to his own. After all, it was the method of transportation favoured by the enchanters and so it made sense that the enchantresses would use them, too.

But the minutes ticked closer and closer to midday and still there was no sign of an enchanted ship on the horizon, and Lex started to worry that she might not turn up at all. He was aware of Jeremiah looking more and more pleased as the moments crept by but that was because he was an idiot who thought it was only about winning, when actually it was about winning *spectacularly*, and that was that bit harder to do if the competition was severely reduced before the Game even began. A no-show from Lorella was therefore the very last thing Lex wanted.

At the same time, however, he didn't want to be shown up by her. And so he was quite annoyed when, five minutes before midday, she finally arrived in a most unexpected way. When the rainbow suddenly appeared in the sky, Lex thought it was something to do with Saydi and her love of all things beautiful, but then he realised that no rainbow – even if it *was* Saydi's sun that day – would ever race across the sky quite like *that*! It was like some sort of glorious shooting star in pink and blue and green, and there were a lot of *oohs* and *aahs* from the crowd below as the rainbow spread across the silver sky to finally end right over the pier. And then Lorella materialised from the end of the rainbow – a human shape suddenly forming out of the multitude of colours. There was a figure-hugging, blue velvet dress and masses of long hair that – for a brief moment – sported all the colours of the rainbow before Lorella herself stepped out of it and the multi-colours sparkling about her slowly faded, leaving behind an exceptionally beautiful enchantress who smiled and inclined her head just a little as the crowd of toffs went berserk.

Lex scowled blackly, thinking that both his own and Jeremiah's arrivals had been most effectively upstaged. The thought made him glance automatically across to Jeremiah's ship. The same sort of thing was clearly running through Jeremiah's mind, for he turned his head to look at Lex's ship at the same time and their eyes met briefly.

But what might have been a shared sympathetic moment was ruined by what had passed between them in the Wither City and they both hastily averted their gazes from one another, glaring back down at Lorella instead and the stunningly beautiful spectacle she was making of herself down on the pier. Well, she certainly knew how to work the crowds, Lex would give her that.

'Arriving by rainbow!' Lex scoffed to Jesse. 'I've never heard of anything so grossly over-the-top in my life! It's pathetic! Isn't it? Jesse?'

The cowboy shook his head and said, 'Sexy as all hell was the first thing that came to my mind, kid.'

Lex scowled at him, pointed a stern finger and said, 'Don't let yourself get taken in by her . . . by her feminine wiles! That's what she wants and I won't have you messing up the Game for me, is that understood?'

'A fella can look, can't he?' Jesse protested, holding up his hands defensively.

'No!' Lex snapped. 'That's what everyone else is doing.' He waved an arm to encompass the noblemen (and women) on the veranda all ogling the enchantress in rather an obvious way. Even Jeremiah was no longer glaring at her. 'We need to be *better* than them!' Lex went on, 'if we're to win the Game!'

Just the phrase *win the Game* sent surges of adrenaline rushing through him and – in that moment, when it was all brand spanking new and just about to begin – Lex practically had to stuff his fist in his mouth to stop himself from shrieking and jumping up and down in uncontrollable excitement at the prospect of what was to come. Another Game! Another Game at last!

Lady Luck was looking quite miffed when she appeared

on the deck of Lex's ship seconds later. No doubt she didn't exactly appreciate having another player in the Game who seemed to have even more of a flair for the dramatic than Lex did himself.

'Come on, then,' she said rather sulkily. 'Let's get down to the pier.'

She plucked them from the deck of the ship and a split second later they found themselves standing on the pier alongside Lorella. A moment later, Jeremiah and his companion arrived with Kala and then Thaddeus appeared alongside the enchantress. The crowd fell hushed and the players, companions and Gods all stood looking at each other in a hostile sort of way. There had, after all, been quite a lot of upset and bitterness and the Game had not even begun yet.

Lex couldn't help nurturing a mild hatred for both Thaddeus and Kala for the petty, cheating way in which they had tried to have him disqualified from the Game merely for being drunk. He found himself feeling un-reasonably irritated by Kala's silly sausage ringlets and little doll-like face – her entire appearance suggesting a sweetness and an innocence that was entirely false. And, as for Thaddeus – why, he practically looked like some sort of actor in a cheap production of a play about demons with that fussy little goatee beard and the OTT long dark cloak. Lady Luck oozed class when viewed beside them, Lex thought smugly to himself, what with her lovely white, toga-like dress and her elegant hairstyle, her masses of blond hair threaded through with strings of pearls. Yes,

Lex decided grimly, both he and his Goddess were in an entirely different class from all the others here.

He cast his eye over the companions next. If they'd been at the feast back at the Wither City, he hadn't noticed them and was not quite sure what to expect. He sort of thought that Jeremiah might have picked a posh fencing instructor with a silly moustache, or perhaps one of his stupid rich friends. What he did *not* expect to see standing at Jeremiah's side was a pretty little girl who couldn't have been more than nine years old. She had lovely long black hair and bright blue eyes. The physical resemblance between her and Jeremiah was undeniable. Unless he had become a father shockingly young, this girl must surely be Jeremiah's little sister. Perhaps *she* was the reason Mrs East had looked so miserable. After all, rich people usually got quite excited at the prospect of their handsome, strapping young sons marching off to a noble and glorious death.

Lex stared at the girl. She noticed and stuck her tongue out at him. He grinned, liking her already. And loving the fact that Jeremiah, whether through stupidity, ignorance or accident, had landed himself with a useless companion and a horrible responsibility to have to carry with him through the Game, whilst Lex had practically the most perfect companion imaginable in Jesse – a swarthy, rough-and-ready cowboy. Once again, all the cards seemed to be stacked in his favour before the Game had even begun! When he was so naturally gifted, how could anyone even *hope* to go up against him and win?

He glanced at Lorella, realising it was probably too much to hope that she would have brought a useless companion, too, but almost half-expecting it just the same. But in fact, when he looked at her, he realised that she did not seem to have any companion at all.

Lady Luck noticed this, too, and said to Thaddeus, 'Might I ask where your player's companion is? You do realise she won't be permitted to play without one?'

'She has a companion, my Lady,' Thaddeus replied in a scornful voice before looking at Lorella and saying, 'Show her.'

The enchantress reached into her pocket and withdrew her hand with her fingers closed around something. When she opened them, everyone leaned forwards a little to see the sprite sitting on her palm. No bigger than the size of a thumb, the sprite wore a tiny pair of dungarees on top of a white t-shirt. Her pointed face and ears were surrounded by a mass of light, feathery hair, one half white and one half blue. A pair of silvery wings were tucked close to her back. And, now that Lex looked closely, he could see a tiny little Binding Bracelet on the sprite's wrist. Lorella dropped her hand and the sprite fluttered up to sit on the enchantress's shoulder.

'The requirements all appear to have been met,' Kala said. 'All that remains is for us to distribute the Divine Eyes and then the round can begin.'

She handed a little crystal ball over to Jeremiah; Thaddeus gave an identical one to Lorella and Lady Luck passed one to Lex, who put it straight in his pocket rather than examining it curiously as the others were doing. Divine Eyes were nothing new to him. He'd carried one with him in the last Game. No one was quite sure how they worked but it seemed that they were somehow able to capture the events of the round and could then be transmitted later on to the giant crystal balls in the Gaming stadiums. It seemed to be something to do with the fact that the Gods watched their players and were somehow able to record what they saw on to the crystal balls.

Kala cleared her throat, stood up a little straighter and raised her voice so that the toffs goggling at them from the veranda would be able to hear what she said. 'The current Gaming champion, Lady Luck, has graciously allowed me the privilege of choosing the first round.' She paused dramatically for a moment before saying loudly and clearly, 'For the first round, then, let it be dead ships!' There were excited mutterings from the crowd and then Kala went on. 'There is one shipwreck down at the base of the volcanoes that, because of the peculiar way in which it was built, has quite a lot of air pockets left in it. In a moment you will all be sent down there by your respective Gods. The first one to return the captain's medallion to me, wins.'

Lex was wary, and he could tell that Jeremiah was, too. Lex knew from experience that they all had good reason to be. The first round in the last Game had involved the seemingly simple task of finding and fixing a broken mirror, but it had soon become apparent that the castle in which they were searching had a number of rather horrible traps – including minotaurs and medusas.

'In order to avoid shrill, hysterical accusations of cheating,' Kala said, with a dirty look at Lady Luck and Thaddeus that made Lex suspect they had already had words about this, 'you will all be put in the same part of the ship at the same moment. Ready?'

She was talking to the other Gods rather than the players, who barely had time to take in what was being said before she was counting, 'One, two, *three!*'

On the exact count of three, Lex and Jesse, and Jeremiah and Lorella with their companions, all disappeared into thin air, and found themselves hundreds of feet below the surface of the sea in the old galley of one of the sunken ships on the seabed.

CHAPTER SEVEN

THE SQUEALING BLUE-RINGED OCTOPII OF SCURLYSHOO

The air was cold and damp and old and musty. It smelled funny – of salt and seaweed and fish. It felt even funnier when Lex took a breath and inhaled the cold air into his lungs.

Of course, being so many fathoms under the sea, the ship should have been in complete darkness, and would have been had it not been for the starfish. They were all over the place – both inside the ship and stuck to the portholes outside, as well. These were sunrise starfish and Lex knew them at once because of the way they were glowing – although it was more of a luminescent greenish-blue than the colour of the sun. He'd seen them before, although never alive. The midnight market back at the Wither City sold a vast array of food on sticks – most of which consisted of the creepy-crawly, long-leggedy, beasty variety – but they also did sunrise-starfish kebabs, and you could always tell what area of the market they were in for, even dead, the starfish still emitted a greenish glow. Lex thought it was gross, himself, but some people seemed to really love munching away on starfish, and they were even considered something of a delicacy back in the city.

The soft green light emitted by them was just enough to illuminate the large room. There were four long rows of tables with a lot of wooden chairs nailed into the floor, all covered with copious amounts of thick, slimy seaweed. There were several paintings on the wall, all depicting a huge, monstrous octopus. Everything was damp and the portholes looked straight out at the cold, black sea. It was a weird feeling to know they were so far under water.

After the six of them appeared in the galley, there were a few odd moments of almost embarrassed uncertainty, for no one was too sure what to do next – not even Lex, who'd done this all before. After all, in the previous Game, for various different reasons, the players had all started the rounds at slightly different times or in different places. They had not all been dumped at the starting line at exactly the same moment like this, in each others' pockets, as it were, and getting under each others' toes. It seemed to be a toss-up between making a mad dash for it or trying to knock the other two over the head with some-thing really heavy. Indeed, it looked like Jeremiah was already reaching for the sword at his belt when his little sister piped up. 'There's three doors out of here and three of you. Why don't you each just pick one?'

'Shut up, Tess!' Jeremiah snapped. 'What did I tell you about talking during the Game?'

Tess pulled a face at him but said nothing. It seemed that Lorella wasn't prepared to stand around discussing the matter and strode away in the direction of the nearest door. She pulled it open, walked through and was gone. Lex decided to do the same. He picked up a starfish that was resting on the floor – just in case there weren't any in the next room and he needed the light – then turned and walked in the direction of one of the other doors at the same moment that Jeremiah turned to walk in the direction of the last one.

Jesse was close behind Lex as he pulled the door open and stepped through, drawing it shut behind them. And immediately something wet and slimy fell from the ceiling, landed on Lex's head, and wrapped long slippery things around his neck. And that was the moment that Lex first discovered that he *did* have a phobia after all. It transpired – most unfortunately – that Lex was absolutely terrified of octopuses.

Of course, he didn't realise that it was an octopus at first. He just started screaming and staggering around, dropping the starfish in his panic, knocking into things and causing them to fall over. It was most unlike Lex to lose his head in this manner. But, even before he knew that the thing on his head was an octopus, he detested the cold, slimy feel of the tentacles wrapped around his neck, squeezing his throat, making his skin prickle with revulsion. When he lifted his hands in an attempt to drag it off, he detested the soft, slimy, *squidgy* feel of the thing latched on to his head. And he detested the weird smell of it and the horrible high-pitched noise it was making.

He couldn't see where he was going and, somehow, managed to fall over on to his back on the floor. No matter how he tugged and hit and pulled, he didn't seem to be able to get the thing off. There was nothing he could do to stop it from choking him to death. The horrible, dreadful, awful, ghastly, horrific, *unimaginable* thought crossed his mind that perhaps he – *he* – *Lex Trent*! – was the one who was going to die in the first round this time, when suddenly a strong hand shoved his shoulder back hard on to the floor, pinning him there. A split second later there was a *squelching* noise and then a sort of wheezing and the grip around Lex's neck suddenly went slack. Then the thing on his head was gone and both his hands clutched at his throat as he gulped in air.

The first thing he saw was Jesse standing over him with a little octopus – a pale fleshy colour with blue rings all over it, about the size of a cat – impaled, long tentacles dangling, on the knife the cowboy held in his hand.

'Poor little sucker,' Jesse said, looking at the octopus sadly.

'What about me?' Lex choked indignantly.

'You're still alive, ain't you? No dead thing I ever came across made as much noise as you.' Jesse shook the knife and the dead octopus slid off it and landed with a splat on the floor beside Lex, who drew back from it in panic, scrambling across the salty, wet boards.

'What the heck is that thing?' he asked, staring at it. 'And are you *certain* it's dead?'

'Sure it's dead,' Jesse replied, shaking blue blood off the knife. 'The rest of 'em ain't, though.'

'The *rest* of them?' Lex repeated, horrified.

It was only then that he realised the long corridor they were in was absolutely crawling with little octopuses – on the walls, the floor and even clinging to the ceiling. And, for the very first time, playing the Game was not one hundred percent fun for Lex. For the very first time in his life, he felt some faint glimmer of sympathy for Lucius when he caught sight of a spider in the bath and trembled in fear just at the sight of it. Lex tried to tell himself that a spider couldn't hurt you and these octopuses obviously could, but he couldn't lie to himself, no matter how well he could lie to other people. The simple fact was that the octopuses could have been utterly harmless and he would still have felt horrified at the very sight of them. It was something about their squidgy heads and long, slimy tentacles – no living thing should look like that; it was just unnatural! They had *squidgy heads* for Gods' sake!

'Do you think they're all over the ship?' Lex whispered.

The cowboy shrugged. 'Seems likely, don't it? Probably been attracted by the air that's still in here. But if we move quietly and don't do anything to startle 'em, hopefully they'll just stay where they are.'

Just the thought of an octopus dropping on to his head

again like that made Lex want to flee the boat and take his chances in the sea outside. But, with a great effort of will, he pulled himself together. All right, so he was unused to this horrible, prickling sensation of fear crawling along his skin; he was unused to feeling irrationally repulsed by something; and discovering your fear of octopuses for the first time when you're in a sunken ship that's *full* of the little suckers is exceptionally bad timing. But that was what had happened just the same and there was nothing Lex could do to change it. He would just have to grit his teeth and bear it. Nothing – but *nothing* – was going to stop him from winning this round. If anything, Lex's success in the previous Game had made him even more competitive than he'd been already, for he had a record to keep now. In the last Game he had won every single round. He'd never lost one yet and he did not intend to start now. The competition was tougher this time, for both Lorella and Jeremiah were bound to prove themselves formidable opponents. Lex could not allow anything to distract him. So he thrust his new-found phobia deep into the back of his mind, stood up, picked up another glowing starfish, cleared his head and tried to think.

'Kala said we need to retrieve the captain's medallion,' he said. 'So the chances are that if we find the captain's skeleton, we'll find the medallion.'

'So what part of the ship will we find the cap'n in?'

Lex thought for a moment and then said, 'It depends what sort of man he was. If he was a brave man, he would have been in his rightful place on the bridge when the ship went down. If he was a coward he'd have been hiding in his quarters—'

'And if he was a greedy man, he would've been hiding in the galley!' Jesse cut in.

Lex glared at him. 'Don't be absurd! *No* man, no matter how greedy, is going to rush down to the galley whilst the ship is sinking to stuff his face one last time. Besides, we just came from there.'

Jesse grinned. 'I was only kidding.'

'Well don't! There's no time for that!' It was important to Lex to win the Game but it probably didn't matter much either way to Jesse. Lex realised then for the first time that he probably should have offered the cowboy some sort of incentive earlier. 'For every round we win, I'll pay you fifty pieces of m-gold.'

Jesse crossed his arms over his chest. 'Make it a hundred.'

Lex scowled at him. It was on the tip of his tongue to remind the cowboy that if it weren't for Lex's timely intervention, Jesse would still be rotting in prison, or else on his way back to the hangman's noose that was waiting for him in the Wild West. But he didn't have any more time to waste so he just snapped, 'Fine!'

They could argue about it once the round was over. And Lex could always go back on his word later if it suited him. His offer of a reward seemed to have the desired effect, though, for now Jesse replaced the knife in his belt, rubbed his hands together gleefully and said, 'So are we going for cowardly or courageous?'

'Courageous,' Lex replied. 'They don't tend to give medallions to cowards. We need to find the bridge.'

So they set off down the corridor, moving slowly, trying not to make any noise and tiptoeing carefully around the octopuses on the floor. Most of them were clinging to the walls but there were a few on the ceiling as well. Here, too, hung several paintings all showing the same octopus. There even seemed to be a large mosaic of one beneath the seaweed on the floor. Lex couldn't help thinking the sea monster a strange choice of décor for the ship. He would have preferred beautiful mermaids, himself, or at the very least a few sleek, silver, friendly dolphins.

Lex was relieved to discover that Jesse seemed to be right – as long as they made no sudden, threatening movements, the octopuses seemed content to leave them be. Unfortunately it all went wrong when they reached the end of the corridor and opened the door, because a lot of water rushed out. It seemed that not *all* of the ship's rooms were dry, after all. It poured out at them, knocking both Lex and Jesse off their feet and carrying them back a little way down the corridor. As sudden, threatening movements went, this seemed to be quite effective at frightening the octopuses who had been knocked into or swept off the walls. They latched on to Jesse and Lex anywhere they could get a grip.

Lex had one wrapped around his right ankle, one on his left arm, one slithering about trying to get a purchase on his chest and one dangling from his right wrist. They were all making that same awful high-pitched noise and it occurred to Lex – through his veil of horror – to wonder whether the little monsters might be poisonous. Surely Lady Luck would never put him in such a position, would she? But of course she would! This was a Game – death and danger were the point!

Suddenly, Lex felt angry. Falling gloriously to your death from a great height, or being dashingly killed by a ferocious, fire-breathing dragon, or getting heroically ripped apart by a band of werewolves was one thing. Getting squeezed and sucked to death by a bunch of horrible little octopuses was something else entirely. As Jesse seemed to be pretty thoroughly occupied with attempting to remove his own octopuses, Lex was going to have to save himself this time. He managed to get up, despite almost falling over again when there were more slippery octopuses getting in the way beneath his feet. The one that had been sliding around on his chest fell off but the two on his arms remained where they were and the one on his ankle actually started dragging itself up his leg!

Lex thought quickly. Unfortunately his knowledge of sea creatures was limited, to say the least. His grandfather had certainly never come across these octopuses – there was no mention of them in any of Alistair Trent's chronicles. But Lex had read other chronicles, too. He was, in fact, always reading, whenever he got the chance. You could learn a lot from a book. And you could never be too well prepared for a Game. Not when a relevant piece of knowledge could make all the difference between life and death. This was the reason Lex had had an entire library installed on the enchanter's ship before he'd left. It was also the reason he was currently carrying a book in his bag called *The Mysteries of the Deep*. He'd packed it as soon as he'd found out where the first round was to take place. It was quite a hefty thing and a great weight, causing the bag to dig painfully into his shoulders. Of course, there was no guarantee that the octopuses would be in there – one book couldn't contain information about *every* sea monster, after all. But Lex was a lucky person and so he was sure that, if he could just get the book out, there would be some information in there that would enable him to deal with them.

Unfortunately, he needed to get into his bag first but, when he reached an arm around to try to swing it off his back, his hand came into contact only with more oily octopuses. There must have been four or five of them latched on to his bag. Jesse was doing even worse than Lex, for he seemed to have lost his knife and there were now a grand total of seven octopuses clinging to him.

'You gotta weapon in that bag?' Jesse asked, starting to look quite panic-stricken.

The water rushing in seemed to have set all the octopuses off, for now even the ones that weren't actually on Jesse and Lex were making their way towards them, all making that horrible high-pitched whining sound.

'No,' Lex replied. 'I'm trying to get to a book.'

'A *book*?' the cowboy said, staring at Lex aghast.

'Yeah.' Lex finally managed to swing the bag off his

back, three of the octopuses flying off in the process to land on the floor at his feet with wet-sounding slaps.

'What good will that possibly do? Is it big enough to squash 'em with?'

'No, I'm going to read about them.'

'*Read about them*?' Jesse repeated, staring at Lex like he was mad.

Lex ignored him and opened the book to the contents page. There was a whole section there about octopuses but the problem was that Lex didn't know what they were called and, without a name, he couldn't look them up. He was just about to start flipping through the relevant section, looking at the pictures, when a name caught his eye and he knew it had to be the right one: The Squealing Blue-Ringed Octopii of Scurlyshoo. Even the name made him shudder.

He flipped the book open to the right page and straight away there was a photo staring up at him of one of the horrible blue-ringed octopuses. There was a large amount of text on the double-page spread but two equally unpleasant sentences leapt out at Lex instantly: *The Squealing Blue-Ringed Octopii is one of the most toxic sea creatures known to man*. And: *The Squealing Blue-Ringed Octopii carries enough venom to kill twenty-six adult humans within minutes*.

When there are four or five of the little suckers clinging to you, whining frantically, that sort of thing is really *not* what you want to be reading. And to think that Lex had had one on his *head*! Why, if Jesse hadn't stabbed it right when he did . . .

There was nothing to be gained by panicking, so Lex kept his head and desperately ran his eyes down the page looking for anything that would help. He skimmed past, *one of the most venomous animals in the world*, and *no known antidote*, as the octopuses clung tightly on to him all the while, about to bite at any second. Then, finally, he found what he was looking for. An innocuous little sentence at the bottom of the page stated that the Squealing Blue-Ringed Octopii – being closely related to land-slugs – had a low tolerance to salt. Thus they spent some of their time in the water and some of the time out of it, on beaches, coves or – Lex supposed – sunken ships that were full of air pockets.

Now, Lex had quite a lot of stuff in his bag seeing as it was a magic enchanter's bag and so was much bigger on the inside than it was on the outside. He was fairly sure he didn't have any salt but he *did* have salty snacks – crispy things that tasted great, and slowly rotted your teeth, according to some people (who were probably very prim, bossy and wore fussy-looking glasses).

Ignoring Jesse, who was demanding to know what he had found out from the book, Lex thrust his hand into his bag, pulled out a bag of salty snacks, ripped it open and shook handfuls of crisps out on to the octopuses that were clinging to him. It was only a hunch, but it paid off. As soon as the crisps touched the octopuses, their skin began to bubble and smoke and they dropped off Lex, squealing even more loudly than they had been before.

Straight away, Lex grabbed a second bag, ripped it open and threw crisps at Jesse. Soon the octopuses on the cowboy were smoking on the floor at his feet as well. The others, who'd been making their way along the floor, stopped, presumably frightened by the noise their fellows were making.

Lex wasn't going to waste time hanging around. He made straight for the open door, calling over his shoulder to Jesse, 'Come on, quick!'

A moment later they were in the next room with the door firmly closed behind them. The previously water-filled room was mercifully free of octopuses, although the rotten boards did creak beneath their feet in a worrying way.

'They're one of the most poisonous sea creatures known to man!' Lex gasped. 'We were covered in them! How the heck did we get out of there without them biting us?'

'They were trying to bite us,' Jesse replied, pulling the sleeve of his jacket outwards so that Lex could see the tiny little pinpricks where the octopuses' teeth had gone through but had been unable to reach the skin.

'Their teeth aren't long enough,' Lex said, staring in horror at his own clothes, all with identical little holes in them. 'If they'd managed to find some bare skin . . .' He trailed off with a shudder.

Before going on, he and Jesse put on the spare coats that Lex had brought in his bag. They would offer more protection from the octopuses and they had hoods to shield their heads. They also each opened a packet of salty snacks to carry with them and fling at any other octo-puses they might come into contact with. Lex had dropped the starfish again when the water had flooded out at them but there were plenty more stuck to the walls in this room, emitting their faint, greenish glow.

'I have to say, these Games seemed a helluva lot more fun from the stadiums,' Jesse grumbled.

Lex said nothing, but the truth was that he completely agreed with Jesse in that moment. This was not fun. At. All. He wondered briefly how the others were faring.

'The sooner we find the captain's medallion, the sooner we can leave,' he said. 'Come on, we need to get to the bridge.'

CHAPTER EIGHT

THE CURSE OF THE SUNKEN SHIP

Lex would've liked to think that the poisonous octopuses were the only dangerous thing on the ship – the only thing standing between him and the captain's medallion and glorious victory for the first round. But he knew better. Games did not tend to work that way – it would make them too boring. Gods – and the human spectators – liked a little variety. The likelihood, therefore, was that there would be several different nasties on board this ship – possibly a mixture of natural inhabitants (such as the octopuses) and things put there specially by the Gods.

When Lex heard a noise coming from behind a closed door a little later he braced himself to throw it open and discover what was behind it. It was no use trying to avoid the horrible stuff, for there were probably more traps around the captain's medallion than there were anywhere else on the ship. The more traps they came into contact with, therefore, the closer to their ultimate goal they probably were. But before Lex could open the door, it was flung open from the other side and Jeremiah burst out.

It seemed that Jeremiah must have heard Lex and Jesse because he came flying out braced for attack, shouting and waving his sword. For a split second Lex didn't realise it was Jeremiah and thought instead that it was something coming to get him, so he used the only weapon he had – he threw his packet of salty snacks in the nobleman's face.

It was a surprisingly effective – if slightly ludicrous – form of attack, for Jeremiah stopped dead, clutching at his eyes with his free hand and yelling. Clearly some salt had got in there and was stinging. He was making a tremendous fuss about it, though. Anyone would think that he'd just had acid thrown in his face.

'Sorry, old bean,' Lex said, not really feeling sorry at all.

'Oh my Gods, what have you *done*?' Jeremiah shrieked, dropping his sword so that both hands could clutch at his eyes. 'I can't see! I'm blind!'

'Well, that's how these Games work, you know,' Lex said cheerfully, declining to correct Jeremiah's misimpression that he had just been attacked with something extremely harmful and possibly deadly.

'It was only a packet of salty snacks, Jeremiah!' Tess said scornfully from behind him. She fixed her brother with a withering look and said, 'Stop being such a baby!'

'Eh?' Jeremiah lowered his hands and looked up with eyes that were a little red but, other than that, perfectly fine. 'Oh. You ass!' he spat venomously at Lex. 'What are you walking around munching on snacks in the middle of the Game for? You'll never win that way!'

'When you've been playing these Games for as long as I have, Jeremiah,' Lex replied, deliberately flippantly, 'you become such an old hand that you can eat and play at the same time. Isn't that right, Jesse?' He gave the cowboy a stern, meaningful look. No point in telling Jeremiah about the Squealing Blue-Ringed Octopii if he didn't know about them already. It would spoil the surprise. And Lex certainly wasn't going to come out and tell a competitor how to deal with a potential threat.

Jesse nodded and put a crisp into his mouth for emphasis, then remembered the Binding Bracelets and hastily handed the packet over to Lex so that he could eat a crisp, too, and they wouldn't swap bodies.

Jeremiah shook his head and bent down to retrieve his sword. 'Well, I think you're a pair of asses.'

'I think anyone who'd use the word "ass" as an insult is a stuck-up toff who has no business doing anything more dangerous than playing a game of croquet!'

To Lex's pleased surprise, Tess sniggered at that, even if she did hastily try to turn it into a cough.

'What happened to your leg?' Lex asked, noticing for the first time that part of Jeremiah's right trouser leg had been ripped away, and there was a jagged gash stretching down his calf – not deep enough to cause any damage, or a limp (more's the pity) – but enough to draw a bit of blood.

'Never you mind!' Jeremiah snapped. Obviously he, too, felt that it would not do to give anything away about threats the other players hadn't come into contact with yet. It looked to Lex like the handiwork of something with claws – a giant crab, or lobster, perhaps. Unpleasant, but hardly deadly.

'Well, it's been fun, but I don't have any more time to waste standing here chatting with you,' Lex said.

Jeremiah gave him a haughty, superior look and turned away to continue the Game as well.

And that was where the problem arose.

They were currently standing in a sort of stairwell with two doors leading on to the landing and stairs stretching away upwards and downwards (with a couple of brass octopuses on the banisters). Lex had come from one of the doors and Jeremiah had come from the other. For some reason, Lex had expected Jeremiah to walk straight past him and back the way Lex had just come but it seemed that he, like Lex, didn't think there was much point in exploring parts of the ship that another player had already investigated. They therefore both went to go up the stairs at the same time.

'Find your own route!' Lex said.

'You find *your* own route!' Jeremiah snapped.

'Look, let's be sensible about this. Why don't we both take the stairs but you go down and I go up?'

Whilst Jeremiah and Lex bickered, Jesse held the crisp packet out to Tess. The little girl reached out to take one but then froze suddenly and shook her head, pointing at the Binding Bracelet on her wrist. Jesse shook his own head, impatient with himself for forgetting again. But then he thought of chewing tobacco and he motioned with his hand for Tess to watch. He took a crisp out of the packet, put it in his mouth, sucked the flavour out of it, and then spat the soggy crisp out on to the floor. No body swap. A big grin spread across Tess's face and she reached for a crisp to do the same.

'I'm not going down!' Jeremiah was saying vehemently. 'There are probably more flesh-eating crabs down there!'

So *that* was what had taken a chunk out of Jeremiah's leg. Lex bet those crabs were nowhere near as horrible as the Squealing Blue-Ringed Octopii of Scurlyshoo, though.

'I'm going up these stairs,' Jeremiah declared. 'And that's that. I would strongly advise you not to get in my way.'

So it was to come down to a race between them, then. Lex decided his best chance would simply be to leg it up the stairs as fast as he could. Jesse could follow in his own time – he was a grown man who could take care of himself. Tess, on the other hand, was a little girl and Jeremiah would have to be even more of a jerk than Lex thought to leave her by herself on this terrible ship.

But just as his whole body was tensed ready to flee, something happened that made them all freeze. There was music coming from above. It was some sort of old sea shanty played on a harmonica. The music was out of place down there on the sunken ship – an oddly lonely sound – a sort of distant echo of the long-gone sailors who had once sailed her.

And that was when Lex first realised that, so far, they had not seen a single skeleton. Where were the crew?

Even if the flesh-eating crabs had stripped the bodies bare, they surely wouldn't have eaten the bones as well. There should be skeletons at the very least. Skeletons all over the place, in fact.

'It must be Lorella playing some trick,' Jeremiah said firmly as Tess drew fearfully closer to his side, clearly unnerved by the eerie music. 'There's no such thing as ghosts.'

Despite this statement, it was clear from the way he looked longingly at the stairs that Jeremiah would now prefer to go down rather than up. Like an amateur, he thought it was better to avoid the obstacles rather than head straight for them. But as Lex was clearly still intending to go upstairs, Jeremiah decided that he'd better, too. They proceeded as a cautious group, for Lex now felt unable to stick to his original plan of legging it up there. Deliberately going towards danger was all very well but running towards it blindly was just plain stupid.

They got closer and closer to the melancholy music until they finally reached the little landing on the floor above and found the cause. A sailor sat there on the banisters with a harmonica in his hand, which he lowered when he saw them coming. They all stared at each other for a minute. The sailor didn't look like a ghost. Or, at least, he didn't look the way Lex had always imagined a ghost to look, in that he wasn't a floating sheet with a couple of eye holes or, failing that, at least transparent. But he didn't look quite normal either. His skin had a strange greyish look, his eyes were sunken, his hair dry.

'What are you, sir?' Jeremiah demanded, pointing his sword at the sailor in an over-dramatic, threatening manner. 'Speak up! Are you a ghost?'

The sailor looked at him in cold silence for a moment before saying, 'We're not dead. We're a cursed crew. We're not allowed to die.' His voice was dry and hoarse, like he never used it. Something about the tone sent shivers up Lex's spine.

'Someone on board pissed off the Gods, did they?' he asked.

The sailor fixed his baleful gaze on him. 'Aye,' he whispered, before shuddering and falling silent. It seemed that whatever the crew had done to get themselves cursed in such a way was not a story this man wanted to dwell upon. Which suited Lex just fine, for he couldn't have cared less.

'Stand aside and let me pass!' Jeremiah demanded.

'No one is stopping you,' the sailor replied coldly.

Jeremiah looked at him suspiciously for a moment before edging past him cautiously with Tess. It was as if he expected the sailor to suddenly attack him. Lex made a show of looking suitably wary and suspicious – as if he was allowing his competitor to go first to make sure it was safe. But the truth was that, unless someone was coming at him with a sword or a mace of some kind, Lex was prepared to cautiously consider them safe for the time being – and thus, potential sources of extremely valuable information.

Once they were past the sailor, Jeremiah grabbed Tess's

hand and raced up the stairs. Lex's lip curled with contempt and he shook his head. What an amateur! The truth was that Lex had no intention of running up the stairs now. He simply wanted Jeremiah out of the way. It seemed that it had not yet occurred to him that, if the crew were all cursed rather than dead, then the captain would be moving around. He could be anywhere on the ship and running about looking for him blindly was not going to get the job done. Lex could hardly believe that Jeremiah had just gone off like that, leaving this rich source of information for Lex to tap alone. Even if this sailor didn't know exactly where the captain was, he should at least know a little more about the potential dangers on board the ship. There was certainly nothing to lose by just asking nicely.

'What are those rings on your hand?' Lex asked, momentarily distracted. They looked horribly familiar and so he was fairly sure that he already knew the answer.

'The octopuses,' the sailor replied. 'We were here before them so they don't seem to mind us most of the time. But sometimes they bite. Because we're already half dead, they can't kill us. But they leave these scars.' He held up his hand to display the pale, white rings. 'And it hurts like you wouldn't believe. Like something has got inside your body and is ripping up your insides. A bite from one of the Blue-Ringed Octopii will stop a live man's heart in under a minute.' He added in a sad voice, 'But our hearts stopped long ago so they present no danger to us.'

'I don't suppose you know where the captain is, do you?' Lex asked.

'He spends most of his time up on deck.'

'Up on deck?' Lex repeated, his heart sinking. 'You mean . . . out there?' He pointed towards a dark port-hole, the black ocean pressing against it in an unnerving manner.

'Yes.' The sailor nodded. 'He wanders the deck. Most of them do.'

Well, that could certainly be a problem. For whilst the cursed crew might not need to breathe, Lex did. In the past he could have magicked himself up there but he no longer had that option – not since Lucius had burnt all his magical enchanted hats, blast him. Lex made it a habit to always carry one of the little mini-hats he used for calling cards as the Wizard in his pocket (you never know when the chance might arise to pinch something), but all they were good for was lighting pipes. They couldn't help him breathe under water. Indeed, now that he thought about it, Kala hadn't actually mentioned what was supposed to happen when someone finally found the captain's medallion. She wanted it returned to her but there was no easy way for a human to reach the surface of the sea unaided and Lex could only hope that the Gods would pull them out of there the same way they'd sent them down.

But he would worry about that later – once he actually had the captain's medallion. And that task in itself had become more complicated now that it wasn't merely going to be a question of plucking the thing out of a dead man's hands. If the captain was wandering about up on deck – walking and talking, as it were – then he might not *want* to give the medallion up. And then there could be trouble.

'What's the captain's name?' Lex asked.

'Jed Saltworthy,' the sailor replied.

The name was vaguely familiar but Lex couldn't place it. 'Decent enough bloke, is he?' he asked, without much hope. After all, this *was* a cursed ship.

'He's the most foul, villainous man ever to roam the Seventeen Seas!'

'Ah,' Lex said, not surprised, but not exactly happy to hear it either. Almost as an afterthought he added, 'What's the name of this ship?'

The sailor gave him an odd look. 'Don't you know? This is the *Scurlyshoo Death*!'

Oh. Shit! Now it all made sense. The captain's name and the octopus décor all fell into place as Lex recalled the story. One hundred years ago there had sailed a magnificent ship called the *Golden Dawn*, captained by a handsome, noble, fearless man named Jed Saltworthy. Until, one fateful day, they were attacked by a giant octopus. It rose up out of the sea, entwined its long tentacles around the ship and almost took the entire thing down to the bottom of the sea with it.

Fortunately, Captain Saltworthy managed to chop one of its tentacles off and this caused the octopus to retreat in agony, but not before it had flung the captain across the deck where he unhappily landed right on top of the broken navigation wheel, one of its jagged giant spokes going right through his leg. He survived the accident but his leg did not. They had to chop it off just above the knee.

The captain was fitted out with a peg leg and the ship was repaired. But it was also renamed. The *Golden Dawn* had perished in the battle with the octopus but, out of the ashes, the *Scurleyshoo Death* had been born, for the ship's new mission was to kill any and all octopuses that it came across, even the harmless ones. But the captain never forgot Gloria, as he had – for some inexplicable reason – decided to name the octopus who took his leg. He would recognise her at once for the fact that he, in turn, had taken one of her tentacles. And so he sailed the seas vowing to track Gloria down and kill her if it was the last thing he ever did. But then, one day, a tornado sank the ship and the *Scurleyshoo Death* and its crew and captain were never heard from again.

'Captain Saltworthy must be absolutely *incensed* to have his beloved ship overrun with octopuses!' Lex said.

The sailor gave him a pitying look. 'Far from it. This is his plan.'

'This is his what?'

'His plan. When the years passed and he couldn't find Gloria, he turned to black magic. He cursed himself, us – the entire ship. We can't die until the octopus dies.'

'Well, how long do these things live?' Lex asked. 'Surely she must be dead by now?'

The sailor shook his head. 'They can live for six hundred years or more,' he said. 'Little horrors. They should have gone down to the Lands Beneath with all the other monsters!'

As one of only four people ever to have gone down to the Lands Beneath, Lex knew that the myths were untrue. There were no monsters down there. Just glass men. On a giant chessboard, so to speak. All the monsters were up here. But there was no point telling the sailor that.

'I still don't see how having the ship overrun with octopuses can be part of the captain's plan to kill Gloria.'

'The Squealing Blue-Ringed Octopii produce offspring once every one hundred years,' the sailor replied. 'The captain managed to find Gloria's nest using his black magic. All the octopuses here are Gloria's young. The captain maintained the air pockets in the ship so that, when the babies left the nest, they'd come straight here. Gloria is away hunting at the moment, but as soon as she comes back she'll follow her children here, believing the ship no longer poses a threat. And that's when the captain will strike and we'll finally be free from this terrible curse once and for all.'

Lex gaped at him. Gloria, the most legendary octopus in the world – to the extent that some people believed her to be a myth – was coming *here* to *this* ship where her *babies* had been lured on board by her mortal enemy! One thing Lex knew was that wild animals didn't tend to react very well when someone threatened their young. When Gloria showed up there was going to be a rather horrible scene and Lex was very keen not to be here when it happened. He was also slightly horrified to find out that the nasty little suckers they'd encountered so far were merely the *baby* version, for they were quite, quite bad enough as it was.

'Can you point us in the direction of the deck?' Lex asked.

The sailor gave them directions and Lex set off, up the stairs, feeling uncharacteristically bleak. The problem was that, if he had to go up on deck to get to the captain, he would not be able to talk, for he would be surrounded by water. And without his golden tongue, what was he? Just some skinny city kid with an over-inflated opinion of himself. He could have throttled Lucius in that moment for losing him his enchanted hats. If he'd still had them he could have performed some spell on himself to enable him to go up on deck and yet still be able to talk. And breathe, obviously.

The sailor had told them that the best way out on to the deck was through the bridge. Which was slightly unfortunate as Lex was fairly sure that was where Jeremiah would be heading. But once they got up there, if the conceited twit was still on the bridge, Lex was fairly confident in his own ability to trick him somehow and send Jeremiah off in the wrong direction.

It was not a simple route to reach the bridge. They had to weave in and out of other rooms, including a once-grand, stately dining room that had clearly been for the captain's private use. The massive walnut table was screwed to the floor, as were the ornate wooden chairs down its length. They were all now covered in a coating of barnacles.

A chandelier hung from the ceiling, although almost all of its crystal was broken. This room might once have been used for impressive dinner parties, with lots of food and wine and stories of sea monsters and adventures. But now it was rather a sad, forgotten sort of place, smelling of damp and decay and seaweed and dead ships.

An impressive bronze statue was fixed to the centre of the great table and Lex wasn't surprised to see that it was an octopus. When he looked closer he saw that it was Gloria herself – he could tell from the fact that she only had seven tentacles. Despite the fact that time and the elements had faded their colours, when he looked at the omnipresent paintings on the walls, he could see that these, too, were all of Gloria.

'The man must have had a screw loose,' Lex remarked. 'If he hated Gloria so much then why did he surround himself with paintings and statues of her like this? The bloody place is like some sort of shrine.'

'One card short of a full deck, for sure,' Jesse agreed.

Finally they made it up to the bridge – thankfully without encountering any more octopuses. There were maps and charts fastened on to the walls, all in various states of decay. Barnacles crunched beneath their feet and long slimy strings of seaweed were stinking in the corners and draped around the wheel.

But the most startling thing about the scene was the view through the large panoramic windows that looked directly out on to the deck. There was a great hustle and bustle of activity going on out there. The deck was being cleared and scrubbed, nets were being raised and cannons were being loaded – all by the hands of a phantom crew.

Jesse whistled. 'Well, blow me, that ain't somethin' you see every day.'

'No,' Lex said, eyes narrowed intently. Perhaps he was imagining it but it really didn't look like there was any water out there – at least not on the immediate deck. There were no bubbles streaming past the windows and portholes; the sailors' hair hung damp about their heads rather than being moved about by the water . . . 'I think the crazy captain has found some way of keeping the deck dry,' Lex said.

'What for?' Jesse asked, frowning. 'It's not like they need to breathe, is it?'

'No, but they've been trying to attract the octopuses, haven't they? Besides, even if you don't need air to breathe, you still need it to talk.'

It was a good point. As any kid who's ever tried to talk underwater in the bath knows, it's not all that easy. And sea water doesn't tend to taste all that nice, either. Lex moved a little closer to one of the portholes and peered out. It definitely looked to him like there was air out there. There were nets full of glowing starfish, which Lex suspected had been put there for the specific purpose of lighting the deck. And by their soft light he could even see water dripping down the clothes of the crew.

Well, there was no point simply standing there staring gutlessly out of the window. There was one way to find out for sure and that was by opening the door. Either he'd get swept away like a sandcastle, or he'd be able to walk out there quite easily. He had no idea where Lorella was and, although Jeremiah didn't appear to be here yet, he could turn up – like the proverbial bad penny – at any moment. Lex had found that the best course of action ninety-nine per cent of the time was simply to march boldly in and hope for the best, relying on luck and his own natural talent for getting himself out of whatever trouble he landed in.

So he stepped right up to the door to the deck – and opened it.

CHAPTER NINE

GLORIA

Fortunately, Lex had been right – no water came rushing in to knock him off his feet. Instead there was just a blast of icy cold, slightly damp air rushing past him. It smelled of salt and seaweed and deep places and dark things. As far as Lex could tell from the light the stuffed nets of starfish were giving off, the force field keeping the sea out was about fifty feet high, stopping just above the crow's nest at the top of the tallest mast. Above that, dark water pressed in in a most disconcerting way. Bits of dust and flotsam had settled on the top, outlining the dome of air that covered the deck where sailors ran about, slipping and sliding on the wet wooden boards. There was also a strange sensation of what could only be described as pressure. As if it was possible to feel the great weight of water pressing down on them from above, kept away only by the strength of the force field. For a fleeting moment Lex wished that he was still playing against Lucius. Then all he would need to do to have him cowering in the corner for the rest of the round would be to scream, 'Look, there's a poisonous octopus!'

There was such a lot of activity on the bridge that no one even noticed Lex and Jesse step out on to it. The captain was sure to be somewhere amongst this lot but Lex didn't know which of the many sailors was the infamous Captain Jed Saltworthy. When Jeremiah or Lorella or both could be upon the scene at any moment, Lex didn't have time to waste twitting about trying to find the captain in a more subtle way. So he cupped his hands around his mouth, raised his voice and shouted, 'Which one of you is the captain? I need to talk to him at once!'

His voice seemed to carry unnaturally far in the strange, damp air down there and practically every single sailor on the bridge stopped dead to turn and stare at Lex with an expression of shock.

And then someone threw a spear at his head.

Lex ducked to the floor so fast that it didn't even come close to hitting him. Jesse, too, had excellent reflexes and was flat on the boards a bare millisecond after Lex. As the spear whistled past them and embedded itself in the wall behind, Lex thought fleetingly that it was a really good thing he had an outlaw as his companion this time rather than an elderly lawyer. If that had been Mr Schmidt standing there, rather than Jesse, his head would now be impaled on a fisherman's spear, like a weird-looking trout. It certainly would have dampened the hero's welcome Lex received on returning to the

Wither City if he'd been carrying his employer's head on a pike. He was sure the rounds had been easier last time . . .

Within seconds, strong hands were hauling Jesse and Lex to their feet and the sailors were bellowing at each other for someone to fetch the captain. These members of the cursed crew all looked more or less the same as the harmonica player they had encountered downstairs – a bit damp and with a greyish tinge to their skin that made Lex think of zombies and walking dead but, other than that, not too bad, all things considered.

But then the legendary Captain Jed Saltworthy himself came into view and he was another thing altogether. Even Lex, who was relatively used to seeing weird and wonderful things, made a disgusted sort of sound in the back of his throat and had to struggle not to let the revulsion show too clearly on his face. In light of his new-found phobia, this was not at all easy.

Jed Saltworthy was not a large man – barely five foot eight – but he was built like a barrel and his coat was so stiff with salt that it looked like it would shatter if you smacked it against the wall. The same was true of his black beard and mane of hair. There were bits of seaweed hanging around him and even a few barnacles crusted to his tough black boot on one side and the wooden peg leg on the other. None of this overly bothered Lex for, although he may have had a thing about cleanliness himself, he had seen enough unclean people not to be overly distressed by it. He wasn't even at all bothered by the peg leg. But there were two things about the captain's appearance that *did* upset him.

The first was that he had an octopus on his shoulder. It had its tentacles wrapped around the captain's upper arm and was just clinging there, looking all revolting and horrible and *squidgy* – enough to make Lex's skin crawl. A sea captain having a parrot on his shoulder was one thing – as long as you didn't mind the bird poo – but a highly poisonous, vicious octopus was something else altogether. Any way you looked at it, it was just plain wrong.

The second thing, even more horrible than the first, was that Captain Jed Saltworthy's skin was covered in blue rings. His hands, his face, his neck – any part of his skin that was showing was sporting blue rings, identical to the ones on the Squealing Blue-Ringed Octopii sitting on his shoulder. He must have suffered hundreds of bites to look such a state – perhaps as a result of carrying one of the monsters around with him like that all the time.

To Lex's surprise the sea captain glared down at them with an expression of almost ferocious approval.

'What's this, then?' he boomed. 'Volunteers?'

'Volunteers?' Lex gasped. 'Volunteers for what?'

'For bait, of course! 'Tis very brave of you, men. Very brave. Well done!'

'Look, there's been some sort of mistake,' Lex said. 'We're not volunteering for anything. We just want your medallion.'

'This old thing?' the captain said, holding up the shiny

gold disc that hung round his neck. 'Certainly, my boy. Take it, by all means.' He raised the chain over his head and dropped it into Lex's outstretched hand. ''Tis the very least I can do seeing as you'll shortly be going to your death.'

'You mad old duffer! We are *not* volunteering to be bait! We're just playing in a Game—'

'Game?' the captain interrupted. 'Octopus-hunting's no game, boy! You should ne'er have joined my crew if you weren't serious about catching these things.' He gave the octopus perched on his shoulder a pat on the head that made Lex wince. 'Beautiful, ain't they?' the captain went on, pulling the octopus off and stroking it tenderly. 'But we can't allow them to rule our waters, can we?' Lex practically had to look away as the insane sea captain actually *kissed* the thing's squidgy head just as the octopus bit him on the neck. They could see he'd been bitten by the fact that blue rings – brighter than the others – suddenly spread out over his skin there. The captain hardly seemed to be aware of this, possibly because he'd suffered so many bites in the past.

'Look, we're not *in* your crew!' Lex protested. 'Don't you think it's odd that you've never seen us before?'

But the captain wasn't listening. He was already beckoning other men forwards. Men who were carrying very large nets.

'I think we can take 'em,' Jesse muttered in Lex's ear.

Lex stared at him. '*Take* them?' he repeated. 'If you mean *fight* them, then of course we can't, you dolt! There must be thirty of them and only two of us!'

Jesse grinned. 'Ain't that always the way? Ready on three?'

'No!' Lex hissed. 'Not ready on three or any other number! Listen – I can talk my way out of this—'

'Fine. You do your thing and I'll do mine.'

'That's not how this works!'

But Jesse wasn't listening. As the sailors approached with their nets, Jesse raised a hand, pointed out towards the black ocean and shouted. 'Look! It's Gloria!'

Twenty men spun around on the spot. Perhaps it wouldn't have worked under normal circumstances but these were cursed sailors who had been waiting for Gloria for hundreds of years. Crying wolf was therefore a remarkably effective way to go. For a moment, even *Lex* thought he'd seen a dark shape moving out there beyond the forcefield.

Not wasting any time, Jesse punched the nearest unsuspecting sailor, elbowed another and kicked a third. And then it was quite clear to everybody that they weren't going to have to deal with Gloria, but with an irate cowboy who didn't want to be used as octopus bait. There was no denying that Jesse was a very good fighter and the fact that he was outnumbered and backed into a corner didn't seem to overly bother him, for the truth was that he had spent most of his life fighting that way. Nevertheless, the fight certainly wouldn't have lasted very long if Jeremiah hadn't appeared on the scene a moment later.

Lex was quite useless in a fight. It wasn't that he was scared; it was simply that he was practical. He knew his own limitations and, although he was strong in a wiry sort of way – as a result of his exploits, first as the Shadowman and then as the Wizard – he was quite thin and not very tall and knew absolutely nothing about how to handle a weapon. He had therefore avoided physical altercations his whole life because he knew he was unlikely to win them. And Lex only played to win. Besides, he didn't want any muscled buffoon giving him some hideous scar that would mar the honest face that played such an important part in many of Lex's scams. He needed his hands, too; he couldn't have any broken fingers slowing him down in his line of work.

As soon as Jesse threw the first punch, Lex's mind was working fast and it seemed to him that the best course of action would be to leave Jesse there to fend for himself – he had, after all, *started* this thing – and leg it back to the bridge with the medallion. Once the round was over, Lex was sure that Lady Luck would pluck Jesse out of whatever mess he was in. The round would be over then, so the rules would not apply. It wasn't like Lex *owed* the cowboy anything, after all. It had been Jesse's own stupid idea to just start punching.

Lex was halfway to the door leading back into the bridge, the medallion gripped firmly in his hand, when he hesitated. What if Jesse got himself killed? Lex couldn't lose him. Not now, in the very first round, when Jesse had yet to teach him a single thing about being a cowboy. And then he'd have no companion for the rest of the Game and so would be at a disadvantage. No, there was only one thing for it. He was going to have to stay and help the idiot cowboy out of the mess he'd got himself into.

Lex turned back round in time to see a sailor rushing towards him. The thief ducked the man's clumsy grab, whirled around and punched the side of his face. It was rather a half-hearted sort of punch for whilst Lex wasn't averse to robbing and cheating people blind, he generally preferred not to cause them any physical injury. At any rate, the punch seemed to hurt Lex as much as it did the sailor, who staggered back with his hand clapped to his face whilst Lex clutched at his hand with a groan. His thumb throbbed so badly that, for a moment, he thought he'd broken it, and his knuckles were smarting like anything.

Well, at least he'd tried. Time to go. Jesse would just have to look after himself. And if he got himself killed, Lex would be really angry with him. Unfortunately there were now five other sailors racing towards him. The annoying thing about it was that there were only *two* running towards Jesse. Evidently the more intelligent sailors had sized up the cowboy, sized up Lex, and decided that Lex was very definitely the way to go. Lex couldn't really blame them. He would have done the same thing himself.

His thoughts of helping Jesse now totally and utterly abandoned, Lex spun on his heel and sprinted towards the door. But, before he could reach it, Jeremiah burst out, sword drawn, Tess close behind him. Lex leapt out

of the way before Jeremiah could impale him, by accident even if not on purpose. The nobleman rushed
forwards and the sailors shrank back a little. Jeremiah *did*
look rather impressive and the sword was extremely large.

'Where is the captain's medallion?' Jeremiah roared.

Lex hastily put his hand behind his back, silently giving
thanks that his competitor was too busy shouting his fool
head off to actually *look*.

'I demand to be given it this instant!'

'Excellent!' came a cry from Captain Saltworthy, from
across the other side of the deck. 'More bait! And such
a strapping lad, too! Bring him to the nets!'

Despite the threat of the sword, the sailors moved
forwards. They were only half alive, after all, and Lex
supposed that if a poisonous octopus couldn't kill them
then a dumb hero with a sword might not be able to do
much damage, either. He ducked out of the way of
Jeremiah and the sailors, and grasped the door handle
with the intention of slipping through to the bridge. But
the door was jammed shut. That oaf, Jeremiah, had clearly
slammed it so hard that it was now stuck in its frame.

'What's that in your hand?'

Lex looked down to see Tess staring at him suspiciously.

'Never you mind,' he replied in what he hoped was
an annoyingly grown-up voice.

'It's the medallion, isn't it?' she said.

'No.'

'You're a rubbish liar.'

'I'll have you know that I'm an exceptional liar, kid,' Lex replied, revelling in being able to call someone *else* 'kid' for a change.

Tess glared at him for a moment before turning her head and shouting loudly, 'Jeremiah! He's got it! Lex Trent has the medallion!'

Jeremiah, who had been flourishing his sword threateningly at the sailors surrounding him, glanced back over his shoulder. Lex couldn't help it. He drew the medallion out from behind his back, held it up so that it gleamed in the light from the sunset starfish, gave Jeremiah his most smug, irritating grin and then flew across the deck to the centre mast. Pausing only to hang the medallion around his neck to leave his hands free, Lex shot up that mast with monkey agility. He was a good climber and he had never been afraid of heights.

He reached the crow's nest in under a minute and from there he had a perfect vantage of all that was going on down below. Jeremiah was surrounded by a large group of sailors and, though he was still waving the sword about rather vigorously, he seemed distinctly reluctant to actually use it. Lex supposed that he'd probably never attacked anyone with it in his life. Pratting about with a posh fencing instructor at a posh school was one thing. Carving a man up for real and seeing his guts pouring out all over the place was probably another thing altogether.

Jesse had no such reluctance to cause physical harm and seemed to be doing rather well, all things considered. There were quite a few groaning sailors lying on the deck around him, at any rate. Captain Jed Saltworthy, meanwhile, was marching about the deck, bellowing for his men to 'ready the bait!' It certainly looked as if Jeremiah East was going to be stuffed into a net and hung out for Gloria sometime soon. Lex would have liked to watch the show but there was no time for dawdling when there was a round to be won.

From the crow's nest, he assessed his situation. The force field was so close that he could have stuck his hand through it. In fact, if he shimmied up the mast just a little further then he would emerge into the sea. That would get him off the ship and away from the batty captain but it wouldn't win him the round since it seemed that the Gods expected them to find their own way to the surface, which presented something of a problem when you were so many fathoms under water. The sea above was pitch black – Lex couldn't see even a glimmer of light from above. They *were* on the seabed, after all. There was no way he would be able to make a swim for it. Once again, Lex cursed his loss of the enchanter's hats.

But then he glanced back down and, in the gloom, he noticed the thick seaweed-covered chains. There must have been six or seven of them – thick, strong, impressive-looking things all ending in an anchor. They were holding the ship to the seabed.

Of course! The ship was full of air pockets. The force field in place over the deck of the ship was itself a giant air pocket. Without the chains holding it down, the ship would simply float up to the surface! That had to be it.

If Lex couldn't leave the ship then he would have to get the ship itself to take him back up to the surface. All he had to do was find a way of releasing the chains. He was just starting to devise a scheme for doing so when a movement out in the dark water beyond caught his eye. He looked. Then he looked again to make sure he wasn't imagining it. He wasn't.

From Lex's vantage point he had a perfect view of the gigantic octopus that was Gloria coming straight at the ship like a bull going for a red rag. It was the most horrific sight Lex had ever seen before in his life. She was coming so fast that he had only seconds in which to brace himself for impact before the huge monster crashed into the side of the ship. The chains all along that side were ripped out and the ship rocked wildly. Everyone on the deck went flying. Lex, despite his best efforts to hang on, was thrown from the crow's nest but managed to get a grip on the netting about fifteen feet above the deck, although the rope burnt his hands horribly.

Gloria was not at all happy. Her awful tentacles – thick as tree trunks – punched through the force field and curled around the deck until she had the ship in a death grip. She looked just like the little octopuses Lex had already seen, except for the fact that she was about a hundred times their size. And the terrible squealing sound she was making was about one hundred times louder.

Everyone on the deck was shouting and running around, trying to avoid Gloria's deadly, thrashing tentacles as the ship, recovering from the first shock of impact, now rocked the other way. The anchor chains on the other side were all ripped out in the process and, suddenly, the ship began to rise.

Lex grinned despite himself. That horrible monster was doing his work for him! They'd reach the surface in no time. Assuming Gloria didn't crush the ship first, of course.

'Fire the cannons!' the captain roared, below.

Lex watched as a cannon was lit and, a moment later, there was an explosion and a cannon ball ripped through the water in a trail of bubbles. It missed Gloria by a mile, of course. She was, after all, entwined around the ship, her tentacles thrashing about all over the deck. The only way a cannon ball would hit her would be if she was positioned right in front of the cannon itself.

Lex tore his eyes away and tried not to think about the octopus. He couldn't let Gloria distract him. And he most certainly did not want Jeremiah noticing his reaction to the octopus and realising that he had a phobia of them. Where was Jeremiah, anyway . . . ?

Lex thought about it too late. He couldn't pick out any players in the chaos below but, just as it occurred to him to wonder where Jeremiah was, a hand gripped his ankle. He looked down and saw Jeremiah clinging to the nets, glaring up at him.

'Give me the medallion!' he shouted above the din.

Lex offered a choice expletive in response and kicked out viciously with his foot, but Jeremiah held fast and then yanked down hard. Under ordinary circumstances,

Lex might have been able to hang on but the rope burn his hands had suffered meant that he instinctively let go as soon as the nets began to cut into his already-raw palms. Fifteen feet was higher than Lex cared to fall. He flailed desperately at the ropes but was stopped in his descent by Jeremiah grabbing his shirt. In another moment the nobleman had whipped the medallion from around Lex's neck and let him go again, plainly intending to drop him to the deck like a sack of potatoes. But he wasn't counting on Lex shooting out his arm to grab Jeremiah's wrist and, when he fell, Lex took the nobleman with him.

They crashed to the deck together, all the breath knocked out of them when they hit the boards, and the medallion flew out of Jeremiah's hand to skitter along the deck amongst the feet of the running sailors. Lex and Jeremiah both twisted round where they lay to stare after it but, already, it had disappeared from their sight. Air bubbles were shooting up around the ship and the sea was getting lighter by the second. They would burst through to the surface at any moment and now, all because of Jeremiah, Lex no longer had the medallion. It was all he could do not to scratch the nobleman's blasted eyes out.

Shoving Jeremiah aside, Lex leapt to his feet and hurried away in the direction the medallion had gone. It was extremely difficult moving about the deck now because the sailors had got spears from somewhere and were trying to stab them into Gloria's tentacles like they were skewering meat on a kebab. They weren't having much success because the tentacles were too thick and strong, and the spears just seemed to bounce right off them. All they seemed to be achieving was to make Gloria even angrier than she already was.

Lex pushed on, avoiding spears and tentacles, and keeping his eyes glued to the floor in desperate search of the faintest glimmer of gold, but he could see nothing beyond scuffling shoes and the more-than-occasional smear of blood. Until a pair of cowboy boots came into view and a voice said, 'Looking for this, kid?'

Lex looked up and a wide grin spread across his face at the sight of Jesse, standing there holding the medallion. Apart from the fact that he stood on a sunken ship's deck rather than a desert, Jesse looked the very epitome of a character from the Western novels Lex had read. His clothes were in disarray, with more than the occasional rip and tear, his hair was a mess, there was a long cut down one side of his face and – most importantly of all – he still had his hat and he was grinning from ear to ear.

'I take it back,' the cowboy said. 'This Gaming thing *is* fun! Don't know why I never tried my hand at it before!'

A sailor suddenly lurched up behind Jesse with a spear but, before Lex could even shout a warning, Jesse threw his elbow back without even so much as turning around and caught the man right on the chin. This caused him to bite his tongue and he dropped the spear and staggered off with both hands clasped to his mouth. Lex practically swelled with pride. Picking Jesse as his companion had been a stroke of genius on his part. With Lex's quick mind and Jesse's superb brawling skills – never mind all the rascally dishonesty they had between them – they made the perfect, *perfect* team.

The next time I play in a Game,' Lex said, 'you have *got* to be my companion again!'

'Let's just see how this one turns out first, eh?' Jesse replied.

Lex said nothing but he already knew how it was going to turn out. He was going to win again. And gloriously, too! Some people were simply born to win and Lex was one of those people. He smirked smugly to himself. It was almost too easy.

But the next few minutes were where it all went horribly wrong.

They could see sunlight glimmering above now as the ship continued to rise and they could tell that they would reach the surface in a matter of minutes. The Gods would be waiting for them there and it would then be a simple enough matter of handing the medallion over.

'Give it to me then,' Lex said, holding out his hand for it.

But Jesse had suddenly gone stiff as a board and was staring over Lex's head at something on the deck. He was motionless only a split second before racing past Lex, taking the medallion with him.

'What the—' Lex whirled around, thinking for a moment that Jesse was betraying him. But he saw, instantly, what the cowboy had seen.

Tess East was standing a few feet away in the middle of the deck – with the captain's little Blue-Ringed octopus in her arms. It seemed that she had just picked it up off the deck, possibly in order to save it from being squashed by the many tramping feet of the sailors who were still running about all over the place.

Lex was horrified. One bite – one bite, the book had said – and those octopuses had enough venom in them to stop the hearts of twenty-six men within minutes. He knew in that moment that he should have told Jeremiah about the octopuses when he'd had the chance. But it was too late for that now. Lex started forwards towards Tess but Jesse got there first. The girl shrank away from the huge cowboy who was inexplicably charging straight at her but Jesse wrenched the octopus from her grasp whilst at the same time pushing her away from it so hard that she sprawled over on the boards. Then he spun round on his booted heel and threw the octopus as far as he could. It flew through the air in an arc – like a bizarre, upsetting sort of frisbee – and spun right out of the force field and into the sea where it smacked on to Gloria and, recognising its mother, promptly attached itself to her, happily.

Jesse then turned back around to Tess where she still lay sprawled on the floor and took a step towards her, saying urgently, 'Hey, kid, did that thing—'

But that was as far as he got before Jeremiah leapt in front of her, eyes blazing with fury, and hit the cowboy so hard across the face that he staggered back and would have fallen flat on the boards had Lex not caught up in time to grab at his shoulders and steady him.

'How dare you raise your hand against my sister!' Jeremiah roared. 'A defenceless child less than half your size! You are a coward, sir!'

Tess was on her feet now, staying close to her brother's side. And clutching the medallion. Jesse must have dropped it when he'd grabbed the octopus from her.

'Shut up, you prat!' Lex snapped. 'Don't you know what just happened? Your sister was holding one of the most toxic creatures in the world!' He looked at Tess and said, 'It didn't bite you?'

She shook her head silently, her eyes wide.

'My companion just saved her life!' Lex raged at Jeremiah.

Jeremiah – because he was, after all, something of a twit – looked suspiciously at Jesse, who was still nursing his jaw, and said cautiously, 'Well, if that's true then I . . . I'm in your debt.'

The cowboy shrugged. 'Think nothing of it, kid. I—'

But that was as far as he got before breaking off to clutch at his chest with a horrible gasp. And that was when Lex first noticed the ugly blue rings rising up on the cowboy's right hand.

'Oh my Gods,' Lex practically whispered. 'It bit you!'

Jesse tried to croak a reply but no words came out. He was still staring in horror at his hand as his knees hit the floor and he crumpled to the deck.

CHAPTER TEN

THE DEATH TWITCH

The *Scurleyshoo Death* burst above the surface into the glittering sunlight. The force field above them vanished, the water all around them disappeared and suddenly the ship was floating on the surface of the ocean for the first time in hundreds of years. The toffs over at the teashop were cheering their fool heads off, clearly quite delighted by the sight of the ship shooting to the surface in an explosion of foam, especially as it currently had a giant octopus entwined all around it. But the only thing Lex was aware of was Jesse, crumpled motionless on the deck. *No known antidote*, wasn't that what the book had said?

Of course people died in the Games. That was partly what made them exciting – there was *genuine* danger and *genuine* peril. But it was not supposed to be *Lex's* companion who died.

A bare moment after the ship broke the surface, the captain succeeded in driving a spear right through one of Gloria's tentacles and was standing there, roaring his triumph in the middle of the deck, when another tentacle suddenly curled around him and plucked him up and over the side of the ship. Suddenly all the tentacles were gone, Gloria was gone and Captain Jed Saltworthy was gone. A matter of seconds later, the crew all vanished: faded away like wandering ghosts. People said later that it must have been because Gloria had bitten the captain's foolish head off and that his death, too, was sufficient to break the curse over the crew, who were finally free to rest in peace.

But Lex was aware of none of this, for he was too over-come with horror at the sight of Jesse, sprawled on the deck. One of the companions in the last Game had been killed by the medusa during the first round but Lex simply hadn't cared. After all, the man had been a mean-looking gangster. He'd probably had it coming. But Jesse had only been trying to save a little girl. It wasn't fair that he was dead. It wasn't *right*.

Matters were not improved when the three Gods appeared beside them on the now-deserted deck. Kala practically snatched the captain's medallion from Tess, smirking with glee over her prize whilst the other Gods stood by sulkily looking distinctly unhappy – as losing Gods usually did.

'The first round goes to me!' Kala crowed gleefully.

Jeremiah – to his credit – did not look particularly pleased about winning. His hand was gripped tightly around his sister's and he didn't appear to be able to tear his eyes away from the cowboy at his feet.

'You humiliated me at the Wither City!' Lex hissed in

a voice that was full of bitterness. 'You cheated me out of the first round! And now my companion is dead because of you! I'll make you pay for this, if it's the last thing I ever do!'

'Give it your best shot, thief!' Kala said with a horrible smile. 'We'll be ready for you!' She placed her hand on Jeremiah's shoulder and they, and Tess, disappeared. The round now over, they had presumably returned to Jeremiah's ship.

'Bad luck, my Lady,' Thaddeus said with mock sympathy. 'But you know what they say: there's always someone who kicks the bucket in the first round. Just be grateful it wasn't your player himself.'

'At least *my* player came close to winning the round!' Lady Luck snapped. 'He did not fall at the first hurdle with those enchanted dolphins as your enchantress did!'

Thaddeus instantly looked less pleased with himself and disappeared from the deck with a scowl, presumably to go and retrieve his player. At the same time, the Goddess of Luck waved her arm and she, Lex and Jesse disappeared from the deck of the *Scurleyshoo Death* and instantly reappeared on the bridge of Lex's enchanted ship.

'How could you let this happen?' Lex rounded on her at once.

'Oh, my dear, I know it's a horrible thing but . . . well . . .' Lady Luck fluttered her hands miserably. 'Little accidents do happen during Games, you know.'

'Little accidents? Jesse is *dead*!' He shuddered even to say it. The words were horrible in his ears, and horrible in his mouth. This was not the way it was supposed to be at all.

'Lex, you know the reality of the Games. This is what you sign up for.'

That might be what other, less talented players signed up for, but it was *not* what Lex signed up for. After all, Mr Schmidt had lived through the whole of the last Game with no serious injuries whatsoever, and he'd been a doddering old lawyer. Jesse had been a swarthy cowboy. It just wasn't fair. And, to make it even worse, Lex couldn't help feeling that he was at least partially to blame for it. After all, if he hadn't gone after Jesse and convinced him to play in the Game then he wouldn't have been there in the first place. Or if he had just *told* Jeremiah and Tess about the poisonous octopuses then Tess would never have picked one up.

'He shouldn't have intervened!' Lex raged angrily. 'It was his own stupid fault! He shouldn't have concerned himself about what Tess East was or wasn't doing! She was the enemy! It was no concern of ours if she killed herself!'

'I agree, dear,' Lady Luck said tearfully. 'It was a silly thing for him to do. And it's a dreadful shame. Really, it is.'

She glanced out the window at the sudden sound of cheers and noticed that Jeremiah's boat was pulling out of the harbour.

'We'd better set off for Olaree, dear,' she said. 'That's where the second round is to take place. We'll go up on deck and bury poor Jesse at sea along the way.'

Lex stared at her dumbly. Would she be this fickle when Lex himself finally died? Shed a tear or two, look suitably pained for five minutes and then flit off in search of the next thing to occupy her flighty mind?

'Look, I can't just tip him over the edge of the boat—' he began, but then he broke off suddenly, eyes narrowed suspiciously. 'Did he . . . Did he just move?'

'Move?' the Goddess replied blankly. 'He's dead, Lex. There are blue rings all over his hand.'

'I thought I saw him move just then.'

'Oh, my dear, I know that's what you want to believe, but I'm afraid that—' But then she, too, broke off with a startled exclamation.

They had both seen it this time. Jesse's hand had definitely moved.

'Perhaps that's a death twitch,' Lady Luck said, peering a little closer.

'Gahhhh!' croaked Jesse.

'Perhaps that's a death rattle,' the Goddess suggested.

Lex pushed her aside impatiently. 'No, he's alive! How is this possible?'

The cowboy was, indeed, alive. As Lex and Lady Luck goggled at him in astonishment, he suddenly propped himself up on his elbows with a great shuddering breath that sounded extremely painful.

'He's alive!' Lady Luck screeched in alarm. 'What wizardry is this? Don't get too close, Lex! He might be a zombie!'

But Lex wasn't listening to her. He was too busy rushing

forwards to help Jesse to his feet, shaking his hand vigorously and saying, 'I'm so glad you're not dead! Do you feel all right?'

'Er . . . yeah,' the cowboy replied. 'I think so.'

'Perhaps you have a special immunity. Did you get bitten by a lot of snakes, or something, back in the West?'

Jesse shrugged. 'No more than usual.'

'Perhaps it's because it was a baby that bit you,' Lex said, reaching for the book.

Consultation of the book revealed that this was indeed a difference between the adult octopuses and their young. It seemed that the babies did not have enough venom to kill a man, only enough to temporarily paralyse him. In the meantime, they were supposed to squeal for the mother who would quickly come over and bite the prey up into little pieces, small enough for the babies to swallow—

'That's quite enough of that, thank you, Lex!' Lady Luck interrupted, fluttering her hands in distress. 'I'm sure poor Jesse doesn't want to hear such horrible things.'

'Oh, no, ma'am; I think they're fascinating little blighters.'

'But doesn't the thought of being chewed up into bite-size pieces and eaten by all those octopuses distress you?'

'Nope.'

Lady Luck looked rather impressed by this, so Lex snorted and said, 'He probably just doesn't have the imagination to picture it.'

'I guess I've never been the imagining type,' Jesse replied amiably.

After reading the book, it seemed that no lasting damage would be done by a baby octopus bite except for the fact that the blue rings would eventually turn into white scars. Lex himself would have been upset about this. The rings were unsightly and rather gross, and it was important to Lex to minimise scars – especially right there on his hand where anyone could see them – but Jesse just shrugged when Lady Luck started fussing about it. It seemed that out in the Wild West they were all rather proud of their scars.

'I'll even be able to beat Popcorn-Face Billy with this,' Jesse said, holding up his ringed hand and looking at it with approval.

'Yes, well, your petty victories aside,' Lex snapped, 'we're now losing the Game because of you! The medallion was right there in your hand! Why didn't you give it to me before rushing off to play the hero? Why did you have to drop it right next to Tess *East*, for goodness' sake? There's no place for heroics in these Games and you'd better get that into your thick head right n—' He broke off, then said, 'Hang on! *Can* we claim hero points for it? He *did* save her life, after all!'

But Lady Luck was shaking her head. 'It won't work, I'm afraid. Hero points can only be awarded for the heroic acts of players, not their companions.'

'But that's totally unfair!' Lex protested.

'I can try and get the rules changed for the next Game but it's too late for this one. Once a Game has started you can't change any of the rules.'

Lex was furious about the entire business. He and Jesse were the ones who had done all the work. All Jeremiah had done was to blunder in stupidly at the end with his sword. It wasn't *fair* that he should have won the round. He hadn't even been the one to pick up the medallion; it had been Tess. But it seemed that, whilst companions couldn't earn hero points for the player, they could win for them, and so there was nothing to be done about it. For the first time, Lex had actually lost a round, and it was a bitter pill to swallow.

The ship set sail for Olaree where they were to spend the next week before the second round. Rooms had been booked for all three players and their companions in an extremely grand hotel. Lex had fully intended to stay on the boat but, when Lady Luck brought him the newspaper headlines the next morning, he soon changed his mind.

He had expected to tear the papers up in a rage at the sight of story after story touting Jeremiah's victory. But, to his pleasant surprise, he found that the focus wasn't on Jeremiah's victory at all, but rather on Jesse's heroic, tragic death. Once they realised the cowboy was perfectly all right, Lady Luck had been all for rushing straight off to inform everyone, but Lex had stopped her.

'Use your head for once,' he'd said. 'There might be some way we can use this to our advantage.'

If nothing else, it might give Lex a slight edge in the second round if all the other players believed he had no companion. What Lex had said seemed to set the Goddess off thinking, for she promptly disappeared, saying that she must edit the Game footage. The Games were not broadcast to the stadiums live anymore, simply because the Gods preferred to pick and choose what people saw. They wanted their own players to come across as daring and heroic and brave. So any unfortunate moment where a player might – for example – break down in tears, was carefully edited out later.

When Lex watched the footage from the round on his Divine Eye he had to give Lady Luck some credit, for she had done a very fine job of it, despite the fact that they had lost. The battle with the little octopuses looked quite horrific, as did the big fight up on deck. There was much emphasis – complete with music and slow-motion play-back – on the moment when Lex and Jesse both ran towards Tess East to save her from the octopus. Lex could practically hear the rapturous applause from the stadiums when Jesse grabbed the little monster off her and flung it out to sea. And then, most deliciously of all, Lady Luck had included the moment when Jeremiah punched Jesse, only she had omitted the part where Jeremiah had spoken and so – to the spectators in the stadiums – the reason for his punching the cowboy would have been completely unclear. Add to that the fact that Jesse apparently crumpled up and died right there on the deck shortly afterwards . . . Well, it was enough to bring tears to the most hardened eye. Indeed, the Lex in the footage even seemed to have manly tears glimmering in his eyes at the end of the round.

'Well, ain't that just touching?' Jesse said when he saw it, smacking Lex hard on the back. 'And there I was thinking you were just a selfish brat who didn't care about no one but yourself.'

'I *am* a selfish brat!' Lex snapped. 'I've never cried for anyone but myself and I don't intend to change my habit now. Those tears were added in later, during the edit.'

'Is that allowed?'

'Of course. The Gods only touch up what is already there.'

On Jeremiah's footage, Kala had done a good job of making him seem handsome and fearless and bold. But, if anything, this only added to the overall impression the public had of him as a cold, ruthless, selfish git – whilst poor, noble, heroic Jesse Layton had given his life to save Jeremiah's little sister. The papers were full of what an honourable, decent, practically *saintly* man Jesse had been, which seemed rather ironic when he was actually an outlaw on the run, with a reward on his head and a noose waiting for him back west for whatever horrible crimes he'd committed there.

Lex might have been slightly annoyed by all the attention Jesse was getting, but the papers were also focusing on poor, grieving Lex Trent. They seemed to have decided that Lex and Jesse had been the bestest, closest of friends for many years and that Jesse's death had crippled Lex utterly.

'It says here that I've spent every day since my dear friend's demise walking the deck of my ship and staring out to sea.'

'*Every* day?' Jesse said. 'Heck, I only died yesterday.'

Lex shrugged. 'Time moves slower when you're grieving. Apparently I'm refusing food, too,' he said, squinting back at the newspaper.

The papers were full of photos from the feast and the first round of Jesse and Lex together looking companionable, whereas any photo of Jeremiah that appeared tended to veer towards the unflattering side, showing him with his eyes half closed or his mouth half open. Overnight, he had become the villain of the piece despite the fact that he had won the first round. Everyone hated his guts. Lex was smugly satisfied. It was worth losing the first round for a result like this.

'I've changed my mind,' Lex said when they reached Olaree the next day. 'I think I might stay at the hotel after all.'

'What for?' Lady Luck said. 'I thought you were going to stay on the ship.'

'It's too good an opportunity to pass up,' Lex replied. 'I've got the part of a grieving friend to play.'

Olaree was a snob town. It was full of posh buildings and fancy sidewalks and rich people. There was to be a welcome dinner for the players that night. Lex's ship arrived several hours before Jeremiah's and, within half an hour, people had left a veritable forest of flowers on the dock beside his boat. Some of the bouquets were quite frighteningly huge and elaborate. Clearly the rich people of Olaree subscribed to the belief that nothing says 'sorry your friend is dead' quite like a spray-painted silver fir-cone. There was even one particularly inventive flower arrangement in the shape of a cowboy hat.

'Why are they making such a fuss about it?' Lex asked, peering out at the harbour from a corner of the window in his room. 'People die in Games all the time.'

'It's several things, dear,' Lady Luck replied. 'It's partly the fact that Jesse is so good looking, in a rough-and-ready kind of way; it's partly that he died heroically saving a child's life rather than merely trying to win the Game; it's partly that Tess East is such a sweet-looking thing and so everyone *wanted* Jesse to save her; and it's partly that you're a young boy, now playing the dangerous Game all alone. People love all that.'

'They're a fickle bunch,' Lex replied, remembering how they had all cheered and cheered for Jeremiah before they decided they hated him.

'Yes, dear.'

'Well, at least it makes it easier for me to cheat and rob them.'

CHAPTER ELEVEN

THE MAJESTIC

Before leaving the ship for the welcome dinner that evening, Lex went to his wardrobe and picked an outfit that was entirely black. He was supposed to be in mourning, after all. He'd always had naturally pale skin and this was emphasised even more by the dark clothes. As a finishing touch he rubbed a small amount of shampoo into his eyes. It stung like hell but, after half an hour, they stopped streaming and merely looked a little blood-shot – like the eyes of someone who hasn't slept a wink the night before because they've been up all night wringing their hands over their fallen comrade. Before leaving the ship, Lex sternly warned Jesse to stay well out of sight, away from the windows, and not to go anywhere near the deck.

The Majestic Hotel was not far from the dock but they had sent a carriage, anyway. Lex was extremely pleased with the hotel from the outset. It was the sort of place that had chandeliers, and desserts fashioned in the shape of swans, and waiters wearing spotless gloves. It was the most decadent, luxurious hotel Lex had ever seen. It was the sort of place that *suited* him. He was made for fancy hotels, not grubby farms. But he was careful not to allow any of his pleasure to show on his face, for he had a moping part to play tonight. Indeed, to anyone who saw him, Lex Trent had the look of a person who hardly knew where he was and didn't care either.

He was aware of people shooting sympathetic glances his way as he followed the porter through the sumptuous lobby to the reception desk. And then – quite perfectly – when he gave his name, the man behind the desk replied instantly, 'Ah, yes. Welcome to the Majestic, Mr Trent. We have a suite reserved for you and your companion on the top floor. Will Mr Layton be joining you shortly, sir?'

Everyone – but *everyone* – in Olaree knew that Jesse was tragically dead. Everyone, it seemed, but this man. The people milling about within earshot gasped at the dreadful, awful, *unforgivable faux pas* and shot anxious glances at Lex. Seizing the moment, Lex willed the colour to drain from his face (a trick he had taught himself some while ago, along with blushing). He swallowed hard and allowed a tremor to creep into his voice as he said, 'Jesse . . . Mr Layton . . . won't be joining me shortly. Or ever. He's dead.'

'Oh, you poor dear!' exclaimed an enormously fat woman nearby who was wearing a lot of lace and the largest floppy hat that Lex had ever seen. She turned a withering glare on the unfortunate receptionist and said,

'It's too dreadful of you, really it is! I never dreamt that any staff of the Majestic could be so insensitive! Don't you know that this poor boy's companion lost his life saving a little girl in the last round?' She was practically quivering with outrage.

The receptionist looked horrified and hastily started apologising. Within seconds, an important-looking manager was bearing down on them all. When he realised what the problem was he dismissed the receptionist on the spot.

Quite a little crowd had gathered around them by this point so Lex took the opportunity to say gravely, 'Please, sir, as a special favour to me, do not dismiss this man. Jesse wouldn't . . . He wouldn't have wanted that.' Cripes, he could practically *feel* the swell of almost ferocious approval emanating from the people around him.

The receptionist was ushered away but the manager assured Lex that he would be allowed to keep his job. Then the manager himself took Lex's bag and escorted him across the lobby to the elevator, during which time Lex had a grand total of three lace handkerchiefs pressed into his hand by women who seemed completely intent on comforting him, despite the fact that he wasn't actually crying. Of course, if Lex had been playing any part but himself then he would have been wailing his head off by now, but he wasn't acting a part as the Shadowman or the Wizard or Trent Lexington. He was – technically, at least – being Lex Trent. And, although he certainly wanted people underestimating him, he didn't really want them believing him to be a weakling who couldn't keep his emotions under control.

So he accepted the handkerchiefs gracefully, for all that he didn't need them, and followed the manager to the elevator with a grim look, as if he was counting the seconds until he could finally be alone.

Even the elevator was a ridiculously posh affair, with a uniformed bellman and everything – because, naturally, it wouldn't do to have the guests pushing their own buttons. The manager told Lex that he had been given the largest suite the hotel had. Lex smirked inwardly at the thought of what Jeremiah and Lorella would say when they heard about that. Even when he was losing, Lex was winning. And that took a really very special kind of skill.

When they reached the thirteenth floor at the top of the hotel, the manager took Lex to the door – the only one, in fact, on that floor – unlocked it and stepped aside for Lex to enter.

It took all of Lex's self control not to react. Never in his entire life had he seen anything so splendidly luxurious. The suite was huge. The living room area was all polished wood, with a grand ornate fireplace and big, solid armchairs that looked as if they'd never been used before. A massive fruit basket, piled high with a veritable mountain of colourful fruits, sat on the gleaming coffee table. Nothing says 'sorry your friend is dead' like a bunch of ripe bananas . . .

'Is it to your liking, sir?' the manager asked.

'It's fine, thank you.'

'The bathroom is through the door to your right. And on the left are the bedrooms . . .' The manager trailed off apologetically for, of course, the second bedroom was now to remain unoccupied.

Lex turned his head away and clenched his teeth to make a muscle twitch in his jaw, as if he was struggling to contain his emotion.

'I expect you'd like to be left alone now,' the manager said hurriedly. 'The entire top floor is devoted to this suite, so rest assured you won't be bothered by anyone. And if there is anything that I, or anyone else in the hotel, can do for you, Mr Trent, day or night, then please don't hesitate to let us know.'

'You're very kind,' Lex replied.

The manager put down Lex's suitcase and left the room, quietly drawing the door closed behind him. Lex crossed over and locked it, then waited until he heard the elevator doors slide shut. Only then did he allow a wide grin to spread across his face. He rushed into the bathroom and goggled at the bath, which was practically big enough to swim in. Then he ran to check out the bedrooms. Both had grand four-poster beds with chocolate mints on the pillows, little fridges that were stuffed full of complimentary drinks and snacks, and even a strange-looking thing that Lex assumed must be a trouser press. There was also a liquor trolley, complete with crystal-cut tumblers and a bucket of ice. If Lex had been a drinking man he would have poured himself a celebratory drink but, as he wasn't, he made do with a celebratory bubble bath.

Lex loved baths and soap and being clean. So if there was a big bathtub going free then Lex was always likely to get in it and stay put well past the time that his fingers got all crinkly. He didn't even care if it was a bit of a girly habit. He liked baths – if they had bubbles in 'em as well then so much the better – and he wasn't going to apologise for it.

He'd been in the tub for about half an hour and was just topping it up with more hot water when the bathroom door opened and a cheerful voice said, 'Fancy place, this, ain't it?'

Lex almost drowned in his own bath water. For there in the doorway stood Jesse, hat tipped back on his head, a bottle of beer in his hand and a stupid grin on his face.

'Oh my Gods, what are you *doing* here?' Lex spluttered, utterly horrified. 'I told you to stay out of sight on the ship!'

The cowboy shrugged. 'Yeah, well, I only take orders from you when it suits me to, kid. Besides, we ain't even playing a round right now. I'm an outdoorsy sorta bloke. I can't stay cooped up on that ship for an entire week; I'll go barmy.'

'You didn't even manage one afternoon!' Lex snapped, grabbing a nearby towel and wrapping it around himself as he stood up in the bath. 'Everyone thinks you're dead! What if someone saw you coming here? Did you even think of that?'

'Relax,' Jesse replied. 'I didn't stroll through the streets. Her Ladyship transported me right here to the room. No one saw nothing.'

'No one saw *anything*,' Lex corrected, being deliberately obnoxious in his anger. 'Haven't you ever heard of a double negative before?'

'Can't rightly say that I have,' Jesse replied, completely unruffled. 'Say, I didn't notice that liquor trolley there before.' And, with that, he turned away from the bathroom and walked back into the lounge.

Scowling and grumbling to himself, Lex stepped out of the bath and hurriedly got dressed. When he went into the living room, the cowboy was sprawled on one of the armchairs drinking beer from one of the crystal-cut tumblers.

'I made it quite clear to you before we started this thing that, if you agreed to take part, you were going to have to take orders from me. I *told* you that was a condition and you agreed to it before you put the Binding Bracelet on!'

'Well, I guess I wasn't exactly telling the Gods' honest truth when I said that,' Jesse replied with a shrug. 'I was in prison, kid, and you were my ticket out. I would've said whatever the heck you wanted to hear to get myself outta that cell.'

Lex glared ferociously at the cowboy. 'You . . . you're a blaggard, that's what you are!'

'Yep. But you knew that before you picked me and you gone went and did it, anyway.'

Well, there was no arguing with that. Lex had known full well what Jesse was, almost from the very moment he saw him. That was precisely why he had wanted him as his companion, and probably would have done even if it hadn't been for Dry Gulch House. There were ways to work around this. As long as Lex paid Jesse for each round they won then he could guarantee that the cowboy would at least try. And there was no denying that he had been useful in the first round. Right up until the end, anyway.

'You can stay because it suits me that you do,' Lex said eventually. 'It means I won't have to sneak back to the ship so that we can eat together. No one will know you're here as long as you stay put in the room and we keep the door locked at all times. In the meantime you can make yourself useful and start teaching me how to be a cowboy.'

'Yeah, about that—' Jesse began.

'If you go back on your word and refuse to do it then, Gods help me, you'll be sorry!' Lex snapped.

'Settle down,' Jesse replied mildly. 'I'll do it. I was just gonna tell you that it'll never work. I mean, look at you. You're a skinny city kid.'

'I was brought up on a farm, actually,' Lex said coldly. 'Besides, I'm not asking you to teach me how to *be* a cowboy; I'm asking you to teach me how to *fake* it.'

'I just don't think it can be done, is all. But if you wanna take a stab at it then knock yourself out, by all means.'

'I'm a fast learner,' Lex replied. 'Just you wait. I'll show you.'

'While we're on the subject, I don't think the Sword of Life is real, neither.'

'Well, the sword is none of your concern,' Lex replied. 'All you have to do is get me into Dry Gulch House. And if you manage that then I'll . . . I'll give you a bonus payment of two hundred pieces of m-gold.'

Jesse narrowed his eyes suspiciously. 'You're making a lot of promises about rewards, kid, but I ain't seen so much as a single dollar yet. How do I know you're good for it?'

'I'm a thief,' Lex replied. 'I can get you your money easily.'

Jesse shook his head. 'You're also a liar. I ain't buyin' it. I can recognise another rogue when I see one. I want my payment handed over to her Ladyship with promises from you and from her that, if I play my part in this circus, I'll get my reward at the end of it. Without that I won't go another step further. I'll walk out that door right now and show the world I ain't dead.'

'You wouldn't have the nerve!' Lex sneered, despite the fact that he knew full well that Jesse absolutely *would* make good on his threats if it came to it. 'Why must I always be plagued with the most *vexing* companions?' he moaned. 'I'd be better off on my own. I'd be better off if you *were* dead! If the Game allowed it, I wouldn't take a companion at all.'

But for all that he was making a tremendous fuss about

it for the look of the thing, Lex was not overly bothered. It was simply a matter of learning how to handle a person. He'd learnt how to handle Mr Schmidt in the last Game and he would learn how to handle Jesse even easier because all the man seemed to care about was money. And for a talented thief like Lex, money really was no problem at all.

'I assume you've no objection to valuables in lieu of payment?' he said, deliberately choosing a fancy legal term in the hope that Jesse wouldn't understand it.

But the cowboy just said suspiciously, 'What sort of valuables?'

Lex shrugged impatiently. 'I don't know. Diamonds or something.'

'Diamonds would be just fine,' Jesse replied, still looking suspicious. 'Just so long as you don't try and fob old Jesse off with fake ones. Got some in your pocket, do you?'

'No, not yet. But in a posh hotel like this there's bound to be rich women carrying their jewels about with them. I bet I'll be able to get you your payment from the very first room I break into.'

His fingers were itching again. Being in posh places like the Majestic always had that effect on Lex. There were, after all, countless valuable things just there for the taking. He wouldn't have done it for Jesse alone, but the thought of carrying out a theft now really rather appealed to him. That pickpocketing business at the Sea Volcanoes teashop had been nothing more than keeping his hand in: something so ridiculously simple that it had barely been fun at all. Pinching something from a hotel room in the Majestic, on the other hand, would be wonderful fun, because it was bound to be at least a little bit of a challenge. He needed to keep his hand in as the Wizard, too, after all. This would be an entertaining diversion amidst all the schmoozing he would be expected to do at the welcome dinner later.

'Yes,' Lex said decisively. 'I'll obtain your payment tonight. After the dinner.'

'Pull that off,' Jesse said, eyebrows raised, 'and I *would* be impressed.'

'Lovely,' Lex replied. 'Nothing matters more to me than impressing you! Now, if you're quite satisfied, can we get on with this cowboy thing?'

'All right,' Jesse said. 'I suppose I can start the lessons on faith. For now. If you wanna pass yourself off as a cowboy, the first thing you need to learn how to do is play poker.'

'Poker?' Lex repeated, pulling a face. 'Are you sure that's what we should be starting with? Shouldn't we be doing . . . I don't know . . . gun-shooting or knife-throwing or tobacco-chewing or something?'

'Here?' Jesse asked, eyebrows raised. Lex had to admit he had a point. The posh, pristine suite probably wasn't the ideal place to learn how to throw a knife.

'Don't make no difference, anyhow,' Jesse said. 'Even if we were on the ship I woulda started with poker. It's the lynchpin, see? Much more so than all that other stuff. I mean, you're not planning on challenging anyone to a duel, are you?'

'Good Gods, no!'

'Well, as long as you stay outta trouble, that stuff won't be as important to you as the everyday stuff. Things like learning how to play poker, chew tobacco and drink coffee black.'

'I already drink coffee black,' Lex replied.

'Not like this you don't,' Jesse said with a grin. 'I'm talking about coffee that's been brewed for so long in a tin pot over an open fire that you can stick a spoon in it and it'll stand up.'

'It sounds dreadful.'

'Yeah, well, you'll have to get used to it because, if you ever ask for cream to be put into the coffee, then everyone will know right enough that you ain't no cowboy. But poker's the most important thing. You ever played before?'

'No.'

'How about other card games?'

'No, I'm not a gambler,' Lex replied, rather contemptuously. 'I don't rely on luck. I prefer to be sure I'll win.'

Jesse stared at him. 'You realise what a dumb thing that is to say, do you? Considering who your Goddess is and all.'

Lex scowled. 'I was an excellent thief and conman even *before* she came along. In fact, that's what made her take such an interest in me in the first place. I'm *careful* and *dedicated* to my art. That's why I sometimes appear to be lucky.'

This wasn't entirely true, and Lex knew it. He *was* lucky. But he was also, as he'd said, careful and hard-working. Indeed, if he'd applied his clever mind to any other profession, he would have climbed his way straight to the top of the ladder in no time. Successfully pulling off thefts and scams did not come *easily*. There was a lot of hard work involved in what Lex did. And he saw himself as completely entitled to every penny he earned.

'Whatever,' Jesse said with a grin. 'The point is that if you've never played card games before then you'll have no feel for the cards. Here.' As if by magic, the cowboy produced a deck from one of the inner pockets of his jacket. 'Have a go at shuffling them.'

Lex took the cards, squinting at them dubiously. They were dirty, dog-eared and all had pictures of naked women on them. Lex shuffled them for a few seconds, didn't drop a single card, and then handed them back to Jesse.

But the cowboy shook his head. 'We ain't done yet, partner. That there was your basic sliding shuffle. Anyone with two hands can do that. But for poker you're mostly gonna need the dovetail shuffle. And you'll also need to learn the Hindu shuffle, the pile shuffle and the Chemmy shuffle. Then we'll go on to the Mongean shuffle and the Faro shuffle. And the false shuffle, too, because they all expect a bit of cheating. Once you've got all that, *then* we'll go on to the game itself.'

Lex stared at him. 'You're joking, surely?'

'That I ain't.'

'All right,' Lex said. 'Show me how each one is done. Whenever I get a spare minute I'll practise, but I want to go on to the game itself today.'

'It's your funeral, kid. But mark my words, you'll need more than just one demonstration before you can master them.'

'Perhaps two, then,' Lex replied carelessly. 'But I have a sharp eye, a good memory and an excellent knack for mimicry.'

'And a large dash of modesty,' Jesse said.

'Modesty is for chumps! Or people who have no talents!'

'Well, I reckon you're probably right about that,' the cowboy replied mildly.

There was a grand total of eight different shuffles that Lex would need to master before they reached Dry Gulch. Jesse demonstrated each one once before they moved on to the game of poker itself. Lex had never played before in his life but, to his smug delight, he quickly discovered that it was precisely the sort of game which he was born to play. To be a good poker player you needed a good memory, an ability to quickly calculate odds in your head and – best of all – you needed to be able to bluff convincingly. Jesse explained that many poker players had 'tells' – something that gave them away when they were lying. Lex couldn't help but sneer at this. He was far, far too disciplined for tells. He could lie brazenly right to someone's face without allowing his expression or his body language to give him away, and had been able to do so for years. Bluffing in poker was, therefore, an absolute piece of cake. Not only that, but he had a good head for figures and was able to calculate the odds and weigh his chances with ridiculous ease.

'Well, I can't see what all the fuss is about,' Lex announced blithely. He could tell that the fact he'd picked poker up so quickly and so easily was annoying Jesse, and he was determined to get as much mileage out of the petty victory as he possibly could. 'This game is so painfully simple that we might as well sit around playing snap and have done with it.'

To Lex's gratification, Jesse's mouth fell open and the cowboy gaped at him like a landed fish. 'Snap?' he managed at last. '*Snap*? Here's a piece of advice I'll give you for free, kiddo, don't ever make that suggestion to any cowboys you meet in Dry Gulch.'

Poker was a mixture of talent and luck, which was why Lex naturally excelled at it. He was dealt more than his fair share of full houses and straight flushes. And, when he didn't get a good hand, he was able to calculate the odds of what Jesse had and, that way, always knew whether he should cut his losses or bluff flawlessly.

'This is so easy it's not even fun,' Lex said after about an hour of playing, throwing down the cards as he spoke. 'I think I've got the knack of it now.'

In fact he was being deliberately flippant. The truth was that he could tell already that he was going to enjoy poker. And if there were a few more players at the table then it would be even better.

'That there was your basic hold 'em,' Jesse replied almost sulkily. 'But there's other variations you'll have to learn yet. Seven-card stud and five-card draw and Omaha and black vulture poker and—'

'Fine, we'll do that later when I have five minutes to spare,' Lex replied. 'I'm going to get changed for dinner.'

'Dinner? Dandy! What are we having?'

'You aren't having anything,' Lex said sternly. 'You're staying right here out of sight. You're supposed to be dead, remember. Look, you do appreciate how important it is that you stay out of sight, don't you? It's bad enough that you're in the hotel as it is. You *must not* leave this room. Even if the hotel is on fire. Got it?'

Jesse shrugged. 'Well, I gotta eat some time. I'm a big fella, not a skinny chap like you. I need food.'

'We'll both eat from the mini-bar before I go downstairs.'

It was a fortunate thing that everyone already seemed to have decided that Lex was so grief-stricken he was refusing food. It would make it less suspicious when he didn't eat a single thing that evening. And leaving good food on his plate would be much easier to do if he wasn't actually hungry. So, before he went downstairs, he and Jesse stuffed their faces on the food that was packed into the mini-bar. There were sandwiches, savoury snacks, chocolate and cake – not to mention the gigantic fruit basket in the living room as a condolence present for Jesse's being horribly killed. They ate until they could not eat any more.

'Well, I guess I'll just go and have myself a little lie down,' Jesse said once they'd finished. 'There's nothing like a snooze after a good meal.'

'Splendid idea,' Lex replied over his shoulder as he

headed into his own room to get changed. He'd brought a slightly smarter outfit for dinner, which was just as well seeing as how he'd got a copious amount of crumbs over his first one – in addition to a smear of melted chocolate across the collar of his shirt whilst greedily trying to consume a particularly large slice of dark, moist chocolate cake. The grief-stricken impression he was trying to convey may have been very slightly spoilt if he had gone down to the restaurant with chocolate stains all over his clothes.

So he put the black shirt and tie on, brushed his hair and rubbed at his eyes a bit before spending a couple of minutes practising grim, pained, mournful expressions at himself in the bedroom mirror.

'Gods, I'm good,' he muttered to himself as he straightened his tie. His face was so pitiful that he almost felt sorry for *himself*! Lex could pull different facial expressions off at will if the occasion called for it but, wherever possible, he liked to spend a few minutes carefully getting himself into character first. It never did to turn your nose up at preparation simply because you were endowed with a Gods-given talent, and were naturally lucky to boot.

Now that he was ready, he lingered in his bedroom only to rummage around in his bag until he found the handcuffs. Lex's bag used to belong to the same enchanter he had stolen the ship from. It was a magic bag that was bigger inside than it was out and could be filled with a practically endless supply of stuff without ever seeming to become any heavier. Lex had therefore packed it full of everything and anything that he might ever conceivably need in a Game, scam or theft. He was sure there were handcuffs in there somewhere and, within a couple of minutes of searching, he'd found them.

Concealing them carefully in the palm of his hand, he then wandered into Jesse's room. The cowboy was – as he had hoped – stretched out on the bed with his arms behind his head and his hat pulled down over his face. This was the very definition of a sitting duck. Poor fool; he was totally unsuspecting. Jesse didn't even look up when Lex walked in but merely said lazily, 'Ain't you gone yet? I thought you'd be down there hobnobbing by now.'

'I just wanted to stress once again how *vital* it is that you don't leave the room this evening,' Lex said, wandering casually nearer to the bed. 'Leaving the ship with Lady Luck's help was one thing but leaving the room could have potentially disastrous consequences for me. You do understand that, don't you?'

'Sure, sure,' the cowboy drawled lazily.

'Good,' Lex replied. 'In that case, I know you won't mind me taking a little precaution.'

And, in one fluid motion, he leant forwards, snapped one cuff around the cowboy's wrist and the other around the bedpost.

Jesse tilted his hat back with his free hand, looked at the handcuffs, looked at Lex and said calmly, 'I sure as hell hope you've got the key to those, partner.'

'It's probably in my bag somewhere,' Lex replied. 'I'll

let you out when I get back. But I don't trust you any more than you trust me. This works both ways – partner.'

Jesse was clearly annoyed but was trying not to let it show. Lex grinned and said, 'Crossing me has consequences. My old companion – dear old Montgomery Schmidt, lawyer and nag extraordinaire – learnt that very quickly. I'm sure you will, too. You may not be the brightest button in the box but you've got half a brain at least.'

'You're too kind,' Jesse replied.

'So I've been told many times,' Lex said before flashing the cowboy one last big smile and saying, 'Have a lovely evening.' Then he turned on his heel and walked out of the bedroom to head to the dinner downstairs.

CHAPTER TWELVE

GREY PEARLS AND VANILLA CUPCAKES

The hotel had several restaurants but it was the largest, poshest one – the one with all the vaulted ceilings and crystal – in which they had the welcome dinner. There were name cards at the various tables – each one seating between seven and fifteen people. Lex found himself on one of the largest tables completely surrounded on all sides by wealthy, fat women who were positively weighed down with jewellery. There was simply no doubt about it – finding something suitable to pinch from one of their rooms later would be no trouble whatsoever.

Jeremiah and Lorella were already seated when Lex walked in. He was pleased to note that Jeremiah looked distinctly unhappy and Tess – who was sitting beside him – looked subdued almost to the point of appearing unwell. Lorella didn't look too happy either. Lady Luck had smugly told Lex that she had been caught by an enchanted dolphin trap almost as soon as she left the galley, right at the very start of the round. The episode had rather taken her down a peg or two.

Lex spent the evening looking suitably morose, pushing the food around his plate and quietly resisting the attempts of the clucking women all around him who were trying to entice him to eat.

'I'm afraid I haven't been feeling very well the last couple of days,' he said pitifully, whilst the women exchanged knowing looks over his head.

After the food had been cleared away, the manager of the hotel got a microphone from somewhere and called for quiet. The room fell silent whilst the man did a little speech about what an honour and a privilege it was, blah, blah, blah, to have all the players assembled at the hotel between rounds. Lex was pleased when Lorella stood up at the end of the speech and said that it was her pleasure to be there. She sat down and Jeremiah obviously then felt honour bound to say something as well for he stood up and – looking distinctly awkward at all the unfriendly looks people were shooting him – said that he, too, was pleased to be a guest at the Majestic. Once Jeremiah had retaken his seat, Lex got to his feet, being careful to look extremely reluctant to do so when he was, in reality, utterly delighted. A greater hush seemed to descend on the room when Lex stood up. All eyes were on him – which was just the way he liked it.

'I'd like to echo what my fellow players have said. I'm truly honoured to be here. And I . . . I'd like to take the opportunity to . . .' Lex trailed off, cleared his throat and continued in a stronger voice. 'If you don't mind, I would be very glad if you would all join me in a toast.' Everyone in the room had their glasses in their hands so quickly that it was almost like magic. 'I'd like to raise a glass to my fallen comrade,' Lex went on, pleased to note out of the corner of his eye that Jeremiah seemed to have slid down even further in his chair and rather looked like he desired nothing more than for a hole to appear in the ground and swallow him up. 'Jesse Layton,' Lex went on, 'was a good man and a true friend. He always put other people before himself. And I know that he gave his life gladly for Tess East and the last thing he would ever have wanted would be for anyone to feel resentful or angry about how the first round ended. That . . . That wasn't his way. Jesse didn't bear grudges and he wouldn't want anyone else to, either. He knew what he was doing when he grabbed that octopus and he did it with no regrets.'

Lex paused, as if he was fighting to keep himself under control, and in that pause he distinctly heard the woman seated next to him whisper to her neighbour, 'He's an orphan, you know. They say the cowboy was like a father to him.'

Excellent idea, Lex thought to himself.

'Some of you may know that my parents died when I was five,' he went on. 'My brother and I were orphaned. We barely remember our real father. But Jesse . . . Jesse was almost like a father to us—' He broke off abruptly at the same time as he willed tears to appear in his eyes for the first time. The seconds dragged on in tense silence before he finally said, 'I'm sorry, I . . . I can't go on.'

And, with that, he sat down and covered his face with his hand. After another moment of silence, the entire room applauded warmly – which was nice. It is always gratifying to be rewarded for a performance. If Lex had been a less disciplined sort of fraud then he might have taken the opportunity to smirk behind his hand, especially as he alone knew precisely where Jesse *really* was – handcuffed to a bed upstairs. But he was far, far too professional for that. Smirking was for when – and only when – he was safely back in his room, securely away from prying eyes.

The women on either side of him put comforting arms around his shoulders and Lex spent the next half hour being thoroughly mollycoddled.

It was towards the end of the evening, when Lex was almost ready to make his excuses and go back to his room, that he became aware of Jeremiah standing up from his table and making his way towards him.

Everyone in the restaurant shot him evil glances as he went. They had all *seen* him hit the dying cowboy who'd heroically saved his sister's life. Lex even heard a few muttered words along the lines of, 'Disgraceful!' 'Outrageous!' and 'Surely he won't have the audacity to actually *speak* to Lex Trent!'

Jeremiah stopped before the table. His head was high, his shoulders were back and he looked right at Lex and said, 'Lex, I just want to say how . . . how terribly sorry

I am. I realise there's no excuse for what I did. My action was unforgivable. But I can assure you that I simply didn't realise what had just happened when I . . . when I hit Jesse. I thought he was trying to hurt Tess. I love my sister and it's my fault she got dragged into this Game in the first place. I'd give anything in the world now to shake Jesse's hand and thank him myself. I . . . tried to give up the win for the first round. I told Kala I shouldn't have won in the first place, but it was too late.' He lowered his voice and went on more quietly. 'I understand that you and Jesse were friends for a long time so I'll understand if you never speak to me again. I just want you to know how heartily sorry I am. If I could swap places with him, I would, in a heartbeat.'

Lex could have throttled him! Jeremiah East was acting like a decent human being, blast him! Already Lex could feel the others thawing – their icy hatred melting away to be replaced with cautious sympathy. Jeremiah certainly seemed genuine, for he hadn't even brought Tess over with him, but had left her back at the table instead. If Lex had been in his place, he would have dragged the kid over for the apology because it was much harder to remain stony-faced when the dear, sweet, angelic-looking child whose life had been saved was gazing at you with big eyes.

As it was, Lex would have loved nothing better than to snap, 'Your apologies be damned! Jesse is still dead and nothing you can say will bring him back, so piss off!'

But that would never do at all, for then he would lose

sympathy. He therefore had no choice but to exercise some damage control. He sat motionless for a moment, as if thinking about what the nobleman had said. Then he slowly rose to his feet, very aware of his own table, and several others nearby, looking at him with baited breath as he turned to Jeremiah and said graciously, 'I believe you, Jeremiah. And I forgive you. I hope we can put this behind us.'

Then he held his hand out to Jeremiah, who looked rather stunned. After a moment, the nobleman gripped Lex's hand firmly and shook it vigorously. Several people actually clapped. Jeremiah then leaned closer and muttered in Lex's ear, 'If there's ever anything I can do for you – anything at all – please don't hesitate to let me know.'

Lex pulled a face inside his head. A sap – that was what Jeremiah really was. Underneath all the arrogance and the bravado and the conceit he was just another silly, gutless sap who could be manipulated so easily that it wasn't even funny.

Playing his part flawlessly, Lex thanked Jeremiah quietly before releasing his hand and looking away. 'If you'll excuse me,' he said quietly, 'I'm very tired. I think I'll call it a night.'

Lex slipped out of the restaurant and swiftly made his way upstairs. He *was* rather tired and looking forward to his bed. But first he had some diamonds to pinch, and he was looking forward to that even more than he was looking forward to going to bed.

How you carried out a theft depended on where you

were thieving *from*. The different locations all had their own set of advantages and disadvantages. Lex had never stolen anything from a hotel before. Most of the things he'd pinched had been from museums and the like. Museums were harder to get into but, once you *had* gained entrance, you were unlikely to be disturbed provided you didn't trip off any alarm systems. Hotel rooms, on the other hand, would be easier to get into than a museum and wouldn't have alarm systems, but the major problem was that you could never be entirely sure when someone was going to come back to their room. You therefore had to work under the constant threat of being suddenly interrupted at any moment. That meant one thing and one thing only: a damned good disguise.

Lex had picked his victim in the dining room downstairs. There had been a big fat woman sat at his table who insisted upon being called Margie and was wearing so much jewellery over her lacy white dress that she positively sparkled like a frosted vanilla cupcake. She had spent much of the evening talking loudly to anyone who would listen about Murray – her 'dear departed 'usband.' She was quite perfect because she was rich *and* she was lonely. Therefore, she was likely to spend a lot of time down in the bar that evening, chattering away. That should give Lex more time to sneak through her room. He had slipped the room key out of her bag whilst pretending to pick his napkin up from underneath the table.

But he certainly wasn't going to *rely* on not being interrupted by her. That was something you learnt early on in this game: expect the worst and prepare for it. Assuming Lex *were* to get interrupted in her room, he would need a viable excuse. And that, naturally, meant dressing up as a member of staff. It wasn't fool proof, of course, for the woman *had* spent the entire evening sitting across from Lex at the dinner table. But people who were that disgustingly rich didn't usually *see* servants. Not really. And Lex would only need to mumble his reason for being in her room before making a speedy retreat. She would not see his face clearly during that time, especially if he was wearing a hat.

And, fortunately, the bellhops at the Majestic all wore hats.

Obtaining a uniform wasn't too terribly difficult. Lex simply slipped out of the hotel and went round to the back. All hotels had back entrances for members of staff to come and go less obtrusively; somewhere the trash cans were kept and where the chefs could nip out for a quick smoke when it all got a bit too much for them in the kitchens. So Lex wandered around and found the place easily enough. From there it was a simple enough thing to wander unobtrusively through the kitchens. Lex had mastered the unobtrusive walk some time ago, now. It was very important to a fraud to be able to walk through a busy place without being noticed. And this was where he blessed his relative lack of height and his generally unimpressive stature. Jesse would find it much harder to walk unobtrusively because of his broad shoulders and height, whereas Lex could just slip right past everyone with barely more than a second glance spared his way. Now that it was a little later in the evening, one might expect the hubbub in the kitchen to have died down a bit. Not so at the Majestic. It appeared that, at this luxury hotel, breakfast, elevenses, lunch, afternoon tea and dinner were not considered to be enough. There was a midnight buffet as well, the centrepiece of which was a magnificent hog roast. There was, therefore, much hustle and bustle going on. Lex slipped through it all easily, grabbing up a big pile of dirty discarded aprons as he went.

Once he was out of the kitchens he wandered around for a while in search of the laundry room. No one stopped him. After all, he *was* carrying dirty washing. In the end he stopped a waiter who was going past and said, 'Er . . . can you tell me where the laundry is? I'm new.'

The waiter quickly gave him the directions before hurrying towards the kitchens. Once Lex got to the laundry he dumped the dirty aprons down and rooted around in the great mounds of clean clothing until he found a bright red jacket that was about his size. Yet another benefit of wearing all black was that it was adaptable: put on a red jacket with a bit of gold braid and he looked like he was wearing a uniform. He grabbed a matching hat and rammed it on his head before walking back to the kitchens. There he lingered just long enough to pick up an unattended plate of cakes – walking off with them with complete confidence as if he was absolutely supposed to take them.

Margie's room was on the fifth floor, number 512. Lex

walked into the elevator with his head held high in a posture of absolute confidence. The quickest way to draw attention to yourself was to look guilty. So he strutted into the elevator and calmly told the attendant that he was heading for the fifth floor. Unfortunately, it got a little bit hairy at that moment because, just as the doors were closing, a foot rammed into the gap to open them again and two people walked into the elevator. Lex knew, of course, that there were bound to be people milling about in the lobby, and possibly using the lifts, who had come from the dining room and had seen him there, or else had seen him play in the first round. But he also knew that most of those people would not really have *seen* him to the point of recognising him in a bellhop uniform. After all, there was no obvious reason why Lex Trent would be wandering about dressed up as a member of staff.

It was, therefore, most unfortunate that the two people who entered the lift now were Tess and Jeremiah East, probably the only two people (with the exception of Lorella and her sprite) who would recognise Lex in such a get-up. Instantly, he assumed a slouching attitude, hunching his shoulders and leaning against the elevator wall in a sulky sort of manner, his head bent at such an angle that they could not see his face.

Luckily, it was irrelevant, anyway, because Jeremiah and Tess paid him no attention whatsoever. Tess was too busy crying and Jeremiah was too busy trying to comfort her. At least she was doing it quietly – Lex couldn't stand bawling kids. He would never even have realised Tess was upset if it hadn't been for Jeremiah leaning down to her level, with his hands on her shoulders as he said, 'People die in Games all the time, Tess. Jesse would have known that when he signed up for it. What happened wasn't your fault.'

'It . . . was,' Tess replied, so quietly that Lex could hardly hear her. 'I shouldn't have picked up the octopus. But I didn't want someone to stand on it . . .' She trailed off with a whimper, but she was scowling through her tears, as if angry with Jeremiah or herself or perhaps both.

Lex rather liked her for that. And the fact that she was getting all wound up and upset about a man who wasn't dead at all, almost – *almost* – made him feel bad. So, as the doors opened for the Easts on the third floor, Lex took a chance by picking up one of the pretty, frosted cupcakes on the plate he was carrying and thrusting it out to Tess. It was a risky thing to do. After all, she only had to look at his face and she would surely recognise him. And how the heck would he explain to Jeremiah what he was doing dressed up in a bellhop outfit? He could try making out that he'd cracked under the strain of Jesse's death, but that really seemed to be stretching it just a bit too far and he was sure Jeremiah would be suspicious. But Lex liked risk. Sometimes he just couldn't help himself. So he held the cupcake out to Tess, even though he knew it might get him caught.

She started shaking her head but Jeremiah said, 'Take it, Tess; you barely touched your dinner.'

So she took the cake from Lex's hand with a muttered word of thanks.

'That's very kind,' Jeremiah said. 'Thank you.'

Lex merely nodded – careful to keep his head lowered – faintly surprised that Jeremiah would even bother to thank a mere bellhop. He supposed it was because there was no one important around to witness it. In another moment, Jeremiah and Tess had stepped out and the elevator continued up to the fifth floor without them.

When Lex got to Room 512, he took out the key and let himself in. It was just a bedroom, and so not as nice as his own suite on the top floor, but still rather impressive, nonetheless. Lex walked in and left the door slightly ajar behind him. Margie probably wouldn't notice her key was missing until she actually got to her room, and Lex didn't really want her going down to reception and possibly returning with a manager to let her in, so he left the door slightly open. He would hear her approach in time to put down anything he shouldn't have been touching and the plate of cakes he was carrying would constitute an effective excuse to explain his presence there.

As soon as he walked in, his eye fell on the large framed photo by the bed. He wandered over to it and saw that it was a picture of Margie with a thin little man wearing a monocle and a bemused sort of expression.

'Dear departed Murray, I presume,' Lex said.

Then he wandered away from the bed and towards the dressing table. There was a hairbrush there and several bottles of perfume. And there were several large brooches.

They were all set with precious stones of various sorts and, taken together, would easily constitute Jesse's fee. But it was all a bit easy and boring for Lex. So he wandered over to the wardrobe; if the room was anything like his, he knew the safe would be here.

Lex had some rudimentary experience with picking locks but, in actual fact, he had no need to try and do so this time. When he saw the keypad, the combination code jumped right out at him. There were letters and numbers on the pad so that guests could chose a numerical password or an actual word. Lex knew it couldn't be anything other than 'Murray', even before he typed in the name and heard the click of the lock as it swung open.

He rolled his eyes. Wasn't there *anything* that could challenge him anymore?

'I'm too good at everything,' Lex muttered irritably to himself as he rifled through the contents of the safe with one hand. 'That's my trouble. Too bloody good at everything.'

The safe was packed full of jewellery, most of which was extremely ostentatious, almost to the point of being gaudy. Keeping his ears strained for noise, Lex rummaged about until he finally found something he liked, for he sure as heck wasn't stealing something ugly. But, finally, there it was at the bottom of the safe – a stunning string of grey pearls. They were extremely valuable and would easily cover Jesse's fee and then some. Lex stuffed them into his pocket. Really, there was so much jewellery in there that the rich old biddy probably wouldn't even notice that the pearls had gone. He took one of the little enchanted hats out of his pocket, anyway, and left it in the safe, for it wouldn't do not to leave his calling card as the Wizard. He balanced the little hat on top of the remaining sparkly pile and then securely closed the lid of the safe with a snap.

He shut the wardrobe door and turned away just as Margie came bustling in. Finally: something to spice up the theft a bit.

'Good evening, ma'am,' Lex droned, lowering his voice and speaking in a sort of monotone. He held up the plate of cakes and said, 'Compliments of Mr Lex Trent; he asked me to deliver these to your room as a gesture of his gratitude that you went to such trouble to look after him tonight.'

It had occurred to Lex at the last minute that it wouldn't do simply to say that the kitchen had sent them up for no apparent reason. That would look far too suspicious, especially once the theft was discovered. But, this way, Lex himself could verify that he really *had* sent a bellhop up to her room with cupcakes, if Margie were to ask him about it later. He could be his own alibi, so to speak.

Of course, Margie instantly gushed all over the cakes and what a dear, dear boy that Lex Trent was. Lex left her to it. He'd intended to tell her that he'd found her room key on the floor outside the door but it didn't even seem to occur to her that she hadn't used it to get in. So he slipped it on to the coffee table as he walked out, strolling cheerfully away with the grey pearls in his pocket.

CHAPTER THIRTEEN

THE WISHING DRAGONS OF DESARETH

Lex walked back into his own room to find Jesse cuffed to the bed, right where he had left him. He was gratified to see that the cowboy looked extremely uncomfortable and that he had twisted round on his side in an effort to rest his arm.

'Well, it's about time,' Jesse said. 'My arm feels like it's gonna drop right off—' He stopped mid-sentence, stared at Lex and said, 'What the heck are you wearing?'

'It's called a disguise,' Lex replied with exaggerated patience. Then he pulled the string of pearls out of his pocket and held it up to the light. 'I got you these. They're more than sufficient to cover the sum we agreed. If you try and get so much as one more piece of m-gold out of me then I'll knock fifty off.'

'Let me see them,' Jesse said.

Lex walked closer to the bed and held the pearls out. Jesse took them with his free hand and examined them closely for a minute. Finally, he nodded, looked up at Lex and said, 'These will do just fine. As long as Lady Luck keeps a hold of 'em for the duration of the Game.'

'I'm disappointed that you don't trust me,' Lex said, holding his hand out for the stolen pearls. 'But some people are just born that way, I suppose. It's quite sad, really.'

'Tragic,' Jesse replied, replacing the pearls reluctantly in Lex's outstretched hand. 'Now let me outta these cuffs. My arm hurts like hell.'

'I have to find the key first,' Lex said. 'Oh dear, I hope I haven't lost it.'

'You have, you little brat, and you'll be sorry.'

'Sorry is a word I only barely understand the meaning of,' Lex replied, before turning on his heel and leaving, very much enjoying the fact that he was annoying the hell out of the cowboy. After an evening spent having to be so polite and likable, it was a welcome relief to finally be as obnoxious as he liked.

Of course, Lex knew exactly where the key to the handcuffs was. But he took his time finding it, anyway, because Lex Trent never did anything just because someone else wanted him to. There had to be something in it for *him* first.

'Here we are,' he said cheerfully when he walked back into Jesse's room with the key. 'False alarm. It wasn't lost, after all.'

'Ain't that lucky for both of us,' Jesse replied.

'I hope you're not going to sulk about this,' Lex replied,

throwing over the key. 'My last companion sulked most of the way through the Game and it got quite tedious towards the end.'

'Well, now, I guess I can't really blame you for not trusting me,' Jesse said as he unlocked the cuffs and freed his hand. He made to reach out for the glass of whisky at the side of his bed but it seemed that his arm was so numb that he clumsily knocked it to the floor instead. He scowled, looked up at Lex and said, 'But if you ever handcuff me to somethin' again, you little pipsqueak, I won't take it half so amiably.'

Lex couldn't help it. He grinned from ear to ear. A challenge! This was just exactly what he wanted.

'I'll get you another glass,' he said, before turning back into the living room.

Lex ordered breakfast to his room the next morning. It was a bit awkward for, of course, he was supposed to be off his food and yet here he was ordering enough bacon and eggs to feed two people. But they had to eat. If anyone asked, he would simply say that the Goddess of Luck was joining him for meals. The Gods didn't need to eat but they enjoyed doing so on occasion. And when they ate, they *really* ate, not having to worry about calories as mortal people did. If Lex put it about that the Goddess of Luck was spending a lot of time in the suite with him – trying to console him after Jesse's death, or something – then no one would think twice about the fact that so much food was going up there.

Aside from the welcome dinner that first night, there were no other organised events the players would be expected to attend. This suited Lex as it would give him more time to focus on his lessons with Jesse. Lady Luck appeared in the bedroom shortly after they'd finished their breakfast and Lex quickly explained to her the new arrangement he had come to with the cowboy. Then he produced the pearls from his pocket and held them out to her.

'So if you wouldn't mind holding on to them until we've finished the Game – I know it's a tiresome business but apparently Jesse doesn't trust me to pay him when all this is over.'

'Very sensible,' the Goddess said to the cowboy. 'Lex can't be trusted at all, you know. He even betrayed *me* once. He wouldn't think twice before stabbing you in the back.'

'Oh, I wish you would stop bringing that up,' Lex said. 'I didn't *actually* betray you, I just *almost* did. There's a difference!'

The point was negligible and Lex had no interest in discussing it any further so he changed the subject and said, 'If we win both the other rounds and come first in the Game, then he gets half of those pearls. If he teaches me well enough that I can pass as a cowboy at Dry Gulch, then he'll get the other half. If he doesn't play his part, then he gets nothing. Understand?'

'Yes, dear,' the Goddess replied.

She left them shortly after that and Lex and Jesse set

about resuming their training. Jesse insisted that learning to drink strong black coffee was next on the list. Rather than ringing down for it, Lex decided to walk downstairs himself. It would give him the chance to show his face, and asking for strong black coffee to take back with him would contribute nicely to the impression he was trying to create of someone so stricken with grief that he was neither eating nor sleeping. It was a winning situation all round, for it would cause Lorella to underestimate him in the next round, it would cause public feeling to warm towards him even further and – best of all – it would half cripple Jeremiah with guilt, and serve him right, the arrogant git.

After dressing all in black and fixing the pained, strained expression back on his face, Lex went down to the lobby. He was pleased, on arriving there, to observe that there was a bit of a disturbance going on. People were flapping about and looking upset and asking questions in very loud voices. And the police were there. Lex tapped on the shoulder of an expensively-dressed man standing nearby and said, 'Excuse me, but do you know what all the commotion is about?'

'It's the Wizard!' the man said. 'The famous thief who's been terrorising the lands. It seems he's struck right here in the Majestic!'

'No!' Lex replied, widening his eyes in shock.

'Yes!' The man nodded vigorously. 'Took Lady Kale-Fortescue's grey pearls right out of her safe! There was no sign of the lock being forced or tampered with. The pearls just disappeared right from inside the locked safe and one of those little hats he uses as calling cards appeared in its place.'

'Astonishing,' Lex murmured.

'I don't know if this chap is some sort of criminal genius or whether he really *is* using sorcery like they say, but those pearls just *vanished* right out of a locked safe that only her Ladyship knew the combination to! It really comes to something when your possessions aren't safe from that villain even somewhere like the Majestic!'

'Terrible thing,' Lex agreed. 'Terrible. Poor Margie. What a dreadful fiend this Wizard must be.'

Feeling well pleased with himself, Lex wandered off in the direction of the restaurant where he caught a nearby waiter and asked him to fetch a bag of the darkest, strongest coffee beans the Majestic had.

'We can brew it for you down here and deliver it to your room, sir—' the waiter began, but Lex shook his head.

'No, I want to brew it myself. One cup isn't enough; I'm going to be drinking it all day. I'd rather do it upstairs myself. Can you bring me a tin can, too, if you've got one? I'm . . . very particular about how I drink my coffee.'

'Very good, sir.'

Very good, sir! Lex hated that phrase. It was so . . . so passive, so subservient! The only way he would ever use it himself was if he was in the process of scamming someone blind. The waiter returned a moment later with the can and a bag of coffee, and Lex went back upstairs with them.

'You can have a go at getting a fire started,' Jesse said. 'And then, once you've done that, we'll brew the coffee on it. You'd better try eatin' beans cooked in the can, too, because they taste different, see, and you wanna be able to eat 'em without a spoon if needs be—'

'Gracious, you'll be wanting me to cook marshmallows on it next!' Lex said. 'Look, I can't see that this is going to be at all relevant. I only want to get into Dry Gulch House and stay there. I'm not going to be riding through the desert having camp-outs and sing-a-longs round the fire!'

'Don't be so sure,' Jesse replied mildly. 'There ain't no fancy cuisine at Dry Gulch House. It ain't like they've got a gang of servants in the kitchens. Most who stay there cook their own food over the open fires in the rooms downstairs. So you gotta learn how to cook it, how to eat it and how to like it, too.'

'All right, fine,' Lex said. 'Tell me how to make a fire.'

So Jesse explained the process of rubbing two sticks together to create friction, getting some dry grass, if possible, etcetera, etcetera. Lex tried for about half an hour before he got bored. He just couldn't get the knack of it. As anyone who's ever tried to do it knows, making a fire in this way is much, much harder than it looks.

'Practice makes perfect,' Jesse said smugly, clearly enjoying the fact that Lex wasn't getting it. 'Just spend a few dozen hours at it and then you'll be—'

'Hey!' Lex said sharply. 'What's that on your face?'

'What?' the cowboy said, instantly looking alarmed at Lex's expression.

'Right there,' Lex said, leaning forwards and reaching out his hand.

Jesse barely had time to take in what was happening as a match suddenly appeared between Lex's fingers and he ran it down the cowboy's stubbled cheek so fast that it instantly flared alight.

'Arghh, shit, kid!' Jesse yelped, jerking back and clapping a hand to his cheek. 'What the hell's the matter with you?'

'I always wondered if that would really work,' Lex said, looking interestedly at the match for a moment before holding it out to light the paper in the fireplace. Sometimes practice makes perfect,' he said. 'But sometimes cheating makes perfect, too. I never do it the hard way when I can cheat and do it the easy way.'

If the worst came to the worst, and he didn't have Jesse's face to hand, then he could always use one of the little Wizard hats by concealing it in the palm of his hand and muttering the magic word under his breath.

Glaring savagely at him, Jesse slowly lowered his hand to reveal an angry red mark stretching down his cheek.

'Ooh,' Lex said with a mock wince. 'Well, hopefully it'll leave a scar and you'll have something else to compete against Popcorn-Face Billy with.'

'Now, look—' Jesse began, lunging towards Lex with the clear intention of grabbing him, his hat falling to the floor in the process.

Lex jumped to his feet but not quite quickly enough. The cowboy sprang up and in another moment had Lex's shirt collar gripped in both his large hands. 'Pearls or no pearls, you're dangerously close to pushing me too far, kid!'

'Get off me, you brute!' Lex snapped, pushing at him ineffectually. 'I'm not going to put up with being man-handled by you! You're my companion; you have to do as I say!'

'In your dreams, you little—'

They were interrupted, at that moment, by a knock at the door. Lex and Jesse both froze.

'Just a minute,' Lex called. Then he lowered his voice and hissed, 'Into the bedroom! Quick! No one can see you here!'

There shouldn't have been anyone knocking on the door, anyway. He'd left the *Do Not Disturb* sign out so that no maid would come bustling in, trying to clean the place up, and he hadn't ordered any room service. Jesse let go of Lex's shirt and, still looking rather put out, crossed the room to the bedroom.

Lex stomped over to the door. 'What is it?' he snapped, as he threw it open.

Tess East was standing on the other side but she shrank back a bit at Lex's tone. Lex was a little bit shocked himself. That dratted cowboy had actually succeeded in making him lose control of himself! *He – Lex Trent* – not in complete control! The thought was almost too awful to contemplate! He could have happily throttled Jesse in that moment.

'Tess,' he said, softening his voice and trying to maintain a grip on himself. 'What are you doing here?'

'I . . . I'm sorry to disturb you. But I wanted to . . . ask for the address of Jesse's family,' she said, looking him right in the eye. 'I want to write to them.'

Of course, Lex had no earthly idea whether Jesse even had family and, if he did, where the heck they were. But he couldn't say that to Tess when everyone seemed to have decided that he and Jesse had known each other for donkey's years. He would have dearly loved to say, 'Jesse didn't have any family. And no friends either, come to that. He was such an insufferable man that no one but me could stand him for more than five minutes at a time. And even if he does have parents, they're probably the sort of simple people who wouldn't be capable of reading a letter, even if you did send them one.'

Instead, he said, 'I'm afraid Jesse's family are all dead. There's no one to write to.'

'Oh.' Tess instantly looked crestfallen. Then her eye fell on something in the room beyond and she said, 'You kept his hat?'

Lex glanced over his shoulder and noticed Jesse's hat lying on the floor near the fire. Damn! He remembered now that it had fallen off when the cowboy had lunged at him.

'Yeah, I kept it,' Lex said, turning back. 'To remember him by. You know.'

'Have you buried him yet?'

Lex was taken aback by the question and the blunt way in which she asked it.

'Er ... no.' Lex couldn't very well say that Jesse was buried when he knew that the cowboy would have to have a 'miraculous' recovery in time for the second round. His plan was to say that the octopus bite had paralysed him for a week, rather than a few minutes. Unless someone happened to be a particular expert on the Squealing Blue-Ringed Octopii, then no one would be any the wiser. And hopefully they would also believe that this paralysis, for some reason, affected the Binding Bracelets so that they stopped working temporarily. 'I'm going to do it before the second round,' Lex went on. 'At sea.'

'Good,' Tess said. 'I want you to bury him with this.' She lifted a chain over her neck and held it out to Lex. A little carved blue dragon dangled from the end.

'What is it?' Lex asked, as he took it and peered closer.

'It's called a Wishing Dragon. One of the Wishing Dragons of Desareth,' she said. 'I don't know why.'

Lex looked at her sharply. Wishing Dragons of Desareth? He hadn't known that there was such a thing. Lex was himself the owner of the three Wishing Swanns of Desareth and, now that he looked at the dragon more closely, he could certainly see the resemblance. Both were intricately carved and perfectly formed. Even though it was tiny, Lex could see the leathery folds in the Dragon's wings, the noble expression on its face and the fierce look in its eyes. It was beautiful, it was priceless and it was – very probably – slightly magical.

'Where did you get this?' Lex asked.

'My grandfather gave it to me,' Tess replied. 'There used to be three. He kept the silver one. He always wore it on his adventures. He used to take all of them with him for luck but, before he went away on his last adventure, he gave the white Dragon to Jeremiah. And he gave the blue Dragon to me. I'd only just been born so mother kept it until I was old enough. They gave it to me before I came away on this Game. I don't want it anymore. I want Jesse to have it.'

It took all of Lex's self control not to wince at the very *thought* of sending this indescribably beautiful, invaluable thing down to the bottom of the sea with a dead man. He glanced at Tess. She had a hard, determined expression on her face and, for a moment, Lex hesitated. She was Cary East's granddaughter, after all. Before the falling-out with Jeremiah, Lex would have been quite determined to like Tess. He *did* like her, even now. It wasn't her fault she had a prat for a brother. Lex himself had a wimp for a brother but he didn't expect people to hold that against him. The blue Dragon was a precious gift left to Tess by the famous grandfather she'd never had the chance to know. Taking it from her would be a dastardly thing to do.

But Lex was a thief. He was the notorious Wizard and he'd been the Shadowman before that. And the girl had just *handed* it to him. How could he *not* take it? Besides which, she was the enemy for the duration of the Game. Jeremiah probably didn't know she was giving away her

Dragon. When he learnt, during the course of the second round, that Jesse wasn't really dead then he would naturally want the Dragon back. It could act as potential leverage very nicely indeed.

'Jesse would have been honoured,' Lex said, closing his fist around the Dragon. 'Thank you, Tess.'

She nodded and turned away at the same time that Jesse walked out of the bedroom so purposefully that it was quite as if he intended to say something to Tess. Lex was horrified. If she hadn't turned around right when she did then Tess would have seen him. The cowboy opened his mouth and Lex knew he was going to say something to call Tess back. Moving faster than he'd ever moved before, Lex practically slammed the door shut before he whirled around, pressed his back against it, glared at Jesse and snapped, 'What's the matter with you? You were going to speak to her, weren't you? Are you soft in the head when it comes to kids, or something?'

'You shouldn't have taken that Dragon,' Jesse said. 'Seeing as there ain't gonna be no burial.'

'I don't know! There might be yet if you keep on like this! I'll kill you myself before the week is out! But I wouldn't send this Dragon down to the bottom of the sea with you or anyone else! It's far too valuable for that. We can use this,' Lex said, holding up his hand and allowing the Dragon to dangle on the chain through his fingers. 'I'll give it back. Eventually. But I'll make Jeremiah work for it first, that's all. You have to take every advantage that comes your way in the Games. This is no place for saints.'

Jesse clearly didn't like it but he didn't push the matter. Of course, Lex wasn't really at all sure that he would ever give the Dragon back. It was too beautiful to give up easily. And it went so well with the Wishing Swanns he already had. But there was no point in telling Jesse that.

Lex had acquired the Swanns during the course of the last Game. He'd got them from an enchanter who had referred to them as the Wishing Swanns of Desareth. It was due to the fact that he'd got them from an enchanter that Lex believed the Swanns must be magical in some way. Enchanters didn't tend to walk around with little ornaments in their pockets unless there was something special about them. But if they *were* magical then Lex hadn't discovered that fact yet. It was true that he used one of them as a sort of key to fly his enchanted ship, but that just seemed to be a matter of the ship needing an ivory object. It was not a power of the Swann itself – it was simply that it happened to be made out of the right material.

After the last Game, Lex had experimented with the Swanns a bit in an effort to get them to do something. He'd tried wishing on them first, just in case. He'd done the obvious and wished for a million pieces of m-gold but it hadn't worked. He'd tried saying magic words whilst holding the Swanns; he'd put them in water and in the sun and in moonlight; he'd tapped them against things and put them under the pillow whilst he'd slept. But nothing had produced any sort of response from them whatsoever and Lex had almost begun to suspect that they were just ordinary things, after all.

But, when obtaining books for the library he was starting on board the ship, Lex had come across a Magical Miscellany that catalogued some of the most famous witches, enchanters and other magical peoples. Whilst skimming through a chapter about a great warlock, he noticed the word *Desareth* in one of the footnotes. It seemed that there had once been a sorcerer by that name who went crazy and killed himself when he was just past fifty. That was the only mention the book made of him and Lex could find no references to the sorcerer in any of his other texts on notable magicians. Of course, it could be that the two were entirely unrelated, but the fact that there had once been a mad sorcerer named Desareth had made Lex wonder whether he was the one who had created the Swanns.

And now he was learning of Wishing Dragons, too. Dragons that had – like the Swanns – once been a set of three. After this Game was over, he would have to make a concerted effort to find out more about them. It could, after all, quite possibly be the case that he was in possession of something immensely powerful and he didn't even realise it. And once he knew what these Wishing animals were, *then* he would decide whether or not he was ever going to give the blue Dragon back to Tess East.

CHAPTER FOURTEEN

jAiLhouse jesse and sid The kid

The rest of the week passed uneventfully. Lex spent most of it closeted away in the suite with Jesse, only occasionally putting in an appearance downstairs to look sad and morose. Jesse insisted on going back to the ship briefly once a day to feed and water Rusty. Lady Luck took him there and back whilst Lex was at dinner. It suited them both as Lady Luck was under strict instructions from Lex not to bring the cowboy back to the hotel until Lex himself returned to the room. Handcuffing him to the bed wasn't likely to work a second time and, this way, Lex could be sure that Jesse wasn't somehow going to stroll into the dining room in full view of everyone, or something equally hideous.

Lex practised for an hour every day with the cards until they finally felt so familiar in his hands that it was almost like they were *part* of him. Every day he drank four cups of the vile, stewed black coffee that they prepared over the fire. After the first two days, he was able to drink it without grimacing.

Chewing tobacco was a little more problematic. Jesse showed him how to tear a piece off a cake of tobacco with his teeth. The idea was then to stick it in your cheek and chew before finally spitting it out along with a foul-smelling glob of tobacco juice. There were spittoons, Jesse said, at Dry Gulch House but many of the cowboys simply spat right on to the floor. Lex was horrified. The whole thing went totally against his natural penchant for cleanliness. But it was the lesser of two evils, seeing as the alternative was to actually smoke a cigarette. There was no way in hell that Lex was doing that – not for any scam. Sacrificing cleanliness was one thing but sacrificing health was something else altogether. So he had no choice but to practise chewing tobacco until the vile taste of it no longer made him sick.

Jesse told him that all cowboys drank all the time but that, too, would not work for Lex. He hated alcohol and he couldn't possibly hope to carry out an effective scam if he was incapacitated as a result of being blind drunk. He would need all his wits about him in order to perpetuate this fraud. So – as with the fire lighting – Lex came up with a way to cheat. He would carry two flasks on his person at all times. Jesse said it was not unusual for cowboys to do so. One of his flasks would have whisky in it but the other would just have water. Whenever he got the chance, he would privately swish whisky around his mouth before spitting it out. That way, people would be able to smell alcohol on his breath. But in public he would only drink from the water flask, thereby giving the appearance of constantly guzzling alcohol when he would really just be sipping water.

He also spent several hours a day handling Jesse's knives and pistols. The cowboy showed him how to spin both types of weapon in his hands and, after several hours of practicing, Lex soon picked this up. It looked very impressive whilst not actually doing anything. Lex certainly had no intention of throwing a knife at anyone. Scamming people was one thing but killing them was something else and Lex was no murderer.

'No one gets hurt in my schemes. That takes real finesse, that does – scamming people without injuries.'

'Just because no one's bleedin' don't mean there ain't no injuries,' Jesse said mildly.

'What's that supposed to mean?' Lex said, annoyed by the cowboy's tone.

'I robbed a bank once,' Jesse said. 'Me and a couple of the fellas. There was a bit of shootin' but no one got hurt. Head banker lost his job, though. And him with a family to feed.'

'Is that it?' Lex asked incredulously. 'Head banker lost his job? Cripes, you probably did the man a favour! Banking is almost as boring as lawyering! Is that why you fled the west?'

'Well, yeah, partly. But I had a price on my head before that. Nah, the main reason I left was because my old gang sorta turned on me.'

'What do you mean, they turned on you?' Lex asked suspiciously. 'What did you do to them?'

'Double crossed 'em,' Jesse replied. 'Or tried to, anyway. They were gonna rob another bank, see? But I knew that one would go wrong. I could feel it in my gut. The cashier was this old chap. Twitchy little fella, he was—'

'So you're soft in the head when it comes to old people as well as kids!' Lex sneered derisively.

'Someone woulda got hurt,' Jesse said firmly. 'So I told the sheriff their plans. Only problem was that this sheriff was a damned simpleton. Botched the capture, he did. And set them off after me. Real mad they were, too. I figured the best thing was to leave town and lie low for a bit.'

'Well, no one gets hurt in my schemes. Not only do I refuse to use violence but I actually go out of my way to avoid it. You can't say fairer than that. That's why I don't intend to ever use knives or pistols in my role at Dry Gulch. I know how to handle them and how to spin the pistols and clean them and that's all I need to know. Seems to me that my lessons are more or less complete already.'

'You still gotta learn how to ride a horse,' Jesse said.

'Well, how hard can that be?'

'And you ain't learnt the lingo, yet.'

'If you mean that pidgin English you persist in using, I think I've got the gist of it from listening to you prattle on all day.'

Jesse crossed his arms over his chest. 'All righty then,' he said. 'Show me.'

'There ain't nothin' to it,' Lex drawled in a perfect

208

mimic of the accent, "cept for draggin' out them pesky vowel sounds and keepin' all the words short and sweet, with a bit of suckin' at your teeth now and then if there ain't no tobacco to be spat.' Switching back to his normal voice, he added, 'Add in a few double negatives and other grievous grammatical breaches for good measure and you're there.'

'OK,' Jesse admitted. 'You gotta grip on the speakin'. But you'll need a nickname. All cowboys gotta name. Y'know, like Quick-Draw McGraw or Popcorn-Face Billy or Rotten-Luck Willy or Snakebite Harry—'

'What's your nickname?' Lex asked.

'Me? Back where I come from people know me as Jailhouse Jesse.'

'Get caught a lot, do you?' Lex sneered. 'Lucky me – I'm being taught all the tricks of the trade by an incompetent cowboy who can't even keep himself out of prison.' He sighed, cocked his head, thought a moment and then said, 'My nickname will be Sid the Kid.'

There was no time for any more planning beyond that because it was the day before the second round was due to begin and they were leaving the hotel. Lex knew that the second round was to take place on one of the Lost Islands but they had been given no more information other than that. He packed up his stuff and got a carriage back to the harbour, whilst Jesse was transported back to the boat by her Ladyship in the usual manner.

'I must admit I'm lookin' forward to comin' back from the dead,' Jesse remarked when Lex joined him on the ship. 'No offence, partner, but having to spend all day talkin' to no one but you is startin' to make me feel a bit barmy.'

'How do you imagine I feel?' Lex replied.

The plan was for Lady Luck to spread the word as soon as Lex arrived at the ship that he had 'discovered' Jesse there alive. She would inform the other Gods, who would inform their players, and a special announcement would be made to the stadium audiences before the start of the next round.

Unfortunately, the plan went slightly wrong.

As soon as they got back on to the ship, Lex and Jesse went upstairs to see the griffins, who were sunning themselves up on deck. They caught all their own food themselves, so Lex had no need to provide for them but he had missed them nonetheless and they had evidently missed him for, as soon as he appeared on deck, all three of them padded over, leaning their great weight against him affectionately.

'I swear they get bigger by the week,' Lex said, stroking their glossy feathers.

Jesse remained in the doorway. Although it seemed unlikely that anyone would be able to see him from the harbour, they were moored right next to Jeremiah's boat and they didn't want to take any chances.

But it didn't make any difference. There was a ladder that stretched up the entire height of the ship. It was what Lex had had to use to embark and disembark throughout the course of the last Game before he'd had the gangplank put in. Now he didn't use the ladder and it had never really occurred to him that anyone else might. But he had been petting the griffins and talking to Jesse about them for about ten minutes when a figure suddenly vaulted over the side of the ship and on to the deck – a figure dressed in royal blue with shiny golden buttons on his jacket . . .

It was Jeremiah.

For a moment, the three of them just stared at each other. The expression on Jeremiah's face went from shocked to relieved to furious. He opened his mouth to speak but Lex got there first. 'Look at this. Turns out Jesse isn't dead after all. Good, eh?'

He wasn't even bothering to *try* to be convincing. Jeremiah would never go for it. And it was rather fun watching the nobleman's face as he realised he'd been had.

'You monster!' he said. 'He was never dead at all! Do you know what my sister has been through this week?'

'The octopus paralysed him,' Lex replied, 'rather than killing him. How was I to know? We genuinely believed he was dead for, oh, the first five minutes. But now I have returned to the ship and found him to be alive. Lady Luck is out spreading the good news as we speak.' Then a thought occurred to Lex; he frowned and said, 'What are you doing here, anyway?'

'I was suspicious!' Jeremiah snapped. 'Tess told me about going to your room to give you the Dragon. She mentioned the cowboy's hat. That was the first thing that tipped me off. And the more I thought about it, the more unlikely it seemed that you would have publicly forgiven me as you did. You laid all that honourable gentleman stuff on too bloody thick, Trent! You're no gentleman; you're a cad!'

'Yes, I am. That's why I always win.'

'You didn't win the last round though, did you?'

The reminder wiped the smile off Lex's face. 'I'll win this one, and the one after that!' he snapped. 'I'll win this Game and have everyone loving me by the end of it!'

'I'm going to tell people what you've done! I'm going to tell them all about how you deliberately tricked everyone into thinking your companion was dead, just so that you could earn sympathy points! It's a disgrace!'

'Good luck,' Lex replied, supremely unconcerned. 'Like I just said, her Ladyship will have already informed the other Gods that Jesse is alive by now. If you go back and say you saw him on the ship, you'll just be telling them what they already know. *You* might know the truth and *I* might know it, but if you try to say I was aware that Jesse's been alive this whole time then it will be my word against yours and – trust me – I'm a much better liar than you are!'

Jeremiah glared at him, grinding his jaw but saying nothing. Lex was right. Jeremiah was already walking on eggshells where public opinion of him was concerned, whereas everyone was practically overflowing with love towards Lex. If he tried to accuse Lex of lying now, then people probably wouldn't believe him and all he would achieve would be to have everyone hating his guts again.

Jeremiah took a deep breath and said, 'I am going to thrash you in the second round like you have never been thrashed before.'

Lex laughed, profoundly delighted by the challenge, and said, 'I'd really love it if you'd try.'

Jeremiah looked at Jesse and said, 'Whatever foul scheme you've been party to this week – no doubt concocted by this hooligan –' he pointed at Lex before turning back to the cowboy – 'you *did* save my sister from harm at personal risk to yourself and I am grateful to you. For what it's worth, I really am glad you're not dead. Now,' he turned back to Lex, 'give me the Dragon and I'll be on my way.'

'Dragon?' Lex said blankly. 'What Dragon?'

'You know full well,' Jeremiah said between gritted teeth. 'One of the Wishing Dragons of Desareth, left to my sister by our grandfather.'

'Oh, you mean *this* Dragon,' Lex said, pulling the chain out from where it was tucked into his shirt. 'You can whistle for it. I've decided to keep it.'

Hardly able to believe what he was hearing, Jeremiah said furiously, 'That Dragon was meant for – and belongs to – the grandchild of a noble Adventurer! Not the thieving grandchild of a mere Chronicler!'

Lex could feel his face going red with genuine anger. 'If I were you,' he said quietly, 'I wouldn't ever insult my grandfather in my hearing again. You're nothing more than a passing amusement to me right now but if you make a true enemy out of me, I promise, you'll regret it!'

'If you won't hand over the Dragon, I'll get it back from you myself!' Jeremiah said, drawing his impressive sword and starting forwards.

Up until this point, the griffins had remained at Lex's side, watching Jeremiah warily but not reacting to him. Drawing the sword had been his first mistake and walking forward in such a threatening manner was his second. Instantly, the griffins formed a line in front of Lex, rearing up on to their hind legs so that the sun gleamed off their razor-sharp claws, snapping their beaks and staring at Jeremiah with such a cold, vicious look in their eyes that it was not hard to believe they could rip him apart at any moment. He had no choice but to come to a dead stop in the middle of the deck.

'I wouldn't take one more step, if I were you,' Lex said lazily. 'You're upsetting the griffins and they can be a bit . . . unpredictable when they're upset. If you back away really slowly and go back over the side of the ship the way you came then they *might* not kill you.'

Jeremiah looked at Lex and the three distinctly savage-looking griffins standing between them and knew he had no choice. So red with anger that he looked rather like a tomato, Jeremiah slowly backed away. When he got to the edge of the deck, he paused long enough only to look back at Lex and say quietly, 'I'll get you for this. And I will have my sister's Dragon back, one way or another.'

'Dream on,' Lex replied. 'And take my advice – think

twice before spiking someone's drink the next time. Not everyone is just some chump who'll take it lying down.'

With one last scowl, Jeremiah sheathed his sword and climbed over the edge of the ship. Lex walked over to the rails with the griffins and watched Jeremiah's descent. When the nobleman was only a few rungs away from the bottom, Lex commanded the ship to rise so suddenly and so quickly that Jeremiah was shaken off the ladder altogether and fell into the cold, salty sea with a splash and a yell.

'*Now*,' Lex said, turning away from the side with a profoundly smug smile, 'we are even.'

CHAPTER FIFTEEN

The Library Tree

The Lost Islands could not be found on any map. This was because they never stayed in any one place for very long. They moved around constantly. No one was quite sure how many Lost Islands there were, although the general consensus seemed to be that there were probably about seven or eight. The reason they were lost was that the Gods moved them periodically. The people all knew this because the Gods had told them so. The Lost Islands were full of forbidden things – things the Gods did not want people to have, but which they didn't want cluttering up the place, down in the Lands Beneath. So they had stashed them all on the islands. They were extremely dangerous places and, if anyone ever went looking for one and – even worse – actually *found* one, the Gods had warned that the consequences would be dire indeed.

It was thought that they must be something to do with knowledge, for it was Herman – the God of Knowledge, himself – who had proclaimed the existence of the Lost Islands over a hundred years ago. Lex was therefore unsurprised when Thaddeus announced that there was something called a library tree on one of the lost islands, since books and libraries certainly fitted in with Herman and knowledge.

It was just past ten o'clock at night and the three players were assembled at the edge of a dark beach with the Gods who had brought them there. Lex had no idea where they were and thought, at first, that they were on one of the Lost Islands already. Then he saw the three rowing-boats on the sand and suspected that they weren't quite there yet.

'Somewhere on the library tree,' Thaddeus said, 'is a book that's missing one of its pages. You will each be given a duplicate page. The first player to replace the missing page in the correct book, wins.'

The players then each found a page being thrust into their hands by their respective God or Goddess.

'Go!' Thaddeus said.

And, with that, the three deities disappeared, leaving the players on the beach.

Jeremiah and Lorella were still clutching their pages uselessly whilst Lex was running towards the rowing-boats. He didn't know where they were, exactly, or where the Lost Island was in relation to them, but he knew the rowing-boats had to be there for a reason. Without even looking at it, Lex thrust the page into his pocket, grabbed the side of the boat and started hauling it down the beach towards the water. A second later, Jesse was helping him and soon the little boat was bobbing on the dark sea with them inside it.

The moon came out from behind a cloud and suddenly Lex could glimpse land ahead. It wasn't far away. Probably no more than a twenty-minute trip if they rowed fast. Clearly, the Gods did not intend the actual finding of the island to be the difficult part and so had started them off quite close to it.

Lex and Jesse rowed as fast as they could. The other players were in their boats by now and Lex could hear the splash of oars behind him. Their boat would be moving the fastest, for it had both Jesse and Lex to row it. Lorella would have to row by herself, as her little sprite certainly wouldn't be able to help, and the same was true for Jeremiah.

Lex's initial plan was to row the boat all the way around the island, rather than pulling up on to the beach. That way he could try to spot the library tree from the water. He didn't know what a library tree was but he hoped there would be something about it that would make it stand out to him, otherwise he'd run the risk of going right past it. As it turned out, this fear was completely unfounded for, as they got nearer to the island, a huge, massive, monstrous dark shape began to form before them.

From the water, Lex strained his eyes through the darkness, hardly able to believe what he thought he was seeing. But, as they approached, there was no denying it: the library tree was so gigantic that it covered the entire island. It was bigger than any building Lex had ever seen in the Lands Above. The roots – which were two or three feet thick in places – were clamped tight around the edge of the island, clinging to it like poison ivy, and trailing down into the sea. There was no shore to speak of because it had been taken over so completely by roots. Lex had no idea how big the tree actually was but it must have been at least two hundred feet high.

They had barely pulled up to the island before Lex was leaping over the side, soaking his feet up to the ankles but hardly noticing as he climbed the tree roots up to the land. As soon as his feet touched ground, the island lit up. Or, rather, the tree did. There were hundreds of little lanterns hung about its branches and they all came on as one. At the exact same moment, the silence was broken by a strange, soft warbling sound that seemed to be coming from all around them.

In the soft glow of light, they could see the tree much better. At first, Lex thought it must be dead, but then he realised it was just black, from the tip of its roots to the end of its leaves.

The humongous trunk, some distance away, looked like it was made up of several trunks that were twisted and knotted together. Branches spread out from the centre in all directions. Wooden walkways were lashed to them with thick coils of rope; rope ladders led from one level to the next and rope bridges ran between branches. There was a complete network of paths, bridges and ladders all around the tree.

And everywhere were books. There were shelves attached to some branches and carved into others. Periodically, giant roots thrust down to the ground from the branches like pillars and these all seemed to have been hollowed out and filled with books, too. There were only leaves at the very top of the tree and these were black.

The tree loomed over them like a grim, sinister guardian. Something about it seemed alive despite the fact that it was completely still. The breeze didn't even rustle the leaves at the top – they just stayed motionless, like they'd been glued there.

'Well, bless me if that ain't the strangest darn tree I ever saw,' Jesse said. 'Looks like it oughta have a pack of vultures peckin' at it.'

It did look dead, or burnt, or something. But there was a rich, damp, earthy smell in the air that spoke very much of living plants and there didn't appear to be any vegetation around except for the tree. The ground was covered in roots and crisp black leaves.

In amongst all the black bark were the occasional splashes of colour. Several large birdcages hung from the branches and in these Lex could glimpse colourful feathers. There seemed to be some sort of songbird in them and they were all warbling away. It was not an unpleasant noise – even if it was unlike normal birdsong – but Lex was sure that the birds were probably some kind of alarm system. Their singing was no doubt alerting someone – or something – to the fact that they were there.

'Come on,' Lex said, starting forwards.

The others were probably only a minute behind them and they could not afford to waste time. They needed to find some way on to the tree. This, as it turned out, was fairly easy, for the nearest pillar-like root stretching down to the ground had a rope-ladder attached to it.

Lex clambered over the roots that were raised up out of the ground to get to the ladder. He shot up it and stepped on to the wooden platform. It felt sturdy and strong, and took his weight without so much as a creak. Whilst Jesse climbed up after him, Lex rummaged about in his bag until he found what he was looking for. By the time the cowboy was standing beside him on the platform, Lex had a large pair of cutting shears in his hands.

'Here,' he said, passing them to Jesse. 'Cut the rope ladder whilst I have a look at this page.'

'Cut the ladder?' Jesse replied with a frown. 'Do you reckon we should?'

'I don't want the others following us up this way,' Lex said. 'It will slow them down a bit to have to look for their own way on to the tree. Do it quickly; they'll be here any minute.'

So Jesse started work on the ladder whilst Lex examined the page Thaddeus had given the players. It was a copy of a handwritten title sheet from a book entitled: *Black Magic For The Darkling Hour*. The author was one Erasmus Grey. Lex gaped at the page in astonishment. He knew who Erasmus Grey was. Everyone did. He'd been a black mage long ago – one of the most famous and powerful mages of them all.

People thought the enchanters were powerful now but, really, they were just a pale shadow of the sorcerers and the black mages who had been before them. After all, the enchanters relied mostly on props – their hats and their staffs – to store their magic and to help them wield it. Without those things, what would an enchanter be but a cantankerous old git in a silly robe? In addition, the enchanters tended to keep themselves to themselves. They were very possessive and generally a mean old bunch, but they were not ambitious. They didn't possess delusions of grandeur or pressing needs to take over the world or impose evil dominion over everyone. Sorcerers and black mages, on the other hand, had been another matter entirely. They were all about evil plans and dark magic and wicked deeds. They didn't need props for their magic – a wave of their hand was all it took. They'd killed each other off in the end so that only the comparatively mild enchanters remained. And now Lex was holding a page to a book that Erasmus Grey himself had written! No doubt it was full of black secrets and old powers and lost spells!

Lex tore his eyes from the page and looked at the nearest row of books, lined up on a huge wooden shelf that was attached to a branch at shoulder height. They were dusty old things that looked like they might fall apart as soon as you touched them. Most of them were bound in leather but Lex noticed a couple that appeared to be bound in wood. Every single volume seemed to have the word 'forbidden' or 'dangerous' or 'secret' in its title. There were about twenty books on the shelf beside Lex. Similar-sized shelves stretched down the entire length of the long branch, supported by root pillars below. There must have been two hundred books at least along the branch they stood upon. There was probably the same number on each of the other branches on this level. And, above them, the branches stretched up so high into the sky that they couldn't see the top through the walkways and foliage.

'There must be *thousands* of forbidden books here!' Lex exclaimed in almost a whisper.

A familiar, powerful surge of greed rushed through him and it was all he could do not to open his bag and start stuffing books into it. Lex knew that knowledge was power – especially knowledge *he* had that no one else did. The Gods didn't want people reading these books, which only made Lex want to read them all the more. His fingers *itched* to grab the nearest book, open the cover and start devouring it.

But he had a round to win and pinching books would only slow him down. He couldn't afford to be slowed down – not this time. Not when it was *so* important that he win spectacularly in order to teach Jeremiah East a lesson he wouldn't forget in a hurry. Lex would have given up all the forbidden books in the entire world to beat that insufferable snob. Once he found the correct book, returned the page and won the round, *then* maybe there would be time to steal a book or two on the way back.

In the meantime, wandering about the tree blindly wasn't going to work. There were simply too many books to hope to just stumble across the right one by chance. Lex was lucky, but even he wasn't *that* lucky. And he certainly wasn't prepared to rely only on luck when winning this round was so important.

'Let's get to the main trunk,' he said, feeling that the best place to start would be the centre.

As he spoke, the other players and their companions came into view. Lex was pleased to see that they both looked miffed already. To make them even more miffed, he pointed at the rope-ladder on the ground and said, 'You'd better hope there's another way up!'

They looked up and glared at him.

'You'd better hope so, too, if you ever want to get down from there!' Jeremiah snapped.

Lex shrugged – exaggeratedly to make sure he'd see it. 'What do I care, so long as I win the round?'

Then he turned on his heel and set off down the walkway towards the trunk, leaving Lorella and Jeremiah to find their own way on to the tree. It was on the tip of his tongue to tell Jesse to point out any more rope ladders he saw so that they could cut those down, too, but then he decided against it. They would waste too much time that way. Lex was happy with a bit of sneaky sabotage only so long as it was convenient and didn't take too long.

They went on along the walkway – carefully, as there were no railings to speak of – and soon found themselves at the huge trunk. The walkway went all the way around it, branching off in seven different directions. It was like a giant cart wheel with the trunk being the centre and the branches being spokes. As soon as they reached it, Lex realised that knowing where to look for the correct book wasn't going to be a problem since a map of the library tree was drawn on the main trunk at intervals. It appeared from this that the tree was about twenty-five levels high. Neat labels on the map spelt out which books were kept where. It seemed that they were grouped according to author. Clearly, if you wrote one forbidden book, you wrote a whole bunch of them. Even so, there were many, many names on the map. The authors didn't appear to be ordered alphabetically but Lex found Erasmus Grey instantly by looking at the top of the map. The book was *bound* to be at the top of the tree – the Gods wanted to get their money's worth after all.

Erasmus Grey's name was, indeed, at the top. Right at the top, in fact. The tree thinned as it got higher and it seemed that Grey had the whole of the top level all to himself.

There was no time to waste. The others would find a way on to the tree in no time, what with the ladders that were everywhere. Lex and Jesse started to climb, both keeping a sharp eye out as they did so. After all, this was a tree full of forbidden books – it had not been built for people to come in and browse. And yet there were maps and walkways. *Someone* walked around these books from time to time. And, presumably, they fed the strange birds in the cages, too.

Before long, Lex and Jesse passed quite near one. It was the strangest-looking bird Lex had ever seen – somewhere between a songbird and a vulture – and twice as large as any bird had a right to be. It had a bald, ugly head and its large wings were hunched about it gloomily as it warbled softly to itself. It was a colourful thing, with feathers of blue, orange and green. It looked sad rather than aggressive but Lex kept his distance, anyway. From the size of it, it could probably have his hand off if it wanted to.

Climbing the tree was not particularly difficult because there were ladders and book-lined walkways everywhere. The only thing that became progressively less pleasant was climbing the ladders as they got higher and higher up the tree. Resolutely refusing to look down helped but, the higher they got, the more everything seemed to creak in an unpleasant sort of way. The other difficulty, of course, was the fact that the walkways had no railings. Whilst not too much of a problem on the lower levels, as they got higher this started making Lex and Jesse a little uneasy. Or, rather, it made Jesse uneasy. Lex wasn't bothered – in fact he quite liked heights. He liked heights and thrills and anything that made him feel truly alive. He loved the sense of adrenaline that coursed through his veins when he knew he could fall to his death at any moment.

'Hurry up!' Lex said. 'What are you slowing down for?'

'I don't want to fall off.'

'But the pathways up here are just as wide as they were down there.'

'Yeah, I know that. But it's psychological, ain't it?'

'Wow – five syllables. I don't think I've ever heard you say such a long word before. Stop being such a pansy and keep up with me!'

But even Lex began to slow his pace a little when they got beyond a certain height. They were, after all, running around a gigantic tree with no safety gear whatsoever – no harnesses, no hard hats, no life lines . . . It was inevitable that they should become more physically tense, especially when climbing the rope-ladders.

They'd been on the tree for about twenty minutes when Lex spotted Lorella down below them. She was climbing a rope-ladder but having some difficulty due to the clothes she was wearing. The grey dress might have enhanced her figure in a very pleasing way but it was not the ideal apparel for climbing, especially as the players all had to drag themselves bodily up on to the wooden platforms when they reached the top, which called for a certain amount of undignified wriggling. In addition, whilst Lorella's long blue hair might have been striking and beautiful, having it falling loose down her shoulders like that was extremely stupid, for it kept getting in her way. She even jerked her own head back once when she put her hand on the next rung and tried to pull herself up only to find that her fingers were clamped down over her own hair.

Lex laughed – loud enough to be sure she would hear. The enchantress glared up at him, her sapphire eyes icy cold with anger.

'Get a haircut!' Lex called down to her, grinning. 'That's my advice.'

Lorella opened her mouth to hiss something back at him but, before she could do so, a grey man appeared on the platform above her. At the exact same moment, an identical man materialised before Lex. Presumably, a third one appeared before Jeremiah, too, wherever on the tree he happened to be.

On first glance, the grey man appeared human but, on the second, it was quite clear that he was not. He was a bit too tall and a bit too thin. Everything about him was grey: his hair, his eyebrows, his eyes. The fine suit he wore was grey and so were his shoes – right down to the laces. Everything about him was immaculate – his tie was completely straight and his hair was combed back so neatly it looked like he'd used a ruler to do it. His skin was pale, his cheekbones were unusually high and there was a cool, superior expression on his face.

'Oh my Gods!' Lex said in mock horror. 'You're a lawyer, aren't you?'

'We are the Librarians.' The two grey men spoke the same words at the exact same moment. 'We are bound to protect the forbidden knowledge in this tree and to ensure that it never falls into the hands of the lowly and the ignorant. Do not test our resolve. We would sooner burn this tree to the ground than let you remove a single book from its branches.'

'We're not here to remove a book,' Lex said. 'We're here to put a page *back*. You don't object to that, surely?'

'Trespassers on this tree will not be tolerated, whatever the pretence,' the Librarian said. 'Leave now or remain at your own peril.'

'Listen—' Lex began.

But, at that moment, the Librarians disappeared. Lex was rather annoyed about that. He'd hoped that they would try to waylay them physically. He was confident that he would have been able to give his own Librarian the slip, but Lorella surely would have had more difficulty, clinging as she was, halfway up a rope-ladder.

'That,' Jesse said, eyes narrowed, 'was too easy.'

'Yes, it was,' Lex replied. 'I suppose they'll be sending things after us now.'

'What kind of things?'

'Beats me. They'll definitely be nasty things, though, so keep an eye out, all right?'

'Yeah.'

CHAPTER SIXTEEN

THE VULTURES AND THE FLYING TREE SNAKE

The first thing that alerted them to the fact that something was happening was the groaning creak of metal hinges. The sound seemed to be coming from all over the tree. A few minutes later, Lex began to have a horrible suspicion as to what exactly that sound might have been when he caught, out of the corner of his eye, a flurry of feathers.

'They've stopped singing,' he said.

'What?'

'The birds,' Lex replied. 'They're not singing anymore. When did they stop?' They looked at each other. 'I think they've been let out of their cages,' Lex said.

It was impossible to know exactly how many birds were on the tree, but Lex had counted seven already and they had only explored a small proportion. They were big things and no doubt had sharp claws and beaks. If a few of them ganged up together, they would probably be able to peck a person to death if they wanted to.

Lex strained his eyes in the half-light. The little lanterns dotted about the tree were hung on long chains from the platforms above. They gave out enough light to illuminate the walkways but not enough to pierce the darkness beyond. But sometimes there was the occasional draught of air – like something large had just swooped by somewhere close. Or there was a rustle of feathers or a blur of movement detectable only out of the corner of the eye.

'Let's just keep moving,' Lex said.

They made it to the next level – about three quarters of the way up the tree – before one of the vulture birds flew through the branches and landed with an inelegant thump on the walkway right in front of them. Lex and Jesse stopped and stared as it picked itself up, shook itself and gave a dismal squawk before turning its baleful gaze on them. It really was an ugly beast. Its green, blue and orange feathers were rumpled and its wrinkly head was bald but for a few wisps of white hair that stuck out at angles. Its beak curved down, giving it an almost comically morose expression, and its eyes were a bloodshot grey.

'That's gotta be the ugliest darn bird I ever saw,' Jesse said softly.

Lex had to agree with him. But it did not seem particularly aggressive. It was just sitting there in a hunched up sort of way on the path ahead.

'I suppose it'll probably tear our throats out as soon as we try to walk past it,' Lex remarked.

'Ain't got the right kind of beak for that,' Jesse said.

'Well, get your pistol out, anyway. You can't be too careful.'

Lex tried shooing the bird away but that didn't work. It just sat there blinking at him miserably.

'Blasted thing!' Lex said irritably. 'I suppose we could try walking around it.'

This was not an attractive prospect for two reasons. Firstly, they were by now extremely high up in the tree and so creeping along at the edge of the walkway was not something either of them felt like doing. Secondly, if the bird *were* to attack them whilst they were trying to walk past it, it wouldn't even need to tear their throats out, for it would almost certainly knock them off the walkway to plunge to their deaths. But they had to get past the bird somehow.

'Just shoot at it,' Lex said to Jesse.

'But it's not tried to attack us!' the cowboy protested.

'I don't care. If it's too stupid to move then we'll just have to move it ourselves.'

'Why don't you try shoving it first?' Jesse suggested. 'Before getting all trigger happy.'

'*Shove* it?' Lex repeated, horrified. 'I'm not shoving it! It'll probably take my eyes out!'

Jesse sighed. 'Here,' he said, passing Lex the pistol. 'I'll try. Me and the animals almost always get along.'

'Yeah, until one of them rips your face off!' Lex said.

But Jesse wasn't listening. He was walking slowly closer to the bird. Finally, he stopped, reached out an arm and gave it a hearty shove. Lex stood back, aiming the pistol and fully expecting the bird to whip around and take Jesse's hand off. But instead it just sat there. Jesse pushed it again, a little harder this time. But it just hunched there refusing to be budged.

'I reckon we can just walk past it,' Jesse said. 'It ain't gonna attack us.'

Lex had to admit it looked like the cowboy was right. He walked over slowly and had just reached Jesse's side when the bird let out a sudden hacking cough that made them both jump. It followed this up with a dry retching sound before throwing up two books along with a couple of pellets that had little bones sticking out of them. Then, and only then, did it fly away.

Lex and Jesse stared at the two books on the ground. They were not wet or slimy or covered in stomach juices, as you might expect them to be when they'd just been thrown up by a large bird. In fact, they were dry and pristine and looked brand new. Both had landed face up and both had extremely startling titles. One was called, *The Life and Death of Lex Trent*. The other was called, *The Life and Death of Jesse Layton*.

They stared in amazement. Lex's book was bound in blue leather, Jesse's in green. Lex's book was noticeably the larger of the two. Jesse reached a hand out towards his book but Lex grabbed his wrist.

'Don't touch it!' he said sharply.

'Why not?'

'I have a bad feeling about those books. You've heard about the Library of Souls, haven't you?'

'That's just a myth,' Jesse replied, but he didn't sound at all sure.

There was a legend that told of a library belonging to the Gods where every person's entire life was recorded in a book. The books wrote themselves, long before the person was born. And, when the time came for a new baby to arrive, the Gods would pick the person whose turn it was to live by choosing souls from the books. If the two books lying before them really *were* from the Library of Souls, then Lex's book would contain within its pages everything he had done and would ever do. It would detail his achievements and his failures. It would state how he would die and when.

Lex shuddered. 'Even if they *are* real, I don't want to know what's in my future. Life wouldn't be fun anymore then.'

'I reckon you're right about that,' Jesse replied. 'Let's just leave 'em be.'

They edged past the books like they were mines that might go off. Lex was glad to leave them behind. People were not supposed to ever see their own books. It wasn't right. It wasn't natural. And Lex had the strong feeling that they shouldn't even so much as touch the front cover with their fingertips.

'One thing I don't get, though,' Jesse said. 'If they really were our life books then how come mine was so much shorter than yours?'

'Because your life is more boring, probably. After all, the typical entry is probably something like, "Jesse Layton woke up, ate some beans, chewed some tobacco, drank some beer, went to sleep." It doesn't take up much space to write.'

'Maybe it's that,' the cowboy agreed mildly. 'Or maybe it's because I'm going to kick the old bucket at a younger age than you.'

Lex stopped suddenly on the walkway. It was true that Jesse's book had been shorter than Lex's, but it had still been a large book in its own right. Perhaps the reason for the difference in length had been because Lex was going to have *more* life, not that Jesse was going to have less. After all, wasn't that what he was after when he went to Dry Gulch? Wasn't that why he'd enlisted Jesse's help in learning how to be a cowboy: to find the legendary Sword of Life? That book must have been confirmation that he was going to succeed!

For a dangerous moment, Lex felt the almost irresistible urge to go straight back to the book and read about where his future self would find the sword. If he could find out the hiding place in advance, it would save him a lot of time and trouble once he reached Dry Gulch. But then he shook himself. He couldn't afford to go back. Not now. Not when they were almost at the top of the tree and winning the final round was within his grasp. Besides which, he still had the strong instinctive feeling that reading from the book would not be a good idea.

So they carried on. They were at a height of about one hundred and fifty feet, and getting near the top. The trunk had thinned as they got higher so that the area they could walk in seemed to be getting smaller and there was less room for books.

Lex had been keeping an eye on Lorella, who had stayed behind them due to the fact that she couldn't climb quickly. She was on a platform directly below them when one of the vulture birds thumped down in front of her and noisily threw up two books at her feet. One was a large blue one called, *The Life and Death of Lorella*; the other was a tiny silver one Lex assumed must belong to the sprite, but it was too far away for him to read the title. The bird flapped off with a squawk. Lorella peered at the book for a moment before snatching it from the ground. Lex stilled as the enchantress flipped open the front cover and flicked through to the last page. No sooner had she started to read than a vicious wind seemed to pour from the open pages of the book, whipping about her, tugging at her dress and hair. She barely had time to get a horrified expression on to her face before she was sucked – entirely – into the book, leaving behind not so much as a single blue hair. The book fell to the walkway with a thump. Lex saw the sprite fluttering about it agitatedly for a moment before she dropped to the floor and heaved at the front cover with both arms to lift it. Then she rifled manically through all the pages, as if expecting to find the enchantress pressed between them like a flower. But there was nothing. Lorella was gone.

'Well, I guess that explains what happens if you try to read from your own book,' Lex said. 'I told you it wouldn't be pretty. I wonder if Jeremiah fell for it.'

His question was answered almost at once when he spotted Jeremiah across the tree on a distant branch. They were on about the same level, which rather upset Lex as he'd hoped he was still ahead. Tess was nowhere in sight. Either she'd got sucked into her book, too, or Jeremiah had left her at the base of the tree. Lex suspected the latter since, if Tess wasn't around to slow him down, that would explain how the nobleman had managed to climb the tree so fast.

They were almost at the top now. And the height was horrible even before the walkways started to shrink. Lex assumed it was the Librarians' doing, as they'd failed to capture all the players with the books the vulture birds threw up. The wooden planks groaned and creaked as they shrank beneath the players' feet. With no railings to hold on to, Lex and Jesse were forced to steady themselves against the bookshelves attached to the branches. Jeremiah had noticed them now, too, and the three of them raced desperately to the top level. The rope-ladders had turned into mere ropes by this time but that didn't hinder Lex too badly for he had become adept at climbing up and down ropes as a result of his cat-burglar exploits as the Shadowman and the Wizard. He left Jesse on the level below and started to climb. He was much lighter than Jeremiah and so had less weight to pull. Although the two of them grabbed ropes at the same time, Lex reached the top platform first.

It was shrinking fast, which was unfortunate seeing as he was now at the very top of the tree – high enough that he would have been able to see the ocean all around them had it not been dark. There were three large bookcases up there, filled with books that had all been written by Erasmus Grey. Lex ran his eyes over the spines in frantic search of the right book, very aware that Jeremiah could be only moments behind him and that the platform on which he stood was shrinking.

To complicate matters even further, he could smell the distinctive scent of burning wood. When the walkways began to shrink, some of the lanterns that had been hung from them had fallen off, smashing on the branches and setting the wood alight instantly. The Librarians had not been bluffing when they'd said they would burn the tree to the ground. The Gods were supposed to keep the island lost but, should someone ever find their way on to it somehow and get too close to the forbidden books, the vulture-birds were the only means the Librarians had of protecting it. If intruders were not sucked into the book then the only thing left to do was to destroy the tree, hence the fact that lanterns were hung everywhere and – although the players didn't know it yet – the library tree's bark was the most flammable in the world. Just one little spark and it would burst into flames.

Before Lex could find the correct book, Jeremiah appeared on the platform beside him. Lex could have ignored him and carried on looking for the book but that would be to leave winning up to chance – a simple matter of whichever of them happened to spot the book first. And Lex never left winning up to chance. He spun on his heel, put a horrified expression on to his face and shouted, 'Watch out for that flying tree-snake!'

Jeremiah glared at him. 'You really think I'm dumb enough to fall for that? There aren't any flying tree-snakes here!'

'None except for the one in my pocket,' Lex replied.

Jeremiah opened his mouth but, before he could say anything, Lex reached into his pocket, drew out the plastic toy rattlesnake he'd put there just for that purpose and threw it at Jeremiah's head. Perhaps if it had been anything other than a snake the plan wouldn't have worked. But as Jeremiah had that unfortunate phobia he instinctively jerked back, arms raised over his head to protect himself – and fell right off the edge of the platform.

Thank you, Mr and Mrs East, Lex thought smugly when he peered over the edge and saw Jeremiah gripping a loop of rope that was caught between two branches. His knuckles were white already for he was dangling over an immense height. In addition, the fire had spread further up the tree and was practically licking at Jeremiah's boots.

'Sitting duck,' Lex grinned.

He turned back round to the bookcases and, almost instantly, his eye fell on the correct book. He dragged it out by the spine, pulled the page from his pocket and was just about to insert it into the book and win the round when he hesitated. He'd as good as won the round already for Lorella had been sucked inside a book and Jeremiah was hanging helplessly from a length of rope. There was therefore no rush – other than the fact that the tree was now on fire and the walkways were disappearing. If he was going to win, he might as well win in style. He would rescue Jeremiah first, thereby earning himself some extra hero points as well as bolstering his image as a noble, self-sacrificing, all-round splendid sort of person.

Lex thrust the book into his bag then leaned over the edge of the platform and called down cheerfully, 'Don't worry, Jeremiah! I'll save you!'

The nobleman glared up at him. 'Don't! Don't save me! I don't need saving; I'm fine!'

'You don't look fine, old chum,' Lex shouted back. 'Hang in there. I'll be right down.'

The platform was barely big enough for Lex to stand on now and he was just reaching out for the rope when one of the books on the shelf caught his attention. It was one word that leapt out at him: *Desareth*. When he turned his head to look at it properly he saw that the book was called, *The Wishing Creatures of Desareth*. This one, like all the others around it, had been written by Erasmus Grey. Lex stared at the book for a split second before reaching out and snatching it from the shelf. He was just stuffing it into his bag when the platform beneath him suddenly vanished altogether and Lex was freefalling for a moment before he managed to grab on to the nearby rope. He received quite a nasty burn as he was only able to use one hand since the other was holding his bag. But, finally, he managed to bring himself to a stop.

The walkways had now disappeared entirely. All that

remained were the ropes. The tree crackled and spat in the heat from the flames; books blackened, shrivelled and burned; vulture birds squawked as they flapped away from the blaze; clouds of grey ash billowed in the air around them. Lex looked down and saw that he was not far off a broad branch, so he let the rope go. He fell on to the branch with a thump and – with a bit of frantic scrabbling – managed to cling on to it and then haul himself to his feet.

'Hey!' Jesse shouted from further along the same branch. 'Hey, we need to get outta here! The whole darn tree's going up!'

'Yeah, in a minute!' Lex called back. 'I have to rescue Jeremiah first.'

He thrust the Desareth book into his bag, pulled out the other one and then ran along the branch to pass both the book and the missing page to Jesse.

'The second I pull Jeremiah up, put the page back into the book, OK?' Lex said.

He couldn't risk taking the book and page with him knowing that Jeremiah might snatch them from him as soon as he was safe, or else find a way to make Lex drop them. If Jesse had them then he could win the round as soon as Lex had saved Jeremiah.

'After all that grief you gave me about the octopus?' Jesse said incredulously. 'D'you really think this is the time for heroics?'

'It's not heroics,' Lex replied. 'I just want the extra points.' Then he turned around and ran back along the branch to the end where Jeremiah still dangled helplessly from the rope.

He had been trying to pull himself up but it wasn't working because he had nothing to grab on to. It was all he could do to cling to the rope. Lex bet his arms must be killing him by now. And surely he must be able to feel the heat from the flames below. They were making Lex uncomfortable and he was aware of ash settling in his hair and flecking his skin as thousands of books burned all around them.

He crouched down low on the branch, leaned over and shouted, 'Give me your hand!'

'Will I ever!' Jeremiah snarled. 'Go ahead and win the round, Trent! I'm not giving you the satisfaction of being awarded hero points for saving me from a situation that you put me in yourself!'

'Now, now, what kind of talk is that?' Lex replied. 'Don't be a quitter. You don't want to die here, do you? Give me your hand!'

'I will not!'

'You won't, eh? We'll just see about that!'

Lex looked around for a conveniently placed rope but there weren't any nearby so he swung his bag off his shoulders and rifled through it until he found the elongating cord and the safety harness. He always packed these things with him, just in case an opportunity to turn into the Wizard should arise.

The cord was extremely long but was currently all wound up within itself. All Lex had to do was press a button on the hand piece and the cord would unravel. It was extremely strong and durable and had aided him many times before. Lex released enough cord to make a loop and secure it around the branch before pulling on a thick pair of gloves with grips on their surface specially designed for just this purpose. He looked at the safety harness but then thrust it back into his bag. There simply wasn't time to fiddle about with all those buckles and straps. The heat from the blazing tree was fast becoming unbearable and the smog of smoke and ash was making them splutter and cough.

'Just piss off!' Jeremiah snapped from below. 'I'll get myself out of this; I don't need your help!'

'Ha! If by "get yourself out of this" you mean cook yourself like a barbecued steak on a skewer then, yeah, you're doing great. Personally, I don't think you can hold on to that rope for much longer. Your knuckles are white and your arms are trembling. You can't save yourself. I know it and you know it. I'm going to swing down on this cord in a minute and I strongly, *strongly*, suggest that you let go of that rope when I grab you.'

Jeremiah glared up at him savagely. But the truth of it was that he really didn't have much choice. He, too, was covered in ash and was now starting to choke on the smoke. Being stuck at the top of an extraordinarily high tree isn't much fun, even when that tree doesn't happen to be on fire. His arms were killing him and the smoke was making it almost impossible to breathe. Lex was right: Jeremiah couldn't save himself, and he knew it.

Lex silently counted to three and then leapt off the opposite side of the branch as far out as the cord would allow, with the effect that he then swung in a descending arc towards Jeremiah. When Lex smashed into him, it was with such force that the nobleman would not have been able to remain clinging to the rope even if he'd wanted to. He had no choice but to grab at the thief's shoulders instead.

Gritting his teeth and trying to ignore the unbelievable weight that was Jeremiah, Lex pressed the button to release more cord and their momentum caused them to carry on swinging. This branch was a particularly long one and overhung the water below – which currently seemed to be an absurd distance away. It was like jumping off the edge of a cliff.

As they began to fall, the cord unravelled itself at lightening speed and Lex only prayed that it was long enough, since he had never had to test it at such a great height before. If he had just been carrying himself then he might have stood a chance of keeping hold of the cord when it finally snapped taut but, with Jeremiah as well, Lex knew that the second they ran out of cord his hands would be wrenched away and they would freefall the rest of the drop.

It must have taken them a mere five seconds to fall all the way down the tree but it seemed like much longer. They were both yelling as they fell – although Lex yelled with excitement as well as fear. He found the fall fun at the same time as he found it terrifying. Or perhaps he found it fun *because* it was terrifying.

The only part of it Lex didn't like was that the fire became more ferocious as they got lower. And, although they were clear of most of the branches, they could still feel the suffocating heat; they still got smoke in their eyes and ash in their mouths.

Finally, the cord ran out with a snap so abrupt that Lex and Jeremiah actually flew *up* a couple of feet when the handle was torn from Lex's hand before falling the rest of the way. Fortunately for both of them, the cord ran out only about a metre above the sea. They fell in with a splash.

The water was relatively shallow there – only about waist high – and Jeremiah was back on his feet with impressive speed, splashing noisily towards Lex who was still coughing up water. When he reached him, Jeremiah grabbed Lex's collar, hauled him to his feet and said, 'If you don't give me that book right now I'm going to take it from you by force!'

'Good luck,' Lex replied. 'It's not on me. Jesse's got it. He'll have won the round by now.'

Indeed, in another moment, Lex and Jeremiah both found themselves plucked from the water and put back on the shore of the beach where they'd started. The three Gods were all there, as were Jesse, Tess and the sprite.

'I won!' Lex exclaimed, speaking directly to Lady Luck. 'I won, didn't I?'

Something would have had to have gone very wrong in those last few minutes for Lex not to have won. After all, he had left Jesse standing there with the book in his *hand*. And, now that he looked, he saw that Lady Luck was holding it. But he still needed her to say it.

'Yes, darling,' the Goddess replied, smiling widely. 'You won. *And* you carried out a magnificent rescue!'

'*Magnificent rescue?*' Jeremiah repeated, his face turning positively scarlet with anger. 'That was *not* a magnificent rescue! It was a—'

But he was interrupted at that moment by the explosion. It lit up the sky and seemed to shake the very ground on which they stood. The humans instinctively threw themselves to the ground, arms over their heads. When they finally dared to look up again, the library tree was gone. All that remained of it was the dark ash settling on the surface of the ocean, along with a few loose pages.

'I suppose Herman put gunpowder in the centre of the tree,' Lady Luck tutted. 'Oh well, it's about time. I don't know why he didn't just destroy those books long ago, if he didn't want anyone to read them. More like the God of Silliness than the God of Knowledge, if you ask me. But what wonderful timing on your part, Lex!' she exclaimed. 'Why, everyone might have been blown to bits if you hadn't won right when you did!'

'I suppose you could say that I saved everyone,' Lex replied, looking as smug as possible.

'Well, everyone except poor Lorella,' Lady Luck said, looking at Thaddeus with rather a self-satisfied expression on her face. 'In your own round, too. Why, it's almost embarrassing!'

'I still have the companion,' Thaddeus muttered, looking extremely hacked off.

Lady Luck laughed. 'A sprite! Oh dear. I really don't think a sprite is going to be much good for the final round I have in mind.'

'Why don't you just worry about your own player?' Thaddeus snapped. 'And let me worry about mine!'

'As you wish.'

And with that, Thaddeus disappeared, taking the unhappy-looking sprite with him.

'Look,' Jeremiah said to Kala. 'I really don't see why Trent should be awarded hero points. I was only hanging from that branch *because* of him! It was *his* fault I was there in the first place! Besides, I didn't ask him to save me!'

'But he did,' Kala said coldly. 'So he gets hero points. That's the way this works. You should never have allowed yourself to be put in that position in the first place. He only threw a toy snake at you, after all.'

Jeremiah went pink with embarrassment. 'I thought it was real for a moment,' he muttered. 'Snakes make me . . . uncomfortable.'

'Wasn't that an unfortunate coincidence for us?' Kala snapped.

Jeremiah clenched his jaw and said nothing. Lex felt smug. Receiving a dressing-down from your Goddess right in front of everybody couldn't be a very pleasant experience. On the rare occasions when Lady Luck was unhappy with Lex, at least she expressed her displeasure in private.

Tess had been sitting on the sand behind Jeremiah looking bored, but at that point she looked up and caught Jesse's eye. He waved. She gave him a shy smile and waved back. And then she and Jeremiah were both gone, taken away by their sulky Goddess.

'Well,' Lady Luck said. 'That's that. A most satisfactory conclusion to the second round.'

'I'm ahead of Jeremiah in points now, right?' Lex asked.

'Yes, dear. He has winning points from the first round but you have winning points *and* hero points. An inspired idea, on your part. Now you'll get to start first in the third round.'

'How about giving me a clue as to what it's about?' Lex prompted.

He'd tried to get a hint as to what Lady Luck's round would entail before but he'd been unsuccessful every time and he was again now. She just smiled and said, 'You'll see. One thing I can tell you, Lex, and that's that it will be glorious!'

CHAPTER SEVENTEEN

i wish my Hands were oranges

Lex was extremely pleased with the footage of the second round when he watched it in his Divine Eye later. As usual, it had been heavily edited in order to make the players look more impressive than they really were. It was, therefore, not clear exactly how Jeremiah had ended up clinging to a rope at the top of the tree. Obviously, Kala felt that his reaction to the toy snake was not something she wanted to share with the public.

Lex's 'rescue' on the other hand, looked spectacular, what with the tree ablaze all around them and time running out. There was even a rousing soundtrack accompanying the part where Lex and Jeremiah plummeted together through the burning tree. Lex was especially pleased with how much soot and ash there'd been on his face and clothes, for it made the whole thing more heroic-seeming, somehow. In addition, from the way the scenes had been put together, it looked like the tree exploded just *seconds* after Lex and Jeremiah landed in the water. By the time Lex had finished watching it, even *he* was feeling impressed with himself. In the last Game, some enterprising company had brought out a limited-edition Lex Trent action figure fighting a minotaur and medusa. Lex rather hoped that this time there might be a Lex Trent action figure with a burning tree and a vulture bird, or something.

But, after the second round was over, the main thing Lex was interested in was the book he'd stolen from the library tree. Lady Luck had been watching him the whole time he'd been playing in the second round, so she must have known he'd taken it, but she said nothing about it. Probably because she didn't much care. Books bored her very quickly. But Lex was thrilled. Not only did he now own one of the last two surviving forbidden books from the tree (the other being the one now in Lady Luck's possession), but it was a book about *Desareth* and his wishing animals! Now, finally, Lex would get to the bottom of them.

He set the ship off towards Dry Gulch, which was a three-day journey at top speed. Then, when Jesse went down to the hold to go to sleep with Rusty for what remained of the night, Lex sat cross-legged on the bed and got out the book. He had not told Jesse about it, nor did he intend to. After all, it was a forbidden book. As such, it was utterly priceless and – perhaps as a result of being so thoroughly dishonest himself – Lex did not trust anyone where utterly priceless things were concerned. But, once the cowboy had gone below and Lex had securely locked his door and closed all the curtains, he opened the front cover of the book and started to read.

It was quite a slim volume and had actually been handwritten by Erasmus Grey himself. In fact, it was not really a book at all, but more of a journal. Lex doubted that Grey had ever intended anyone else to read it. It seemed that Grey had had something of a preoccupation with Desareth, who had already died about one hundred years before Grey was born. Desareth, Grey wrote, was brilliant. But he was also mad. Mad as a cracker. If he'd been sane, he could have set his hand to anything and succeeded. He could have ruled the world. *Worlds*, even. As it was, his brilliance was so great that it managed to shine through his madness . . .

Lex skipped the almost adoring account of Desareth and his life and jumped forward to the bit about the Wishing Creatures. It seemed that they were one of the projects on which Desareth had worked the hardest for the longest time. Once Lex had read about what they were, how they worked and what they did, it all clicked into place. Suddenly it all made sense.

The Wishing Creatures granted spoken wishes. This had been one of Lex's very first theories but he had dismissed it when he had picked up one of the Swanns and wished for money, and it hadn't worked. Now he knew why. The Wishing Creatures *did* grant wishes. But they each only granted one *particular* wish. You had to know what to wish *for* or it wouldn't work.

Grey wrote that each animal belonged to a set of three and that there were twelve known sets in existence: dolphins, dragons, elephants, griffins, mermaids, monkeys, phoenixes, swanns, tigers, unicorns, witches and wolves.

At the back was an index of all thirty-six animals along with their wishes. Some of the wishes were listed as 'confirmed', some as 'rumoured' and some as 'unknown'. After all, unless you were Desareth himself then presumably the only way to find out what a particular creature's wish was would be to guess it.

Lex ran his eye down the list and saw that some of the wishes were extraordinary and magnificent. The green Elephant, for example, granted the wish that every apple the owner touched would turn into gold. The blue Mermaid's wish caused the first person the owner saw after making their wish to fall desperately and permanently in love with them. And the golden Phoenix's wish could cure any illness.

Others, however, were rather less impressive. Indeed, a couple of them didn't seem to make any sense at all. That, Grey wrote, was where Desareth's madness started to show itself. Why go to all the trouble and expense and effort of making these Wishing Creatures, only to give them an utterly pointless wish? The red Monkey's wish, for example, could produce an unlimited number of hard-boiled eggs. And the orange Griffin's wish turned sand into mud.

Even worse than the pointless wishes, however, were the dangerous ones – the worst one being the black Wolf, which granted the owner their wish that they'd never been born. Lex shuddered to think how *that* wish had been discovered.

Naturally, Lex hoped that the Creatures he already

owned would have wonderful, fantastic powers. He ran his eye down the index at the back in desperate search of the Swanns. The first one he found was the white one. According to Erasmus Grey, the white Swann's wish would silence any musical instrument. Desareth, apparently, had hated music of any kind, so perhaps to him this had seemed logical. To Lex it was utterly useless and he was profoundly disappointed. Other creatures turned apples into gold and all his rubbishy Swann did was silence music. He tried not to feel too despondent. After all, it might be a good party trick at some point.

He looked down the list at the next entry, which was the red Swann. But this one was no better. The red Swann's wish, it seemed, was to cause people to swap places. But it transpired that there were several conditions. Firstly, the wisher could not themselves be one of the people to swap; secondly, the names of both men had to be known to the wisher in order for it to work; thirdly, both men had to be in close proximity to one another; and fourthly, and most ridiculously of all, one of the men had to be dead.

'This is frickin' ridiculous!' Lex muttered under his breath. 'I might just as well have the one that turns sand into mud!'

Why the heck would anyone want to swap two men who were physically near to each other, anyway, when one of those men was a corpse?

But the next creature was the worst one of them all. The list had not been done in any kind of order and the next one Lex's eye fell upon was the blue Dragon. It seemed that its wish was to turn the wisher's hands into oranges.

Lex had to read the entry twice to make sure he'd read it correctly. Grey had marked this wish as 'confirmed', meaning that someone, somewhere, at some point had actually *made* this wish and it had come true.

Lex took the Dragon out of his pocket and glared at it ferociously. What sort of a person said *I wish my hands were oranges*, anyway? Lex would have thrown the Dragon out of the window and into the sea if it hadn't been for the fact that Jeremiah might give him something to get it back for Tess, and he could hold the Dragon over the nobleman's arrogant head until then. Perhaps he might even be able to get him to speak the wish once the Dragon was back in his possession. It would serve the stuck-up git right to have to go through the rest of his life with oranges for hands.

Lex tossed the Dragon aside on the bedspread and searched the list for the remaining Wishing Creature he owned – the black Swann.

'I suppose it probably just turns pumpkin pies into poo,' he said sourly – and rather sulkily – as he ran his eye down the list.

But when he finally located the black Swann, it did not have a useless wish, or even a dangerous wish. In fact, it had no wish at all in the book, for Grey had marked it as 'unknown'. The bright side was that the Swann *might* still have a half-useful wish, but the problem

254

was finding out what it was. It could be just about anything. Lex spent more than an hour that night trying out different wishes in the hope of stumbling across it but, really, it was quite hopeless. He was so pissed off by the end of it that it was on the tip of his tongue to say he wished he'd never found the Swanns, but he forced himself not to, just in case it were to come true. Indeed, whilst the black Swann was in his possession, he was going to have to try and remember to be extremely careful what he wished for.

CHAPTER EIGHTEEN

SLOW SID

On questioning Lady Luck, Lex learnt that the library tree had housed only originals. Some of the books had been copied but Herman had ordered these all burned when he first banned the books. However, just because the God had ordered it so, didn't necessarily mean that it had actually *happened*.

'So, theoretically, there could be copies of a forbidden book out there?' Lex said.

'Yes, dear, I suppose so. They'd risk a lot of trouble if they were found out, though.'

Well, if there was anything worth risking trouble for, Desareth's Wishing Creatures was surely one of them. Lex nurtured a faint hope that he was the only one who knew about them, but he strongly suspected there must be others out there who knew of the Creatures and were looking for them, too.

He would just have to put them out of his mind for now. He needed to have all his attention focused on infiltrating Dry Gulch House as a cowboy and then finding the Sword of Life. And then he was going to win the third round, *and* the Game. After he'd done all that, *then* he would turn his attention back to the Wishing Creatures of Desareth. He would track them down somehow and he would have them for himself. If they belonged to someone else then he would pinch them; if they were lost then he would find them; and if they were long buried then he would dig them up. Between the information in Erasmus Grey's book and Lex's own natural talent for getting what he wanted, he would have those Creatures – as many of them as he possibly could.

The enchanted ship took three days to reach Dry Gulch. They soon left the sea behind them and, as they journeyed on, the landscape became less green and more brown and scrubby. Lex knew they were getting close when cactuses and tumbleweed started to appear an awful lot.

He used the first day to fine-tune the skills Jesse had taught him back at the Majestic: card-shuffling, poker-playing, pistol-twirling, knife-spinning, coffee-drinking, bean-eating and so on. Of all these things, it was bean-eating that Lex disliked the most. Not because he had anything against beans *per se*, it was simply that Jesse insisted he eat them without a spoon.

'Don't find spoons out in the desert,' he'd said.

Which was all very well, but eating a can of beans without a spoon meant getting yourself in a terrible mess. With a hell of a lot of effort, Lex might have been able to do it neatly but the problem was that no cowboy would make any effort whatsoever, and that meant that Lex couldn't either. He would even be expected to wipe his mouth with his sleeve and belch loudly once he'd finished!

'For such a pernickety fella, I'm surprised you chose this line of work,' Jesse remarked.

Lex's obsession with cleanliness was his one flaw as a conman, but he kept his feelings under control – he was disciplined enough to grit his teeth and bear it. He'd always had a thing about being clean, even as a small child. When his grandfather had taken Lex and his brother to the fair, Lex had wanted to do anything and everything there was to do – except for the goo slide. Kids could go down a slide and land in a big pool full of slimy goo at the bottom. It was extremely popular but Lex threw a very loud tantrum as soon as his grandfather merely *suggested* he might like to go on it.

After the first day of travelling, Lex had his first go on Rusty. They were confining the griffins inside several times a day so that Jesse could take the horse up on deck and let him get some fresh air and exercise. Lex had never been on a horse before in his life (unless you counted the pony at the fair). There had been a horse back at the family farm but that had just pulled the wagon. And now Lex had only two days to learn how to ride.

It did not quite turn out to be the piece of cake he'd expected. There was more to it than just sitting there on the horse's back. It had to *look* right, too.

'You gotta look like you were practically born in the saddle,' Jesse said. 'Like you and the horse are one living thing. Don't hold the reins so high. Lean back in the saddle more. And don't be lookin' down at the horse like that all the time – look straight ahead at where you're goin'.'

After an hour of walking around the deck, Lex began to feel more comfortable in the saddle. It was what came next that was more tricky. Walking was one thing – the other three gaits were something else altogether. First, Lex had to learn how to squeeze with his legs so that Rusty would pick up into a trot and, later, a canter. This required more strength than he would have thought. Fortunately, Lex did have fairly strong legs as a result of all the rope-climbing and building-scaling he did all the time as the Wizard. But the other problem – the most major one – was trying to stay on the horse's back. It turned out that trotting and cantering were much bouncier gaits than walking.

Lex fell off. A lot.

The first time it happened, he'd taken a corner too sharply, his foot had fallen out of the stirrup and then he'd lost his balance. Over the side of the horse he went, landing on the deck on his back with a horrible thump. It was like all the air had been driven out of his body with a club. Lex would never have believed that falling from such a relatively-low height could hurt so much. Thankfully, he'd managed to avoid hitting his head but pain shot through his back and his right arm. He'd heard of people falling from horses and breaking their backs or snapping their necks, paralysing themselves for the rest of their lives and, for an unpleasant moment, he had a clear vision in his mind of that happening to him. Lex knew he would never be able to live life in a wheelchair – never!

A shadow fell across him, and Jesse's unconcerned voice said, 'Well, get up then. Ain't no use just lying there gasping like that. Best thing to do when you fall off is to pick yourself up and get right back on. That's if you want to carry on at all, of course.'

Lex dragged himself to his feet. Aside from being stiff and sore he appeared to be unharmed. He practically snatched the reins from Jesse and said, 'Of course I want to carry on!'

He put his foot into the stirrup and swung himself back up into the saddle.

'It probably ain't strictly necessary, y'know,' Jesse said, watching him. 'I mean, you won't be on horseback once you're inside Dry Gulch House, will you? It just looks better if you turn up on one, that's all. And you can get away with walkin' for that. You don't have to go galloping right up to the front door.'

But that wasn't good enough for Lex. He knew full well how important first impressions were. He'd read enough cowboy books to know that the single most important part of pulling this scam off successfully would be for him to be at ease with his horse. Whether that ended up being a five minute performance or a five day one, Lex didn't care. Jesse was right – going to all this bother was probably unnecessary. *Probably*. But Lex didn't work with '*probablys*'. And that was why he always won.

He had no intention whatsoever of arriving at Dry Gulch House any way other than on horseback. He might only have one shot at this and he wasn't going to blow it just because mastering horse riding was difficult for a city kid. He would dearly love to be able to leap out of the saddle mid-ride and actually stand on the horse's back whilst holding the reins as it cantered along. But if he didn't have time to learn how to do that then, by heck, he was at least going to learn how to canter and gallop.

He fell off Rusty quite a lot that day. Time and time again, in fact. But he sustained no serious injuries and was rather annoyed when, about five hours after he'd started, Jesse announced that it was, 'Time for a break.'

'I don't want a break!' Lex snapped. 'I want to carry on until I get it right!'

'That may be,' Jesse replied calmly. 'But Rusty needs to have a break and get some food and water in him. After he's had a rest, you can carry on in the afternoon. If you still want to.'

Lex thought that last sentence had been spoken in rather an odd tone and he found out why a moment later when he dismounted. His legs were like jelly. As soon as his feet hit the deck, his knees buckled and he collapsed into an untidy heap on the ground. Jesse laughed heartily. 'Always strikes newbies like that,' he said. 'Not used to it, see?'

'I'll get used to it fast enough!' Lex snapped, dragging himself upright with some difficulty. The truth was that every muscle in his body ached – both from the numerous falls and from the extended amount of time he'd spent on Rusty's back.

'Go take a hot bath while I see to Rusty,' Jesse said. 'I know you're right fond of soap and if you have a bit of a soak in the tub then your muscles won't seize up so bad.'

Lex stomped off to the bathroom feeling annoyed, no less because of the fact that Jesse was right. If he ended up so stiff he could hardly move then that wouldn't exactly help his image as a cowboy, either.

After having a long bath, he went back on deck that afternoon and spent another few hours on Rusty. By the end of that day he had improved immensely – and was able to get the horse to trot and canter on command, whilst managing not to fall off. He still bounced around in the saddle a lot. But he didn't fall off. It was a start, and he still had all of the next day to practise. Lex would have liked to keep on riding all night but Jesse, blast him, insisted that Rusty ought to rest, and so should Lex. But Lex had no time for resting. He spent much of that night practising with his cards, knives and pistols. He even had another crack at eating beans straight from the tin and drinking some ridiculously strong black coffee.

After a couple of hours' sleep, Lex was up bright and early the next day to get back to work on Rusty. He no longer fell off – now it was just a question of getting it to look right. Cantering in particular took Lex some time to get the hang of. It wouldn't do for him to be bouncing around in the saddle, perilously close to falling off at any moment.

'You gotta move *with* the horse,' Jesse kept saying.

'Yes, I understand that!' Lex snapped. 'It's what I'm *trying* to do!'

He had not expected learning horsemanship to be so difficult. He'd seen people on horses before and it had always looked so easy – like the horse was the one doing all the work and the rider simply sat there. The reality was not like that at all. But, at around five o'clock that afternoon, something shifted and suddenly it all seemed to click.

'There!' Jesse yelled. 'That's it! You're doing it!'

But Lex didn't need Jesse to tell him. He could *feel* the difference. Now he was moving in perfect time with Rusty like they really were just one animal. It was simply a matter of getting the rhythm right and now, finally, Lex had got it.

'Nothing to it, really,' he said as he slid off Rusty's back. His legs were killing him but he managed to grit his teeth and bear it.

'I gotta say you seem to have picked it up pretty quick,' Jesse replied.

'I told you I was a fast learner,' Lex said. 'I'm going back to my room now to practise the other stuff.'

Lex spent the rest of the day doing just that. After so many hours of practice, he had mastered all eight card shuffles and could spin the pistols and twirl the knives with no danger of dropping them. He could spit almost from one side of the room to the other and be sure of hitting whatever target he aimed at. And he could even drink the horrible sludge they called coffee, without gagging. Now that he had horse riding down, too, Lex felt pleasantly well prepared for cheating his way into Dry Gulch House the next day.

They arrived at Dry Gulch a little after three o'clock in the afternoon. Lex set the ship down on a patch of desert beside the inn the players were supposed to be staying at. It was conveniently located right in the middle of the town, which was actually rather a boring one. Lex had expected it to be full of cowboys but, in fact, it seemed instead to be full of peasants and townsfolk walking around with horses and baskets of apples and the like. Lex pulled a face in disgust at the dull scene. It was like being at a country fête. They might as well set up a stall selling punch and have done with it. The people did not even seem particularly excited – or even interested – at the arrival of the players.

'What's the matter with these people?' Lex said to Jesse. 'Don't they know who we are? Why aren't they cheering? You told me you had Games out here.'

'Sure, we do,' Jesse replied. 'But there ain't many folk what goes to 'em. You need money to bet on players and that's somethin' that tends to be in short supply around these parts. Besides, most people round here are farmers. They ain't got time to waste watching Games.'

'What about the cowboys?'

'Well, we don't mind a bit of gamblin' when we've got cash in our pockets, but most of us would rather bet on cards than people.'

Lex supposed that was fair enough. After all, you relied on your own skill when playing poker, not on the skill of a person you had never met and didn't know. And it worked in his favour not to have to worry overly much about one of the cowboys at Dry Gulch House seeing through his disguise and recognising him.

The enchanted ship was to remain in the town. Lex couldn't very well take it with him when he was trying to pass himself off as a cowboy. Jesse led Rusty down the gangplank and on to solid land, which must have been a welcome relief to the horse when it had had to make do with exercising up on deck for the last two weeks.

They paused in the town only long enough to shop for supplies. Lex needed a costume and he needed a horse. Both turned out to be a little more complicated than they had expected. The clothes store sold suitable items: the hat and the shirt and the neckerchief and the trousers and the boots. But they didn't stock them in Lex's size. Most cowboys tended to be large, brawny men – not skinny teenagers.

'But this is ridiculous!' Lex exclaimed in frustration, as he stood before the mirror in an outfit that was far too big for him. 'Surely all cowboys start out as teenagers, don't they?' He looked at Jesse and said, 'I mean you didn't just hatch out of an egg looking like that, did you? Do people here just walk around naked until they're twenty-one?'

Jesse shrugged. 'Like I said – it's all farming land. Most teenagers round here are of the strapping kind.'

Fortunately, the store owner said they would be able to alter the clothes so that they would fit Lex. This involved a bit more expense and delay but was, at least, a solution. They left the tailor to it and made their way to the stables in search of a horse. Beside the others, Lex was able to see just how handsome Rusty really was. He had a glossy sheen to his coat and a bright look in his eyes that not all the other horses had.

'How come he's in such good condition?' Lex asked Jesse suspiciously. 'When you're a down-and-out cowboy, on the run half the time and in jail the rest?'

'Never stayed in jail for very long,' Jesse replied. 'Me and Rusty might have a wanderin' sorta life but I always exercise him every day, keep him well groomed and feed him the finest food, even if it means I have to go hungry myself. The horse has to come first.'

Putting another's needs before his own was something of an alien notion to Lex. He did not know horses like Jesse did, so he let the cowboy look them all over and pick one out. In the end, he chose a dappled grey mare called Sally.

'Sally?' Lex said, pulling a face. 'Are you sure that's the right horse? She's a bit small, isn't she?'

'Strong, though, and healthy,' Jesse replied. 'No jitters. Besides, you'll want a small horse. A big one would only make you look even shorter and skinnier than you really are.'

Lex supposed that made sense. It was, at least, much easier getting on to Sally's back than it had been getting on to Rusty's. They made their way back to the clothes store so that Lex could change into his new outfit and ditch his old one. By the time he was kitted out and back on the horse, he was starting to feel like a real cowboy. He could feel Sid the Kid coming to life inside him. To a true fraud and conman, it wasn't a case of *pretending* to be Sid the Kid, it was a case of *becoming* him. The hat and the boots helped a lot. Looking the part always helped. And, whilst Lex may not have been the usual beefy, brawny sort of cowboy, with the horse and outfit he looked like a cowboy just the same. Now all that was left was for him to act like one convincingly enough to get into Dry Gulch House. Once he was inside, he was sure that the sword would be as good as his. For surely, if anyone were capable of discovering its secret hiding place, that person must be Lex Trent.

As they rode out of town, Lex thought he could come to like horse riding. It was a handy skill to have for someone like him because, if he got caught and had to run, he could only go so fast on his own two legs. If he were able to pinch a horse, on the other hand, then he would practically fly out of there and his pursuers would be left choking on the dust!

'How many times have you been to Dry Gulch House?' Lex asked, as they continued on at a sedate walk.

'Let's see. First time I went was two years ago, now. Then I went back twice last year and once this year. So that's four. It ain't a bad place to stop at, if you happen to be passin' through Dry Gulch.'

'It's not expensive? I mean, it is a mansion, after all.'

'Not too shiny inside anymore, though,' Jesse replied. 'Just because you can't take anything outta the house, don't mean you can't ruin what's already in it.'

Lex winced. Doubtless the house had once been full of wonderful, beautiful things until those idiot cowboys had gone and spoilt it all. It was approaching dark when they finally neared the house. It was one of the ugliest things Lex had ever seen in his life. It seemed to have been constructed from several different materials, including wood, brick and limestone. You could tell, just by looking at it, that it had been designed by a madman. There was no logic, no structure, no order. In some places the building was four storeys high, in others it was barely half a storey. Some parts of the house had no windows at all, others had ones that were hardly bigger than a man's thumb. Chimneys were dotted around in a very odd manner across the uneven roof. And what looked very much like a bath-tub was sticking out of the corner of the house all by itself on the third floor. In fact, there was a cowboy in it now, still wearing his hat, splashing about and singing noisily, pausing only long enough to take long swigs from a liquor bottle.

'How the heck,' Lex said, 'did he get into that tub?'

'You gotta climb out through a window above it,' Jesse replied. 'You think that's weird, just wait till you see the rest of the house.'

Bright lights shone from the windows, whatever their size, and Lex thought he could hear the faint notes of a honky-tonk piano coming from inside.

'Well,' Jesse said, 'shall we?'

They dismounted their horses and tied them up at one of the long posts outside.

'Someone'll come and take 'em round to the stables once they know we're stayin' here,' Jesse replied. 'They almost always have spare rooms but I guess it'll depend on whether your little act is good enough to cut the mustard.'

'You'd better hope it is,' Lex replied.

'Now, now, we had a deal,' Jesse replied. 'All I had to do was teach you everything I know about being a cowboy, and I've done that. You gotta pull this off by yourself. I had my doubts at first, but you were tellin' the truth about being a quick learner and I think you'll probably manage it.'

'Glad to hear it. Now, let's go find out.'

They went up the four steps to the porch and walked in through the front doors. Or at least tried to. Just as Lex was about to put his hand on the doorknob, the doors flew open. He and Jesse both managed to jump back in time to avoid being flattened but, when two big cowboys came rushing out, Lex was unable to get out of the way quick enough to avoid one of them barrelling into him. He and the cowboy got tangled up together and ended up rolling down the steps to the ground. By the time they'd managed to disentangle themselves in the dust, the second cowboy had jumped on to his horse and was already riding away fast.

'Daw-gone it!' the other cowboy exclaimed as he leapt

to his feet. In another moment there was a pistol in his hand and he was aiming shots towards the fleeing cowboy. He missed, which seemed to infuriate him even more. He spun round on his heel, back towards Lex still sprawled in the dust, and the expression on his face as he looked down on him was not at all friendly.

'That man insulted me!' he exclaimed. 'And because of you he got away! Seems to me it's only right that you should take his place in the duel! What's your name, boy?'

But before Lex could say so much as a single word, Jesse said conversationally, 'That's Slow Sid.' He sauntered over with his hands in his pockets. The other cowboy might have looked a bit meaner and had a few more scars than Jesse, but they were about the same size. 'Sad, really,' Jesse went on. 'He used to be Sid the Kid – I'm sure you've heard of him? – but then, coupla years back, he went and fell off his horse and caught his head a right crack on a rock. And that was that. Sid the Kid was no more and all that was left was poor old Slow Sid. Don't know who he is or what he's doing half the time, now. Ain't that right, Sid?'

Jesse looked down at Lex pointedly. Lex was furious. How dare he? How *dare* he? He had not spent all those hours practising and practising passing himself off as a half-decent cowboy only to have to play a simpleton the whole time he was here! At the back of his mind he was aware that Jesse was trying to prevent him from getting shot in the face, but that wasn't the point. Lex could take care of himself – he didn't need anyone coming to his rescue. But what was done now was done and, if he didn't want to raise suspicion, he really had no choice but to play along. So Lex lowered his voice, unfocused his gaze slightly, looked up at Jesse with the most gormless expression he could muster on short notice and said, 'Horse hit Sid onna head.'

'Well, the horse didn't hit you; the floor did,' Jesse replied. 'But, yeah, you fell off the horse first, so I hear. That's what happens if you insist on riding horses what ain't been broken in yet.'

The other cowboy glared down at Lex for a moment, still looking mightily peeved but no longer murderous.

'Huh,' he grunted, and then finally walked off.

Once he'd disappeared back into the house, Jesse looked down at Lex, a little smile tugging at one corner of his mouth and, reaching down a hand he said, 'You need some help there, Sid?'

Lex would have dearly loved to hiss some unpleasantry back at him but, for all he knew, the scar-faced cowboy was watching from the windows. Others' attention may have been drawn their way by the altercation and Lex couldn't risk anything that might give him away. This was show time, now. Granted, it might not be the kind of show time he had planned upon, but it was show time just the same. Shouting-at-Jesse time would just have to wait.

So, making a real effort to look mildly confused, Lex gripped Jesse's hand and allowed the cowboy to haul him to his feet. Then he dusted himself off and gazed around stupidly, as if not too sure of where he was. His hat had fallen off in the kerfuffle and lay on the floor in the dust. Lex purposefully ignored it and started to stagger towards the front doors. Jesse clapped the hat back on his head from behind, as Lex had known that he would. He didn't bother to adjust the lop-sided angle but simply carried on towards the door. He pulled it open and, this time, managed to get all the way inside.

Once there, he stopped short. The entrance hall was enormous, with a great sweeping staircase going up to the next level. Portraits lined the walls from floor to ceiling. Every single one was of the same person – a rather strange-looking man with greying hair, a thin face, impressively bushy whiskers and an expression of mild puzzlement.

There must have been two hundred portraits there, all of different sizes, all of the same man. Some of the paintings were traditional head-and-shoulder portraits. But others were much larger and showed the entire person. They were – to put it mildly – ridiculous. One picture was of him sitting at a table having tea with a giant fox (who was wearing a waistcoat); in another, he was sitting on a toilet with his trousers around his ankles. One particularly large painting showed him brandishing what looked very much like a smoked trout against an enormous white dragon that seemed set to roast him where he stood at any moment.

In every picture he wore the same dark suit, the same daft monocle, the same bushy whiskers and the same amiable expression of foolish, mild puzzlement.

It was a little hard to see some of the paintings properly, especially those hung lower down, because most of them had a hell of a lot of darts sticking out of them.

'Nathaniel East,' Jesse said behind Lex. 'In every single painting, the mad old coot. Painted them all himself, so they say.'

It must have taken him years. The paintings were so detailed and some of them were so large that Lex thought it must have taken Nathaniel practically his whole life to paint them. He could not have produced all of these during the five years he'd lived in Dry Gulch. For some unknown reason he must have brought them with him when he'd travelled out to the Wild West.

'Can't be taken down, see?' Jesse went on. 'Because of the witch's sticking spell. So the fellas just use 'em for dart practice mostly. Let's go through to the bar.'

Adopting a rambling, shuffling gait, Lex followed him. He would have known where to go, even without Jesse, by following the raucous sounds of talking and laughter and the rather jolly music of a honky-tonk piano.

The bar adjoined the entrance hall to the left. It was a large room, that easily accommodated the twenty or so people there. Everyone in the room was a cowboy. You could tell by the hats and boots. A lot of the furniture had obviously been moved from other rooms, for none of it matched. It seemed that, although the witch's sticking spell meant that none of the items could be taken out of the house, some of them could be moved from room to room. Any spare table or chair had been brought there.

Lex even saw two men drinking at a chess table, the chessmen still fixed firmly in place – glued into a stale-mate from the looks of it.

'Let's go get ourselves a drink, Sid,' Jesse said, already striding purposefully towards the bar.

Lex obediently followed along behind him.

'Hello again, Sam,' Jesse said to the man behind the bar.

Lex was pleased to note that he was bald and had a .waxed moustache that curled at the ends, just like in the books.

'Howdy, Jesse,' Sam replied. 'Back again? Ain't you got bored of lookin' for that sword yet?'

Lex almost jumped where he sat. Jesse had told him right back in the jail cell at the Wither City that he didn't believe the Sword of Life existed. He had neglected to mention that he had searched for it himself.

'Just passin' through this time,' Jesse replied. 'Needed somewhere to stay for a few days. You got any rooms?'

'Yep.' Sam turned around and picked off a key from the board on the wall behind him. He put this on the bar in front of Jesse, glanced at Lex and said, 'Who's your friend?'

'This here is Slow Sid,' Jesse said. 'We're travelling together for a while.'

'Pleased to know you, Sid. I'm Sam. What can I get you?'

'Glass of milk, please,' Lex said, scooping up the nearby beer mats and absently starting to shuffle them.

'Sid!' Jesse said sharply. 'What have I told you about that?' He looked at Sam and said, 'He means milk and rum. Obviously.' He added a nervous laugh at the end of that, which Lex thought was rather a nice touch.

'Obviously,' Sam replied, eyebrow raised.

'Yeah,' Lex said, giving the barman his best eager-to-please smile. 'Milk and rum.' He turned his smile on Jesse, who nodded approvingly. 'Without the rum,' Lex added – to which Jesse shook his head despairingly.

'What are you hanging around with this halfwit for, anyway?' the barman said suspiciously. 'You're a one for always bein' out for yourself, so what's in it for you, Jesse, eh?'

Uh oh, Lex thought. Off the top of his head he could think of a couple of half-decent explanations but the problem was in trying to convincingly produce them when he'd been sitting there affecting a complete lack of awareness of anything that was being said.

But, as it happened, he didn't need to come up with something because, quick as a whip, Jesse said, 'What's in it for me? Well, I'll show you.'

And, suddenly, Lex found the beer mats plucked from his fingers and a pack of cards pressed into his palm instead. He looked up at Jesse, who raised an eyebrow meaningfully. Lex knew instantly what he had in mind. He looked down at the pack in his hands for a bare moment before breaking into a perfect Faro shuffle. It was one of the more difficult ones to do but Lex pulled it off flawlessly.

'Little bit of Sid the Kid comes back when he handles the cards. We split the winnings,' Jesse said blithely.

'You're using him,' the barman said with a knowing chuckle.

Jesse gave a lazy grin. 'Dunno 'bout that. Works all right for us, don't it, Sid?'

Lex grinned stupidly and took a big slurp of the milk Sam set down in front of him. It left a moustache but he didn't bother to wipe it off.

CHAPTER NINETEEN

PLANTAGENET THE DREAM-FOX

They spent the rest of that evening in the bar. Slow Sid was clearly something of an enigma to the other cowboys and it seemed to bring them great amusement to take it in turns buying him glasses of milk.

Of course, whilst he was sitting in the bar, Lex could not be looking for the sword, but he didn't mind. This was groundwork. Groundwork that was going splendidly well. Already Lex could see that Slow Sid was going to serve him much better than Sid the Kid ever could. It was, after all, one of his own rules that he should always be underestimated as much as possible, by as many people as possible. In his preoccupation with learning how to become a cowboy, he had become *too* good. The other cowboys might have been wary of Sid the Kid, with his mean card skills and his impressive knife spinning and the keen, sharp mind that made up for his lack of brawn.

Sid the Kid could never have wandered the house at night. Slow Sid, on the other hand ... Well, no one would think twice about a nincompoop lost in the halls.

The trick, therefore, was to get himself known to as many of these cowboys as possible. And that evening spent in the bar was the perfect way to do it. With a little bit of help from Jesse, everyone became very interested in Slow Sid. It was cleverly done, Lex couldn't deny that. Because Jesse was, at the end of the day, every bit as much of a rotter as Lex was, the cowboy didn't even need Lex to tell him what to do. He could do it all by *himself*! Whilst maintaining a perfectly amiable manner towards Lex, Jesse brazenly exploited him for the others' entertainment.

They bounced off each other beautifully. At one point, Jesse proclaimed that he'd never seen anyone dance like Slow Sid. He then promptly sat down at the honky-tonk piano and started to play a lively, jolly little tune. Lex leapt up on to the bar, secretly delighted by the cowboy's improvisation, and broke out into the most absurd jig he could manage. The cowboys cheered merrily. It was probably no lie to say that they had never seen anything so silly in their lives.

It was perfect. Even if there were cowboys staying in the house who were not in the bar that night, they would be sure to hear about Slow Sid later and, if they were to catch Lex wandering around at night, then they would surely put two and two together and assume he was just a halfwit who couldn't find his room, rather than a thief and an adventurer who was looking for the Sword of Life. As Slow Sid, Lex could get away with doing practically anything.

It was about midnight when Lex and Jesse finally left.

After the dancing, Lex had affected a sudden fatigue and apparently gone to sleep with his head on the bar. Seeing that he was to provide no more amusement to them, the other cowboys had settled down to talk to Jesse, flicking cigarette butts at Lex from time to time but paying him no attention other than that.

Finally, Jesse collected Lex from the bar and they made their way back out to the main entrance hall. Up the stairs they went, past the portraits and up to the large landing at the top.

The corridor leading there was uncommonly thin. Only just wide enough to accommodate Jesse's broad shoulders. Anyone with a plump stature would not possibly have been able to squeeze through. It was lit with electric lights along the ceiling. Doors led off from both sides.

Jesse glanced over his shoulder at Lex and said quietly, 'Not a bad start, eh?'

The corridor appeared to be deserted but Lex did not respond to Jesse's question. Breaking character was a risky business and a bad habit. Lex never allowed himself to do it until he could be absolutely sure the coast was clear. So he ignored Jesse and simply continued walking down the corridor in the slow, shuffling gait he had adopted as Slow Sid. Jesse looked faintly surprised but had the sense to say nothing as they continued on down the hallway. A moment later he stopped in front of a room with the number nine painted roughly on it in chalk. He unlocked the door and they stepped in.

Because the corridor had been so narrow, Lex had been

expecting the room to be small, too. But, actually, it was extremely large. The corridor had obviously just been another one of Nathaniel East's quirks, rather than a result of a genuine need to conserve space.

The large room they stepped into was fairly ordinary in so much as it had a large four poster bed, a wardrobe, a sink and a window that looked out from the front of the building. A hammock was strung across one corner. But the odd thing about the room was its colour scheme, for everything in it was a garish shade of lime green. The walls, the floor, the ceiling, the furniture. It was extremely wearing on the senses and Lex instinctively wanted to wince and shield his eyes from the horrible sight. But he kept staunchly in character as Slow Sid whilst Jesse groaned aloud and said, 'Aw, man, not the snot room!'

Lex couldn't help thinking that, if someone had snot that colour, then that person must have something very seriously wrong with them indeed. But he said nothing as Jesse closed the door behind them. Instead, he rambled over to the wardrobe and opened the door to check inside it. Then he wandered over to the bed and looked underneath it.

'What are you doin'?' Jesse asked, staring at him. 'Lex?'

Lex ignored him and went to look behind both of the heavy lime drapes that fell all the way to the floor alongside the window. Only once he'd satisfied himself that there was no one else in the room with them did he relax and drop the act.

'This is the ugliest room I ever saw in my life!' he declared.

Jesse breathed a sigh of relief then and said, 'You gave me a horrible turn for a minute there, kid. I was almost thinkin' that perhaps you really did hit your head in that scuffle outside and the entire evening *weren't* an act, after all!'

'I never break character in public,' Lex replied. 'Never. So don't ever talk to me out there unless you're talking to Slow Sid. And thanks a lot for landing me with that character, by the way! Having to play your pet monkey all week was not what I had in mind!'

Of course, Lex was secretly rather pleased with the Slow Sid development, but there was no point in admitting as much to Jesse.

The cowboy merely shrugged and said, 'You'd have found yourself fighting a duel with scar face outside if I hadn't stepped in when I did.'

'Rubbish!' Lex retorted. 'I can look after myself. If you'd just given me another moment, I would have got myself out of it all right. Next time you decide to help me, don't!'

'Noted,' Jesse replied. 'Let me know how that works out for you. And, since you're so keen on staying in character, I guess I'll just have to take the bed whilst you take the hammock.'

'Help yourself to the bed, by all means,' Lex replied. 'It's probably riddled with lice. What do you people sleep in, anyway? And don't tell me you sleep in the nude.'

Jesse shrugged. 'Shirt and long johns, usually.'

'Good,' Lex said, pulling off his jacket. 'I'm going to go and do a bit of sleepwalking.'

'Knock yourself out,' Jesse replied. 'You won't find the sword.'

'That's another thing,' Lex said. 'You never told me you'd been here looking for the sword yourself.'

Jesse shrugged. 'You never asked, kid.'

'Huh. Well, sit back and watch me succeed where you failed. It should be an enlightening experience for you.'

Lex stripped down to his shirt and long johns. Barefoot and with his hair messed up a bit, he could instantly pull the sleepwalking card if need be. Or else he could simply say he was looking for the bathroom. Thus attired, Lex left Jesse snoring in the bedroom (the big dolt was asleep as soon as his head touched the pillow) and set off to explore Dry Gulch House.

An hour later, Lex had still not seen everything there was to see. The house was enormous. More of a castle than a house, really. And the problem was that it had no logical structure. It was like a maze. Certain parts of the house were therefore easy to miss. Even parts that you *had* seen would not be easy to get back to once you'd left them behind.

It was clear that the most used parts of the house were the bar downstairs and the bedrooms. Other than that, it seemed like most of the cowboys didn't wander into the other areas. After all, people had been searching for the Sword of Life for over a hundred years, now, and had never found it. Most people thought that it couldn't be found at all or that it was a myth and had never existed to begin with. It was easy to see how a person could get lost for hours – maybe even days – inside the house. It was almost as if it had been built to confuse and disorient. Some rooms were completely dust free, whilst others were coated in a layer of the stuff several inches thick.

The thing that jumped out about the house straight-away – other than how utterly bizarre it was – was the fox motif that was everywhere. Practically every single room had at least one fox in it somewhere. Sometimes it was easy to spot – a large wooden statue in the centre of the room, for example. Other times, you had to look more closely. The fox might be a tiny model glued to the skirting board, or it might be carved into a leg of a table, or appear just once somewhere on the wallpaper. Sometimes there was just a fox's head, in others there was a complete fox. And he was always wearing a waistcoat. Lex thought back to the painting in the entrance hall of Nathaniel having tea with a giant fox and supposed it must be the same one.

A second thing jumped out at him and that was the prevalence of the number thirteen within the house. Chandeliers had thirteen arms; wallpaper flowers had thirteen petals; tables were set with thirteen chairs; and unused fireplaces were stacked with thirteen logs. The number thirteen bothered Lex more than the fox did. Everyone knew that thirteen was a magical number. Everyone knew that Nathaniel had been friends with a witch who had cast a sticking spell over the contents of the house for him. Lex knew as well as anyone that magic could be tricky, and that it could be dangerous, and so the thirteens everywhere made him proceed even more cautiously than before.

At one point, he passed through a huge library with shelves upon shelves of books. There was even a ladder to reach the ones all the way up at the top. These books couldn't possibly compare to the thrill of the library tree, of course, but Lex was quite excited by the sheer number, just the same – until he realised that they were all identical. The library housed one volume and one volume only – *The Life And Times Of Nathaniel East*, by Nathaniel East.

Lex pulled a face in disgust. All this shelf space, wasted on just one book. He reminded himself that Nathaniel East was Jeremiah's great-great uncle. It therefore should have come as no surprise that the man's house was full of portraits of, and books about, himself. Vanity clearly ran in the family.

Lex pulled one of the books off the nearest shelf and flicked through it. It was a slim volume that seemed to be a rambling account of the dreamworld Nathaniel had clearly lived in. Lex recognised two of the chapter headings from the paintings in the entrance hall. In those chapters, Nathaniel told of how he had, several times, taken tea with a giant fox named Plantagenet. Apparently, they would sit and chat for hours over the cucumber sandwiches and sugar tongs. It seemed that the fox had many fascinating stories to tell and those afternoons were, Nathaniel wrote, some of the most pleasant he'd ever spent. In the other chapter, he blithely told of how he had once defeated a great white dragon wielding nothing more than a smoked trout.

'Smoked trout!' Lex muttered derisively. 'It ought to have been a swordfish, at the very least!'

He took the book with him. There really wasn't much point in trying to pinch it when the sticking spell over the house would not allow anything to be removed from its walls, but he could at least take it back to his bedroom and have a flick through it later.

He continued on through the house. He was attempting to draw a rough map as he went but – as other architects had found before him – it was almost impossible to capture Dry Gulch House on paper. The rooms ranged from the almost ordinary, to the astonishingly impractical, to the outrageously bizarre. Lex walked through one room with a lofty ceiling from which hung thirty or so open umbrellas. Glass bubbles were set into the wall and twenty or so bath-tubs, overflowing with rubber ducks, stood below.

In another room, Lex found a sort of chapel with three stained glass windows, on which were written obscure poems. The first read:

> *I, Nathaniel East, here doth claim,*
> *That all who try to slur my mortal name,*
> *Will fail and fail, again, again,*
> *For I have not hidden it in vain.*

The second read:

> *Time will tell, as time does well,*
> *What will change, what stays the same,*
> *Who will triumph, who will fall,*
> *For I have seen it all before.*

And, finally, the third:

> *Plantagenet shall guard the sword in a fond embrace,*
> *Until the cowboy king shall take it from its rightful place.*
> *For noble cause in a heroic race.*
> *Much danger, peril, death, all else do risk,*
> *If they wouldst try and take it with the kitchen whisk.*

Lex had heard of the windows before. Most people thought they were a riddle, telling where the sword was hidden. Lex accepted it looked that way but, after all, Nathaniel East had only hidden the sword once he realised his house was being ambushed by a gang of outlaws. If these windows had been put in when the house was originally being built, then he couldn't possibly have known that was going to happen. Some sources suggested that Nathaniel East had believed he could see the future. But, just because the nut believed it, it didn't mean it was true.

Even so, there was no denying that the poems on the window certainly seemed to point towards the hiding place of the sword. Lex wrote the verses down in his notebook next to the map he was sketching. There had been various different interpretations of the riddle. The obvious one for the 'cowboy king' was a cowboy who was tougher, meaner and stronger than all the rest, which didn't hold well for Lex if Nathaniel's prediction was true since he was, in fact, a completely fake cowboy. Underneath the act, he was no more a real cowboy than he was a duck-billed platypus.

But he noted the riddle down, anyway. He already knew who Plantagenet was, for the book had stated that this was the name of the giant fox. Unfortunately, knowing this did not help Lex much, for the simple fact that the fox motif was literally *everywhere* in the house. Finding the right fox did not narrow down potential hiding places by much, if at all.

Lex opened the book again, hoping for more information that might furnish some further clue. He skimmed through the relevant section and learnt that Nathaniel had believed this Plantagenet to be what he called a 'dream-fox'. Lex rolled his eyes, for doubtless this meant that Nathaniel had only ever seen Plantagenet when he'd been asleep, and yet the mad old fool hadn't had the sense to realise that this meant the giant fox wasn't real at all, but merely a product of his own loopy mind. In addition, Nathaniel noted how Plantagenet always came to see him at the same time: thirteen o'clock. Lex narrowed his eyes at this. Thirteen o'clock – the witching hour. If there ever *were* such a thing as a dream-fox, then thirteen o'clock would be the time it would come. It certainly explained why the number thirteen appeared so often within the house. Could it actually be that a giant fox really *had*—

Lex shook his head, impatient with himself. If he didn't watch out, he'd end up as nutty as Nathaniel. He'd never heard of a dream-fox before – never in all the books he'd read. And Lex was *very* well read.

He went on, past staircases that led up into ceilings and windows set into the floor. At one point, the entire floor was made out of glass. It looked directly down on to the umbrella room. Lex could tell because he could see the umbrellas – all of different colours – opened out beneath his feet.

He spent a few minutes in the entrance hall examining the paintings there. He noted that the one with Nathaniel having tea with a giant fox was entitled, *Taking Tea With Plantagenet*. Not only that, but the fox appeared in several other paintings, too, usually in the background and sometimes partially obscured. One painting of Nathaniel showed him serenely strolling, stick in hand, through a battlefield. An *ancient* battlefield from the looks of things because the warriors all seemed to be half naked, and wielding bows and arrows. Indeed, even Nathaniel's top hat had an arrow sticking through it. And there, at the bottom right-hand corner of the painting, was a fox's tail, only just visible.

In another painting, Nathaniel stood, balancing on one leg, in a river, surrounded by pink flamingos. He had his umbrella up, despite the fact that it wasn't raining. And on the nearby bank, peering through a bush, was what looked suspiciously like a giant fox in a waistcoat.

Lex spotted the fox in a few more paintings but it was always partially hidden or obscure. The teatime one was the only one that showed him clearly. Clear enough to see that he couldn't possibly be real.

Lex moved on to the fourth floor. At one point, he opened a door and almost went through it before realising – just in time – that there was no floor beyond – just a sheer drop to the courtyard below. Later on, he came across a sort of games room that might have been fun were it not for the fact that all the balls on the snooker table, and all the chessmen on the chess table, were nailed firmly in place.

He did not come across another person during his explorations. The cowboys staying in the house were all either asleep or still down in the bar. But, in actual fact, Lex could have easily got away with wandering about the house, even as Sid the Kid, for it was just so easy to get lost, which was probably why the other cowboys stuck to the bar and the bedrooms rather than attempting to navigate the rest of this madhouse.

As Lex went on, he began to feel a little disheartened, for the house was just so *big*. It had taken years to build and it would take years to search. Jesse had been here on four separate occasions looking for the sword and had no luck. Hundreds had attempted the task before him but with no success. Lex had only four days before the third round began. Four days to do what everyone before him had failed to do.

He had an excellent sense of direction but, when he

started trying to make his way back to his bedroom, he found it extremely difficult, even with the map he'd drawn. The problem was that most of the rooms had doors leading to several other rooms. It was not simply a case of one room following on from another in a logical order.

At one point, he came across a room that was full of doors. There was a grand total of twenty, set around the walls. Lex opened every single one of them, sure that many must lead to the same room. One door led nowhere: when Lex opened it, there was just a brick wall behind it. And another led to a room so small there was no way any human would ever be able to get into it. But the other eighteen doors all led to different rooms. How was that even possible? Surely there should not be enough space for them all. Granted, they were all narrow rooms but even so . . .

Lex felt a mounting sense of frustration. The house was too big and there was no logic to it. He could be the cleverest person in the world and still be unable to crack the riddle on the stained-glass windows. Trying to unravel the messed-up mind of a madman was like trying to untangle a never-ending ball of string.

Still, there was nothing for it but to forge on. Lex spent most of that night exploring the house. In fact, due to the fact that he got hopelessly lost, he was later back to his room than he'd intended, and only fell into his hammock a bare hour before the sun began to rise.

CHAPTER TWENTY

THE BLACK SWANN AND THE SECRET TEA PARLOUR

The next two days were a tiresome, irksome business for Lex. His time was split between playing Jesse's pet monkey for the entertainment of the other cowboys down in the bar, and searching for the sword at night. It was worse than looking for a needle in a haystack. If Lex had had a proper riddle to work with, he would have cracked it already by now, but all he had to go on was a madman's drivel that might not even hold the answer at all.

Something unexpected happened on the second morning, though: Jeremiah came to Dry Gulch House. Lex was in the bar when he arrived. Jeremiah came on his own, by carriage – the fool. He must have brought the carriage with him on board his ship, for it had the East coat of arms emblazoned in gold on the door. No doubt he had travelled across the desert in it when he reached the Western shore and was forced to leave his ship behind.

Lex was sitting by the window eating a tin of beans when Jeremiah arrived. Someone had given him a spoon but, for the look of the thing, he felt compelled to spill most of them down the front of his shirt, anyway.

No one actually noticed Jeremiah until he walked into the bar. When he came in, dressed in his fancy royal-blue coat with the golden buttons, hair brushed, jaw shaved and generally looking as clean cut as a man can be without being a woman, he couldn't have stuck out any more than he did. Everyone went quiet, staring at him in amazement. Everyone knew that only cowboys were allowed into Dry Gulch House, now. Peasants weren't allowed, farmers weren't allowed and noblemen *definitely* were not allowed.

'I am Jeremiah East,' he announced to the room. His booted feet were planted firmly apart on the floor like he owned the place. It was clear that he was pleased with the fact that everyone had gone silent at his appearance. He had no idea that this was just the calm before the storm. 'This house was the rightful property of my great-great-uncle, Nathaniel East. It was unlawfully taken from him a hundred years ago by savages. I have consulted a lawyer who has assured me that, despite the time that has elapsed, no deed of ownership was ever passed. This house is therefore still the property of the East family. You are all trespassing. I will give you one hour to vacate the premises. I expect you all to provide me with contact details so that later we can negotiate reparations for the vandalism done to the house. If you carry out my instructions to the letter then I will agree to waive my lawful right to collect rent for the period during which this house has been illegally occupied.'

Lex goggled at him. He'd known Jeremiah could be stupid, but he hadn't realised just *how* stupid. As an ex-law-student, Lex knew that everything Jeremiah had said was, technically, true. But things like that just didn't *matter* out here. Not here in the Wild West where disputes were decided by duels and the sheriff was just someone to throw stuff at on a slow-moving day.

The scar-faced cowboy Lex had crossed earlier was the first to react. He stood up from the table where he'd been drinking and told Jeremiah – with rather a lot of unnecessary swearing – to get out. Jeremiah actually looked shocked and outraged by this. It was clear that he had expected his little speech to work flawlessly.

'The law is on my side,' he said, going quite pale with anger. 'I have the documentation with me, if you'd like to examine it. It's quite bad enough that my poor uncle was slaughtered right here in his own home by a gang of savages like you, without having his house overrun by them as well! You ought to be ashamed of yourselves! You're a corrupt, contemptible lot of cowards and I want you out of my family's house *right now*.'

Calling them cowards was going just that little bit too far. These were men who produced far too much testosterone as it was, and prided themselves on being tough and manly and other such meaningless things. Yet there Jeremiah stood, looking rather smug and clearly thinking that he had just put everyone in their place, when, actually, the most likely reaction now was for one of the cowboys to stand up and shoot him straight in the chest.

'Y'know I'm getting the sort of feeling that history is about to repeat itself,' the scar-faced cowboy said. 'First the uncle, then the nephew. We'll put your head up in the trophy room, kid.'

'You wouldn't dare touch me!' Jeremiah sneered.

Lex could have groaned aloud. He believed it! The idiot *actually* believed he wouldn't be harmed here, when the fact was that he was seconds away from either being shot, or dragged outside to be strung up from the nearest tree. Lex had to wonder how the nobleman had even managed to survive into adulthood. He shook his head in despair (but only on the inside). The parents were to blame, really. This was what a posh school and too many private fencing classes could do to a person. But Jeremiah getting himself killed was the last thing Lex wanted. After all, he didn't want to win the Game by default. Where would be the fun in that? He wanted to win gloriously. And that would be difficult to do with both Lorella and Jeremiah dead, and no one but Tess and a little sprite left to compete against. It would be like being the only adult on a toddlers' wrestling team: you'd win all right, but there would be no glory in it. No, this wouldn't do at all. Lex was just going to have to save the nobleman from himself. Again.

Before anyone else could do anything, Lex quickly scooped up a spoonful of beans from his tin, drew the spoon back, took careful aim and flicked them right at Jeremiah's face. Lex was sitting only a few tables away and his aim was good. The beans splattered right across Jeremiah's right cheek.

'Boring man,' Lex announced blithely to the room in general. 'Boring speech. But nice coat.'

The other cowboys erupted into cheers and laughter at the same moment that Jeremiah roared in outrage. The nobleman's head whipped around, looking for his assailant. Lex could have lowered his head and hidden his face under his hat, but he didn't. Their eyes met and it was worth the risk to see the expression of utter amazement and fury on Jeremiah's face at the sight of Lex sitting there in Dry Gulch House, calmly eating a tin of beans – or calmly dribbling a tin of beans, as the case may be. Disciplined as he was, it was too much for Lex and he broke one of his own rules then by breaking character just long enough to wink at Jeremiah. Then he instantly slipped back into Slow Sid and continued to eat his beans, staring vacantly out the window as if he'd already forgotten Jeremiah was even there.

'Oh my Gods, that's Lex—' Jeremiah started to shout above the din, but was instantly cut off by a crust of bread hitting him on the nose. A moment later, he was being positively pelted with food. Everything and anything edible within easy reach was hurled at Jeremiah. It was mostly beans. Soon they covered his coat and his skin and his hair. It would have been glorious fun to watch but Lex forced himself to calmly finish his lunch whilst gazing blankly out of the window because that was, after all, what Slow Sid would have done.

Jeremiah tried to throw a punch at one point but the danger had passed by then. The cowboys were in too good a mood to think about killing him now. A lot of blood all over the place would completely ruin the atmosphere. So he was unceremoniously hurled out of the front door instead where he landed on his back in the dust by the front steps.

Lex hoped he would just get back in his carriage and drive away but instead Jeremiah stood up and, still bellowing in anger, actually started coming back towards the house – like someone just *begging* to be hanged by his neck until he was dead. The cowboys had clearly had enough of the game by then, for one of them fired a shot. It was not intended to kill but, still, the sound seemed to tear through the air as the bullet bit the ground between Jeremiah's feet. The nobleman stumbled back, white as a sheet. The sudden quiet from the rest of the cowboys indicated very clearly that the fun was most definitely over.

'If you don't want to be strung up from that tree right there,' the scar-faced cowboy said, pointing at the nearest one. 'Then get in your fancy carriage, drive away, and don't ever let us see your sorry face here ever again!'

Jeremiah – bean-stained and dusty – stared at the cowboy for a moment. Then his eyes swivelled round to the window where Lex was watching. All eyes were on Jeremiah and – as this was make-or-break point – Lex broke character a second time, just long enough to emphatically mouth the word, 'Go!'

To his relief, Jeremiah finally turned on his heel and stalked back towards his carriage with his head held high like there weren't really beans dribbling all the way down his back. Lex only breathed a sigh of relief once Jeremiah had climbed up into the driver's seat, grabbed up the reins and ridden away, back in the direction he'd come.

'He's really going to hate you now,' Jesse remarked in their lime-green bedroom the next morning.

Lex shrugged. 'He hated me anyway. Besides, this is all his fault. He started it by spiking my drink in the Wither City.'

'You really are one to hold a grudge, ain't you?' Jesse said.

'I never forget an insult,' Lex replied in a hard voice. 'A person might wrong me once but, by the Gods, they won't do it again!'

'Well, if you feel that strongly about having a bit of somethin' extra put in your drink in what was just a childish sorta prank, then think how Jeremiah must feel about having his uncle killed and a family mansion stolen away by a gang of ruffians like us.'

Lex was slightly startled by that, for he hadn't thought of it in that way before. But he had to admit Jesse had a point. If Dry Gulch House had once belonged to the Trents, Lex would have been every bit as outraged as Jeremiah – more so, probably – and utterly determined to get it back. Only he would have been cleverer about it. He would not have simply marched in, expecting self-righteousness and legal technicalities to carry him through. He would have made *sure* he succeeded. And he would never have waived his right to rent – never! He would not simply have got the house back from the cowboys, he would have had his revenge on them, too.

But he shrugged Jesse's comment off carelessly. 'The Easts have plenty of other family mansions. I'll bet they don't even miss this one. It's not like any of them would want to live here, especially after what happened to Nathaniel. Anyway, enough of all this talk about Jeremiah. I need to carry on looking for the sword.'

Although it was now morning, Lex had decided to continue his search straightaway, after snatching a few hours sleep, rather than waiting for nightfall again. It didn't matter much, anyway, since the other cowboys tended to spend all their time in the bar. There was, therefore, no reason why Lex shouldn't search during the day as well. Especially as he was fast running out of time.

'Ain't you tired of that, yet?' Jesse asked. 'I told you, that sword ain't real. You're lookin' for somethin' that don't even exist!'

Lex scowled. The truth was that, even if the sword *were* real, he was starting to think that he might be forced to concede defeat for the simple reason that he was going to run out of time. In a house this huge, it could be hidden in any number of places. After hours of exploring, there were still rooms he hadn't been into at all. Let alone the countless secret passageways he knew the house to contain but which he was yet to discover. It could take him a year or more to locate the sword.

And yet the thought of having to admit failure was a bitter pill to swallow for Lex. He had bragged to Jesse about finding the sword. The idea of having to admit that that had all been a lot of talk was intolerable. Jesse would gloat insufferably. He would rub it in and pour salt into the open wound. Lex knew he would do that because it was exactly what he would have done himself.

'The sword *is* here!' he snapped. 'Just because you were unable to find it doesn't mean that I won't. It's right here, somewhere in this house. I just wish I knew where that sword was. Then I could—aarghh!'

He broke off with a cry of pain as something very hot suddenly started to burn through his trouser pocket. He reached his hand in, grabbed the velvet pouch and flung it on to the bed. It was practically smoking. Gingerly, he picked the pouch up between thumb and forefinger to tip the contents out on to the bed. The Wishing Creatures of Desareth tumbled out together. The white and red Swanns and the blue Dragon lay there as usual. But the black Swann was steaming hot. In fact, as Jesse and Lex watched, it even started to char the sheet.

The black Swann – the one whose wish was recorded as 'unknown' in Erasmus Grey's book. And Lex had just said aloud that he wished he knew where the sword was hidden. Now the Swann was burning hot to the touch. When Lex had been very little, he had played a game with his brother, which involved one of them hiding an object for the other to find. The seeker would move around the room whilst the hider said they were getting hotter the nearer they got to the hidden object, and colder the further away they went from it.

Could it be . . . Could it really be that the black Swann's wish was not to turn pumpkin pies into poo, as Lex had feared, but to locate missing objects instead? Could it be that just one of his Wishing Creatures could actually do something *useful*?

'What are those things?' Jesse said, peering down at the stone animals on the bed.

Lex ignored him and used a corner of the sheet to pick the black Swann up gingerly. 'I wish I knew where my brother, Lucius, was,' he said, loudly and clearly.

The Swann did not go instantly cold as he had expected, but remained hot instead. Lex frowned at it for a moment before the idea occurred to him that perhaps the Swann could not locate more than one missing object at once. Perhaps it would not 'reset' itself, so to speak, until Lex had found the sword.

He picked up the other Wishing Creatures and thrust them into his pocket before looking around for something with which to pick up the Swann. He couldn't carry it in his bare hands for any great length of time without it burning his skin. He could try using a piece of the sheet but he feared the Swann would burn right through that, too.

'Here,' Jesse said, crossing over to the fireplace and picking up the cast-iron tongs. 'Use these.'

Lex took the tongs and used them to pick up the black Swann. It left behind a big circle of black on the sheet. Hopefully no one would notice. They hadn't exactly been white to begin with. And they were already riddled with burn marks where cowboys had clearly fallen asleep with lit cigarettes in their hands.

'So,' Jesse said, staring suspiciously at the Swann. 'D'you mind tellin' me just exactly what it is you've got there?'

'Yeah, I do mind. Don't be so nosy.'

It was no use, though. Jesse, despite appearances, wasn't stupid. He'd heard Lex say that he wished he knew where the sword was right before the Swann started to burn through his pocket. He'd seen Lex's reaction – known that little cogs were turning in the thief's brain. He knew that Lex suspected the Swann might lead them to the sword, somehow. And with something magical hopefully guiding the way, there was no chance that Jesse wasn't coming, too.

Lex was not best pleased. After all, he knew that the cowboy wanted the sword and that he'd been to Dry Gulch House on more than one occasion to search for it. But there was nothing he could do to stop Jesse from coming. Resolving to keep a very sharp eye on the cowboy, Lex stepped out into the corridor. First they went upstairs, and the Swann cooled enough that Lex was able to hold it with his bare hands. So they went downstairs, and the Swann got even hotter than it had done in the bedroom. It was a little difficult to follow, for the Swann was so hot that a shift in temperature was only noticeable if it was a larger one. Lex was a little worried that other cowboys might see them wandering around and think them a strange sight, what with the glowing-hot Swann Lex was carefully carrying in the tongs – although it was, perhaps, the sort of odd thing Slow Sid might do for no apparent reason. At any rate, no one appeared beyond the recesses of the bar.

Eventually, by a patient process of trial and error and after several false starts, they finally found themselves back in the library. And there the Swann started to smoke. The smoke stopped if they moved into any of the other rooms leading off from the library, but started again the instant they went back.

'So it's in here somewhere then, right?' Jesse said. Lex did not like the eager way he'd said it.

'That, or there's a secret room here somewhere,' Lex replied.

Lex suspected the latter. A library was, after all, a classic place in which to conceal a secret room. The problem, though, was that, as far as Lex knew, secret doors were usually opened in libraries by pulling out the right book, or combination of books. It was a little hard to work out which ones to move when every single volume here was exactly the same.

Whilst Jesse wandered around tapping on walls like a fool, Lex stood and looked at the bookcases. There were thirteen of them in total. They were tall, heavy, wooden things – identical but for the fact that the thirteenth one over in the corner had some sort of wooden carving

perched on top. It was so small that it was barely noticeable, and Lex couldn't even tell what it was from the
floor. He strongly suspected, but went up the ladder,
anyway, to check. The little carving was, as he had thought,
a fox. Sitting on its haunches and complete with little
waistcoat, it calmly surveyed the library below.

Plantagenet shall guard the sword in a fond embrace . . .

Lex fiddled about with it a bit but it didn't seem possible
to move it in any way.

'What have you found up there?' Jesse called from
below.

Lex ignored him. Each bookcase had twenty-six shelves.
Lex went down the ladder until he was at the thirteenth.
Then he counted along until he was at the thirteenth
book. To all outward appearances, it was exactly the same
as all the rest – but it was the thirteenth book on the thirteenth shelf of the thirteenth bookcase, being watched
over by a little wooden Plantagenet . . .

Lex pulled the book out. At first, absolutely nothing
happened. He was just about to sulk because his idea
hadn't worked when, suddenly, with a creak and a groan,
the entire bookcase began to swing forwards. Lex shot
down the ladder before he could get squashed and stared
in delight at the now-revealed doorway that had previously been hidden behind the bookcase. He snatched up
the tongs and the black Swann and rushed straight into
the secret room before Jesse.

The light coming in from the library illuminated the
place enough for them to see what it was, despite the fact

that it was covered in a three-inch coating of dust and a thick matting of spider webs. It was a parlour. A tea parlour, from the looks of things. Decorated in what had once, possibly, been pink and cream, it was a smallish room, with one table in the centre. A huge glass chandelier hung from the ceiling, adorned with pink and blue glass flowers. Despite the coating of dust, it was clear how beautiful it had once been.

The table was covered with a tablecloth and several lace doilies, still laid out with tea for two. There was an exquisite silver teapot along with a matching milk jug and sugar bowl. Two delicate bone-china cups and saucers were set before the two chairs facing each other on opposite sides of the table. And in the middle was a plate set with miniature cakes that the years had turned rock hard. Apart from the dust, it was almost like the table had been set yesterday. As if Nathaniel East was going to stroll into the room at any moment to take tea with his imaginary fox.

And there, hung above the fireplace, was the sword. It was everything Lex had expected it to be – large, bejewelled and magnificent – one blade blue, the other red. Unlike a normal sword, this one's handle was not at the end, but in the middle, with the two blades stretching out from it in opposite directions. Lex and Jesse spotted it at the same time and moved forwards as one.

But, as soon as Lex took his first step, the black Swann became so hot that it burst – quite literally – into flames. Lex almost jumped out of his skin, and instinctively whipped back his arm. The flaming Swann flew out of the tongs and went up towards the ceiling where it smashed into the chandelier. Dust and dead bugs rained down on Lex as the Swann fell back down to the carpet. When it landed, it was smoking but no longer on fire. Lex looked up and met Jesse's gaze.

'Well, now,' the cowboy said with a grin. 'Weren't that a lucky thing that you weren't holdin' it just then? It woulda taken your hand off.'

'Yeah, well,' Lex said, dusting dead bugs off his clothes and trying to sound casual. 'I'm always lucky.'

Unfortunately for Lex, he spoke just a little bit too soon on that occasion. The sentence was barely out of his mouth before there was a creaking and a groaning from overhead. The next moment, the cord holding the chandelier snapped. Doubtless, it was a combination of age and being hit with a flaming Swann but, suddenly, the chandelier was falling down right to the spot where Lex stood.

He dived for cover. And almost got out of the way in time. Almost. But not quite. One twisted glass arm struck him across the side of his head, the glass shattering with the force of the blow. The rest of the chandelier smashed directly on top of the tea table, raising a great cloud of dust and causing the table to collapse beneath it.

Lex reeled away from it all, his head whirling. He sneezed once from all the dust. Then blood started running into his right eye from the gash on his head. He was vaguely aware that this was not one of those 'get back up and brush yourself off' sort of injuries – which infuriated him seeing as he had finally, *finally*, managed to find the sword. It was *right there* and all he had to do was reach out and *take* it . . .

But it was no good. There was nothing Lex could do to prevent the wrecked parlour fading from his vision as everything went silent and black, and he crumpled to the floor in a dusty, bleeding heap.

CHAPTER TWENTY-ONE

Lumpy bumpy cake and two smoked trout

When Lex woke up, the room was different. There was no dust for a start. No cobwebs, either. The panelled walls were splendid in pink and cream; the glass chandelier was resplendent and unbroken, garlanded with dozens of perfect, translucent flowers that speckled the entire room with pink and blue light. The Sword of Life hung above the white marble fireplace looking all the more impressive for the fact that it was no longer covered in the dust and grime of a hundred years.

The table in the centre was also restored. The white cloth and lace doilies were spotless and the silver tea service gleamed. Set daintily on a round plate in the middle were some of the prettiest cakes that Lex had ever seen.

But the thing that *really* caught Lex's attention was that there was a giant fox, dressed in a smart waistcoat, sitting in one of the chairs at the table – cup and saucer in hand, drinking tea and watching Lex with intelligent brown eyes.

'Good day to you,' the fox said cheerfully when he saw Lex looking at him. He had a warm, mellow voice, and spoke with a refined accent. 'So kind of you to join me for tea. My name is Plantagenet. Do draw up a chair.'

Staring like his eyes were about to pop out of his head, Lex slowly got to his feet. Only then did he realise that he was no longer the same himself. He'd been wearing cowboy clothes that were covered in dust and blood before. Now he seemed to be wearing the clothes of a gentleman – dark trousers and a waistcoat, not unlike the one the fox was wearing. He could also feel how neatly brushed his hair was.

'What is this?' he demanded.

Plantagenet looked at him. 'What is what, dear boy?'

'All this.' Lex waved his arm to encompass the room. 'The parlour going back to the way it was; these clothes; *you*! You're a giant, talking fox. You're not real!'

'Well, not in the strict sense of the word, perhaps,' the fox said, pouring tea out into the second cup. 'Do you take cream and sugar?'

'I don't want any tea!' Lex replied. 'I want to know what's going on!'

'Sit down and drink your tea and I'll tell you,' Plantagenet said mildly.

Still feeling unsure, Lex pulled up a chair and warily sat down across from the fox.

'That's better,' Plantagenet said, pushing the cup and saucer towards him. 'Help yourself to dessert, by all means. The lumpy bumpy cake is excellent.'

'I don't want any lumpy bumpy cake!' Lex snapped. 'This room was in ruins! Everything was broken! A chandelier fell on my head! Oh dear; I'm not dead, am I?'

The fox laughed. 'Gracious me, no! You'll be fine. You know who I am, of course?'

'You're the imaginary talking fox Nathaniel East thought he could see.'

'Yes, indeed.' Plantagenet sighed and said, 'Poor dear Nathaniel. A most amiable companion, he was. He could see the future, you know. He told me the cowboy king would come for the sword one day.'

'And that's me, is it?' Lex said, feeling faintly surprised. It did, after all, seem unlikely that Slow Sid could really be anyone's idea of a cowboy king.

'You're masquerading as a cowboy, aren't you?' Plantagenet said.

'Yeah.'

'And are you not also a king?'

'What?'

'King Lex Trent I?'

Lex thought back to his crowning during the course of the first Game. The royalty had been temporary, and Lex had only been a king for a few seconds, but his name was inscribed on the Royal Monument back in the Wither City.

'Er . . . sort of,' he said.

'There you are, then,' Plantagenet said happily. 'You're the cowboy king, come for the sword as Nathaniel foretold that you would. You'll have to catch up with it, though, I'm afraid – the sticking spell doesn't apply to the sword, you see. Listen.' The fox put down his teacup and leaned forwards across the table slightly, his voice taking a more serious tone as he went on. 'Here's a word of advice for you. Take a smoked trout along on the next round of the Game. It saved Nathaniel's life once, and it'll save yours, too. Best make it a pair of trout, just to be on the safe side. Don't forget, now. Good luck. And maybe I'll see you again one day.'

And, with that, Plantagenet vanished. And so did everything else.

Lex opened his eyes to a lot of dust and pain. *Now* he was in the right place. Coughing and spluttering, he propped himself up on his elbows and opened his left eye. Then he rubbed the dried blood from his right eye so that it was no longer glued shut. The first thing he noticed was that the Sword of Life was gone. So was the black Swann. And so was Jesse.

'That bastard,' Lex said thickly. 'That *bastard*! I'll get him for this!'

He staggered to his feet, his head throbbing savagely. He had no idea how long he'd been there, or how long Jesse had been gone. He was going to have to find out, and quickly, too.

But first things first. Lex needed to get a smoked trout. That was what Plantagenet had said. He was the talking fox after all, so he ought to know. To Lex's slightly muddled mind, getting the trout seemed like the task with top priority. So he left the wrecked tea parlour and zigzagged his way round to the kitchen. It wasn't much of a kitchen to speak of, really. After all, they mostly just served tins of beans. But there had been fish for breakfast a couple of times. Lex must have been quite an odd sight, bursting into the kitchen, covered in dust, with a bleeding head and screaming for trout.

'Want a glass of milk, Sid?' the barman said with a smirk. 'Calm you down a treat.'

'Listen, Mack,' Lex snapped, grabbing fistfuls of the barman's collar in both hands. 'I ain't Slow Sid anymore, see? One more blow to the head and I'm back to my old self. This is Sid the Kid you're dealing with now. And if I hear just one more crack about milk then you'll be using your hat to pick up your teeth. Got it?'

It was all hot air, of course – after all, Lex was half the size of the barman. But the man shrank back, anyway. Doubtless it was the shock of it. Like a small, soppy dog turning suddenly vicious. Plus, the genuine anger in Lex's eyes, as well as the blood smeared down one side of his face and crusted in his hair, did make him look a little deranged.

'Smoked trout!' Lex barked. 'Give me two, right now!'

'All right, Sid,' the barman said, holding up both hands in a placating gesture. 'Whatever you want.'

He rummaged in the larder and, a moment later, produced two large smoked trout. Lex snatched them from him.

'Where,' he growled, 'is Jesse?'

'I dunno,' the barman replied.

Lex pushed past him impatiently and went to the bar to question the cowboys there. As soon as he entered the room, he grabbed his pistol from its holster, raised it above his head and shot a bullet right into the ceiling, causing plaster to shower down upon the floor. Everyone fell silent and turned to stare at him.

'Listen up,' Lex said in a hard voice. 'Slow Sid is gone for good. As soon as I find Jesse Layton I'm gonna string him up by his neck till he's dead. Five gold pieces to the first man to tell me where he is.'

'He rode out about an hour ago,' one cowboy piped up. 'In a right hurry, he was, too. He went due west.'

'Due west isn't a location!' Lex snarled. 'Can't anyone do better than that?'

The words were barely out of his mouth before Lex realised that he didn't actually need to know where Jesse was. He could find out at any time just by eating something. The Binding Bracelets would cause them to switch then, and Jesse wouldn't get his body back until the two ate together again.

Lex was just looking at the uncooked trout in his hand, and about to force himself to take a bite out of one of the raw fish, when a new cowboy entered the bar. The first words out of his mouth were, 'Hey, Sam, did you hear about poor old Jesse?'

'What about poor old Jesse?' Lex snapped, whirling round to face the newcomer.

'Captured,' the cowboy replied. 'Seems his old gang

heard he was here. I guess someone recognised him from the reward posters. They're gonna hang him at noon, so they say.'

All thoughts of swapping places with Jesse disappeared instantly from Lex's mind.

'Say, and there's another thing,' the cowboy said. 'There's some posh fella walkin' round the town telling everyone that there's an impostor here at Dry Gulch House. He's even giving out posters, look. Says it's really some city kid called Lex Trent.'

As he spoke, the cowboy took a crumpled poster out of his pocket and straightened it out so that the whole room could see it. It was a promotional poster from the stadiums showing a large image of Lex's head. The cowboys stared at the poster for a moment. Then, slowly, all eyes turned towards Lex.

'Is this true?' one of the cowboys said in a dangerous voice, stepping forwards to loom over Lex in a distinctly threatening way.

Under normal circumstances, Lex would have been able to get himself out of that mess. He would have thought of *something* to prove to everyone there that he really was a cowboy and that Jeremiah was just out to make trouble. But, because his head was still a little muddled, all he seemed to be able to think about was the smoked trout still hanging from his hand. So when the question, *what would Sid the Kid do in this situation?* rose up in his mind, all Lex could think was, *The fish! Slap him with one of the fish!*

So he did.

There may have been a number of ways of proving himself to be a cowboy. Slapping another cowboy in the face with a smoked trout was not one of them. There was a bellow of anger from the struck cowboy and suddenly everyone in the bar was lunging for Lex. But his natural instincts kicked in then and he ducked past them all and fled out to the stables, leapt on to Sally's back and dug his heels in.

As he galloped past the entrance to Dry Gulch House in a cloud of dust, several cowboys aimed shots after him. Fortunately, they all missed – possibly because he was moving too fast – and Lex was very glad, in that moment, that he had learnt how to gallop, after all.

He only slowed down once he was a considerable distance away from the house. Then he took a moment to collect himself and think about what he was going to do. Jesse had gone, taking Lex's sword and Swann with him. The cowboy must have known that he couldn't hold on to them for long because Lex was bound to use the Binding Bracelets to swap them. His intention, therefore, must have been either to ride into town and sell the items, or else hide them somewhere until the Game was over and the Binding Bracelets were off . . .

Lex glanced down at the Binding Bracelet on his wrist and suddenly felt quite cold with horror. Jesse could switch them! If he was able to talk his captors into giving him some food – a last meal, so to speak – then he could swap the two of them and Lex would find himself in Jesse's place! Lex might not have thought the cowboy capable of that at one point, but Jesse had shown his true colours today – leaving Lex behind with his head practically bashed in and taking the sword with him. Lex wasn't at all sure that Jesse wouldn't swap them, if he got the chance. He therefore had to make sure he found him first. The outlaw at Dry Gulch House had said he thought Jesse was to be hanged at noon. Lex would have to hope that information was correct. Hopefully, that would give him enough time to find the dratted cowboy first.

But, even once he'd found Jesse, Lex would need a plan. He could not simply go riding in – a lone kid on a horse. He'd just get strung up by his neck, too. Lex pinched the bridge of his nose and tried to think. He was alone in the middle of a deserted dusty path with no idea where Jesse was or how to go about finding him. His head hurt, his throat was dry and Heetha's sun was beating down savagely already, making him thirsty, sweaty and rather drowsy. He felt that, if he could just lie down in a cool patch of shade and sleep for a few minutes, his head would be much clearer when he woke up. But that wouldn't do. Not at all. He had some vague notion that people who had recently hit their heads should not go to sleep in case of concussion but, quite aside from that, he might at any moment find himself in Jesse's body with a noose around his neck.

Struggling with muddled thoughts was an unpleasant, unfamiliar experience for Lex. But, suddenly, a plan came to him. He could only hope that it was a good one. Not like the fish-slapping plan, which hadn't worked out at all. He dug in his heels and Sally set off down the path at a canter.

It took about twenty minutes to reach the town. When Lex got there, he went straight to the undertaker's. He could tell it was the undertaker's because of all the cheap wooden coffins on display in the window. And there, parked right outside, was what Lex was looking for – a hearse. Or, at least, a long, flat wagon with a coffin on the back.

'Good,' he muttered to himself.

After surreptitiously checking to make sure that the coffin was not an empty one, Lex then proceeded to corner passing farmers and ask them where the cowboys went for hangings. He was sure they would know. After all, they would need to have some idea of where the place was, if only to stay away from it. Sure enough, he soon had a set of rough directions. People seemed eager to tell him, just to get rid of him. He certainly cut an alarming sight, what with the dried blood, and the sweat making streaks in the dust down his face, and the – by now rather worse-for-wear – smoked trout still dangling from one of his hands.

According to the townspeople, it was about a half-hour journey on horseback. With that information, Lex had everything he needed to carry out his plan. All he had to do now, was steal the hearse. The problem was that it was not hitched up to a horse. If it had been, then Lex would have simply leapt on to the wagon and driven away before anyone could stop him. But he was going to have to hitch Sally to the wagon, which could be a problem seeing as the undertakers had large glass windows, and he would surely be spotted within moments.

Lex was standing there trying to work out how he was going to do it when he suddenly heard a loud, irritatingly familiar voice.

'Impostor at Dry Gulch House! Please take these posters and pass them on to any cowboys you see! Impostor! Lex Trent is really a trickster, posing as a cowboy!'

Lex rolled his eyes. Whilst walking around the town he had spotted hundreds of posters identical to the one he had seen in Dry Gulch House. They'd been stuck to almost every available surface. If you didn't know any better, one might think that the people of Dry Gulch were Lex's most avid, enthusiastic fans. Goodness only knew where Jeremiah had got so many posters. Presumably, Kala had somehow provided him with them. Well, Lex might have had his cover blown – partly by Jeremiah and partly by his own pathetic response to the poster – but he was damned if he was going to stand there listening to Jeremiah's self-righteous spiel as well.

He marched up to the nobleman – now dressed in a bean-free blue coat and dark trousers – and tapped him, rather hard, on the shoulder. 'Give it a rest, can't you?' he snapped when Jeremiah turned around. 'Your stupid plan worked. I'm out of the house. Congratulations!'

To Lex's surprise, Jeremiah gaped at him with a horrified expression on his face. 'What . . . what happened to you?' he said, finally finding his tongue. 'Did . . . did the cowboys do that?'

For a moment, Lex had absolutely no idea what Jeremiah was talking about. Then he caught sight of his reflection in a nearby window and almost jumped in shock himself. The blood, dirt and sweat made him look really quite alarming, and the gash on his temple reminded him of how much his head hurt. Lex looked back at Jeremiah, all ready to snarl his defiance and tell the nobleman that he could keep his petty victory because the cowboys hadn't so much as laid a *finger* on him, and he had found the Sword of Life before they'd chucked him out, anyway . . .

But then he met Jeremiah's eyes and his plan changed direction abruptly. For Lex spotted it at once – that flicker of guilt. Guilt was one of Lex's favourite things. It was just so darn *useful*. A person burdened with a guilty conscience could be made to do almost *anything*. Jeremiah was trying to hide it – and it was only a flicker – but there was no doubt whatsoever that he seemed to be feeling a twinge of guilt, the lightweight.

'What did you think was going to happen?' Lex asked. 'That they would just give me a slap on the wrists and send me on my way?'

'No, I just . . . I thought that they'd throw you out like they did me, and—'

'I barely escaped with my *life*!' Lex snarled. 'Jesse wasn't so lucky. They've dragged him away to be hanged.'

'*What?*' Jeremiah fairly goggled at him.

Despite the danger and the heat and his aching head, Lex found himself thoroughly enjoying the moment. 'I understand why you hate me,' he said, taking the opportunity to rub salt into the wound, 'but I'm surprised you feel that way about Jesse. Whatever I might have done to you, he *did* save your sister's life. But I suppose you don't care about that. All you care about is how much you hate me. Well, congratulations. Now Jesse really *is* going to die because of you.'

'Now, look!' Jeremiah snapped, grabbing Lex's arm. 'Is any of this true or are you just lying through your teeth again? Why the heck would they hang Jesse just because *you* were posing as a cowboy?'

'Jesse helped me. He was an accomplice, so in their eyes he's just as guilty as I am. Worse, in fact, because he's one of them and so ought to know better.' Lex threw Jeremiah's hand off impatiently and said, 'Use your brain, if you have one! Do you really think I would bash my own head in for the sake of a scam?'

Jeremiah glared at him. 'I think there's nothing you wouldn't do for the sake of a scam! You're a blaggard and a rogue! You don't care about anyone but yourself and you're quite happy to lie shamelessly in people's faces to get what you want! I saw how you did it at the Majestic when you had everyone believing Jesse was really dead. Even *I* thought you were grieving! So forgive me if I don't fall for the same trick twice, but I know what an excellent actor you are and I'd bet money on the fact that the state you're in now is due to nothing more than careful planning, good make-up and fine acting.'

And with that, Jeremiah lunged out his hand and knocked the dried blood from Lex's temple, clearly expecting it to flake away to reveal ordinary skin beneath. Instead, he simply re-opened the gash and it started bleeding again.

Lex did not need to act this time. Jeremiah's clumsy fingers had made contact with the most sensitive part of his already-sore head. If his headache had been bad before, that touch almost seemed to split his head in two. He pushed Jeremiah away with one hand whilst jerking the other up to clamp over his temple, warm blood trickling through his fingers as he groaned in pain.

When he was able to see something other than stars again, he glared up at Jeremiah and said, 'Are you *completely* deranged? Did your mother drop you on your head one too many times as a baby? What the heck's the matter with you?'

'I'm sorry,' Jeremiah replied. 'I honestly thought you were putting on an act.'

'I'm not!'

'Well, obviously, I can see that now!' Jeremiah said, looking quite peeved. 'But you only have yourself to blame! When you walk around fibbing all the time about everything, you can't be surprised when people don't believe you on the odd occasion when you *are* telling the truth!'

'Whatever!' Lex replied sourly. 'If you'll excuse me, I

need to go and try to save Jesse from the mess you've landed him in. No doubt it'll be futile and we'll both end up dead, but I'm sure that'll please you no end.'

'Oh, don't be ridiculous!' Jeremiah said. 'Naturally, I'll help you rescue Jesse.'

'You'll what?' Lex frowned. He knew the nobleman felt guilty, but he hadn't realised he felt *that* guilty.

'This is your fault,' Jeremiah said firmly. 'Not mine. If you hadn't lied and cheated your way into Dry Gulch House then Jesse wouldn't be in the predicament he's in now. So don't think you've managed to guilt me into anything. But he did do Tess a great service back on the *Scurleyshoo Death* and I owe him for that. So I'll help you.'

Well, two rescuers were better than one. And, if anyone shot at them, Lex could always use Jeremiah as a human shield.

'What's your plan?' the nobleman asked.

'First we need to steal that hearse,' Lex said, pointing across the street to the undertaker's. 'Do you think you can distract them long enough for me to get Sally hitched to the wagon?'

CHAPTER TWENTY-TWO

The Hanging

Jeremiah was not overly happy about stealing the hearse, but he went along with it, anyway. Lex had had a lot of practice at hitching horses to wagons back at the farm he'd grown up on, and even knew how to adapt an ordinary saddle to the task. He was therefore able to do it extremely fast and the undertaker didn't suspect a thing until it was too late, distracted as he was by Jeremiah's posh voice and shiny buttons – for wealthy clients meant expensive coffins and thus a larger-than-usual ham to take home to the dinner table. Once Jeremiah saw that Lex was ready, he made his excuses, left the shop and leapt up on to the cart alongside the thief, who flicked the reins to get Sally moving forwards. She soon picked up quite a pace and – aside from a bit of shouting and name-calling from the under-taker – they made a clean getaway.

'You stink of fish,' Jeremiah said, once they were clear of the town. 'Why the heck are you carrying those trout around like that, anyway?'

'Er . . .' Lex looked down at the battered trout still in

his hand. He could hardly tell Jeremiah that he had them because a giant, talking fox had told him to get them. He'd sound nuts. He found it difficult to believe, now, that he had actually gone to the kitchens and demanded a pair of smoked trout. Clearly he hadn't been thinking straight. Really, it was a wonder he'd got out of that house alive.

'Never mind,' Lex said, stuffing the fish into his bag. 'It's not important.'

'So, what's the plan, exactly?' Jeremiah asked.

'Well, we'll ride in, pretending to be there for the body, obviously,' Lex replied.

'But the coffin's got the name *Clint Davis* written on it on a little brass plaque,' Jeremiah pointed out.

'Oh well; I'm sure they won't notice,' Lex said carelessly. 'And even if they do, I bet most of them can't read. Once we're there, maybe you can cause a diversion whilst I get Jesse.'

'*Me*? What am I supposed to do?'

'I don't know; use your imagination. Do a cartwheel or something.'

'But—'

'Let's just concentrate on getting there, all right?' Lex said. 'We'll worry about the rest later.'

Time had got away from Lex in the town. There was only an hour to go until noon. If Jesse was going to switch them, then he'd probably do it when the noose was actually around his neck and he was on the very verge of being hanged. He wouldn't want Lex to have time to talk his way out of it, after all.

Lex urged Sally to go faster along the dusty track, past the cactuses and tumbleweed, praying that the directions he'd been given were accurate. He could see the huge rock formations the farmers had mentioned and, after about twenty minutes, he slowed the cart down to go around one and was profoundly relieved, on turning the corner, to see a little gaggle of cowboys grouped around a tree, right where the farmers had said they would be.

They turned to glance at the advancing cart, which Lex forced himself to keep slow, so as not to arouse suspicion. The cowboys watched its approach warily. Lex counted six of them. And a mean looking bunch they were, too – big, brutish and clearly unfamiliar with the concept of regular bathing. Their horses were standing nearby, and Lex instantly spotted Rusty a little to one side.

And there – balancing with some difficulty on a wooden stake – was Jesse with a noose around his neck. The rope was just short enough and the noose was just tight enough to make the cowboy extremely uncomfortable. It was cutting into his neck and causing red welts to rise up on his skin. Really, Jesse was being half-hanged already. The area he had to stand on was extremely small – it was only because he had such a good sense of balance that he hadn't fallen off yet, especially seeing as his hands were tied behind his back. But he couldn't keep it up all day. And as soon as he fell off that stake, the rope would go taut and that would be that. He looked positively astonished at the sight of the approaching wagon but Lex couldn't work out whether that was because he was pleased to see them or dismayed.

'What is this?' one of the cowboys demanded as soon as the wagon ground to a halt. 'Why have you come here?'

'We've come for the body,' Lex replied blithely. 'Can't have it lying around stinking up the place. Not in this heat.'

The sun beat down upon them quite relentlessly. Lex wished he had his hat, but it had come off when the chandelier had fallen on him. Flies, drawn out by the heat, buzzed around his face and he had to keep swatting them away.

'Never bothered anyone before. Besides, you don't look like undertakers. Especially that one—' one of the cowboys began, gesturing towards Jeremiah and his expensive coat and posh haircut.

'Oh, come on!' Lex replied in an impatient voice. 'Obviously we're not undertakers! Don't be so daft! We stole this hearse. I have a personal vendetta against that man,' Lex said, pointing an emphatic finger at Jesse. 'He stole from me and then left me for dead.'

'Aw, come on, kid, it was only a little knock on the head, after all—' Jesse began in rather a strangled voice – the noose clearly making it painful for him to speak.

'Shut up!' Lex snapped. Turning back to the cowboys he said, 'I want the satisfaction of seeing that bastard hanged and then – if you don't object – I'd like the body. I'd be happy to pay you for it, of course.'

That caused a pleased smile to spread across their faces. 'Sure,' one said, 'we'll sell him to you. He'd only be wasted on the vultures, otherwise.'

Jeremiah leaned closer and hissed in Lex's ear, 'Just what sort of rescue *is* this?'

Lex nudged him hard in the ribs to shut him up.

'Look, fellas,' Jesse said hoarsely, starting to sound rather desperate. 'Ain't there some way we can work this out?'

'No, there ain't, you good-for-nothin' double-crosser! If you've got any final prayers, say 'em now, because your time in this world is done.'

'*Lex*—' Jeremiah tried once again.

'Sshh!'

'What's the matter with him?' one of the cowboys asked, staring at the nobleman.

'Him? Oh, he just . . . he just heard this rumour, that's all.'

'What rumour?'

Lex rolled his eyes and said, 'Some nonsense about that half-wit –' he pointed at Jesse – 'learning some sort of dark magic on a library tree during the Game that we've been playing.'

'Say, I heard he was in a Game,' one of the cowboys said. 'How about it, Jesse? Are you gonna curse us all a hundred times over before we hang ya?'

'I was with him the whole time on that tree,' Lex said firmly. 'Almost the whole time, anyway. He didn't see any magical secrets. And even if he did, he wouldn't have the sense to know how to use them. Hang him. Go on. Do it now. What are you waiting for? I want him dead!'

'Lex,' Jesse croaked. Lex turned his head to meet his

eye. There was a beseeching look in the cowboy's face that was almost painful. 'Please . . .'

With his face set like stone, Lex looked at Jesse and said coldly, 'I told you – more than once – that there would be consequences if you crossed me. Well, you crossed me. And now you're going to pay for it.'

'This is outrageous!' Jeremiah exclaimed standing up. 'I won't stand by and watch a man being killed in cold blood—'

He broke off as Lex gripped his wrist and yanked him back down. 'Close your eyes, then!' he snapped.

'Any last words, Jesse?' one of the cowboys grinned.

'When I say "go",' Lex whispered urgently in Jeremiah's ear, pressing the reins into his hand, 'whip the horse up as fast as you can. Doesn't matter which direction. Just get the cart out of here.'

Then he hopped down on to the ground, as if he wanted to get a closer view of the imminent hanging. As casually as he could, he moved a little closer towards Rusty.

'Yeah, I got some last words,' Jesse said, glaring ferociously at Lex. 'You just better hope this rope don't break, you little brat, because if it does then I'll be coming straight for you, soon as I've finished with these guys.'

'Brave words for a man what's strung up by his neck,' one of the cowboys laughed. 'Shame you ain't gettin' outta this in one piece. Not this time. This is for double-crossin' us. I sure hope it was worth it.'

And – with that – the cowboy kicked the stake out from beneath Jesse's feet.

CHAPTER TWENTY-THREE

THE GREAT ESCAPE

The red Swann was already in Lex's hand and he started to mutter the wish under his breath as fast as he could the moment the cowboy's leg moved towards the wooden stake, praying to the Gods all the while that the name on the coffin was correct.

'I wish that Jesse Layton and Clint Davis would change places!'

To those watching, it seemed that, at the very moment the noose tightened around Jesse's neck, the cowboy disappeared and some fat bloke appeared in his place, dangling lifelessly at the end of the rope. Everyone stared. Some yelled in fright. Others reached for their pistols. After all, nothing protects you from a swinging fat man like a few rounds of bullets.

Lex shouted, 'Go!' and positively vaulted on to Rusty's back. Jeremiah whipped up the horse with such zeal that the wagon shot straight towards the open desert. Lex paused just long enough to shout, 'It's all true! Jesse Layton *has* become a sorcerer! He'll see us all dead for this!'

Then he dug in his heels and raced after the wagon. As he did so, he could just see, out of the corner of his eye, many of the other cowboys scattering towards their own horses, setting off in random directions in their haste to be away from the most unnatural hanging any of them had ever had the misfortune to witness.

They'd been riding for quite some time before Lex finally slowed Rusty down to a halt. In the blistering heat, such a mad-dash ride was extremely unpleasant. Lex's shirt was clinging to him and he was so thirsty that his throat burned and itched like he'd been drinking sand. Jeremiah stopped the wagon beside Lex and looked over at him with a slightly wild expression on his face as he said, 'What in the world just happened back there? Where's Jesse? Is he in the coffin? Is he all right?'

'I dunno,' Lex replied. 'Let's ask him.' He slid off Rusty's back, then clambered up on to the back of the wagon, thumped on the wooden lid of the coffin and said loudly, 'Hey, Jesse! Are you in there and, if so, are you all right?'

'Let me outta this thing!' Came the muffled response. 'I feel like I'm being cooked! And it stinks like the bejesus, too!'

'For Gods' sake, Lex, let him out!' Jeremiah said.

'First things first,' Lex replied firmly. He rapped on the lid of the coffin again and said, 'What did you do with my sword?'

'Sword?' Jeremiah said. 'What sword?'

'Here's the deal, Jesse,' Lex said calmly. 'You're not getting out of this coffin until I say so. And, believe me,

I'll see you buried in it before I let you out without getting my sword back first.'

There was a long moment of silence before Jesse's voice came out reluctantly. 'Rusty's got it, dammit. Didn't have time to do anything with it. It's in one of the saddlebags.'

Lex hopped off the wagon and went straight over to Rusty. Inside the larger saddlebag he did, indeed, find the sword, along with his black Swann.

'Lex, what the heck just happened back there?' Jeremiah demanded. 'How did you manage to switch them like that?'

'I'm a great magician,' Lex replied, transferring the Swann to his pocket and the sword to his bag which, being magical, easily accommodated it.

'What is that black swan?' Jeremiah asked. 'It looks like our Dragons. And that sword, Lex – where did you get it?'

Lex ignored the questions and went back to the coffin to undo the brass clasps and let Jesse out before he could be cooked to a crisp.

'You wretched little brat! I'll get you for this!' were the first words out of the cowboy's mouth.

He sat up in the coffin, looking hot, sweaty and dishevelled. An angry red mark ran all the way around his neck. It looked extremely painful, which pleased Lex. Even though Jesse hadn't actually been responsible for the blow Lex had taken to the head, he felt a bit of resentment towards him for it, anyway.

'Get me for what?' Lex replied carelessly. 'Saving your life? You ought to be thanking me!'

'You cut it too fine!' Jesse snarled. 'I almost had my neck wrung like a turkey whilst you were pratting about making your little performance!'

'The performance is important, you simpleton!' Lex replied. 'Otherwise they might have thought I had something to do with your miraculous escape. They needed to believe I wanted you dead. Besides, don't you think you ought to be more careful how you talk to me? Don't forget that it's *me* who's really the sorcerer, not you!'

'If you're a sorcerer then I'm a blinkin' ballerina!' Jesse growled. 'You ain't no magician! You're just a kid with a few magic Swanns!'

'Magic Swanns?' Jeremiah repeated. 'What the heck are they?'

'They grant wishes, or something,' Jesse replied. 'That's how he did it.'

'Well, whatever! I still saved your neck, you ungrateful wretch! After you stole from me, too, and left me for dead!'

'Did I heck!' Jesse scoffed. 'It was only a little crack on the head. I've had worse and lived to tell the tale. So, yeah, I took the sword. But I only did exactly what you'd have done in my place.'

'That may be,' Lex replied in a voice of ice. 'The difference is that I wouldn't have got caught! I heroically, selflessly, save your life and then you actually have the nerve to lecture me about the way I went about it! All right, so I let you sweat a bit first but you ought to consider yourself lucky that I saved you at all!'

'No way you'd have let me die, seeing as you had no idea where the sword was!' Jesse retorted.

'Well, maybe I saved you because I wanted the sword, and maybe I saved you for your charming company!' Lex snapped. 'I guess now we'll never know! No doubt you would have used the Binding Bracelets to switch places with me if you'd been given the chance to get your hands on any food!'

To Lex's surprise, Jesse looked utterly gobsmacked by this. Then he looked highly offended.

'Hey!' he said angrily. 'Stealing the sword was one thing – it weren't even yours to begin with – but letting you hang for my past is somethin' else. The thought never even entered my head!'

'Surely you can't expect me to believe that?' Lex snarled.

'Will you two *shut up*!' Jeremiah said loudly. He glared at Lex and said, 'You dragged me here under false pretences! They weren't about to hang Jesse because he helped you get into Dry Gulch House but because he double-crossed them; you weren't interested in saving his life – you just wanted the sword; and I'm starting to think the cowboys weren't the ones who roughed you up, either.'

'No one roughed him up,' Jesse snorted. 'A chandelier fell on his head.'

'Yeah, that sounds more like it!' Jeremiah replied, looking quite vicious. 'No doubt you were doing something you shouldn't have been doing at the time, too! If that sword you're talking about is the one I think it is, then it once belonged to my uncle! Which means it now rightfully belongs to me!'

'Does it ever!' Lex scoffed. 'I'm the one who found it!'

'That doesn't make it yours!'

'It does in my book! I'm the one who got my head bashed in to get it! I'm the one who's probably gone half crazy for it and, no doubt, will be seeing giant talking foxes for the rest of my days because of it!'

'What in the world,' Jeremiah said, 'are you talking about?'

Lex cursed silently. He hadn't meant to say anything about Plantagenet. He'd end up strapped down in a loony bin, for sure. He told himself that it had just been a dream. To prove it to himself he took the trout out of his bag and threw them defiantly down on the sand where, given the heat, they would probably be cooked within minutes.

'I'm hot; I'm tired; I'm thirsty; I'm probably concussed; I've done what I came here to do; and I've had it up to here with the pair of you! I'm going back to my ship!'

'Well said, old chum.'

Lex almost jumped out of his skin, and whirled round on the spot to stare in dread at the wagon. There, perched on top of the coffin, was Plantagenet. He looked just as he had before – dressed in a waistcoat, and even holding a cup and saucer.

Lex stared at him for a moment before looking back at Jeremiah and Jesse. He'd hoped to see suitable expressions of shock on their faces but, instead, they just looked slightly puzzled.

'Can't you *see* him?' Lex hissed.

'Who?' Jeremiah said blankly.

'*Him!*' Lex pointed back at the wagon. But when he looked back, there was no one there. Plantagenet had gone, almost as if he'd never been there to begin with.

Lex pinched the bridge of his nose, but it didn't help and he swayed where he stood.

'Is this another one of your acts?' Jeremiah demanded.

'No, I'm not feeling well!' Lex snapped. 'It's this heat! No doubt you two would just love it if I dropped down dead – then you could pinch all my stuff and leave me out here all alone in the desert. But I'll be damned if I'm going to be left for dead twice in the same day! So I'm leaving right now! You can find your own way back! See if you can manage to stay out of trouble for five minutes without me!'

'You should probably see a doctor,' Jeremiah said. 'Head injuries can affect people in funny ways, and that looks like a nasty one.'

'I don't need any doctor!' Lex snapped. 'And I don't need you sticking your nose in where it doesn't belong!'

'Aw, just let him go,' Jesse replied. 'With any luck, he'll keel over before he gets back, and the vultures will peck him to death. Save us all a lot of grief.'

Lex ignored him. He picked up his bag and, after a brief hesitation, snatched the trout off the sand before making his way back to Sally. He unhitched her from the wagon, climbed up on to her back and then set off in the general direction of what he hoped was Dry Gulch.

Secretly, he was completely and utterly horrified. It seemed to him that he'd either suffered some sort of serious brain damage that caused him to see Plantagenet, or else he'd gone mad. But he couldn't afford to go mad! Not now, when he was in the middle of a Game, and close to winning it, too! He cursed the black Swann, and the chandelier, and the sword, and Jesse for causing him to get hit on the head like that. He'd been perfectly fine up until then. He thought angrily to himself that he seemed to be completely incapable of getting through a Game without some seriously debilitating thing happening to him. Last time, he had spent the better part of one week as a whiskerfish; this time he was seeing giant, talking foxes wherever he went!

After a while, Lex became aware of the sounds of a wagon trundling along at a brisk pace behind him. He risked a glance over his shoulder – just to make *absolutely* sure that Plantagenet wasn't the one driving it. To his relief, it was just Jeremiah and Jesse. Lex pulled a face and turned back. Why the heck was Jesse giving Jeremiah a lift? Didn't he understand the concept of them being on different sides?

Still, Lex slowed Sally down just a little. For, although he knew the way back well enough, what he really wanted to do as soon as he got to his ship was raid the larder. And he couldn't do that unless Jesse was there. So he went on just far enough ahead to look defiant, but not so far that he would lose sight, or sound, of the wagon behind him.

CHAPTER TWENTY-FOUR

THE GOLD-DUST MINES

After a good meal, a good bath and a good night's sleep on board his ship, Lex felt one hundred times better. His headache had gone entirely by the next morning and Heetha's horrible sun had been replaced with Saydi's. As Goddess of Beauty, her sun always brought the loveliest – not to mention the most comfortable – weather on the Globe.

Lex had the sword; he had triumphed against the odds and he had even managed to rescue his companion from certain death, as well. Now, finally, the third and final round was to start today and already Lex felt that he couldn't wait. He and Jesse were back on speaking terms – mostly because Lex found he couldn't overly resent Jesse for taking the sword, when it was exactly what Lex would have done himself. He respected Jesse more for being a man who was entirely, unashamedly, out for himself, than he would have done if he'd been some charitable, do-gooder sap. Besides, just because he didn't trust Jesse, didn't mean that he didn't like him.

'You're not entirely useless,' Lex said generously. 'Which is a step up from my last companion, at least.'

Of course, spending half the night gloating over the Sword of Life had improved Lex's mood immeasurably. Just as the legend went, the red blade was hot to the touch whilst the blue blade was icy cold. The red blade took life; the blue blade gave it back. Lex couldn't help thinking that it would be a dodgy weapon to take on to the battlefield though. After all, if some twit happened to get the blades mixed up then they could actually give years *back* to their opponent, rather than killing them dead, which would be rather an unfortunate mistake to make in a fight.

Lex didn't know when he would use it or how. But – one day – he would need more life. And then, somehow, he would find the courage to stab himself with that blue blade. He had no way of knowing how much life was stored up within the sword, although the stories said it was a hundred years or more. Lex would take whatever he could get. He was an adventurer, after all. And living life was what Lex was all about. It would be frightening – plunging that cool, blue blade into his chest. But Lex was no coward. And there was almost nothing he wouldn't do to wring more experiences and adventures out of this world before he finally croaked it.

But, for now, he stowed the sword away in his bag. It was another benefit of the enchanter's magical bag that it seemed able to contain objects completely. Bottles of water could be spilt without so much as a drop of liquid seeping through. By the same measure, it seemed that sharp objects could not penetrate the fabric. Lex was therefore able to carry the sword about with him without any danger of accidentally impaling himself with it during the course of the Game. This was a particular advantage where this sword was concerned since, the fact that it had two blades stretching out in opposite directions, with the handle in the middle, made attempting to sheath it at your belt without cutting yourself rather difficult.

The players gathered, as per Lady Luck's instructions, on a dusty track just outside Dry Gulch the next morning. They were reduced in number, of course, for Lorella was gone, leaving only the little sprite to play in her place. Possibly that explained the sulky, resentful expression on Thaddeus's face. Lex had to wonder why the Gods bothered playing at all when they always got into such strops as soon as they started to lose.

As in the previous Game, the players' points were wiped clean for the third round so that any of them might have a chance of winning. The advantage of the points he'd already earned, however, meant that Lex would get to start the third round before the other players. Flushed with confidence from his victories at Dry Gulch – both obtaining the sword *and* rescuing Jesse – Lex didn't really see how he could possibly *not* win the next round, especially as he was to get a head start. He was positively itching to find out what the third round was to entail so that he could set his mind immediately to the task of winning the Game and triumphing over Jeremiah.

'The third and final round,' Lady Luck said with a smile, 'is to take place in the Gold-Dust Mines.'

The players fairly goggled at her. There had been a great gold rush about a hundred years ago at the Gold-Dust Mines. It was believed that they were amongst the richest – if not *the* richest – ever to be discovered. Profiteers and entrepreneurs had fled to Dry Gulch hoping to make their fortunes. But – sadly – it appeared that gold was not the only thing down in the mines. There was a ferocious, vicious dragon down there, as well. It had been the last of its kind one hundred years ago. The others had long since died out. Although dragons generally regarded humans as walking snacks, this one was particularly aggressive. It didn't just kill when it was hungry, but all the time in between as well. It hated everyone and everything and was fiercely possessive of its home. Many believed it to be dead now, but no one dared enter the mines, just in case the fearsome beast still lived. For this dragon was sadistic. It did not simply bite your head off, but ripped out your insides whilst you were still alive and had a little play with your intestines before it finally ate you. No one wanted to die that way.

Several people had tried to slay the beast before. Large, muscled heroes and mercenaries had been brought in to see if they could rid the mines of the scaly menace. But all had failed: chewed up and spat out, armour and all. And so the mines had finally been forced to board up and close down entirely. Too many miners had been killed and there was a little gaggle of widows wailing outside the entrance seven days a week by then. So the place was shut and everyone agreed that it would not be reopened until they could be absolutely sure that the dragon was dead.

The problem, though, was that dragons were known for their longevity and so it might very well still be down there, even though a hundred years had passed.

'Is the dragon dead, then?' Jeremiah asked.

'I hope not,' Lady Luck replied. 'It's the subject of the third round. First player to drive a blade into its heart, wins.'

The sprite looked utterly crestfallen by this, which was to be expected seeing as she was about the size of a thumb and therefore would not be able to wield any blade larger than a toothpick. Jeremiah, on the other hand, looked extremely pleased. No doubt, this was the sort of round that suited him perfectly. After all, it would not require much brainpower to slaughter the dragon – just a strong arm and a complete disregard for the sanctity of life. Having been privately and expensively educated in a posh academy, Jeremiah had probably spent more time out in the forest hunting small, defenceless animals, than he had in the classroom learning how to read and write. History, maths, science, philosophy and all those other academic subjects were probably rather pointless to a member of the aristocracy who was only going to sit around, bossing people about once they were grown up, anyway.

Lex, on the other hand, was not happy about the third

round. He was not happy at all. He was an adventurer. He loved exploring new places and doing never-done-before things. He did not kill stuff. He'd never killed anything before in his life – not even on the farm. Lex did not care for blood and gore and death. Those things weren't fun at all. All right, so the dragon was a terrorising, murderous, blood-maddened beast but, skulking down there in the mines, it was not doing anyone any harm now. Lex tried to tell himself that this was no different from the first round in the last Game where he had defeated a minotaur and a medusa by turning them into stone. They may not technically have been dead, but life as a lump of rock couldn't really be all that great. Still, this round left a bad taste in his mouth and he found himself extremely annoyed with Lady Luck for devising it. She knew full well that Lex was no warrior, so how the heck did she expect him to win this thing? OK, so he had a head start and a magic sword, but this was not the sort of task that Lex excelled at. Winning this round did not require cleverness, it merely required strength. Any old fool could weight-lift. Lady Luck really ought to have known better, but that was the price you occasionally had to pay for having the most dim-witted deity out there.

'This is a stupid round,' Lex said bluntly. He knew it wouldn't make any difference, but he felt the pressing need to express his displeasure, anyway.

'It's hardly that,' Lady Luck replied. 'Slaying a dragon is the ultimate mark of a true hero. The player who pulls this off will have people talking about him for decades.'

Big deal, Lex thought. So what if a lot of silly people gushed about you long after you were dead? But there was nothing for it. If he wanted to win the round then he would have to kill the dragon. And, once Lex started something, he would do anything to finish first. If he came second then, really, he might as well kill himself and have done with it, for he would only die of shame and self-loathing later on, anyway.

'You are twenty points in the lead, Lex,' Lady Luck said. 'So you have earned yourself a twenty-minute head start. Jeremiah will then follow. And Lorella's companion, Mab, will go twenty minutes after that. Good luck.'

And, with that, Lex and the other players disappeared from the dusty path and found themselves standing directly outside the boarded-up Gold-Dust Mines.

Lex lost no time, but started forwards at once, pausing only to glance back and smirk at Jeremiah over his shoulder. It was clear that the nobleman loathed having to stand there for a full twenty minutes whilst Lex got started on the round. The boards had been removed from the entrance, presumably for the purposes of the Game. Lex didn't hesitate, but walked straight through with Jesse close behind him.

'No one said nothin' about any dragon-slaying,' the cowboy grunted.

'What's the matter?' Lex replied. 'You're not scared of the dragon, are you?'

'You're damned right, I'm scared of it! That thing's responsible for the deaths of hordes of men! What makes you think we have any chance of killing it when so many others have failed before us?'

'We'll do it,' Lex replied, 'because that dragon is all that stands between me and winning this Game.'

'Well, I think it's a right shame,' Jesse replied. 'It ain't doing no harm down here now. We oughta just leave it be.'

'You can leave it be if you like,' Lex replied, 'but I plan on winning this thing. Besides,' he added, 'if I die during the third round then there's no guarantee that Lady Luck will give you those pearls. She can be sulky like that.'

Jesse grunted again, but kept pace with Lex as they moved deeper into the mines. They were dark and wet and damp. They didn't smell too good, either. Water dripped from the rocky walls, giving the place a sort of mildewy scent. The general consensus seemed to be that the dragon had been sleeping for several months after the mine first started being built, and things were trouble free during that time. After that, something the miners did, woke the dragon up and that was when the killings began. The mine was, therefore, unfinished. They had only had time to lay some of the paths and railway tracks, and to dig some of the shafts, before they had been forced to close down. When they finally decided to abandon the place, everything was left exactly where it was. Lex and Jesse passed several large piles of picks and shovels as they walked in.

When they were only a few feet from the entrance they had to stop. It was too dark to proceed any further, and it certainly didn't take a genius to work out that wandering around an abandoned mine without light was not a good idea. Never mind the danger posed by the dragon, they could fall down an uncovered shaft, or have a ceiling fall down on them, or anything.

'Don't even think about lighting a torch,' Jesse said.

Lex rolled his eyes. 'I know that,' he replied.

Lighting any kind of match down there would not be a good idea at all seeing as they didn't know what gases may be present. They would need some other source of illumination but, fortunately, Lex had just the thing in his bag. The enchanter's bag was huge inside but Lex could usually find the things he'd put in there himself without too much difficulty – perhaps because they were near the top. Every now and then, however, rummaging around he would discover something he'd never seen before. Last night on the ship he had had a good old rummage and found a caged glow-canary. The yellow bird shone like a beacon and had traditionally been used in mining because it could detect the presence of gold. When it came within ten metres of the stuff, its glow changed from white to yellow.

No one entirely understood glow-canaries, for it seemed that they did not need food and water in the same way most species did. Indeed, they periodically seemed to go into a state of hibernation, and would only come 'alive' when someone woke them up again. There were several ways of achieving this. Saying 'wake up' in a loud voice usually did the trick. Poking also worked. Lex had owned the enchanter's bag for several months now and he had never come across the canary before. But once Lex woke it up, the little bird seemed quite happy, stood on its little perch and cocking its head this way and that in an alert, curious manner.

If it had been any other bird that had been in the bag without access to food and water for all those months, Lex would have discovered a dead, rotting corpse in its place but, as it was a glow-canary, it was alive and well, and now it was going to come in extremely handy.

Lex took the cage out and, instantly, pure white light shone all about them, illuminating their way perfectly.

'What else you got in that bag?' Jesse asked, staring.

The truth was that there could be any number of things left by the enchanter in there but, because it was Jesse asking, Lex shrugged and said, 'Nothing of any value.'

They moved on. The narrow path that was cut into the rock led downwards. When they got to a certain point, it branched out in three directions. Lex chose the middle one because he had a feeling about it – and when you're a person who's as lucky as Lex, you never ignore your gut feelings.

They walked for some time through a twisty, turny corridor. It was an adrenaline-pumping walk, going deeper and deeper into the mines when they knew that some-where in there lurked a terrible, ferocious, murderous monster. Lex wasn't over keen on monsters because they tended to eat first and ask questions later. You couldn't really scam a monster. Or talk it out of killing you. Or trick it into killing itself, instead. Lex, therefore, vastly preferred humans, for his silver tongue was not wasted on them. Still, he did experience something of a thrill in going into a highly dangerous mine that no one had been inside for more than a hundred years.

So far, though, the only odd thing Lex had noticed were the holes in the ground. They didn't look like they had appeared there naturally and yet they obviously weren't anything to do with mining. Lex decided there must be moles down there, and thought nothing more of it.

Until a rabbit popped its head up. On first appearances it was a perfectly ordinary white rabbit, but something about the look in its pink eyes stopped Lex dead in his tracks. He recognised that look. He had seen it before, back on the enchanted ship. And he had seen it later on at the farm, just before the crazy animal burnt the barn down. It was a mad, rabid, evil look that you weren't likely to forget in a hurry.

'Shit,' Lex breathed. 'I think that's a—'

But before he could even finish the sentence, the rabbit opened its mouth and shot a plume of fire at them. Lex and Jesse both jumped back but, before the rabbit could emerge all the way out of its warren, Jesse drew his pistol and shot at it. He missed, but the sound was enough to send the rabbit back down into the hole.

'Jeepers, I hate those fire-bunnies,' the cowboy said.

'You've seen them before?' Lex asked.

'You get 'em out in the desert sometimes. Nasty little buggers they are. Dying out now, thank the Gods. Ain't seen one in years.'

'Let's hope there aren't too many more of them,' Lex said as they went on. He knew from past experience just how much damage one fire-breathing rabbit could do and he did not fancy being stuck down here with one, let alone more.

'Are they carnivorous?' Lex asked, remembering that first time he'd come across one on the enchanter's boat and it had tried to chew through his boot.

'Oh yeah,' Jesse replied. 'They'd gladly make a feast of you if you let 'em.'

'Hang on a minute,' Lex said, a horrible, terrible, awful suspicion suddenly occurring to him. 'What if . . . What if there isn't any dragon?'

'What makes you say that?' Jesse asked, frowning. 'It killed all those men, didn't it?'

'Did it? No one ever saw the attacks, did they? They only found the charred bodies later.'

'Yeah, but . . . those bodies were blackened to a crisp. Half eaten most of the time, too. No way one little bunny could do that, even if it could breathe fire.'

'Not *one* perhaps,' Lex replied. 'But if there was a *pack* of them . . .'

'But the fire-bunnies are dyin' out,' Jesse said, starting to sound a little desperate. 'Everyone says so. Besides, other miners reported havin' seen the dragon.'

'Well, of course they did,' Lex replied dismissively. 'Down here in the mines, getting increasingly scared, with more and more people dying, I'd be surprised if there wasn't a man among them who wasn't convinced

347

he'd seen the dragon at some point. Who knows – perhaps a few of them really *did* catch a glimpse of one of the fire-bunnies. They would probably have been genuinely sure that it was a dragon they'd seen. Besides, if miners were being attacked in the tunnels whilst they worked then how would a dragon even *fit* into those narrow corridors? How would it be able to move around the mine at all?'

'Some of the descriptions are quite detailed though,' Jesse pointed out – although he sounded anything but certain.

'But none of them match,' Lex muttered. 'Although I suppose it would've been dark down here and they would have legged it as soon as they saw anything. Hopefully, there are fire-breathing rabbits *and* a dragon down here.' That sounded odd, given the circumstances, so Lex added, 'Well . . . you know what I mean.'

'I sure do,' Jesse replied. 'I don't much fancy wanderin' round this old mine looking for a dragon that don't even exist, and maybe never did.'

'You and me both,' Lex grunted.

The problem, though, was that sending players down to an abandoned mine to slay a dragon that wasn't real sounded *exactly* like the sort of stupid thing Lady Luck would do. Lex couldn't help wondering what would happen to the Game if that was the case. How would they decide the winner if the third round was one that couldn't possibly be won?

After about twenty minutes of navigating their way

through the corridor, Lex was starting to worry that it didn't lead anywhere useful at all. The mine was unfinished – for all they knew, this corridor would suddenly come to a dead end.

But then they came out into the cavern.

As previously stated, there is more than one way to wake up a glow-canary. Shouting and poking will do the trick. But another thing that works like a charm is to bring a glow-canary that's already awake into close proximity with sleeping ones. Something about the light the awake one sheds will rouse the sleeping ones within seconds.

Jesse and Lex, therefore, had to shield their eyes because, after a good half hour spent wandering the dark mine, they were not prepared for the bright light of three hundred or more glow-canaries. The cages hung from the cavernous ceiling far above them and the light illuminated one of the largest rooms Lex had ever seen in his life. It was massive – and it was only because there were so very many glow-canaries that they were up to the task of illuminating it at all.

The room contained a railway track. Or, at least, the hub of one. The track ran out of the room in several different directions. Presumably, the little carriages had been intended to transport equipment in and gold out. But they had never got very far with the actual mining and Lex assumed that the railway, too, was unfinished.

He and Jesse moved cautiously into the cavern. They walked past laid and unlaid track, and a couple of steam trains with names like I. M. Daring. A multitude of rusty tools lay around on the gravelly floor, too. There was something a little sad about the abandoned scene – with all that stuff just left down there to rot. When the great gold rush had started, bright-eyed, hopeful people had flocked to Dry Gulch thinking that they were going to make a fortune when, in actual fact, they had met only with disaster, death and destruction before they were finally forced to close up the mine, cut their losses and flee.

Jesse and Lex passed through the cavern at a brisk walk. The canaries had started to talk to each other and that worried Lex. Whilst they may have only been chirping softly, the fact was that there was at least one fire-bunny down here and, possibly, a dragon as well that might be alerted to their presence by the noise.

'Damned birds,' Lex muttered under his breath.

At least the fact that the mine was unfinished meant that it shouldn't take too many hours to explore it. If they covered every scrap of ground and failed to find a dragon then they would know that it was useless.

They were about halfway across the cavern when there was a dull rumbling. They could feel it as well as hear it. The very walls and floor seemed to tremble and bits of rubble fell from the ceiling. Now *that* sounded more like a dragon and this cavern would certainly be big enough for one. From the sounds of it, the thing was gigantic and, suddenly, the thought of attempting to *kill* it seemed . . . well . . . completely and utterly absurd. Lex was a clever thief, not a warrior. How the heck was he supposed to manage it?

But then the rabbits came. They poured out of the tunnel from which Lex and Jesse had entered, as well as the other three tunnels alongside that one. Perhaps, back in the days that the mine was being built, there had just been a small pack of fire-bunnies. Now there were hundreds. And hundreds. And *hundreds* of them. And they were all swarming directly towards Jesse and Lex, some of them even shooting little plumes of fire from their mouths in their excitement.

'Oh my Gods,' Lex whispered.

He and Jesse spun on the spot and ran along a line of track towards one of the exits, out of the cavern. A single cart was perched in the dark arch, poised to run along the track sloping downwards into the next room.

'Get in the wagon!' Lex shouted, leaping in.

'Get *in*?' Jesse gasped, aghast. 'Have you gone barmy? We don't know where that track goes! It ain't safe! It might not even hold our weight—'

'Get in here right this second or I'm leaving without you!' Lex snapped. 'I don't care where it goes! We can't escape those things on foot and they'll be on us any moment now!'

Jesse glanced over his shoulder. And Lex took the opportunity to grab his arm and drag him bodily into the cart. The cowboy lost his balance and flipped into it head first. There was barely room for the two of them and the force of Jesse's bulk landing inside was all that was needed to push the cart forwards on to the track.

As it turned out, the next room wasn't a room so much

as another huge cavern, even bigger than the first one. As before, the caged glow-canary – still clutched in Lex's arms – set off all the rest. There were hundreds of them hanging from the ceiling again. No doubt they had been brought in to illuminate the area so that the workmen could see the monstrosity they were building. It looked like some sort of wooden roller coaster. Tracks on stilts weaved everywhere within the great space, from all directions, branching off this way and that to other parts of the mine.

Unfortunately, so much track meant that certain routes had to bend and dip rather horribly in order to fit in with the rest of it, and the track Lex and Jesse were on went, almost instantly, into a two-hundred-foot drop. Jesse barely had time to right himself in the cart behind Lex before it was plummeting downwards.

The two of them screamed their heads off. The rickety little wheels of the cart blazed along, leaving a trail of sparks and making a horrible, tearing, rusty, screeching sound, as if they were about to come right off the track altogether.

But then, suddenly, it levelled out. Despite the initial drop, they were still astonishingly high. Then they found themselves shooting upwards, carried along by the force of their own momentum. They came to a brief slow at the top of the curve – just long enough for Lex to glance back and see that the rabbits had reached the entrance and, unable to stop themselves, a whole load of them were toppling through the arch like lemmings, freefalling the two-hundred-foot drop to the tracks below. That seemed to kill them, which was reassuring. Finally, they managed to stop themselves and, instead, piled up in the archway, blowing fire out into the cavern. They were far too far away to be able to reach Lex and Jesse, for that brief, frenetic wagon ride had carried them right out to the middle of the cavern.

'Perhaps we oughta try and get out—' Jesse began, but it was already too late.

The cart tipped over the top of the curve and then they were speeding off again. This time the drop was not so steep, but the track was long and straight instead, heading directly towards a tunnel on the opposite side of the cavern. Jesse was relieved at first, for this would surely get them off this helter-skelter of death. But then Lex said, 'Uh oh.'

When you're speeding along on an ancient, unfinished mining track, the very last thing you want to hear coming out of anyone's mouth is, *Uh oh.*

'What?' Jesse asked.

'The track runs out up ahead.'

Jesse looked over Lex's shoulder and saw that he was right. The track ran out abruptly. Where it should have continued, there was just empty space stretching out ahead – and they were speeding right towards it. Perhaps it had collapsed due to age and damp, or perhaps that part of the track had never been built to begin with. However it had happened, the track disappeared out from under the cart a bare second later and Lex and Jesse found themselves hurtling through the air with a great cavernous drop stretching out beneath them.

CHAPTER TWENTY-FIVE

THE DRAGON

'Jump!' Lex shouted.

But jumping from a falling cart is actually harder than you might think. They therefore didn't so much jump, as throw themselves over the edge towards a stretch of nearby track about ten feet below them. They smashed into it, causing it to move beneath their weight in a worrying sort of way, before it, thankfully, steadied. The cart, meanwhile, fell three hundred feet before it hit another piece of track and was smashed to bits.

Jesse, who was clinging to the track beside Lex, reached over and smacked the back of the thief's head.

'Ouch! What was that for?' Lex demanded.

'Dragging me into that cart!' Jesse growled.

'Oh, shut up. If I hadn't, you'd have been eaten by the bunnies by now.'

'Yeah, 'cos my position is so much better now, ain't it?'

'Well, I won't save you again if you're going to be that ungrateful,' Lex replied. 'Stop whining; it's not that bad.'

He slowly got to his feet. His glow-canary had fallen

a little further along the track, so he crept forwards and picked it up. The bird appeared to be unharmed and was still shining brightly, as were the other ones hanging from the ceiling.

'Come on,' Lex said. 'We can walk to the other side.'

This was easier said than done, for they were at an incredible height and the track was narrow and had a tendency to shift beneath them. Lex forced himself to keep his eyes on the archway ahead and not to look down. Inch by slow inch, they finally made it to the other side. It didn't do anything for their nerves that a large part of the track groaned, creaked and then collapsed almost as soon as they did so.

'It's probably rotten to the core, after all these years,' Jesse said. 'It's a miracle we survived at all.'

'But we did,' Lex said briskly. He turned away from the cavern as he spoke, though, for it *was* quite horrible seeing nothing but air where the track you'd just been standing upon seconds ago had once stood. 'Let's finish looking for this dragon.'

'What dragon?' Jesse said. 'I'd bet anything that you were right and there never was one. It was most likely them bunnies all along. A hundred years ago, there'd probably have only been ten or twenty of 'em but that's more than enough to roast a man and pick the meat off his bones.'

'You may be right,' Lex replied. 'I think you probably are. But I'm not taking any chances. I'm going to explore every square inch of this mine before I'm satisfied there's no dragon.'

'We'll probably end up getting killed when a ceiling collapses on top of us,' Jesse grumbled. 'This place is gonna come caving in before too long.'

'Let's make sure we get in and out before that happens, then.'

They pressed on. Everywhere they went, they woke up more glow-canaries that lit their way. Fortunately, they had all been left behind when the workers decided to flee and so the way was illuminated for Lex and Jesse better than they had expected.

Lex had nurtured a faint hope that perhaps the fire-bunnies were all on the other side of the mine – that they were unable to cross the cavern with its great wooden roller coaster. This hope, however, turned out to be sadly, ridiculously, optimistic. The rabbits were everywhere. They could tell by the warrens and rabbit holes. Lex and Jesse fled past every rabbit hole, dreading that a rabbit head might suddenly pop up and roast their feet. In fact, this very nearly happened on one occasion. They missed the rabbit hole and didn't even realise a rabbit was there until a blast of fire suddenly scorched the back of Lex's legs. He yelled and jumped up in the air. When he looked back, sure enough there was a vicious fire-bunny glaring at him with a surprisingly angry expression on its face, considering the fact that *it* was the one that had almost barbecued *Lex*. The rabbit had burnt the back of his trousers but, thankfully, his legs were unharmed. Jesse threw a rock at it and it disappeared back into the tunnel.

'What the heck is their problem?' Lex said in exasperation.

'Fire-bunnies hate everyone and everything,' Jesse replied with a shrug. 'Little monsters. Say, I sure as heck hope that there's more than one way outta this place, 'cos I don't fancy having to go back the way we came.'

Neither did Lex. Hordes of fire-bunnies aside, there was no guarantee that they could get back across that network of wooden railways without the whole damned thing collapsing beneath them. Besides which, without getting in a speeding, runaway cart again – an experience that even Lex was keen to avoid repeating – the whole journey would take much longer.

'We oughta start lookin' for a way outta here,' Jesse said after about half an hour. 'There's been no sign of the others. Chances are they turned back long ago. We'll end up getting ourselves killed and Jeremiah will win by default. You don't want that, do you?'

'Not particularly, no,' Lex replied, aware of the fact that Jesse was attempting to manipulate him. 'But I don't want to be the twit who cut the third round short because he didn't think the dragon existed when, in fact, it did the whole time. Jeremiah could be slaying it as we speak. We keep going.'

But for all Lex knew, Jesse was right. And, personally, Lex was feeling less and less sure that the dragon was real. He knew people, and he knew how easily they could get themselves wound up about nothing. One of the single most distinguishing features of a dragon was its ability to blow fire. And the fact that there were masses of fire-bunnies down here seemed too large a coincidence to ignore. But there was still the chance that the dragon *was* real, and Lex couldn't possibly give up on the third round until he was absolutely certain that it was not.

As they went on, Jesse continued to whinge about the fact that they were wasting their time but he might just as well have been singing nursery rhymes for all the effect he was having on Lex.

Then they walked into another room and something happened to the canary. If either Lex or Jesse had been paying the birds any attention, they would have noticed that the light they shed was getting progressively brighter and more golden. When they stepped into the new room, a dazzling, sparkling light seemed to burst out of the bird, illuminating the entire cavern. They had finally found the gold. It glittered all around them in huge heaps of wealth. Lex had never seen so much in all his life. It was piled in great mounds up towards the ceiling, like particularly lovely stalactites. There was also a lake, so smooth and still that it seemed like a mirror. The gold piled up all around it and spilled into it. There was probably loads of the stuff beneath the surface, as well. The glow-canary Lex carried was the only one in this room. Presumably the workers had never got any further than this.

Possibly, this was because of the huge dragon sprawled on top of a great heap of gold in the middle of the room.

Apart from its massive size, it was not at all what Lex had expected. It was snoring contentedly, for one thing.

And, although it may once have been a greenish colour, now it was mostly grey. Its scales seemed to have changed colour with age. Sound asleep, it was completely unaware of the humans' presence. Lex saw now why Lady Luck had thought he could win. Lex may have been no fighter but even he was capable of stabbing something that was asleep . . . Or was he? Was he really *that* despicable that he would slaughter a geriatric dragon in its sleep, just so that he could win a Game?

'It did *kill* all those people,' he said, in a feeble effort to convince himself.

'Did it?' Jesse asked. 'Seems to me it was probably those nasty little fire-bunnies all along.'

Lex walked through the gold to get closer to the dragon. He was a few metres away when the thing woke up. It slowly lifted its head and looked sleepily towards Lex with white eyes. The dragon was almost completely blind, so it must have been its sense of smell that made it move towards Lex. It got up slowly, ponderously, as if its limbs ached, and then it slithered inelegantly off the pile of gold. When it got to the floor, it crumpled on to its front legs and its long neck and head smacked on to the ground in a really pathetic way. Slowly, it picked itself back up and shuffled over towards Lex.

Lex stood completely still. He thought he should probably be terrified and running, or else reaching for his sword and screaming. But it was difficult to feel afraid of something that seemed so distinctly unthreatening. It did not look at all like a creature poised to attack. Indeed, it was so old that it seemed to be all it could do to walk. When it reached Lex, it thumped down to the floor in front of him. The dragon's head was as big as Lex. When it opened its mouth in a yawn, Lex saw that it had hardly any teeth left in its head. And yet its breath was the most foul that Lex had ever smelled – a sort of grim mixture of stagnant water and very old fish. Rotten, dead fish, possibly.

'Eww!' Lex exclaimed in horror.

Even worse, a second later, the dragon licked him, dragging its huge tongue up the front of Lex's shirt, practically soaking him in dragon saliva in the process. Then, drooling happily, it bent its lizardy head and rubbed itself affectionately against Lex's shoulder.

'Oh my Gods,' Jesse whispered, moving closer to them. 'It's tame.'

He reached out a hand and ran it along the dragon's head. The monster pressed into the caress happily. It seemed to revel in being touched and spoken to. At one point, it even rolled over on to its back as if wanting them to rub its belly.

'There's no way this beast ever killed anyone,' Jesse said.

'No,' Lex replied.

Clearly the things that had terrorised the mines had been those blasted fire-bunnies, after all.

'You raise a hand against this dragon and I'll knock your head off,' Jesse said calmly.

'You don't get to tell me what to do,' Lex replied, without heat. 'I will spare this dragon because it pleases me to.'

Lex knew the rules of the Game meant that he must kill the dragon, or at least try to. But Lex had always turned his nose up at rules – even if they were set by the Gods. Besides, why kill a dragon when you could *own* one, instead? If Lex could find some way of taking the dragon with him from the mine, he would prevent Jeremiah from winning. Then Lex would be the proud owner of what was quite possibly the last dragon left alive on the entire Globe. Just think how impressive *that* would be!

The only problem was that, now the points had been wiped clean for the third round, there would be no victor in the Game. Lex might draw with Jeremiah by default, or the Gods might even disqualify him. Both were equally unpleasant pills to swallow. Lex might just as well lose altogether than share the limelight with that insufferable snob. It was almost enough for him to reconsider slaying the dragon, after all. But then he looked at the grey old thing, drooling happily as Jesse scratched it behind the ears, and he knew he couldn't – *wouldn't* – kill it. It would be like chopping a dear old lady's head off whilst she was in the process of trying to give you a home-baked pie. The Game and the Gods be damned. There were limits, and Lex didn't kill. He might cheat and lie and steal, but he didn't go out and kill things for fun. That was the sort of thing the posh snobs he stole from did, and one of the reasons Lex found it so easy and guilt-free to take their stuff.

No, they would get the dragon out of here somehow. All right, so it seemed like an impossible task, considering the fact that they were deep underground in a mine that was practically falling down around them and the dragon was old and feeble, not to mention enormous – and most of the tunnels were quite narrow. But there had to be some way to do it. Lex thrived on seemingly-impossible tasks. The dragon had got in here somehow, after all. Now they were just going to have to get it out.

Lex looked up at the ceiling. It was so high that it might even go all the way back up to the surface. If the old dragon could find some last burst of energy from somewhere, then perhaps it could smash through the ceiling and fly out. But, given that it could barely walk, that seemed unlikely.

Lex was still trying to work out what to do when Jeremiah came rushing into the cavern from the opposite side. He was dusty and dishevelled, as if a few bits of ceiling might have fallen down on him along the way, but he was free of scorch marks, so had obviously managed to avoid being attacked by the fire-bunnies. Tess wasn't with him and Lex assumed that, as with the second round, he had left her behind, out of harm's way.

The nobleman's sword was already in his hand and, when he saw the dragon, Jeremiah instantly charged towards it. The dragon turned ponderously and then began lolloping towards the nobleman, clearly pleased and excited at the appearance of a new human who might give him a scratch behind the ears, too.

Lex was utterly horrified. Not only was Jeremiah going to kill the dragon but he was going to win the Game, as well. It was the most awful worst-case scenario imaginable.

The scene seemed to slide down into slow motion as Lex sought desperately for a way out of what was about to become a complete disaster. Then, suddenly, a plan came into his mind. A desperate, last-measure plan.

Lex swung his bag off his back and reached inside to get the Sword of Life. He would pierce the dragon's skin with the blue blade, thereby giving *back* all the life stored within it. This would make Jeremiah think he'd lost, and would hopefully give the dragon enough strength to fly out of the mine, taking Lex and Jesse with it. There was no time to think about the fact that he would be giving years of life away to a dragon, rather than keeping them for himself.

Lex dropped the glow-canary and pulled the sword out of his bag. This caused one of the smoked trout to fall out on to the floor with a wet-sounding slap. There was no way the dragon could possibly have heard that sound. And yet, one moment it was thundering towards Jeremiah – who now looked quite pale with fear but was drawing back his sword regardless – and the next the dragon spun round on the spot as fast as its huge bulk would allow, an eager look in its almost-blind eyes. It turned back at the same time that Lex threw the sword, blue blade first.

It shot through the air, straight and fast, and buried itself in the dragon's heart. Lex had never felt so awful or guilt-ridden in his life as he did when the dragon crumpled to the ground with a grunt. Jeremiah threw his own sword down in a rage, clearly believing that Lex had just succeeded in slaying the dragon. For a long, horrible moment, Lex thought so, too. Perhaps that wasn't the real Sword of Life at all, but a mere replica. Perhaps he had just killed the dragon for real.

But then, slowly, its scales started to change colour. From pale grey, they deepened into an emerald green – all except a single stripe running down the dragon's back, which remained grey. The three humans stared as the dragon stirred. It got back to its feet, shook itself once, and then lumbered on towards the smoked trout as if nothing had ever happened. It didn't even seem to feel anything when Lex pulled the sword from its chest – and there was no wound left behind. The green scales just closed up over it. Meanwhile, the dragon gobbled up the trout will all the enthusiasm and excitement as if it had been the most delicious thing it'd ever tasted. Then it pranced about in front of Lex with all its new strength and vigour. Its eyes had lost their white sheen and were now a vibrant amber.

'You idiot!' Jeremiah crowed smugly. 'You stabbed it with the wrong blade!'

'No,' Lex replied, 'I didn't.'

'The challenge of this round is to kill it, not give it back more life!'

Sword in hand once again, Jeremiah was striding back towards the dragon with a purposeful air Lex didn't like the look of one bit. He and Jesse both stepped in front of the dragon – not that that made much difference, for the beast was far too big to be shielded by humans – but the gesture was startling enough that it temporarily stopped Jeremiah in his tracks, just the same.

'Get out of the way!' the nobleman said. 'That thing's a killing machine. It'll have both your fool heads off in a minute!'

'Oh, don't be such a galloping twit!' Lex snapped. 'Can't you see it's tame? It probably never hurt a human in its life!'

Even now that it was no longer old and drooling, the dragon did look quite absurdly friendly. Especially now that it was nuzzling the back of Lex's head with its snout. Not to be deterred, however, Jeremiah said, 'What about all those mining deaths, then? They closed the mine down and left all that gold here just because they felt like it, did they?'

'No, it was the fire-bunnies.'

'Fire *what*? What the heck are you talking about?'

Lex stared at him. 'Surely you've seen them? This mine is full of hundreds and hundreds of fire-breathing rabbits!'

'Oh, that's rich, even for you!' Jeremiah sneered. 'Surely you can't expect me to fall for that! Just how stupid do you think I am? Fire-breathing rabbits! I never heard anything so ridiculous in all my life! You're making it up to throw me off my guard, and then you're going to slay that dragon yourself and win the Game!'

Lex glared at him. 'If I was going to make something up, believe me, I would come up with something much more convincing than fire-bunnies! They're far too ludicrous to be made up! I'm telling the truth! Just look at my burnt trousers!'

'Nothing you say is going to convince me,' Jeremiah

said firmly. 'Now, stand aside or risk getting your head chopped off!'

Then the idiot drew back his sword arm and prepared to throw . . .

But then there was a familiar rumbling sound. Lex and Jesse exchanged a horrified look, whilst Jeremiah stood staring around stupidly.

'What's that noise?' he asked.

'The bunnies are coming,' Lex replied.

From the sound of it, there were even more of them this time than there had been last time. Their stampede was causing bits of dust and gravel to fall from the walls and the ceiling, and the water of the lake to ripple. There were only two entrances into the cavern. Lex had entered through one, Jeremiah through the other. At almost the exact same moment, hordes of ferocious fire-bunnies poured in from both entrances. Their eyes were angry, red and bloodshot; they were slavering from the mouth and blowing fire through their nostrils. Jeremiah screamed and Lex couldn't blame him. That was not the way bunnies were supposed to look at all.

They were surrounded. Trapped. There was no way out of the cavern with still more bunnies pouring in from both entrances towards them where they stood in the centre of the room.

Presumably, the dragon was safe from the rabbits. After all, they'd had more than a hundred years to eat it and hadn't done so. Possibly they could not bite through its scales. But, unless they got out of this room, and quickly too, the three humans were all going to be eaten alive.

Lex looked at the dragon and the bunnies and the ceiling – his mind working faster than it had ever worked before. And – suddenly – he knew what he had to do.

'On to the dragon!' he shouted. 'Now!'

Then he grabbed his bag and the glow-canary, turned on the spot, and dragged himself up on to the dragon's back, gripping scales the size of dinner plates to climb the animal like he would a rock wall. He sat down right behind the dragon's neck. Jesse quickly followed and so did Jeremiah. The dragon seemed quite happy to have the three humans sitting on its back and, indeed, the beast was so large that it probably didn't even feel their weight. But that alone did not make them safe. Already, the rabbits were swarming towards them and, once they reached the dragon, there was nothing to stop them from climbing up it after their prey, just as the humans had done. There must have been close to a thousand fire-bunnies in the room by now but, clearly lacking a single aggressive bone in its body, the dragon seemed quite unconcerned by all the rabbits swarming towards it, and it was quite clear that it wasn't even thinking of attacking them. Which meant they had to try to escape. But getting a dragon to fly upwards is not as easy as getting a horse to trot forwards, as Jeremiah was already finding out. Sitting at the back, clinging on to Jesse, the nobleman was shrieking, 'Fly, you stupid beast, fly!'

Which, unsurprisingly, had no effect on the dragon whatsoever. But Lex knew something that would. He opened his bag and fumbled desperately for the last remaining trout, as well as the fishing rod he had spotted in there earlier. Finally, he got them both. The rabbits were climbing up the dragon as Lex hooked the fish on the end of the line and then threw it up into the air as far as he could.

The dragon spread its wings instantly, and Lex, Jesse and Jeremiah were forced to cling on desperately as the huge thing beat its great wings, causing ripples to run along the surface of the lake. Slowly, it rose up into the air, quite oblivious to the trails of fire the little rabbits were shooting at it below.

Doggedly following the trout Lex dangled before it, the dragon swooped upwards towards the roof of the cavern. Lex risked one last glance back at the frantic, maddened rabbits beneath them and – only for a moment – thought he caught, just out of the corner of his eye, a brief glimpse of what looked just like a giant waving fox. But, when he moved his gaze to get a better look, there was no giant fox down there. Just more and more furious rabbits.

Lex had to look back towards the ceiling then because the screams of the other two were distracting him. As Lex had hoped, the dragon did not slow down when it reached the top, but merely went right on through, head first. The dragon's great bulk was more than enough to shatter the earthy ceiling and they burst out of the mine in a shower of dirt and stones and into the bright, sparkling sunlight beyond.

CHAPTER TWENTY-SIX

A PAIR OF DOUBLE-CROSSERS

The dragon seemed to forget about the trout for a short time after it emerged from the mine. It had not, after all, seen the sun or breathed fresh air for over a hundred years. With some of its youth now restored, it was enjoying its freedom more than ever and soared joyously out over the desert below.

This did get slightly worrying for a while. Especially when the dragon began to climb steadily higher towards the clouds with no sign of turning back any time soon. But, by waving the trout around particularly energetically, Lex managed to get the dragon's attention back again. He used the fishing line to dangle the fish lower than the dragon's snout and soon they were heading back down towards the ground. The dragon spread its wings just in time, and they came to land outside the mine with a thump that made the ground shake.

The Gods were already there, along with the sprite, who perched on top of a nearby cactus, looking despondent.

'That,' raged Kala as soon as the dragon touched down and instantly devoured the trout (and half the fishing line), 'was the most astonishingly poor show I have ever witnessed!' Pointing at Lex, she went on, 'You deliberately saved that thing's life and didn't even try to kill it! If I were your Goddess, I would turn you into a wooden chessman right here and now!'

'Whatever for?' Lex asked. 'I won, didn't I?'

The Gods stared at him for a moment before Kala found her tongue and gasped, 'Won? *Won*? You were supposed to *slay* the dragon!'

'That's not what I heard,' Lex replied blithely – but not *too* blithely, for he was talking to a God, after all.

Lex did not give up a win easily and, during that brief flight on the dragon's back, a plan had formed itself in his mind.

'Lady Luck said that the first person to drive a blade into the dragon's heart, wins,' he said. 'Well, I was the first person to drive a blade into its heart.'

There was silence for a moment before Kala raged, 'You were supposed to slay the beast and you know it!'

'But she never said that specifically, my Lady,' Lex said, trying to sound respectful. 'She said that the person who managed to slay a dragon would be talked about for years and years, but she never actually said that was what *we* were supposed to do. All she specifically said was "blade in the heart".'

'He's right,' Thaddeus growled, after another brief silence. 'Technically speaking, he's won.'

'I ought to be awarded some hero points, too,' Lex said. 'For saving him.'

He jerked his thumb over his shoulder towards Jeremiah, who was still clinging to the dragon's back and looking rather sick.

'Oh, hero points or no hero points, what does it matter?' Lady Luck beamed. 'You've won, Lex! And you've rescued that dear, sweet dragon!'

Lex had to resist the urge to roll his eyes at yet another demonstration of Lady Luck's utter fickleness. An hour ago, she had been ordering them to kill the beast, now she was all eager to pet and coo over it.

Jeremiah chose that moment to slide off the dragon's back, land with a thump on the ground and be noisily sick. Which was good because, when the dragon spread its wings in a most impressive way just a moment later, Lex and Jesse were the only two on its back and that final image would be the perfect one to show in the Gaming stadiums before Lady Luck passed Lex yet another trophy and the Binding Bracelets fell from their wrists, marking the end of the Game.

The celebratory dinner that took place in the Wither City after the Game was over, was a very different affair from the one that had taken place before it. No one was laughing at Lex, for one thing. In fact, many people were grovelling all over him, whilst Jeremiah sat at a table by himself, looking forlorn. Lex revelled in the victory. Towards the end of the evening, of course, he was getting rather fed up with people toadying all over him. He decided to call it a night and quit whilst he was ahead.

When he got back to the harbour, he saw that Jeremiah must have been thinking along the same lines, for he was there about to embark on his own ship.

'Hey,' Lex called across the dark pier. 'Wait up.'

The nobleman stopped reluctantly and watched Lex approach, with a suspicious expression on his face.

'You've come to gloat, I suppose!' he said peevishly when Lex stopped in front of him.

'Not at all,' Lex said. 'I've come to shake your hand.'

Jeremiah narrowed his eyes. 'Why?'

'To show there's no hard feelings.'

Jeremiah stared at him. 'Well, why should *you* have any hard feelings, after all?' he snapped. 'You stole my sister's Dragon and my uncle's sword and you think you got away with it! Well, you haven't! I'll tell you what I'm going to do, Trent – I'm going to—'

'Oh, save it,' Lex said mildly. 'I've come here to give you back those things.' As Jeremiah watched in astonishment, Lex swung the bag off his back, rummaged through it and then straightened up with the Sword of Life and the blue Dragon of Desareth in his hand. 'Here,' he said, holding them out to Jeremiah. 'It was wrong of me to take them. I'm very sorry.'

'You're giving them back . . . just like that?' Jeremiah asked. 'No tricks?'

'No tricks,' Lex replied. 'The Game's over now and these things are of no use to me. Especially the sword now that the life that was stored up in the blue blade has all been used up. Better that you have it back and slaughter a few peasants with it. Or a few armies. Perhaps I'll steal it back from you in twenty years or so when it's useful to me again.'

'Well,' Jeremiah said finally. 'Thank you. And . . . thank you also for . . . you know . . . taking me with you from the mine and not leaving me behind to get eaten by the rabbits.'

Lex shuddered. 'No man should get eaten by rabbits. No matter how much of a stuck-up toff he is. Oh, that reminds me. I wanted to give you this back, too.' And from his pocket he produced the purse he'd stolen from Mrs East at the teashop.

'What is—' Jeremiah began.

'Your mother's purse,' Lex replied. 'I pinched it, back at the Sea Volcanoes.'

Jeremiah stared at him, speechless for a moment, before putting the purse in his pocket. 'The next time I play against you, Lex,' the nobleman said quietly, 'I will win.'

'Well, I doubt that very much,' Lex replied airily, 'but dream about it, if you like. Let's not spoil the moment by arguing. I don't much like you, Jeremiah, and I daresay the feeling's mutual. But for the sake of our grandfathers – who were both fine men – let's try to part on good terms.'

Jeremiah looked suitably serious at the mention of their grandfathers and nodded. 'Agreed,' he said pompously. 'For their sake, if not for ours.'

Lex smiled. Moulding people was so easy that, really, it was like they were made of clay half the time. When Lex stepped forwards to embrace Jeremiah, the nobleman looked taken aback and not best pleased, but he allowed it for a brief moment – clapping Lex awkwardly on the back before hurriedly releasing him. But that was all the time Lex needed. He said goodnight and goodbye to Jeremiah and then walked back to his own ship with the nobleman's white Dragon of Desareth nestled securely in his own pocket. After looking it up in Erasmus Grey's book, Lex had found out that the white Dragon could transport the wisher back to his home instantly – no matter how far away he happened to be from it at the time. Lex couldn't very well allow Jeremiah to walk off with something so useful. The opportunity to pinch it was just too good to pass up.

All in all, it had been a profoundly satisfying victory. Lex set sail that very night and, by the time Jeremiah noticed his Dragon was missing, Lex was far, far away. The only thing that marred his pleasure was Jesse – the dratted cowboy had done a runner. And he had taken Lex's book about Desareth's Wishing Creatures with him.

Lady Luck had presented the cowboy with the grey pearls as soon as they got back to the Wither City but he had declined to go to the celebratory feast under the guise that he'd had enough of the Game by then, and was glad to be done with it. But when Lex got back to the ship, Rusty was gone and so was Jesse. Lex was only mildly miffed about this at first. After all, if another Game were to arise then he could always track the cowboy down and invite him along, but the speed and stealth with which the cowboy had left alerted Lex to the fact that something was most definitely up. So he carefully combed through the ship until he found the thing that was missing.

The Wishing Creatures of Desareth, by Erasmus Grey, had been securely tucked away in the safe Lex had had installed in his bedroom on the ship. But when he opened it, all that remained was a note from Jesse that read:

Howdy, partner,

Here's a piece of friendly advice, kid: you need a better safe. This one is pathetic.

Hope you don't mind, but I've taken the book. Seems only fair, seeing as you have four of the Wishing Creatures of Desareth, and I ain't got none.

Thanks for all the fun and, hopefully, we'll see each other again sometime (but not too soon, eh?). Give my love to the griffins.

Your friend and mentor,

Jesse Layton.

Lex stared down at the letter in his hand. 'Friend and mentor, my foot!' he muttered darkly to himself.

He stood there a moment longer, waiting for the hot, horrible anger to sweep over him at the fact that someone had stolen from *him* for a change. But it never came. Instead, all he got was a strange feeling of thrilling excitement. What Jesse didn't know was that Lex had an almost photographic memory and could therefore remember practically everything he'd read in the book. He also had the black Swann of Desareth, with which he should be able to track Jesse down. He would find the cowboy eventually and get his book back. After that . . . if Jesse wanted to compete against Lex for the other Wishing Creatures out there, well . . . the cowboy would certainly be a worthy adversary, and Lex was in permanently short supply of those.

He read through the letter one more time, his smile growing wider at every word.

'Perfect,' Lex said gleefully as he put the letter in the safe and slammed the door shut. 'Just what I always wanted: a brand new challenge. And with a half-decent opponent, too. Bring it on, Jesse. I'll be ready for you.'